I0609039

Thomas Edward Oliver

Jacques Milet's Drama

Thomas Edward Oliver

Jacques Milet's Drama

ISBN/EAN: 9783337394585

Printed in Europe, USA, Canada, Australia, Japan

Cover: Foto ©Andreas Hilbeck / pixelio.de

More available books at **www.hansebooks.com**

Jacques Milet's Drama,

"La Destruction de Troye la Grant;"

Its Principal Source; —

— Its Dramatic Structure.

by

Thomas Edward Oliver,
(A. B., Harvard University)
Salem, Massachusetts,
U. S. A.

A Thesis accepted by the Philosophical Faculty of the

University of Heidelberg

for the degree of

Doctor of Philosophy.

Heidelberg.
Buchdruckerei von E. Geisendörfer.
1899.

TO

MY UNCLE

HENRY KEMBLE OLIVER, M. D.

IN

GRATITUDE AND AFFECTION.

It gives me much pleasure to express here my deep sense of gratitude for the many kindnesses shown me by Professor Dr. Fritz Neumann of Heidelberg, whose instruction it was my great privilege to enjoy.

Professor Neumann suggested the subject of the present thesis and was ever ready with friendly counsel during its preparation.

Table of Contents.

Introduction.

Milet's Drama.

Appendix.

Index.

Introduction.

1. The extraordinary vitality of the Trojan legend in the middle-ages with its many ramifications in every land, forms one of the most interesting chapters in the history of literature. This chapter in its more general features has been admirably treated by such scholars as A. Joly. Hermann Dunger, and Wilhelm Greif, while, in addition to these men. many others have devoted their attention to the numerous special problems in this vast field that have arisen from the desire to determine the correct classification and inter-relation of the manifold mediaeval versions of the story of Troy. Of this extensive research work we can here only present such features as seem necessary to furnish an adequate introduction to the following pages.

2. As is well known, it is not to Homer nor to Virgil that we must look for the direct sources of those mediaeval versions of the Trojan legend, which attained great popularity and wide-spread ramification in every European tongue. Although Homer and Virgil served also as direct sources of mediaeval imitations (Greif § 3, § 4; Dunger, Pages 21–23) these were almost exclusively written in Latin and attained only a limited popularity. It was a necessary step to a wide-spread, popular interest in the story of Troy, that some author should clothe it in the language of the people. Such an author arose in a troubadour, Benoît of Sainte-More, who, at the Norman-French court of Henry II of England, composed about 1184[1]) his great work. „Le Roman de Troie" in some 30,100 eight-syllable verses in couplets. This production is one of the great monuments of

[1]) This date seems well supported by M. Joly P. 113, who bases it upon verse 13,442 of Benoit. This contains a reference to „riche dame de riche rei" who cannot well be other than Eleonore of Guienne, wife of Henry II.

mediaeval literature, not only because of its intrinsic merit, but also because, owing to its well-deserved popularity, there arose a long series of translations and adaptations in all Europe, either of the whole work or of selected portions. That Benoît of Sainte More should therefore receive the greatest credit as the father of this vast branch of literature, cannot be too strongly emphasized, and all the more so when we realize how far above his manifold imitators he stands, and also from what sources he himself drank.

3. Modern research has restored to Benoît the merit which he alone deserves, by showing in all its bareness the skeleton out of which he formed the living body. That skeleton we still possess in two mediocre works written in Latin, one the „Historia de excidio Trojae" of a certain Dares Phrygius of the 6th or 7th century, the other the „Ephemeris belli trojani" of Dictys Cretensis of the fourth century (Joly P. 677). Just why Benoît preferred these works to others of equal or of greater literary merit, is not very evident. It may have been chance which brought these alone to Benoît's notice. More probably however it was his mediaeval credulity in the statements of Dares and Dictys that they were present as eye witnesses of what they described, for he not only repeats these statements (that of Dares 5,073, 21,588 and elsewhere, that of Dictys 24,301—6), but constantly refers to Dares and Dictys for the truth of what he writes. The further interesting fact that of these references (see list by Greif P. 15 foot-note) nearly half are misleading and have no basis in the Dares or Dictys we possess, served as one argument in a conflict of opinion as to whether or not a more complete Dares or Dictys existed in an original Latin or Greek form, from which more complete version Benoît, perhaps, drew his inspiration. G. Körting, R. Jäckel and Clemens Fischer argue for a more complete Dares (respectively Dictys), the existence of which means, to them, a limitation of Benoît's originality. On the other hand Joly, Dunger, Greif and others plead for Benoit. Gaston Paris now takes an intermediate position. He still believes that a more complete Latin Dares existed, but he no longer thinks that Benoît used the same. (see Romania III, P. 131; Revue Critique 1874 No. 19. P. 292.)

4. M. Joly has given a most just estimate of Benoît's literary merit, and the comparative study of Benoît with two of his successors, which study was necessary in the preparation of the present thesis, has only strengthened our belief in the fairness of M. Joly's criticism. Benoît is certainly one of the greatest figures in mediaeval literature. He was indeed too great for the middle-ages, for how else can we understand the ease, with which a century later, between 1272 and 1287 (Barth P. 8—9), an Italian, Guido de Colonna, usurped, through a translation of Benoît into corrupt Latin, the fame of his predecessor and became in the latter's stead the source of all the more important, subsequent adaptations of the Troy legend? The importance of this usurpation is further seen in the fact that Guido's work itself, copied and recopied in a constant stream of manuscripts during two centuries[1]) found its way into print in a first edition of 1477 and remained in print until nearly the advent of the sixteenth century. The last dated print we have is 1494. So complete was this usurpation that Guido's work was long considered the original and Benoît's the translation! (Joly P. 882.)

5. 1) We must not however be too severe with Guido, for through him the Trojan legend received another long lease of life. Moreover as M. Joly has pointed out (P. 887) Guido took Benoît at his word in the latter's repeated assurances that he found everything in Dares and Dictys. Guido probably thought Benoît merely a translator of Dares and Dictys and hence his absolute neglect to give Benoît any credit. It however still seems strange that Guido makes no mention of Benoît even in those places where Benoît mentions himself, verse 128; 2,049; 2,054; 5,073; 19,079. Particularly striking is the passage 125 fol.

Ceste estoire nest pas usee
Nen gaires leus nen est trovee
Ja retraite ne fu unquore
Mes Beneeiz de Seinte More
La controve et fait et dit.

and also the following: 2,045 fol.

De sa vie ne de son fait
Ne sera plus por moi retrait
Gie ne le truis pas en cest livre
Ne Daires nen volt plus escrivre
Ne Beneiz pas nel alonge
Nen velt fere acreire menconge
Daires nen fet plus mencion
Mes qui or velt oïr chancon
De la plus halte ovre qui seit
Si come Beneiz laparceit etc.

---

[1]) see Appendix § 247 B¹ for list of them possessed by the National Library alone in Paris.

The first of these passages is in Benoît's introduction which Guido otherwise repeats almost verbally.

2) Although thus Guido never mentions Benoît, yet he refers all the more to Dares, and this he does, as Benoît had done, in many cases where the episode in question is completely absent in Dares. This fact, together with other arguments, is used by Joly (P. 883) and Barth (P. 14) to show that Guido did not, as Dunger (P. 61—4) maintains, know even that Dares which we possess, not to speak of a more complete Dares. Barth (P. 13) sufficiently disposes of the idea that Guido used Dictys, and Greif agrees with him (§ 76). Greif however asserts that Guido knew and used Dares (§§ 72—76). Of the arguments he gives for this, it has yet to be determined how many would disappear when a really critical edition of Guido, based especially upon the earliest manuscripts, shall have been made. We are inclined to think the evidence insufficient, especially when based only upon *one* print as Greif has done (§71.), for it is equally probable later copyists inserted from Dares' texts passages which Greif ascribes to Guido. In any event the close comparison of Guido and Benoît, necessary in the following study, furnishes further evidence of the slavishness with which Guido followed Benoît.

6. During the last part of that period in which we have already (§ 4.) noted the continued popularity of Guido's work, Jacques Milet a young French writer, (concerning whose life Haepke in the introductory paragraphs of his thesis recently published has gathered together all that we as yet know), moulded the mediaeval Troy story into dramatic form. Milet's drama contains 27,984 verses in varying metre, and is so divided as to require four days to play. It was composed in the years 1450 - 1452, and its popularity is attested by the existence of a last print in 1544. — The question now naturally arises, what work or works served as the source of Milet's production? It requires only a hasty reading of Milet to show that his work has the closest resemblance in its general features and plot to that great family of mediaeval versions of Troy, of which Benoît of Sainte-More is the worthy father. No thorough investigation has however as yet been made to establish Milet's relation to his predecessors, and as proof that the need of such an investigation still exists, we beg leave to pass in chronological review the various opinions that have been expressed. and thereby to show that their conflicting evidence rests upon inadequate and even superficial knowledge.

7. 1) The Brothers Parfaict (Edition of 1736, Vol. II. P. 418.) say „le Poëte à la réserve de quelques traits d'un livre intitulé Histoires de Troye, a suivi Dares Phrygien (Auteur fort connu et dont il n'a fait quelquefois que corrompre ou estropier les noms propres.)"

2) Although the „Histoire Littéraire de la France" has not yet reached Milet, we find the following in Vol. XIII P. 428, (date 1814) under „Benoît, Poète Anglo-Normand": „Il paraît que cet ouvrage (= Benoît's) eut un grand succés et qu'il conserva même assez long-temps sa réputation. Traduit en prose dans le 14e siècle, *il* fut mis sur le théâtre dans le suivant. Jacques Milet le fit imprimer (sic) sous le titre de Destruction de Troyes la Grant mise en rime françoise et par personnaiges."

3) Brunet („Manuel du Libraire." 1861, Vol. II. P. 658) speaking of the edition of 1544, the only one in which the drama is attributed to Jehan de Mehun, says: „C'est la seule édition où ce mystère soit attribué à Jehan de Mehun. Celui-ci n'en est pas l'auteur mais il paraît certain qu'il avait composé sur le même sujet un poème qui n'a pas été imprimé. Peut-être Jacques Millet n'a-t-il eu qu'à donner à ce poème la forme dramatique pour en faire un mystère, et c'est ce qui aura engagé l'éditeur de 1544 à rappeler le nom du premier auteur". Commenting on this hypothesis as to the source of Milet, Petit de Julleville only says: („Mystères" Vol. I. foot-note P. 570) „Nous reproduisons cette hypothèse de l'auteur du Manual du Libraire, mais elle paraît peu plausible". The brothers Parfaict more correctly ascribe this mistake in the edition of 1544 to a misreading of the initials J. M. (Edition of 1736 Vol. II. P. 419).

4) Curt Wunder (1868) in his thesis seems wholly ignorant of the existence of Benoît, for the latter's name is not mentioned at all! That Wunder was ignorant of the true source of Guido is shown on P. 8; 9; and P. 10. Foot Note 3. where he represents Guido as going directly back to Dares and Dictys.

Indeed the only possibilities which Wunder gives as sources of Milet are Dares and Dictys (Page 8) „und die vorzüglichsten Nachahmer derselben. Unter diesen ragen hervor: Josephus von Exeter, Iscanus genannt (de bello Trojano libri VI, in Hexametern), und Guido von Colonna, der das Material, welches Dares und Dictys bieten, nach Gutdünken verschmilzt und erweitert.“ This omission of Benoît seems incomprehensible, the more so because before Wunder's work, the relation of Guido to Benoît had been hinted at by several scholars[1])

Wunder first (Page 8) eliminates Iscanus as source-possibility of Milet, and then (after noting that the plot of Milet is the same as that of Dares to Chapter XXXIX of the latter, and then follows Dictys from Dictys' fifth book.) he concludes: (Page 9.)

„Milet hat also entweder den Dares und den Dictys in der angedeuteten Weise benutzt, oder — die Vermuthung liegt nahe — er hat aus einem Schriftsteller geschöpft, der seine Geschichte aus Beiden zusammenstellte, als welcher von uns oben Guido von Colonna bezeichnet wurde. Und in der That stellt eine Vergleichung zwischen seiner Geschichte und dem Drama die Entnahme desselben aus der ersteren ausser allen Zweifel.“

There now follow in Wunder (Pages 9—11) several cases of agreement between Milet and Guido, which he advances as proof of Guido's being Milet's source, without being aware that all of them with *one* exception are equally applicable to *Benoît* as Milet's source. This one exception is the manner of Hecuba's death, which in Benoît is related otherwise than in Guido and Milet[2]), but, even when we add to this proof of Milet's relation to Guido, the presence in Milet of Latin quotations from Guido, which Wunder notes (Page 31.), we are surely not justified in following Wunder when he concludes (Page 11.) „Dergleichen Uebereinstimmungen wären noch sehr viele beizubringen, wenn nicht diese schon uns zu dem Schlusse zu berechtigen schienen, dass Guido von Colonna's Historia destructionis Trojae als Haupt-, ja wohl als *alleinige* Quelle für Milet's Drama anzusehen ist.“

The simple fact of Wunder's total negligence of Benoît points to the inadequateness of his work, but we have felt it wise to insist upon this defect, because no one of those, who later refer to Wunder[3]) has seemed to realize the complete

[1]) F. Douce; J. C. Dunlop; Fromman: Cholevius. (see Dunger P. 61; Sommers, Introduction Vol. I. Page XXV foot note 2.)

[2]) see this essay § 231[2].

[3]) see § 7[7]; [11]; [12]; [15].

 7^{5-6}.

absence of Benoît in Wunder's thesis, and the consequent insufficiency of the proof he advances. Moreover, even when we allow the fullest possible weight to Wunder's evidence, it surely cannot warrant him or us in believing that Guido's work is the „alleinige Quelle" of Milet's drama. Far more evidence than Wunder advances, is necessary to support that opinion, even if we overlook his omission of Benoît.

5) In Tivier's thesis (1868) „Etude sur le mystère du siège d'Orléans et sur Jacques Milet auteur présumé de ce mystère" we find on the other hand no mention of Guido as source of the Destruction de Troie. In fact no direct source is given and Tivier only implies (Page 202) in a vague way that the souvenirs of the Trojan war came to Milet disfigured in the „chronique du faux Dares et l'oeuvre du trouvère Benoît de Sainte-Marthe" (for More?). Tivier therefore thinks the influence of Virgil (especially the second book of the Aeneid) and of Homer greater than we shall find reason to believe; he however deserves credit for pointing to one or two cases where that influence in all probability exists (§ 189; 224^{4-7}).

The general insufficiency of Tivier's thesis is shown, when, speaking of the episode of Troilus and Briseida (P. 292 ff.) and other resemblances of Milet's work with Shakespeare's „Troylus and Cressida", he says (P. 297): „Nous avons montré, que, non seulement il (= Milet) s'était rencontré avec Shakespeare dans une entreprise commune, mais qu'il avait eu sans doute l'honneur de lui servir de modèle."

Tivier however, here and in his later work (see § 7^8) gives an appreciative estimate of the literary merit of Milet.

6) With M. Joly (1869—70) we come to the first consideration of *both* Benoît and Guido as possibilities of being Milet's source. In a first statement M. Joly is in doubt whether Milet knew Benoît himself, but in later passages he seems to assume that Milet did know and use Benoît. The first statement is (Page 845): „Je ne saurais dire s'il avait lu le vieux poème lui-même, mais tout au moins il connaissait les traductions en prose dont nous parlions tout à l'heure (= Pages 827—843) [En effet dans son prologue, dont nous allons parler, il n'est question que de „prose laye" (laïque, vulgaire)]. C'est là et dans le livre de Guido qu'il a pris les éléments de son oeuvre ou plutôt son oeuvre même." The other passages in Joly are: (Page 847) „Nous croyons inutile d'analyser le Mystère: ce serait répéter ce que nous savons déjà et

refaire le Roman de Troie. L'imitateur n'en a rien laissé; il a non plus rien ajouté d'essentiel, si ce n'est, comme nous le verrons tout à l'heure l'empreinte très marquée de son temps. On retrouve dans l'imitation l'oeuvre originale tout entière, autant du moins que le permettent les nécessités de la mise en scène. Tous les discours que Jacques Millet rencontre dans le poème de Benoît, il les reproduit avec empressement, souvent même il les étend, — — — — — — puis de temps en temps le combat s'arrête et les héros échangent à la façon homérique des discours empruntés le plus souvent textuellement au livre de Benoît."

And later (Page 852) „il lui (= Benoît) emprunte le plan de son oeuvre; il lui emprunte le caractère de ses personnages. Il les a trouvés dans Benoît, non pas seulement indiqués, mais complètement développés. C'est à Benoît que revient à cet égard tout le mérite de l'invention.

7) Dunger (1869) only says (Page 65) „ihm (= Guido) folgt Jacques Milet in seinem 1484 herausgegebenen Mysterium." Dunger refers to Wunder's dissertation without further comment on Milet.

8) In Tivier's „Histoire de la lit. dram. en France" (1873), he seems to have abandoned his idea of a common authorship of „Le Siège d'Orléans" and „La Destruction de Troie", which he had tried to prove in his thesis (see § 8[5]); he is ignorant of the works of Wunder, Joly and Dunger, for he mentions neither Benoît nor Guido as possible sources of Milet. He only says (Page 387) „La seconde (journée) qui résume trois chants de l'Iliade" and introduces several instances of Milet's resemblance to Virgil. His ignoring of Benoît and Guido therefore leads him to greatly over-estimate Milet's originality.

9) Barth (1877), without referring to any authority except Dunger (Foot Note P. 32 of Barth) says. (P. 33) „Sowohl Jacques Milet als auch Raoul de Fevre folgten ihm (= Guido) in ihren Dichtungen."

10) Petit de Julleville („Les Mystères" 1880) seems ignorant of all possibility of Guido. He says (Vol. 2. P. 573) „Dans ce poème de trente mille vers l'invention se réduit à peu de chose. L'auteur n'ignorait pas entièrement l'Iliade, mais il a puisé surtout dans l'ouvrage si populaire au moyen-âge de Dares le Phrygien ou plutôt de l'auteur, quel qu'il soit, qui a écrit, sous ce nom, le „Daretis Phrygii de excidio Trojae Historia". Il s'inspire aussi beaucoup de Benoît de Sainte-More, auteur du Roman de Troie.

11) Meybrinck (1886) says (§ 5) Guido „ist wiederum die Vorlage gewesen für einen französischen Dramatiker des 15. Jahrhunderts, Jacques Milet". Meybrinck refers to Parfaict;

de Julleville; Bib. du théâtre français; Tivier (§ 7[8]); and Wunder. On Page 6, Meybrinck says: „Nirgends wird (in Milet) dessen (= Homer's) Name genannt, während Milet sonst Colonna genau folgt." We quite agree with Meybrinck's good opinion of Milet's literary merit (P. 69) although Meybrinck has failed to signal the great unevenness of Milet's production.

12) Greif (1886) refers to Wunder's thesis (§ 80) and then, speaking of Milet's relation to his source, he says „dass die Anlehnung an Guido eine ziemlich enge ist, dass ausserdem in der Partie v. 24,681 ff.[1]) sich eine Benutzung des 6 (?) Buches der Aeneis bemerkbar zu machen scheint." Greif further thinks Milet knew the Alexander-Romance, and the „Achilleis" of Gualtherus ab insulis (de Castellione) (See for the use by Milet of the latter. § 168[3]).

13) Sommers (1894) only says (Page XXXVIII. of Introduction to Vol. I.) „Jacques Milet dramatised in 1450 Guido's Historia". He gives no authorities for this particular statement, although elsewhere he mentions Joly, Dunger and other writers on the mediaeval Troy legend.

14) L. Constans in the large „Histoire de la langue et de la lit. fran." which is appearing under the direction of Petit de Julleville says (Vol. I, 1896, Page 216). „Dans la seconde moitié du XV siècle notre Roman (= Benoît) était encore populaire puisque Jacques Millet en tirait un mystère etc — — Elle (= Milets work) suit le poème assez regulièrement."

15) Haepke in his recent (1897) study of the language of Milet's drama with a view to a future critical edition, says (end of § 7): „Liegt auch bis jetzt noch keine Specialuntersuchung über die Quellenfrage der „Destruction" vor, so habe ich mich doch durch eine summarische Untersuchung davon überzeugt, dass an Wunders und Greifs Ansicht festzuhalten ist, unser Drama gehe direkt auf Guido de Colonna zurück, ja dass die Anlehnung eine sehr enge ist."

16) It seems hardly necessary to point out that the confusion and insufficiency of the opinions, we have just noted, have found equal expression in those manuals and histories of literature which make any mention of Milet's work.

---

[1]) = Priam's allegorical monologue, see § 202—5.

8. 1) In view of the uncertainty shown in the above opinions, the question of Milet's relation to his predecessors Benoît and Guido may still be declared unsettled. The investigation of this relation forms one feature of the following pages. It seemed to us probable, inasmuch as so many mediaeval French dramatic productions are adaptations of earlier epic versions of the same subjects in the French itself, that a like fact ought to hold good at least in part for Milet's drama. It was undoubtedly this same thought, that led many of the above writers to make the statement, that Benoît served as direct source of Milet, without furnishing any sufficient proofs of that affirmation. In our present study of Milet's source, we have made a thorough examination of the versions of Benoît, Guido, and Milet, with the following questions constantly in mind:

a) Is Milet indebted directly to Benoît?

b) If so, to what extent?

c) If not, what is his debt to Guido?

2) As the first two questions formed the original stimulus of our study, we employed the following procedure: For every episode of the drama, we compared Milet's version *first* with Benoît, noting all resemblances and all deviations. We then repeated the process by comparing Milet with Guido. Naturally, since the three versions were in general so similar, it was necessary to pass over everything which was *alike* in the three and sift out only the deviations. These deviations could be of two sorts, either *mutual* deviations of *two* versions from the third, or deviations of *one* version from the other *two*. The first sort would show us the extent of the influence of the *earlier* of the two versions upon the *later;* the second the amount of originality and independence of each version. Of course as regards Benoît, his deviations from his successors only form a small part of his originality, since he is the creator of all episodes common to the three versions (except in so far as he in turn is indebted to earlier sources).

3) Our thesis contains the results of this process of sifting and comparing, and we can affirm with the greatest certainty that there exists *no* direct relationship between Milet and Benoît, that on the contrary wherever, in an episode common to all

three, Benoît's relation differs from Guido, Milet invariably follows Guido, not Benoît. Negatively also, wherever Guido omits anything in Benoît, Milet omits it also. Indeed throughout Milet there is a constant succession of points of contact with Guido both of this affirmative and negative character, and, when we note the nearness and continuity of these points of contact. we are eminently justified in assuming, regarding what lies between, common to all three versions, that Milet is also indebted therefor to Guido and not to Benoît. That a few isolated cases of apparent direct influence of Benoît upon Milet exist, is to be expected from the great length of the work. Each one of these cases however is readily explained, often indeed without calling attention to its isolation from its fellows and its proximity to the never-ending succession of points of contact between Milet and Guido. The references to such cases are in the Index under „*Benoît,* seemingly influences Milet".

It is thus proved that the words at the end of Milet's own prologue are true: „Cy sensuit listoire de la destruction de troye la grant translatee de *latin* en francoys mise par parsonnages". His main source at least is a work in Latin and that work is Guido's. That here and there traces of other influences, occur, in no case however of Benoît, will be seen.

9. 1) We wish now to direct attention to another possibility, of which the Brothers Parfaict (§ 7[1]) and M. Joly (§ 7[6]) have already given hints: In Milet's prologue where in allegorical language, he speaks of the Trojan ancestry of the French kings as the reason of his wish to write the history of Troy, he adds (Verse 277):

Et pource que bien ie savoye	Si ay voulu eviter reddicte
Que aultreffois a este escripte	Et ay propose de la faire
En latin et en prose laye	Par parsonnages seullement.

2) Without going into the question whether with „latin" Milet meant more than Guido's work, we would like to raise the query, just what work or works he refers to, as knowing so „bien", in the words „prose laye" That this means the language of the people as opposed to Latin, the language of the church and the learned, is evident. Does it however mean French alone, or are we to suppose Milet knew of prose ver-

sions in other tongues? The Brothers Parfaict name a French book „Histoires de Troie", which Wunder (Page 8) interprets as meaning „Les cents histoires de Troye, Paris in 4° (Brunet VI, 13,231)" by „Christienne de Pisa († 1420)."

Wunder names no other possibilities, but Joly (see first passage quoted § 7⁶) says Milet must have known the prose translations of Benoît, without however giving any proof of this statement. Not only would it be an interesting study to examine what one or ones of these prose versions of the Trojan story may have been know and used by Milet, but much still remains to be done in the determination of the relation of each of these works to Benoît and to Guido respectively (see in this last connection Paul Meyer, Romania XIV Page 1).

3) It seems to us, considering the closeness of contact of Milet with Guido, that the influence of any other mediaeval Troy version, if such influence exists at all, must be very limited, and its traces isolated. Moreover against the idea of Milet's use of such additional source or sources, may be cited the words of his prologue. (301)

Si retournay a descouvert
Dedens mon habitation
Ou ie trouvay ung livre ouvert
Faisant des troyans mencion
Lors commencay sans plus attendre
A faire listoire de troye.

Of course these words alone are of very little weight. We think however that, if influences of mediaeval origin other than Guido exist, they came to Milet only in the form of more or less vague souvenirs. We regret that we were unable for lack of time to add the investigation of this question to the present study. We hope however that our establishment of Milet's relation to Benoît and to Guido will very materially aid in some future solution.

10. Although we thus felt forced to restrict our study of Milet's source to his relation to Guido and to Benoît, the very process of determining this relation put us in possession of a large amount of material, which enabled us to see clearly, in what measure Milet is indebted to his source, the nature and extent of his originality, and how he moulded his material into dramatic form. Our attention had been called to the desirability of such a study of Milet's dramatic ability by a passage in Greif (Page 67): „In einer späteren Untersuchung werden wir uns ausführlicher über Milet's Verhältniss zu seiner Quelle verbreiten, besonders über die Art und Weise wie er den Stoff dramatisierte.“ These lines were written in 1886, since when the promised study has not been forthcoming. It therefore seemed advisable, inasmuch as many interesting features of Milet's dramatic talent had come to light during the investigation of his source, to embody them also in the present work. With this purpose in mind it was at first our intention to treat the two questions, that of Milet's source and that of his use of the same, in two distinct parts of this thesis. It however soon became apparent that the two studies were so intimately related, the one with the other, as to render their separation not only difficult but inadvisable. We therefore decided to treat both matters at the same time. If a lack of clearness is in some cases the result, it is to be hoped a carefully prepared index may help to remedy the fault. Our process has therefore been, to analyze each episode or scene of the drama, with a view to showing:

1) The absence of the influence of Benoît.

2) The extent of indebtedness to Guido.

3) The amount and nature of Milet's originality.

4) The manner in which Milet, combining the elements borrowed from his source, with the suggestions of his own imagination, moulded both into dramatic form.

II. 1) We regret for many reasons that critical editions exist neither of Benoît nor of Guido nor of Milet. Although these are very much to be desired, we do not think that the results of this study would be much affected by them. We did not feel able to draw into our field of study the manuscripts of Benoît, Guido or Milet, especially in view of their large number. Yet, as most of this work was done in the Bibliothèque Nationale of Paris, we were able to make use of the several prints of Guido and of Milet which are there (see § 247 B²; 247 C). For Benoît we were limited to the edition of M. Joly, the promised edition of L. Constans not having yet appeared.

2) A few abbreviations which we have used may not be at first apparent:

B. signifies Benoît. The verse numbers refer to Joly's edition.

G. is used for Guido. As no modern edition as yet exists, we determined to use the first edition of 1477 as basis for our references. The pagination is however defective, the first four of each eight sheets alone being numbered on the recto side, thus: a 1, a 2, a 3, a 4. To complete the pagination we continued the enumeration with: a 5, a 6, a 7, a 8. For recto and verso, r and v are used, and the line of the page is indicated by another number, thus: a 7 r 24; m 5 v 16. etc.

M. abbreviates Milet. The numerical references are to Stengel's „Autographische Vervielfältigung" of the edition of 1484.

d. after a number means *„stage direction"*.

B-G. used together signify the version common to Benoît and Guido only; similarly G-M. that common to Guido and Milet; B-G-M that common to all. In the Index, *beg.* is for „beginning"

The division into chapters was made for the sake of convenience.

With these preliminary explanations we beg leave to present the results of our work.

The First Day of the Drama.

Chapter I.

The Embassy of Anthenor to the Greek princes.

Milet 1—1,129; Benoît 2,873—2,910; 3,173—3,632; Guido D 4 v 8 — D 7 v 14.

12. This chapter offers us but a few minor illustrations of M's dependence upon G, for M. has in the main taken the general trend of the story common to B-G and moulded it into dramatic form. The chief interest therefore centers in observing how he did the moulding, although an occasional point indicative of M's source will present itself.

13. The first day of the drama opens with a monologue by Priam, its central, figure, who thanks the deities that his city has been rebuilt[1]) better than before. Passing then to a recital of his injuries and especially of his great grief at the shameful fate of Exiona, his sister, he gives vent to his desire for revenge. To that end he will summon his court. He therefore sends his messenger, Macabrum, to bid the princes of Troy come to the palace. Priam mention's all these by name, and Macabrum, as he leaves each prince, declares his purpose to visit the next, giving in each case the names. This simple and naïve way of introducing us to the growing list of personages is employed throughout the drama on every similar occasion.[2])

[1]) See § 239 for M's allusions to the first destruction of Troy.

[2]) In this connection a slight error is to be noted in verse 105: „Je men vois tout fin droit parler | a anthenor sans plus attendre.“ As it is Anchises to whom he immediately speaks and Anchises who replies; moreover as Macabrum later (verse 122) addresses Anthenor at the same time as his son Pollidamas, the „anthenor“ in verse 106 is an evident error. Strange to say the latest edition 1544 is the only one which has the correct reading „Anchises“. All others of the National Library have „anthenor“.

Priam had bidden Macabrum summon *all* his sons, but Hector is not named with the other four (129—131; 233—236), and although mentioned later by name (239; 347; 1,000; 1,004), he does not actually appear until after the return of Anthenor from Greece (1,026). This omission is in harmony with B-G, but M. omits all reference to the cause there given, namely that Priam had sent Hector to Pevoine (B. 3,189, G. = Panonia. D 4 v 16). M's only explanation is in the words of Anthenor upon the latter's return (976—8): Car ie scay bien quil n'estoit pas en la ville quant ie party | Mais il est venu dieu mercy.

14. 1) The princes prepare to go to Priam, Anchises bringing Enee and Ascanius (179). This is only interesting as indicative of a characteristic of which we find many more striking examples in Milet later, namely his love of scenes illustrative of filial or of family affection. These scenes form one of the few relieving features which sustain our interest in an otherwise too often wearisome waste of words:

Enee: Ascanius il fault mouvoir
Pour aler a la court du roy
Ascanius: Pere ie suis prest quant a moy
Daler partout ou vous plaira.

2) The princes meet and join company as they proceed to Priam. This is also an idea utilized often by Milet in similar assemblings. They greet one another in most friendly manner. Anthenor praises Troillus to his son Pollidamas: (236)

Et troillus qui tant me plaist
Car de parfaicte hardiesse
De vaillance et de proqesse
Apres hector n'est nul pareil
Il est blanc et si est vermeil
Comme une rose au moys de may.

3) Another pleasing little scene, indicative too of the growing disposition to characterize the personages, follows the above:

(267) Paris:
Or ca donc puis quil est ainsi
Vous yres devant anchises
Anchises: Non feray Paris
Paris:
Si ferez, vous estez le plus veil de tous
Pour dieu alez devant
Anchises:
Mais vous
Car devant vous n'yroy ie mye
Anthenor:
Alons ensemble ie vous prye
Et ne faisons cy plus d'arrest.

Milet shows further his very considerable originality in the characterization of his personages. He here adds quite a human flavor by representing Priam as very impatient:

226—228.
Amy bien m'est tart que ie voye
Ceulx a qui envoyé t'avoye,
Car i'en ay besoing grandement.

also 275—284.
Dea macabrum il me desplaist
Que ie ne voy vers moy venir
Ceulx que ie t'ay fait convenir,
Si suis esbay donc ce vient

Macabrum:
Ha s'ire pas a moy ne tient,
Car icn ay fait bien mon devoir;
Mais ie voys de present scavoir,
Se i'en verrè nulz d'eulx venir.

Priam:
Va tost sans plus toy cy tenir
Et les faiz haster vistement.

There was no indication of such impatience in B-G.

15. 1) The princes finally appear, Priam addressing pleasing words of welcome to each, and particularly affectionate ones to his sons. In this M. has an opportunity to further emphasize his characterizations. Thus Priam speaks to Paris:

(310.)
Beau filz paris vostre grande beaulte,
Et vostre corps qui est plain de bonte
Donne a mon cueur grande esjouissance.

To Troylus: (346.)
Ha troillus beau filz, comme ie croy,
Apres hector n'est nul pareil a toy,
Quant ie te voy de pitie ie lermoye.

M. found these characterizations already in B-G. but he is quite original in depicting Priam's especial affection for Anthenor above all the other courtiers:

358—360 Ha anthenor pour dieu n'arrestez pas,
Acollez moy ie vous prie bras a bras.
Ha beaulx amis bien soyes vous venus.

2) Priam now addresses the assembled court. He reminds them of the grief he has had the past ten[1]) years (377) at the fate of Exionne, and of the other wrongs done him by the Greeks. Priam's language is vigorous and brings to light more sharply his character than do the corresponding speeches in B-G. Essentially the same thoughts are expressed in all three versions, but one idea occurs which we find only in G and M.

G. (D 5 r 14)
„sed quod bellorum eventus semper ambiguus et dubia sunt facta pugnantium."

M. (453—456)
Mais pource que l'advenement
De guerre si est incertain,
Que nul ne peult certainement
Jugier des combatans a plain, etc.

Before therefore trying warlike measures, let them endeavor to secure Exionne by peaceful demand. Priam asks Anchises,

---

[1]) see the various inconsistences of time, in these references to the earlier destruction of Troy, in Appendix § 239.

as the eldest, for advice, who counsels sending Anthenor to the Greeks (480). In B. Priam himself appoints Anthenor without asking for any advice (B. 3,240) but G. says (D 5 r 27) that Priam appointed Anthenor „suorum fidelium approbatione", which probably suggested to M. Priam's less independent action.

16. Anthenor prepares to go, bidding Athimas tell the shipmaster Sorbin to make ready the ship. Then Anthenor in prayer (519—530) beseeches the gods to protect him and to allow the success of his mission. B-G. know no such supplication, this being one of the many scenes entirely original to M. which help greatly to bind together the movement of the drama and to render it smoother. There follows a little scene of farewell between Anthenor and his son Pollidamas with the refrain.[1])

(539) Adieu mon filz pollidamas
Adieu jusques au retourner.

Anthenor and his companions arrive at Manise the city of Peleus. In B. Anthenor delays three days before disclosing his mission (B. 3,276). G. knows nothing of this, nor does M refer to any delay, on the contrary: (577)

Athimas:	Anthenor:
si me semble que mieulx vauldroit	Or ca donc pour le faire court
qu'alissions tout droit a la court.	Alons y sans dilation.

In B-G. Peleus demands Anthenor's mission. In M. he states it without being asked. Original to M. here and elsewhere is the manner of greeting an enemy: Anthenor (585 ff.) asks „le grant dieu de terre et de mer" to protect Priam,

et fortune par sa maniere	Et tous ceulx qui a la priere
diverse et fiere	qu'il leur requiere
Vueille ses enemis confondre	Ne vouldront a son gre respondre.

Peleus refuses Anthenor's request for Exionne and orders him away.

17. Anthenor journeys to Thelamon and gives a similar hostile greeting (687—690). As a proof of his statement of what the Greeks did at Troy, Anthenor says „Je le scay bien car ie y estoye" a statement not found anywhere in B-G. In M. Anthenor is one of the many who, at one time or another, declare they were at the earlier destruction of Troy (see § 239⁴

---

[1]) see Appendix for a list of the refrains § 246.

treating of such references). In this dialogue with Thelamon there are several sure indications of M's dependance upon G:

1) M. 715--718. Envoyès luy sans resistance
Sa seur et il vous pardonnera
De tout son cueur et sa puissance,
Et iamais plus ne vous herra.

G = D 6 r 16. Si restituendam sibi eam benignitas vestra providerit, etc.

2) Thelamon's words (719) le mesmerveille de l'inconstance De ton roy; D 6 r 21. de tui levitate regis admiratione multa commoveor.

3) 727. Si eu de mon sang respandu; D 6 r 26 in mei cruoris effusione.

4) The threat: 741—742 Se tu ne pars de mon pays
Ie feray ton corps dommager.

D 6 v 8. quod nisi instanter feceris scias te sine dubio mortis periculum incursurum.

5) Anthenor goes then to Thaie (see § 243 proper names) to Castor and Pollus. His visit gives us no particular point of M's contact with G. to chronicle, except a similarity of expression: D 6 v 25 „tu vitam tuam tibi parum caram esse monstraveris."

M. 822 „Qui devers nous t'envoie ie t'affie
Bien peu prisoit ton corps et ta vie."

G. omits to let Pollux speak, although B. had not. In M. Pollux takes part in the dialogue as in B, but this similarity is readily understood since the necessity of letting each important personage speak explains Pollus' speech in M.

Anthenor visits next „roy Nestor" (871). B. in the corresponding place has „reis nestor" (B. 3481.) whereas G. has „dux nestor" (D 6 v 31). This slight resemblance has no weight however, for M. uses the titles „roy" and „dux" indiscriminately: „Nestor duc" 5,667; and the less so because a few lines beyond (895) in his reply to Anthenor, Nestor says: „Se ce ne fust pour ma noblesse", which is taken directly from (D 7 r 9) „nisi me mea frenaret nobilitas". B. has no such idea.

18. Ordered away by Nestor, Anthenor retnrus at once to Troy. In B. there is a description of a storm which in G. finds an extraordinary expansion, this being one of G's much vaunted additions to his original. M. omits even a reference to it, and passes by also in consequence Anthenor's special thanksgiving in the temples for his safe arrival. (B. 3561—4. D 7 r 31). Instead there is a pleasing scene of welcome in which Pollidamas „qui doit estre de XVIII ans ou environ" greets his father in the following refrain:

(950) Ha cher pere moult estes las
Moult avez fait longue demeure.

Anthenor then bids Athimas summon Anchises, Liconius Amphorbius and Hector to come before Priam. Athimas obeys and greets Andromache (1,007) at the same time with Hector. In affectionate words Hector bids his brothers come with him. They all agree, expressing love and obedience to him. „car vous estez le plus ancien“. All come before Priam and seat themselves „fors Anthenor“ (1073) who makes his report to Priam. The speech calls for no comment except to note a peculiar phrase in the relation of Thelamon's refusal to surrender Exionne:

1102 Si dist que point ne la rendroit, Et que ia tant qu'il vivroit,
Car a grant peine l'avoit eue, Vous n'en aures ne pie ne queue.

The speech is essentially the same in all three versions.

Chapter II.

Priam's Council with his nobles and with his sons relative to the sending of Paris to Greece.

M. 1,130—1,752; B. 3,633—4,150; G. D 7 v 15 — E 5 v 13.

19. In general M. found the dialogue already so completely developed in this section that he had little to do except to extend it slightly and to insert a few connecting links. If the previous chapter showed but few points of undoubted contact of M. with G., this chapter has a great abundance. Indeed some passages are scarcely more than literal translations from G, this being one of the most striking portions of the drama in that respect.

20. Priam's speech: In M. no particular anger is shown by Priam at the conclusion of Anthenor's speech (1,030). B-G. on the contrary emphasize this trait (B. 3633 — D 7 v 12). Priam's speech to the nobles is essentially the same in B-G-M. One idea however is common only to G-M.

1,162—4. Nous devons tous mettre noz corps
Nostre avoir et nostre chevance
Pour noz peres lesquelz sont mors.

D 8 v 9—11: ut quilibet vestrum (other editions = nostrum) — personas et res proprias debeat fortune committere ad instaurationem damnorum nostrorum et ad nostrem gravis injurie ulcionem.

At the conclusion of the speech M. has an extension of dialogue (1178—1225) terminating in Priam's thanking the nobles and requesting them to withdraw:

(1228) Partez vous hardiment d'icy
Je vueil parler a mes enfans.

B. makes no mention of their withdrawal, there being nothing to distinctly indicate they were not present during Priam's interview with his sons

B 3705. Molt s'en est li reis esjoiz ·
Puis a apelez toz ses filz.

M. is beyond doubt indebted to G. (D 8 v 19) recendendi licentiam affectuosis verbis tribut unicuique remanente rege in suo palatio cum omnibus filiis suis etc.

21. Then follows Priam's address to his sons, the refrain „Et de tous points vuide de ioye" occurring four times. In G-M the sequence of thought is exactly the same, in B. quite otherwise: Priam begins his speech in tears (1244; D 8 v 25). In B. the tone is more imperative, in G-M. more that of an appeal to the filial duty of his sons, in which Priam emphasizes his age and weakness and his consequent dependence upon their youth and strength. B. gives no such reasons. Priam's last words are to Hector and show his affection for him.

22. Reply of Hector: In M. alone Hector „parle en plourant" (1336 d). It is sufficient to give a list of the striking instances of M's dependence upon G; the sequence of thought is again the same, and very different from B, although many of the same ideas there find expression; completely absent in B are the following:

a) the naturalness of the desire for revenge. G. adds a peculiar argument to his expression of the above thought: (E 1 r 24) si vindictam appetimus de injuriis nobis illatis non sumus degeneres hominum a natura cum etiam animalia irrationabilia videamus hoc voto potiri (!)

b) M. first translates, and then quotes outright from G. „quia personarum qualitas iniuriarum qualitatem minuit et augmentat iniquitatem".[1]) (M. 1352. G. E 1 r 23.)

[1]) The quotation is the same in all M. prints except that 1544 has placed it at the side of the page opposite its translation. G. has „cum" for „quia" and omits „iniquitatem" in all prints. These variations of M. might serve to determine what group of Guido Mss. he used.

c) Hector, as first born, acknowledges his desire above all the sons, to demand vengeance.

M. (1361—1372.)

Mais pource que premier suys,
Cher pere, de vostre lignee,
Croyes qu'il n'est nul de voz filz
A qui tant la vengence agree
Comme a moy, c'est chose prouvee
Car elle me touche plus fort
Et si sera par moy vengee
Du roy laomedon la mort;
Car ie doy par ma propre dextre
Venger mon sang et mes parens
Et doy tousiours le premier estre
Pour les secourir en tous sens.

G. (E 1 r 26 — E 1 v 2.)

Nullus est ergo inter filios vestros care pater qui de nece avorum nostrorum magis teneatur vindictam appetere sicut ego qui sum primus in eorum ordine geniture et ideo primus esse debeo in ulciscendi fervore prae ceteris. Ergo cum omni aviditate desidero vindictam meorum inimicorum appetere ut etiam in cruore meo mea dextera cruentatos interimat qui crudeliter meorum avorum et civium effundere cruorem.

d) Second Latin quotation from G. (E 1 v 7.) It is absent in the edition of 1544. (M. 1392) quid enim prodest alicui bene forte in principibus agere aliquid subito si illi contingerit et fortuna veniat sinistro (Edition of 1477, Guido, after *agere:* „quod demum terminari contingunt sine sinistro).

e) Third Latin quotation (E 1 v 11), also absent in the edition of 1544; (M. 1400.) Illud enim potest dici felix principium cuius exitus felix est. (G. 1477 has „felix potest dici — — — felix fuit".)

f) (1401) Vous savez que *auffrique*[1]) et europe Est de tous points aux grecs submise. (E 1 v 15) noscis totam *affricam* et europam hodie graecis esse subjectam. B. simply says (3791). „Veez Europe que il ont | La tierce partie del mont." B. then gives a lengthened account of the power of the Greeks (3793—3806) and includes as allies of the Greeks „toz icels d'Ase", which is in direct discord with

h) M. who here and elsewhere, considers Asia[2]) as the domain of the Trojans (1409) „si n'est pas auiourdhui pareille La puissance de toute Asie a celle des Grecs." which is a literal translation of (E 1 v 19) non est equalis hodie asie potentia potentatui tot virorum. In this connection an important item is in B. alone (3,810—17), namely Hector's emphasis of their lack and need of ships.

[1]) see Africa in proper names § 241.

[2]) see Asia in proper names § 241.

i) The foolishness of exchanging repose and peace for the turmoil of war: 1417—1424. E 1 v 24 27.

j) Exiona is not worth such a price. B's superiority is here strikingly manifest for there is no trace of such a brutal thought: 1425—40. E 1 v 28 — E 2 r 3.

B. says at the end of Hector's speech (B 3823). „Sor ço redistrent lor talent | Li plosor qui sont en present | En plosors sens le volent faire | Ennui sereit de tot retraire. | Apres els toz parla Paris.“ This passage might well have suggested to M. an expansion of the dialogue. He did not expand it however, but follows G, who has no corresponding passage and makes Paris speak immediately after Hector.

23. Speech of Paris: The sequence of thought in G-M. is exactly the same, as well as many details. B. is quite different:

a) (M. 1448 d) „Paris se lieve nu teste“. E 2 r 11 „se erigens“. B. does not mention this detail.

b) The dream of Paris is alike in G-M, in the following points:

1) The hunt took place in „Ynde mineur“ (M. 1489) „in minori india“ (E 2 r 28). Joly's text gives „Inde la major“, although manuscript *B.* gives „menor“, which might indicate the group of Benoît Mss. from which G's version arose. In describing this scene Curt Wunder says in his dissertation § 14 „auf dem *Berg Ida*“ (!), but M. makes absolutely no mention of Ida. Here as in a few other instances Wunder does not follow strictly the story as told in M. Guido alone says later „in ipsius nemoris solitudine quod ydra (in Edition of 1486 ida) vocatur perveni solus“ (E 2 v 7). Benoît gives a wholly different location (B 3850.) El vals de Tariens | Lez la fontaine ou nus n'aboivre | tres desoz l'onbre d'un geneivre.

2) It was Friday: 1497 „jour de vendredi“, E 2 r 30 quodam die veneris. Perhaps G. chose this special day because of the role of Venus in the dream. B. is not explicit „l'autrier es kalendes de Mai“ (B. 3842).

It was toward evening. M. 1501 Si advint que sur la vespree E 2 v 2 circa vesperarum confinia.

3) B. makes no mention of Paris' horse, but G-M. have several details in common:

1517—18.	E 2 v 12.
Mon cheval estoit tout pollu Par les gouttes de sa sueur	Cum equus meus totus esset modidus nimio per sudore.
1521—26.	E 2 v 14—16.
Adonc descendy a pie Pour dormir iusques au lendemain. Prins mon cheval et le lye A une branche par le frain. Et la m'endormy au serain En attendant la matinee.	descendi fessus ab equo et ipsum in ramo cuiusdam arboris michi propinquo cum habenis fremi sui studui colligare. Deinde stravi me solo quod adhuc multo vigebat in gramine arborum umbraculis prohibentibus eis siccitatem etc.

4) In B. the goddesses are Juno, Venus and *Minerva;* in G-M. Juno, *Pallas,*[1]) Venus. In G-M. they remain in the background while Mercury addresses Paris. Mercury states specifically the promised gifts of *all* the goddesses; in B. only that of Venus is specified. In G-M. Paris requests that the goddesses stand before him naked. Curiously enough M. makes no mention of the apple as the cause of dispute among the goddesses, and refers only in vague terms to „le don“ (1574, 1578, 19,944, 19,949). All the illustrated editions however except that of 1544 represent one of the goddesses holding an apple. B. describes no particular examination of the deities by Paris, but G-M. give it in considerable detail, M. more than G., M. adding the thought „lors regarday ioyeusement“ (1589).

M. adds a detail unknown in B-G.

1531. Il me fut advis que ie vy
Ardre des torches plus de vingt
Et lors le dieu mercure vint.

B. has two details not repeated in G-M: Mercurion calls to Paris three times B 3858. Mercurion had suggested Paris as arbiter B 3878.

24. The speech of Deyphebus:

a) 1609—1616	E 3 r 30 — E 3 v 2.
Tres puissant roy ie vous supplie Que me vueilles escouter, A celle fin que ie vous dye Mon couraige sans riens celler. Ie dy que qui vouldrait penser, Quant on entreprent quelque affaire, A tout ce qu'il peult succeder, On n'oseroit nulx beaulx faitx faire.	si in omni negocio quod est aliquis aggressurus vellent singula qui possent esse futura particulari deliberatione terminari numquam aliquis esset qui alicuius rei onori subiceret animosus.

[1]) Referring again to this scene, M. says also Pallas 19,944,

b) 1617	E 3 v 2
Car se les laboureurs pensoient, Que les oiseaulx prinssent le grain, Croyes que pas ne le someroient	nam si semper agricole diligenti deliberatione pensarent quanta a raptu volucrum aufferenda sunt semina numquam forte semina sulcis darent.

B is utterly different 3913—3924.

c) the rest of the speech is also alike in G-M.

25. The warning of Helenus: This speech is so much alike in all three versions that no sequence of dependence is seen. At its close however B. simply says all were silent and depicts no particular astonishment (B 3969). Yet G. says (E 3 v 28) „sapientis vacillavit regis animus et turbatione repletus extitit non modicum stupefactus", which M. takes up and extends to the whole assembly in the stage direction after 1688. „et tous les princes seront tous esbahis et regarderont l'ung l'autre et (ce) voyant le roy priam comme esbay fera admiracion".

26. Troylus' vigorous speech: Here the resemblance of G. to B. is much more striking than that of M. to G. In B. the whole speech expresses the greatest contempt for the priesthood, and G. takes up and intensifies the sharp satire[1]) (B. 3977—4,002) (G. E 4 r 3—17) It is interesting to note that M. leaves this all out, only retaining one sentence:

M. 1690 Vous troublez vous pour les ditz outraigeulx
D'un prestre plain de pussillaminite,

of which we find the counterpart in G. (E 4 r 4,) ad quid turbamini circa plura ad vocem unius *pussillaminis* sacerdotis". Other points of contact with G are:

a) 1695	E 4 r 10
Car ce qu'il dit, vient de legierecte Non pas de sens ne de soutivecte	cum ex sola procebat stulticie levitate
b) 1699—1700	E 4 r 12
Laissez les aultres faire leur voulente Sans empescher leur bon consentement	Sinat alios qui labe verecundie obducuntur debitas in armorum conflictu exposcere ulciones.
c) 1702	E 4 r 14
Lachez les nefz, baillez le voille au vent	Jube navigia solvere.
1708	
Que le voille soit droit au vent mis.	

At the close of Troylus speech M. leaves the course of events outlined in B-G, omitting a large section and passing

[1]) See another example of G's dislike of the clergy in his relation of the corruption of the priest Thoas § 210[0].

directly to the expedition of Paris to Greece.[1]) Priam expresses his joy and gratitude to Troylus for his valiant speech (1715) „car les soultilz argumens de logicque | Ne sont pas tant a louer que prouesse". Then bidding Paris and Deyphebus prepare for the journey, he sends Macabrum his messenger, to command Anthenor, Enee and Pollidamas to accompany his sons.

Chapter III.

The Departure of Paris for Cytharea.

M. 1753—2,088. B. 4,151—4,202; 4,235—4,272. G. E 5 v 14 — E 6 r 24; E 6 v 9—30.

27. Here Milet allows his fancy free play and although G. disposes of the incidents related in few words, and B. in still fewer, M. expands them into a pleasing passage, depicting the departure of Paris, the filial affection of the sons for Priam and his love for them. It is one of the most pleasing scenes in the whole drama, and shows beyond question Milet's talent. In Benoît, after Priam has spoken to the „baron", exhorting them to obey Paris and to meet valiantly their enemies (B. 4,167 —4,198) they enter the ships and „Congie prennent a lor amis." (B. 4,199). That is the whole scene in B. In G. there is an

[1]) In this omitted section (B 4,015—4,150; G- E 4 r 21 — E 5 v 13) the contents are briefly: Priam sends Deyphebus and Paris to Pevoine (G- Panonia) to procure soldiers. During their absence he calls a „parlement" of Trojan nobles, repeats his grievances, the failure of Anthenor's embassy, and asks for advice, M. certainly showed judgment in omitting these scenes of repetition, but perhaps not as much in neglecting entirely the role of Panthus, the son of Eufobius, who tells the assembly of the prophecy of his father that great disaster would come to Troy, if Paris brought a wife from Greece. All contradict him. Priam has ships built and Hector goes away to assemble valiant knights. Cassandra makes a prophecy similar to that of Panthus, which is not believed. G. follows B. closely, adding somewhat to the warning efforts of Cassandra, and repeating from Ovid that the soul of Pythagoras had passed into Euphorbius. G. adds also a long discourse on fate.

almost identical speech by Priam. There follows then the statement (E 5 v 23). „Rex Priamus *Anthenori* et Enee de quibus supra relatum est necnon et polidamas ipsius anthenoris filio mandat et precipit ut cum paride in greciam cum ipso navali exercitu se accingant — quibus devote annuentibus etc.“ Anthenor is also distinctly mentioned as accompanying the expedition (E 6 r 20) „in consilio sapientium *Anthenoris* et Enee qui vobiscum sunt in presenti negocio“. B. does not mention Anthenor with the others in the corresponding place at all: (B. 4178 Priam speaking): „Deyphebus o vos (= Paris) sera. | Et vos i ireiz, Eneas | Ensemble o vos Polidamas.“ We only learn much later (B. 4361) that Anthenor was in the expedition, at the council held to decide upon the attack on the temple of Venus. M. follows G. in mentioning explicitly *Anthenor* at the outset of the expedition, (1734, 1744 d, 1759, 1895 d etc.), and uses the above passage in G (E 5 v 23 fol.) to build up the scene (1733—1770) wherein Priam sends Macabrum to bid *Anthenor* prepare for the voyage.

28. In B. the scene of parting is of the briefest (B. 4195): „Ni ot puis altre parlement | Es nes entrent comnnement | Dreit vent orent et coie mer | Por corre tost et por sigler | Congie prennent a lor amis | Tost ont esloingnie lo pais.“ G adds a few details: (E 6 r 20) — „Et finito colloquio universus exercitus naves ascendit. Paris et deyphebus in lacrimis a rege obtenta licentia naves intrant etc.“

This is undoubtedly the starting point of Milet's entire scene of departure (1771—2,006) to which he adds the farewell speech of Paris and the affectionate dialogue of the two brothers Paris and Deyphebus. The entire scene merits quotation, but space does not allow us. Suffice it to say that it is one of the most pleasing parts of the drama, its chief charm, aside from the sentiment expressed, consisting in the simplicity of the words used. M. introduces Hecuba who laments greatly the departure of her sons, and reproaches Priam for sending them into danger. Priam and both the sons comfort her and she is finally appeased. Priam then gently urges the departure with the refrain (1896).

Or sus sans faire grant langaige,
Partez beaulx enfans il est temps

29. Priam remains alone with Hecuba and utters a prayer for the safety and success of his sons. He then comforts the disconsolate Hecuba, bidding Hector do likewise. Priam at last shows some impatience at Hecuba's continued lament, but Hector replies:

1952 Tres cher pere, pas n'est chose nouvelle
Que femme pleure, c'est chose naturelle
Car vous savez que amour de femme est tendre.

The scene of embarking opens with a refrain by Paris:

1988 Sire anthenor, comment vous va
Estes vous tout prest de partir.

and closes with pleasing farewell words by Paris to Troy and all those dear to him. Paris then exhorts Deyphebus so to act as to merit honor. Deyphebus assures him of his fidelity and love, promising to do all Paris asks. Paris thanks him with

(2,058), Ha mon trescher frere feres
Et ie vous ditz qu'a tousiours mais
Vous aymeray toute ma vie.

after which Sorbin, the ship master, announces

(2063) Nous sommes cy en la partie
De grece dicte cytaree.[1])

30. Immediately following are a few lines suggesting the influence of Guido: Sorbin says (2065)

Pource seigneurs s'il vous agree
Iencreray les nefz[2]) en ce port.

---

[1]) This direct passage to Cytharee leads us to note here the omission of things common to B-G, showing still further the independence of Milet: The fleet numbers 22 ships (B 4,155; E 5 v 22), The departure is in the spring wherefore G. takes the opportunity to make another display of his astronomical knowledge (E 5 v 15 ff.). Paris and Deyphebus return from Pevoine. Priam's only parting speech is addressed to the „baron". On the journey the Trojans pass the ship bearing Menelaus to visit Nestor in Pirre (G = Pira.) but neither party recognizes the other. Menelaus is thus absent when the Trojans arrive. In M. a faint trace of this episode is in verse 2,161, Helen's prayer to Venus „Ie vous (= Venus) requier que brief soit sa (= Menelaus') venue". Yet further on we find M. had evidently forgotten what his source contained, for we hear Menelaus saying 5,322 that he was visiting Peleus in the city of Manise when Helen was captured. A later mention of Menelaus' absence is in the words of Helen herself 25,254. Car il m'avoit seulle laissee.

[2]) There is a slight confusion in regard to the number of ships. In 2066 we have the plural, also in the stage direction after 2000, then in 2545, 2626, 2627 d. Yet in stage direction after 2,006 we have „la navire". Later in 11,143 we note „plusieurs nefs".

Anthenor: Ami ancre les pres du bort
Affin que nous venons a terre
(adont Sorbin gette l'encre en mer puis dit)
Ilz sont bien.

B. did not have this detail of anchoring, but G. mentions (E 6 v 13) „anchoris in profundum maris injectis".

To Paris' question to whom Cytharee belongs, Anthenor replies that its king is Menelaus, brother of Agamenon[1]) and cousin of Nestor. They land and meeting three Greeks, Protheus, Thideus and Egenus, Paris asks what their assembly means. Protheus replies it is the celebration of „la solennite de venus" (2,084) The three Greeks followed by Paris and the Trojans go to the temple of Venus.

Chapter IV.

The Meeting of Paris and Helen. — The Capture of Helen.

M. 2,089—2,619. B. 4,235—4,616. G. E 6 v 30 — F 2 v 31.

31. 1) Although M. handles the material of these scenes with considerable originality, this chapter is again one of the most striking for illustrating M's dependence upon G, and his ignoring of B.

All are in the temple of Venus, and Paris offers his prayer and sacrifice. B. had said this took place in the temple of Venus, but strange to say, he had added 4274. „un sacrefice appareilla | A la deesse *Diana*. G however knows nothing of Diana and states (E 6 v 29.)" devotis orationibus oblationes suas in *multa auri et argenti copia immensa prodigalitate* (Paris) profudit" M. omits also all mention of Diana and specifies with G. the nature of Paris' offering:

(2093) Ie te presente du mien cent escus
Qu'ay apportez de troye proprement
(adont les gette sur l'autel de venus).

---

[1]) Agamemnon in Greif's copy of the Dresden edition is probably a copyist's mistake, as all other editions have Agamenon. which spelling is also found everywhere else in Greif's copy of the Dresden edition.

2) M. alone shows the ingenuity of making this prayer of Paris the connecting link between the earlier promise of Venus and the subsequent capture of Helen: (2095.)

Je te requiers de bon cueur humblement,
Se deité ne fault point ne ne ment,
Qu'il te souviegne de la doulce promesse
Que i'euz de toy quant feis le iugement
De la beaulte de ton corps excellent
Souviegne t'en trespuissante deesse.

32. 1) In Milet's method of relating *why* Helen came to the temple, we see another trace of G's influence: In B. *Renommee* 4,299 (G = loquax fama E 7 r 12) had reached Helen's ears, but the message it brought is different in B. and in G: In B. Renommee simply tells of the arrival of Paris and the Trojans, but nothing is said of the beauty of Paris as a part of the news. Indeed it is only later when Helen is in the temple that, seeing there the handsome youth, she asks, and learns that it is Paris (B. 4,327). Moreover we fail to detect in the words of B. any trace of curiosity on Helen's side even as a part of her motive in coming:

B. 4,306.
Ne se prise ne tant ne quant
S'ele a ceste feste ne vait.
A ses privez dit et retrait
Qu'ele a piece a un veu voe
A rendre a cel jor devise.
Sor l'autel velt ses dons offrir,
Co dist, et ses respons oïr.

2) G. however seized this as a good opportunity to display his hate and contempt of the fair sex. (E 7 r 12) „sed loquax fama — — ad aures Helene de p u l c h r i t u d i n e p a r i d i s etc." and E 7 r 15 vane voluntatis desiderabilis appetitus qui mulierum animam consuevit subita levitate corripere helene animam inconsulta flagrancia concitavit ut optaret ad ipsius festivitatis solemnia se conferre gaudia visura festiva et etiam inspeetura ducem frigic nationis (Then follows a long passage E 7 r 19 — E 7 v 21 in which G. strongly censures the folly and sin of dancing, music, religious fêtes and all other opportunities for the sexes to meet. It is quite an oriental conception of the sphere of woman, and possesses particular interest by contrast with Benoît).

3) M. who is nowhere the woman-hater that Guido is, omits all this, but still G's influence is distinctly traceable: The personality of Protheus is substituted for Rumor as the bearer of the news to Helen. As in G. however the beauty of Paris is the chief news:

Protheus, 2131
Et la i'ay veu ung troyan
Si tresbel que c'est merveille,
Si se dist filz au roy priam[1])

---

[1]) M. does not make plain however where Protheus obtained this knowledge, as Paris had not told him. This is a slight naïveté in M's. exposition.

Mais par ma foy ie m'esmerveille
De sa grant beaulte non pareille
Et de sa maniere plaisante
Pource dame ie vous conseille
Qu'aliez au temple sans attante.
Helene:
Esse chose si excellente
Que tu me ditz?
Protheus: Certes ouy.
Helene:
Oncques homme tant ie n'ouy
Blasonner que tu le blasonnes,
Mais puis que ce conseil me donnez
Je vueil aler pour adorer
La deesse sans demourer.

Thereupon Helen goes with Florimonde, whose role of confidante original to M. we will presently note (§ 36). Helen prays to Venus for the safety of Menelaus and for his quick return. This last line is the first of the three references to Menelaus' absence which M. contains (see Foot note to § 29). Helen also prays for strength to be faithful to Menelaus. B-G do not have this detail at all. B makes no mention of the actual occurrence of Helen's prayer; G. devotes to it only (E 8 r 2) „ibique suas oblationes deae veneri".

33, 1) The actual meeting of Paris and Helen now follows. In M. it is given with an amusing naïveté.[1] (2163 d). „lors se taist helene et doit paris passer et repasser par devant elle et la regarder du coing de l'ueil et puis se tire loing d'elle et dit ce qui ensuit en s'esmerveillant" „Ce qui sensuit" is a description of the beauties of Helen which have so seized hold of Paris. B. in this place gives no description at all, but simply says (B. 4334, the subject being Paris):

Et son dolz senblant apercut.

G.[2]) however gives a long and detailed description, a part of which M. repeats in the same order but with less detail. The parallel passages follow:

2171—74.
Elle a les chevoulx reluisans
Et tous de fin or galoppez
Et deux laz qui sont bien duisans
De quoy ilz sont enveloppes.

E 8 r 13—16. Miratur enim tam in ea rutilante fulgore flavescere crines multos quos nivei candoris protractus in medio crinium dyameter equaliter divedebat et aurea fila hincinde serpentia sub certi lege federiis coegerant involutos.

---

[1]) The subsequent meeting of Achilles and Polixene forms a pendant to this scene (§ 126.)

[2]) Fischer (P. 20) says that both Herbort v. Fritzlar and Konrad von Wurzburg also insert in this place their descriptions of Helen.

2175—78.
Le fronc plain sans *rigousites*
Aussi cler comme vif argent
Et les deux temples des costez
Composees moult proprement.

E 8 r 16—20. sub quibus subsidebat frontis lactea et niviosa planicies ad eius fulgencia tympora usque descensa ubi crinium aureorum cumulus perlucida visione turgebat et cuius frontis detestabilis nulla *rugositas* planiciem sulcaverat adequatam.

2179—2181.
Dieu quel beaulte quel plaisance
Qu'esse que de veoir ses deux yeulx
De la forme de tous les dieux.

E 8 r 25—27. (after the eyebrows) Miratur igitur oculos duorum siderum radios describentes quorum orbes quasi gemmarum iuncturis artificiose compositi etc.

2182—85.
Elle a les soulcis gracieulx
Qui sont velus moderement
Je croy certes que c'est la mieulx
Faicte dessoubz le firmament.

E 8 r 21—23. Miratur etenim in tam nitide frontis extremis convallibus gemina supercilia quasi manufacta sic decenter elevata flavescere ut geminos exemplata velde in arcus etc.

2186—89.
Son nez est se bien compose
Comme de manuel ouvraige
Et si est aussi dispose
Selon la forme du visaige.

E 8 r 30—31. Miratur etiam in illa mire pulchritudinis nasi sui lineam regularem qui maxillas dividens in geminas partes equales etc.

2190.
Sa faicture est belle a oultraige.

E 8 v 6. miratur etiam pulchritudinem faciei etc.

2191.
Et si a la bouche pollie.

G. describes the mouth in great detail: E 8 v 2 lips. E 8 v 14 teeth etc. He then continues his extravagant description by speaking of the chin, neck, throat, shoulders, back, hands, fingers, nails, breast and general figure.

2) The above is the only description of Helen in M. B's description is not in this place, but later (B. 5,099—5,120) in the catalogue of portraits of the leading Greeks. There the description is very general, but one or two details are given, none of which appear in M.:

B. 5111 Por verte li plosor diseient
Que si frere la resenbleient.
also 5,113 Enz el mileu des dous sorciz
Qui dougié erent et tretiz
Aveit un seing en tel endreit
Que merveilles li aveneit.
and 5,117 Li cors de lie ert biaus et gras
Molt par se vesteit bien de dras.

When G. arrives at this passage in B. he refers to his

own previous extravagant description: (F 7 r 8) „Dixit (= Dares) enim primo helenam speciositate nimia refulsisse de cuius statura et forma satis aperte supra retulimus. Hoc addito quod ipse dixit helenam ipsam inter duo supercilia quamdam babuisse et modicam tenuem cicatricem que miro modo decebat eandem.“ As M. omits this entire series of portraits, it is easily understood how he neglected this striking detail of Helen's beauty. Even more comprehensible is M's complete ignorance of B. 5, 111—112, since G. did not contain a similar statement.

34. Let us return now to the meeting of Paris and Helen: Paris continues to express his great admiration for Helen's beauty. Helen sees him and gives vent to her pleasure in a long monologue (2214—2269) for which G. furnishes the leading ideas (F 1 r 7—17.) and in which Helen describes her wonder at his beauty and her growing love for him. The refrain, „*si ne m'en plaist il gaires moins*“ occurs frequently as Helen battles with her conflicting thoughts. Paris approaches, and greets Helen: 2270.

	Helene:
Dieu gard la belle dame helene,	Dieu gard le iouvencal plaisant,
La plus belle qui soit vivant,	Le filz de priam roy de troye,
Qui est de tant de beaulte plaine,	Et luy doint ce qu'il va querant,
Qu'il n'est nulle qui soit devant.	Et de ses amours avoir ioye.

(adont Paris se recule ung peu arriere et se pourmaine, puis dit)

I'ay a ceste fois apparceu	Que ie ne suis pas trop deceu,
Au doulx regard que i ay eu d'elle,	Car, se ie l'ayme, ainsi fait elle.

This is all that M. gives of their first interview, for Paris then goes to consult with his companions regarding the capture of Helen. B. gives hints of a much longer interview than M:

4350	and adds 4355
Tel leisir orent de parler,	Heleine sot molt bien de veir
Qu'alques i distrent de lor buens.	Paris la revendreit veeir.

G. adds considerably to this, lowering greatly the dignity of Helen, by letting her signal for Paris to approach in reply to the latter's signs. The actual interview is also much vulgarized: F 1 r 28 „sic vacantibus aliis ad ea que iocose fiebant in templo nec advertentibus illorum insidias amatorum unus alteri quidquid gestierat in animo resolutis in suspiria vocibus propallavit et quidquid de optatis eorum fieri deberet inter se brevi prescripsere sermone.“

Milet in this scene certainly shows a finer sense of delicacy than G. or even than B. by omitting everything in the nature of a lovers' interview, especially G.'s mention of plans „de optatis eorum fieri". M.'s treatment is in harmony with his subsequent delineation of Helen's character.

35. The council of Paris and his companions takes place in M. (2,293 d) *„devant l'autel de venus"*, and the Trojans do not leave the temple until afterward (2397). In B-G. Paris returns to the ships (B. 4354; F 1 v 5). In the speech of Paris two features point unmistakeably to G:

1) 2296.	F. 1 v 8 „omnibus notum est vobis
Vous saves bien que nous avons	qua de causa priamo regi nostro pla-
Ceste charge cy entrepris,	cuerit nos in greciam transmisse; fuit
Pour avoir la dame de pris	enim eius totalis intentio ut exionam
Exionne seur de mon pere	sororem ipsius nostro studio rehaberet."

B. gives this idea but a secondary place: (4368)

Nos a li reis Prianz tramis
Por fere a cels honte et domage,
Qui le firent nostre lignage.
Il n'est rien de ma ante aveir
Ja en ço n'aiez vos espeir.

G. alone repeats the idea of the impossibility of securing Exionne by force and he alone, followed by M. suggests another means to secure her, namely:

2) F 2 r 7. Ex eius (= Helenae) captione spes nostra certa resultat quod ob commutatione ipsius defacili poterit rex priamus suam recuperare sororem.

M. 2312 On nous vouldroit voulentiers rendre
Exionne en la rendant.

B. has no trace of such an idea.

3) In M. Paris' speech is followed by an extended dialogue (2318—2397) which is only hinted at in B-G. (B. 4435—4441; F 2 r 12): Anthenor counsels an attack upon the temple, but Enee speaks against it. Enee's speech is interesting since M. forgot it, when later (23,051—056) (see § 193[5]) he lets Priam blame Eneas as well as Anthenor for having counselled the attack! When the attack is planned, Paris exhorts the Trojans to act „sans noise faire" 2393; the same phrase occurs in B. 4448, with no equivalent in G. This coincidence might count for something, were it not one most readily caused by the context.

36. The Trojans now leave the temple and there follows between Helene and Florimonde a scene of considerable originality: Helene wishes to remain that night, (2400)

Pource que ceste feste cy
Est de grande solennite.

She then passes to an extravagant praise of the beauty of Paris (2406 - 2457) and declares her love for him. She appeals to Florimonde in the refrain *„Que vous en semble florimonde?"*

Florimonde wisely advises her mistress to direct her thoughts elsewhere, but Helene justifies herself, weakly, with (2474)

Florimonde c'est par le cours Qui quiert tousiours avoir secours
De nature et de ieunesse, De plaisir fonde en liesse.

Helen then becomes silent.

37. 1) The Attack: Paris in a refrain reminds his men:

(2482) Seigneurs la nuyt est aprouchee.
Il nous fault tous appareiller.

Enee counsels (2491) Il fault laisser dedans les nefz
Aulcuns de noz gens bien armez
Pour garder, qu'on ne leur mefface,

which points directly to (F 2 r 18) „relictis navibus in tuta *custodia armatorum*". In B. the purpose of leaving men is quite different and it is not repeated by G. (B. 4453.):

Et cil qui remandront as nes | aient sus trait ancres et tres | que si tost com auron chargie | seions nos del port esloignie.

Another indication of G's constant influence is: M. 2511. „Tires voz espees toutes nues." G. F 2 r 21. „in ore gladii". Original to M. is the idea in 2512: Et n'espergnez ne clercs ne prestres.

2) We now notice something common to B. and M., but, curiously enough, absent in G., the *binding* of the prisoners:

B. 4486 et maint en i prennent et lient. B. 4497 pris en ont et liez assez. M. 2516 qu'ilz soient liez vistement. M. 2521 d. chascun prendra son prisonnier et le liera.

This coincidence might possess weight were not the thought of securing the prisoners one most readily supplied from the context,[1]) and were not the above passages in M. in the closest possible connection with (2521 d) „et paris se lievera tout soudainement et prandra helene par la main et dira". This cannot possibly have come from B, 4487:

„La bele la cortoise Helene | I pristrent (subj. = li Troien in 4479) tote primeraine", but only from G. (F 2 r 23) „Reginam helenam et omnes eius comites paris propria manu cepit."

38. 1) Paris bids the prisoners and booty to be placed in the „challans" (M. 2537) and „bateaulx" (M. 2545). I know not whether he intends these words as synonyms of „nefs". The limits of the stage might preclude two sorts of craft, even if one were smaller than the other. Yet Guido mentions two:

---

[1]) M. uses this idea of binding prisoners later in two places where B-G. omit it (see § 89).

„naves“ and „in schaphis“ (E 6 v 13), with which latter the Trojans effect their landing. B. has only „nes“. In the mention of the booty from the temple both M, and B. describe its nature in more or less detail (B. 4498—4503; M 2540—2545). G. does not. But the words of B and M. are far too general to be compared.

2) Paris now congratulates all upon the success of the expedition, and M. still further smooths out the flow of the story by making him say, (2555) in giving thanks to Venus:

Venus, qui me feist la promesse,
Qu'elle me donroit belle femme,
Or a elle fourny ma ieunesse.

He then proceeds to comfort Helen who had begun to mourn her fate. He promises her all honor, and a lawful marriage. She beseeches him for clemency both for herself and her companions, extolling the virtue of mercy.[1])

Chapter V.

The Return to Troy.

M. 2,620—3,106 („disner“ middle of first day). B. 4,617—4752; 4783—4916. G. F 2 v 31 — F 5 r 1.

39. Milet does little more in this series of incidents than to resolve the narrative into dialogue, reproducing very freely all the essential ideas of the earlier versions, which latter continue to show the closest possible resemblance.

The Trojans (2619 d) „naigent fort jusques ad ce qu'ilz soient arrivez au port de thenedon qui est pres de troye“ M. omits here its distance although B. had said (B. 4594) „set lieues“ and G. (F 2 v 20) „per sex miliaria“ (see Thenedon in proper-names § 241). Paris bids the men disembark „car il est besoing de mengier“, orders the ships to be unloaded and the tables set. „Athimas et Sorbin alumeront des piches et porteront devant eulx et helene se serra en ung banc puis dira“ (2627 d).

[1]) M. omits the whole incident of the resistance offered by the castle in Cytherea before the embarking of the Trojans (B. 4507—4558. G. F 2 r 30—F 2 v 12). G. differs only slightly from B. who names the castle twice, Helee. G. omits the name entirely. B, places it on the sea-coast. G. on an eminence above the temple (F 2 r 31.)

40. Then follows the scene of Helen's bemoaning her fate, which M. adapts very freely from his source and resolves still more, than there, into dialogue between Helen and Paris. A part of Helen's lament has already been given in M. 2586—2609 before leaving Cytherea (see § 38) wherein M. shows good judgment, the dramatic treatment requiring Helen to begin her lament immediately upon being captured and not to wait, as the epic versions represent her, until the arrival in Tenedos (seven days B. 4585. G. F 2 v 19). M. adapts so freely his material to the dramatic form, that it is difficult to establish points of contact with his source, the more so because G. follows B. here with the greatest closeness. Yet we venture to present the following:

1) Paris to Helen. 2674 Vous aves ia tout le visaige | Noircy de lermes ou peu pres. which was perhaps suggested by (F 3 r 3) dum pectus et faciem continuis fluvialibus lacrimis irrigaret (subj. = Helena). B. says only, 4621 „plorot et molt grant doel feseit“.

2) M. 2691 d, adont helene doit torcher ses yeulx, from corresponding place in G. F 3 r 25 „tersis lacrimis“. B. makes no mention of such an action, but on the other hand Helen continues her weeping 4,748.

3) In B. Helen only asks mercy for herself, and the other prisoners beseech for grace independently of her: B. 4694

Chascune donc merci li crie | As pies li chient les plosors
Qu'il ait merci de lor seignors | Qui sont es liens e si destreiz.

This passage might well have suggested to M. an extension of the dialogue to the other prisoners, the more so as he is very fond of such extensions, but G. did not take the hint, and M. omits it as well. Instead, in G-M, Helen beseeches for clemency for her fellow-prisoners as well as for herself. The language is almost identical:

M. 2700—2711.

Et se par la vostre bonte
Et tresexcessive clemence,
Vous monstrez vostre charite,
Soubs cueur plain de magniffcence,
Aux chetifs plains de desplaisance,
Et a moy qui suis prisonniere,
Les dieux, comme i'ay esperance,
Le vous rendront en la maniere,
Car humanite se ingere
D'avoir pitie des patiens,
Et les dieux en telle maniere
Sont les biens faits retribuans

G. F 3 r 28.

Si quid ergo mihi captive et aliis captis mecum boni confertur a quoque, sperare poterit talia conferrens a diis gratiam cum afflictis compati humanitas suggerat et diis placeant pietatis humane.

Helen had already used a similar plea for herself and her companions in the lament before leaving Cytherea. M. 2594. (See § 38.)

Ie vous recommende aussi | Pource qu'ilz sont de mon pays
Tous les prisonniers qu'avez pris, | Se vous estez preux et gentilz etc.

41. In the whole description of Helen's lament B. makes no reference to Paris' preparing a feast for her, or of her refusal to eat. B. has only the general statement: B 4749. Molt la Paris reconfortee | A merveilles la enoree | Molt la fist la nuit bien *servir* | Co poez saveir sanz mentir." I understand that *servir,* while perhaps including serving of food, is by no means restricted to it. G. however mentions both that Paris prepares a feast and that Helen refuses to eat:

F 3 r 6. que (= Helena) crebris ululatibus inquieta nullo cibo aut potu potitur. F 4 r 4. Et adveniente sero paris eam studuit deservire non minus blandiciis quam preciosis cibariis habundanter. Without doubt these lines suggested to M. the scene 2716—2755, a scene not without a certain humor:

Paris: „Or ca madame et m'amye | Levez vous si yrons souper
Helene: Certes Paris ie n'yray myc
Paris: Or ca madame et m'amye | Vous y vendrez ie vous affie.
Helene: Puisqu'il vous plaist, ie y vueil aler.
Paris: Or ca madame et m'amye | Levez vous si yrons souper
Or vous seez sans plus tarder | Dame helene, car il me plaist.
(Tandis que Paris parle a helene on doit mettre la nappe)
Helene: Devant vous non feray sans doubter
Paris: Or vous seez sanz plus tarder | Il me plaist de le commander
Helene: Ie le feray puisqu'ainsi est.
Paris: Or vous seez sans plus tarder | Dame helene, car il me plaist.
(Lors helene se siet)
Or ca sans faire plus d'arrest | chascun se see en son endroit
Et si faictes comment qu'il soit | Que nous ayons les menestrelz.
Enee: Veez en cy de bons ouvriers | Cornez, menestrelz, il est temps.

(adont se seront tous, premier paris et helene empres luy puis deiphebus puis anthenor puis enee puis pollidamas et les demoiselles se serront d'ung coste et d'aultre et quant la viande sera sur la table, dira)

Paris: Dame helene comme i'entens | Vous ne faictes point bonne chere
Laissez ceste douleur amere | Et mengiez ie vous emprie.
Helene: Grant mercy.
Paris: Pour dieu, ie vous prie | Oblies toutes voz douleurs
Car ie scay bien qu'apres voz pleurs | Vous aures des joies nouvelles.

Then Paris bids Pollidamas command the other captive „damoiselles" to eat. He does so, but receives from Florimonde the curt reply:

Certes nous ne nous hastons mye | Damoiseau, la vostre mercy.

42. Paris now prepares to journey to Troy sending Athimas ahead to announce his coming. B. makes no mention of festivities being *prepared* to welcome Paris. G. however does: (F 2 v 31.) „et universe plebi sollemne festum instituunt universi (= troye majori)“ and later F 4 r 12 „immensa tripudia in omni genere musicorum“. The traces of these passages are seen in the directions given by Paris to his messenger Athimas:

2771. Et qu'on quiere tous instruments
De musique et tous ornemens
Et toutes choses de plaisance;

also in Athimas' words to Priam 2796 „Et vouldroit (= Paris) que a grant assemblee | Luy et ses gens feussent receuz.“

Athimas delivers his message and Priam orders horses to be got ready and bids his sons accompany him. Helenus is the only one to disturb the joy of the moment by lamenting, and in reply to the demand of Troillus he gives as his reason (2836): Je voy la destruction de troye | A laquelle nous sommes venus.

The actual scene of meeting is essentially the same in all versions. M. introduces the incident of Paris' dismounting to honor his father, but strangely omits the leading of Helen's horse by Priam afoot. Priam does not dismount until they arrive at Troy (2917 d).

43. B. makes no mention of the royal palace in connection with the return to Troy. G. adds such a detail (F 4 r 24) „in multa veneracione deduxit (= Priamus) quousque ipsam (= Helenam) in suam excelsam aulam regiam introduxit“, which is reflected in M. (2918.)

Priam: Belle descendez il est temps,
Puisque nous sommes au chastel,
Car il nous fault entrer dedens
Si verrez comment il est bel.
Je l'ay fait tout de nouvel,
Depuis que troye fut desdruicte;
Puis le temps de la tour babel
Ne fust telle besongne construicte.

Helen dismounts — — „et priam prendra helene par la main“.

The above passage in G. served also as pretext to M. for introducing here the descriptions of Ilion and of the royal hall, which, in B-G. occur in the general description of Troy before Anthenor's voyage to Greece (B. 3,029—3,120; D 3 v 31 — D 4 v 9). The three pictures of the castle show great independence, yet a comparison yields the following:

1) Height (B. 3,041) N'esteit si estreit de desus | V. C. teises n'eust et plus[1]).

[1]) This would give the fabulous height of about 3,000 feet! See La Curne de Sainte Palaye, Dictionnaire de l'ancien francais. Vol. 10. p. 52 „toise“. It is there given as a measure varying according to different trades, but averaging six feet. Ducange under „tesa“, „tesia“ says „mensura sex pedum“.

For „teises" G. substitutes „passus" thus moderating the extraordinary height by about one-half: (D 4 r 2). „cujus altitudo summitatem quingentorum passuum attingebat." M. follows this exactly (2,938) „selon ce qu'il est mesure | il a cinq cens pas de haulteur."

B. alone states that the castle had „dis estages" (B. 3,069) Curiously enough M. omits the detail that it reached the clouds (B. 3,047; D 4 r 6).

2) The windows are described more in detail:

M. 2950

Les fenestres sont votellees
De petis pilliers de crystal,
Et les sommettes cinellees
De fin azur fait a esmail;
Et par ung merveilleux destail
D'ouvraige menu figurees,
Les colonnes sont de courail,
Et les basses toutes dorees.

D 4 r 13 sic et ejus fenestras non insigniverat opus forte mormoreum cum major pars earum extructa fuisset ex quadris fulgencium cristallorum sic fenestrarum ipsarum columne sic capitella et bases ipsarum.

(see Haepke Page 41.)

44. The descriptions of the hall: B. is very general. G. and M. go more into details and agree in the following points:

1) Both length and breadth are given: D 4 r 19. prolixe longitudinis sed latitudinis consonantis.

M. 2966 Elle est longue a grant merveille,
— — — — — — — —
Ec si est de largeur pareille.
M. adds: de haulteur semblablement.

2) M. 2,970.

toute vestue noblement
De diverses tables mabrines,
Et voustee pareillement
Toutes de riches portes cedrines.

D 4 r 20

tabulis vestita marmoreis
et ex lignis cedrinis et hebani eius tabulata testudo

3) M. 2974.

Et veez cy le siege royal,
(the richness of whose jewels M. alone describes 2974—82.)
Au devant y a une table
Toute d'ivire composee
Par ouvraige non comparable
Et de longuer bien mesuree.
De deux costez environnee
De bancs tous ouvres de cipres
La bordure est estranglee
De quarreaulx d'azur pres apres.

D 4 r 23

in huiusmodi sale capite regium erat solium institutum ubi mensa regia longa proceritate distensa locata extiterat tota composita eboris et hebani subtilibus ex iuncturis. Sic et ab utroque latere mensarum ordo distensus commodas dabat discumbentibus sessiones.

B's mention furnishes no such striking resemblance to M: B. 3,099:

A l'un des chies fu fez li deis,
Ou mangera Prianz li reis.
Les tables i sont arengiees,
Ou mangeront ses granz mesniees.

M. omits all reference to the altar at the other end of the hall and to the statue of Jupiter, both of which G. copies from B. adding a few details.

45. Helen thanks Priam for his courtesy to her, a prisoner. There follows now another pleasing scene of family affection: Hecuba arrives with Cassandra,[1]) and welcomes Helen with friendly words and a kiss. Hecuba then kisses Paris who kneels before her. She thanks God for their safe return, bids Deyphebus come kiss her and expresses her gratitude to Anthenor and Enee. She then tells Polixene to embrace and welcome her two brothers. Polixene does so in charming lines (3,042—65). Addressing Paris:

3,045
Quant ie regarde voz deux yeulx,
Qui me semblent si gracieulx,
Tout le cueur me rit de plaisance.

and 3,054
Baisez moy mon frere tres doulx,
Car i'ay pleure souvent pour vous
Quant vous estiez en ce voyage.

46. The marriage of Paris and Helen now follows. Here Milet shows considerable originality in the dialogne, and also, in consequence, in the characterization of the personages, especially Helen. Paris asks Priam to give him Helen in marriage, and adds

(3,070) Dame helene s'il vouz agree,
Il convient faire ung mariage
De nous deux avant la vespree.

In her reply, Helen has forgotten all her sorrows:

3,077.
Se me voulez avoir a amye
Ie suis vostre, pas ne le nye,
Et estre vueil tousiours a vous
Et affinque ie le vous dye
Ie vous ayme par dessus tous.
Paris:
Belle tenez l'annel d'amours
Par cueur de desir amoureulx
Ie vous vueil servir a tousiours
Et serviray de cueur ioyeulx
Baisez moy, fin cueur gracieulx
Baisez moy comme vostre amy.

Helene:
Le reffuser n'est pas le mieulx
Car en vous n'aige pas failly
De vostre anneau ie vous mercie
Que vous m'aves cy presente;
Si le prens comme vostre amye
De tres loyalle voulente
Paris:
Belle ie suis entalente
De servir amours loyaulment
Helene:
Et i'ay mon cueur du tout boutte
A vours aymer parfaictement.

---

[1]) Although Cassandra accompanies Hecuba at this time she takes no part in the dialogue at all. This is remarkable, because in both B. (4,863—916) and G. (F 4 v 2—F 5 r 1.) her rôle is very marked and exceedingly dramatic. It is difficult to understand M's omission of Cassandra here and his later intro-

In this marriage-scene we see no hint of a religious ceremony. G. had said F 4 r 29. „in templo pallidis". There is further no mention of marriage festivities as in B-G. On the other hand we note the use of the ring as symbol, wholly unknown to B-G.

Priam now closes the scene with the refrain, taken up by Anthenor: (3,098) „Seigneurs il est dorenavant | Temps de retraire en sa maison". Each one retires „En sa maison et se fera cy pause pour disner."

Chapter VI.

The Summoning of the Greek princes.

M. 3,107—4,486. B. 4,753—782; 4,917—5,072; the portraits of the leading Greeks 5,087—5,270; the enumeration of the Greek allies 5,587—694. G.[1]) F 5 r 2 — F 6 v 29, followed by portraits of Greeks and Trojans to G 1 v 14, and enumeration of the Greek force to G 2 v 12.

---

47. This series of scenes shows how M. expanded his source. He requires 1,379 lines to tell what B had told in 183 lines and G. in a like small space. As a result the dialogue in M. is largely extended and there is a most wearisome length to most of the passages:

48. Cytheus goes to Menelaus[2]) to tell him of his misfortune. In this scene we have several points of contact with G:

M. has substituted a definite person, Cytheus, as the announcer of the news, for the „fama loquax" of G. (F 5 r 7), and the „Renomee qui tost s'espant" of B (4,753). M. had done the same earlier, when Helen learns of Paris' arrival in Cytherea (§ 32[3]).

A quotation of the passages shows clearly M's dependence upon G.:

---

duction of her, 6.479. unless he thought her appearance then more dramatic. If so however, why let her appear here at all? For this later appearance where M says essentially what B-G. say here, see § 63.

[1]) G. makes the passages corresponding to B. 4783—4,916 and 4,753—782 exchange places, thus bringing each to its more logical connection.

[2]) Wunder (P. 15) adds here „in Sparta", but this name does not occur in this place nor anywhere in M.

M. 3,119, Menelaus:
Comment messaiger qui a il?
Citheus:
Monseigneur ie vous certiffie,
Que les troyans sont arrivez
En Citharee tous armés,
Si ont de voz gens mis a mort.
Menelaus:
Haro vecy grant desconfort.
Citheus.
Ha monseigneur encores pis
Il y a ung nommé paris,
Qui se dit filz au roy priam,
Si est le plus plaisant troyan,
Qui feust en toute l'assamblee,
Si a tant fait qu'il a amblee
Madame helene, vostre femme.
(lors menelaus se pasme et quant etc.)

F. 5 r 10.
cui (= Menelaus) postquam patefacta sunt omnia et singula de disrobatione templi vidilicet in insula cytharee dominio suo subjecto de nece suorum interfectorum ibi nequiter a troyanis, de captivitate mulierum et aliorum deductorum in troyam.

et demum de raptu sue helene quam plusquam se ipsum amore tenerrimo dilegebat, tantorum dolorum aculeis factus est anxius quod pronus cadens in terram debilitatus est (spiritu) et factus est deviciens in loquela.

The desire for a climax terminating in the news of the capture of Helen is very evident in G-M. No such desire is shown in B, nor has B. any mention of the fainting of Menelaus:

B. 4,762.
Reis Menelaus la l'on noncie,
Qu'il aveit sa feme perdue,
Et Paris li aveit tolue.
A Troie l'en aveit menee;
Ja poeit estre en sa contree

After Menelaus returns to consciousness he speaks in M. a long monologue (3,132—237.), for which either B. 4,767—70 or G. F 5 r 10—20 could have served as basis, except that G and M. alone make special mention of the desecrating of Helen's beauty. (F 5 r 20; 3,180.) M. alone represents Menelaus as loading Helen with reproaches and as contrasting his goodness and faithfulness toward her, with her treacherous infidelity.

49. 1) Menelaus now sends Citheus to summon Agamenon. G. here adds that he summoned Castor and Pollux at the same time (F 5 r 30.) An echo of this summoning of Castor and Pollux is seen in M, where Menelaus later includes them in the list of kings whom he bids to come help him (3,465). B. says nothing of their being summoned, but represents them as setting out immediately in pursuit of Helen and Paris. (B. 5,041—72).

2) M. makes no mention in this place of where Menelaus was, when he heard of Helen's capture. It is not until 5,320 that we read in his speech to the Greek kings:

Vray est que n'a pas grandement
Seurvint dedens mon pensement
D'aler le roy peleus veoir
Droit a manise.

This is an inexplicable deviation from B-G. where it is stated at least twice that Menelaus was with *Nestor* in *Pirre* (G. = Pira). B. 4,206; 4,228; G. E 6 r 31; F 5 r 9.

3) Moreover both B. and G. say that Nestor returned with Menelaus, after playing the part of a comforting friend. B. 4,770—4; G. F 5 r 23—28. In M. all trace of Nestor in this connection is absent. Indeed he has to be especially summoned: 3,473; 3,867. (see foot-note to § 29.)

4) Another point of interest is found in the name of the kingdom of Menelaus, whither he now returns: B. says 4,770 „Arriere a Parte[1]) retorna". G. says very indefinitely F 5 r 26 (compare F 5 r 29, F 6 r 5) „celer se accingit ad reditum regni sui". M. therefore, forced to find a name, quite naturally adopts Cytharee, where Paris stole away Helen.[2]) The Greek kings, coming in obedience to the summons of Menelaus all declare they are going to Cytheree. (4,142; 4,579; 4,626; 4,650; 4,680; 4,792; 4,823; 4,927; 4,959; 5,065 etc. etc.) Moreover Helen is often called queen of Cytherea 2,794; 20,882.

50. Citheus goes to Agamenon in Methenes (3,237) and tells him of the rape of Helen. After a lengthy censure of the Trojan people and a vow of vengeance, Agamenon goes to Menelaus and comforts him. The speeches in G-M. are almost identical, but lack of space prevents their being quoted here. B., while corresponding closely to G., contains no thought which M. could not find as well in G; on the other hand there are many points of contact between M. and G. alone:

a) 3,353—5 = F 5 v 5—7.
b) 3,356—64 = F 5 v 7—9.
c) 3,365—73 = F 5 v 9—11.
d) 3,374—76 = F 5 v 11—13.
e) 3,377—88 = F 5 v 13—17.
f) 3,434—36 = F 5 v 22—25.
g) 3,443—48 = F 5 v 28—31.

[1]) In B. Parte is the city of Menelaus: 5,591; 8,167; 29,520; the residence of Castor and Pollus 2,093; the first place of assembly for the Greek kings 4,782; 4,921; 4995.

[2]) By thus adopting Cytharee, Milet ignored the passage in G. (E 7 v 26 ff.), where G. states that Helen crossed by ship from her husband's city and kingdom on the mainland to the island of Cytharea, another part of his dominions. Yet, although M. says also that Cytharea is an island, we nowhere find mention of the Greek princes needing ships to reach it! In lines 33—36 of M's „Instrument" (after verse 23,386) we find the name Serpedon as the kingdom of Menelaus together with Cytherea.

Menelaus is quieted by this speech of his brother, and following his suggestion sends Citheus to summon the Greek princes. He gives Citheus a list of the latter (3,460—76). We have already noted the presence of Castor and Pollus, and of Nestor in this list. (§ 49.)

51. 1) This long passage of the summoning of the Greek princes is a curious illustration of the way Milet expanded his source. He relates in 1,029 lines (3,457—4,486) what B. says in ten verses (B. 4,985—95), and G. in an equally small space (F 6 r 1—4). Citheus proceeds to deliver his messages, and we have a series of scenes like those at the beginning of the drama when Macabrum summons the Trojan princes (see § 13). Citheus repeats at each visit the cause of his coming at more or less length, and in most cases kneels to deliver his message. He goes first to Achilles and Patroclus who are together. Achilles promises to come (3,514) „avant qu'il soit moys et demy".[1])

2) Citheus goes to Diomedes. Meanwhile Achilles asks Patroclus to accompany him as his „frere d'armes" (3535—6). Patroclus desires greatly to avenge his father killed by the Trojans (3531) (see § 239[1]). Citheus continues his journey, delivering his message to Diomedes who promises to come in two days (3,559), then to Ulixes, Prothesilaus, and Naulus. The last two were not mentioned in the instructions given Citheus by Menelaus (3460—76). Naulus already knows of the rape of Helen:

3529 Car Castor n'a pas longuement	Lequel tout le fait me conta
Et Pollus par icy passa	Et qu'il aloit apres sa seur.

52. The continuation of the speech of Naulus is Milet's version of the fate of Castor and Pollus. A few remarks are requisite here:

1) B. says (5,041—72). Quant al port de *Lesbie* furent | Si tot n'orent tere perdue | Que tormente lor est venue. | G. and consequently M. make no mention of Lesbie.

2) B. speaks of the existence of superstitions regarding the fate of Castor and Pollus, and gives no definite assurance himself of their death: (5,064) Mes qui qu'en feist dol ne joie. | Ne pot estre por riens seu | Que il esteient devenu. G. speaks also

---

[1]) See § 245 B. for list of time-measurements used by M. showing his freedom in that respect.

of these superstitions, and adds to them the myth of their having become stars, the „gemini". G. nevertheless denies all these superstitions, and says the two brothers were drowned (F 6 v 11), qualifying however this statement with „prout vere putatur" M. omits all the superstitious ideas about their fate, and declares unreservedly that they were drowned. 3,641 „car la mer les a anglotis" and 4,335 „Si sont tous deux en mer perilz". In support of this M. adds „Si n'en sont eschappez nulz vifz. Fors que *ung seul* qui le m'a (à Naulus) compte". Therefore M. simply emphasizes the assertion of G.

53. 1) Naulus vows vengeance and recalls to mind the Trojans' treatment of Jason. He himself is however too old; his son Palamides will go in his stead. Then follows a long exhortation to Palamides (3,667—802) in which Naulus bids him be worthy of his ancestors. He warns him also against speech that is not guided by wisdom. The passage is very prolix and without poetic value. Equally wearisome is Palamides' reply (3,803—50.) Naulus then dismisses Citheus, who goes to Nestor and his son Archilogus. Nestor promises to come with his son.[1])

---

[1]) The verse 3,904 requires notice. Nestor says: „Ie luy (= Menelaus) merray foison d'artillerie". This line has already attracted the attention of Meybrinck (page 32, 33) and he rejects the idea that M. here means artillery in the modern sense of the word, saying only: „Ich möchte artillerie eher als Collectivbezeichnung für Waffen überhaupt auffassen, wie es ja auch sonst im Sinne von Rüstkammer oder „Waffenwagen" gebraucht wird (vgl. Schultz „Das höfische Leben zur Zeit der Minnesinger" II, 186.)"

M. however could have used the word in the modern sense, for gunpowder artillery was known at his time. See Larousse's Dictionary under „Artillerie" page 729, where we learn that gunpowder artillery was used at Florence in 1326, and in France in 1328. The Encyclopedia Brittanica under „Artillery" says that Edward III of England used cannon in the modern sense in 1338. The earlier meaning of the word „artillerie" is a very general one applied to weapons of all sorts, including engines of the catapult type (See Godefroy and La Curne de Sainte Pelaye), and only by a gradual process did it assume its modern restricted sense. That Milet however did not use the word in this modern sense is, to our mind, clear from the verses which follow. These are simply a catalogue of what he meant by „artillerie" i. e. „harnoys, becz de faulcon, dars, haches, espees"; „masses de plomb" were used in gunpowder cannon but also in catapult engines. Had he meant gunpowder artillery he

2) Then follows a long passage (3,879—986) wherein Nestor urges Archilogus to learn the art of war, for he is no longer a child. Nestor will confer knighthood upon him and outlines the ceremony and the main features of the knightly code. Archilogus promises loving obedience (3,987—4,050). Nestor bids Archilogus help him arm, contrasting the honor of filial service to the ignominy of a serf's work. He then promises Citheus to go to Menelaus in two days, and dismisses him.

3) In the visit to Ajax, we note the latter's declaration that he will himself kill Paris, a prophecy that is really fulfilled. M. remembered this as he wrote the verses here.

54. Citheus then goes to Thelamon and greets also the latter's son Thelamonius Ajax. Thelamon says his great age will prevent his coming[1]), but his son shall represent him. A short scene of exhortation follows between father and son, as in the previous instances. Thelamonius Ajax promises Citheus to come in six days to Cytharee (4,206). Citheus goes then to Prothenor and Cediron. The latter promise to come in three days (4,284). Citheus thanks them and returns to Menelaus. Meanwhile Prothenor and Cediron order their respective servants Micheus and Sergestus to arm them. Citheus then arrives before Menelaus and reports everything, including the fate of Castor and Pollus (4327—44). Thereupon Menelaus again gives vent to his grief.[2]) He doubts the goodness and justice of the gods especially „Venus dame de joye" (4,409), whom he had always served loyally „Plus que Juno ne que pallas". We note

---

would have specified, it seems probable, the several sorts of gunpowder machines of his day „mortiers, couleuvres, couleuvrines, canons, veuglaires, bombardes, crapeandeaux, pots de feu, serpentines, tuyaux de tonnerre etc. He would have also spoken of the projectiles used: plommées etc. (See Larrousse under Artillerie.)

[1]) Note that in B-G. Thelamon actually goes to Troy, and besides other combats, fights Panthasilee. When M. relates this fight, he substitutes the son Thelamonius Ajax (§ 185[3].)

[2]) This passage (4,345—424) contains one of the few examples of stanza formation in Milet. The scheme is a b a b b c b c, i. e, eight eight-syllable verses. There are ten such stanzas each ending with the refrain. „Car mal sur mal n'est pas sante." A similar passage with 10-syllable verses is 516—524—532 (—538.) In several other cases it is reasonable to suppose copyists' changes have altered the original schemes.

the same grouping together of these three goddesses as in the relation of the dream of Paris (§ 23[1]). Agamenon comforts his brother, who promises to compose himself before the arrival of the Greek princes.

Chapter VII.

The Greek princes assemble at Cytharea and go to Athens.

M. 4,487—6,101. B. 4,990—5,040 and 5,569—5,586. G. F 6 r 3—15 and G 1 v 15—27. Enumeration of Greek allies in B. 5,586—5,695; in G. G 1 v 28 — G 2 v 12.

55. This passage is another example of the extraordinary expansion by M. of the scant material in B-G. In general this assembling of the Greek princes has the same characteristics as the previous assembling of the Trojan princes to go to Priam's court (see § 14). Each Greek prince has some one to help him arm. Achilles starts first with Patroclus and with his Mirmidons, Orgiam, Cebat, Missellet, Abimalet (4492—94). Prothesilaus and servant Adamas follow. Diomedes and his „seneschal" (4507) meet Achilles and his companions, recognizing them by Achilles' standard (4516—19) and Patroclus' banner (4524—6). The two parties join company[1]) and proceed together. They are seen approaching by Citheus. Menelaus welcomes them, bidding them however wait until the others come (4,612). In similar manner Ulixes and his body-guard „permenis et cloacus" (4615) meet Prothesilaus and servant Adamas, and the two parties are welcomed in like terms by Menelaus.

56. 1) Nestor and Archilogus with banner-man Methenez start next. We have already noted how the omission of Nestor's accompanying Menelaus home as in B-G., explains his being

---

[1]) As the Greek princes meet, most of them say they are going to Menelaus or Cytharea. Nestor and Ajax Thelamonius say however „Agamenon" 4,919, 5,175. In both the latter cases, the rhyme is responsible.

summoned now (§. 49[3]). Nestor's rôle is here very interesting: He speaks of his great age and endurance in warfare, then, à propos of Paris, he ridicules the effeminacy of lovers as a warning to Archilogus:

(4768–78) Quant par amours sont jeunes gens souppris,
Ce n'est que char tendre comme rosee;
Trop sont douilletz et trop delicatifz,
Tousjours sont matz, angoisseux et pensifz;
Plus simple sont que nouvelle epousee.
Par ma barbe qui est roide et meslee,
Ce a telle amour mettoies tu pensee,
Tous les membres te vouldroie trencher
Et demincer plus menu que poiree,
Car en amours n'a point cueur de duree
Mais en soulcy le convient trebucher.

Archilogus assures Nestor that his thoughts are quite elsewhere:

4785 Ie n'ay talent de croppir en la cendre,
Pour ung baiser ou pour regard attandre.

2) Ajax and servant Corinthus also commence their journey to Menelaus. They meet and join Nestor. Nestor talks with Ajax, contrasting their skill and endurance in war with that of the younger generation:

4948
Ilz ont apprins a mollement
Coucher en lit, non pas en paille,
Quant il auront eu le harnois
Sur le doz de nuyt et de jour,
Comme nous avons aultreffoiz
Sans prendre repos ne seiour,
Et seront dedens un estour
A bailler coupz et recepvoir,
Ie croy que de leur folle amour
Ne leur pourra gaires challoir.

At their arrival in Cytharee before Menelaus, the latter welcomes his cousin Nestor with especial joy (4976.) „Acolles moy ie vous emprie." As in previous cases, however, he asks them to await the arrival of the others.

57. Ajax Thelamonius now takes leave of his father Thelamon, promising to do well his duty. Thelamon repeats his exhortations to knightly conduct:

5,012.
Et si te vueil bien commander,
Qu'entre dames et damoiselles,
Tu te gardez de rien parler,
Qui puisse toucher l'onneur d'elles,
Et que soyes entre pucelles
Gracieulx et de beau maintien
Sans trop regarder les plus belles.

Thelamon then warns his son of the dangers of love, citing his own experience and that of Jason. The passage is rather curious. Love makes

(5,030)

Les plus saiges devenir lours
Et les vieulx tourner en enfance.
Combien qu'on y preigne plaisance
Et qu'aucuns en louent les taches,
Si respons a leur consequence,
Que thoreaulx ne quierent que vaches;
C'est a dire que gens oiseux
Qui a rien faire sont vaccans
Sont communement amoureux
Ainsi que thoreaulx aux champs.

Thelamon bids his son good-bye and the latter departs. Prothenor and Cediron also start with their banner-carriers, Mitheus and Sergestus. They meet Ajax Thelamonius and all go to Menelaus, before whom the same greetings take place as before.

58. Agamenon now (5,256) announces to his brother that all[1]) have come, and bids him lay before them his grievances and ask their aid. Menelaus approves this advice (5,303 d). „adont menelaus s'encline vers tous les princes, lesquelz se doivent lever tous en estant et puis raseoir, puis menelaus dit". This speech of Menelaus, like most such in M., is much spun out (5,304—431): He repeats his grievances, which concern the honor of all Greece; he reminds them of the vengeance taken for the insults offered Jason and Hercules, and asks their advice and aid. Only lines 5,320—3 are noteworthy:

Vray est que n'a pas grandement
Seurvint dedens mon pensement
D'aler le roy p e l e u s veoir
Droit a m a n i s e.

We have already taken due notice of this passage (§ 49).

As the kings remain silent, Agamenon adds his plea for vengeance to his brother's words, addressing several of the kings in person. This speech (5,432—527) is also very prolix. Nestor and Achilles promise all aid in their power, and Menelaus thanks both profoundly.

59. The election of Agamenon to the leadership is the next event of the drama. (5,572—867.) M. has made a long scene out of a mere incident in B-G. B (5,003—18) simply says the Greek princes elect Agamenon „empereor". There is not even a suggestion of the possibility of the election of another. G. prefixes his statement of the election of Agamenon with (F 6 r 8.) „pro huius autem executione negocii ante omnia statu-

[1]) Palamides is here completely forgotten, although Menelaus had said, 4992, that he was expected to come. No explanation of his absence is asked or given until he finally appears 8,002 (see § 75).

erunt *aliquem* eligere in ducem et principem etc." It was undoubtedly this „*aliquem*" which suggested to M. his expansion of this incident, wherein he represents Agamenon as unwilling to accept and as disparaging himself, bidding the princes elect another. M. assigns the traditional reputation for cleverness to Ulixes; it is he who suggests the need of a leader. Throughout the drama this idea of Ulixes' wisdom is maintained (see Index). Dyomedes nominates Agamenon, who, after long urging by Menelaus, Ulixes, and Dyomedes, finally agrees to accept. This scene of the election of Agamenon has its counterpart on the Trojan side in the selection of Hector (see § 84).

60. 1) Achilles now suggests the start for Troy (5,868) and Agamenon approves, in order that they may come to Athens „dedens deux jours". Menelaus sends Cithens ahead to inform Menesteus of their coming. The latter thereupon goes to meet the advancing princes. Cithens sees them approaching and names them:

(5,940) Si sont ce croy que ducz que roys
Plus de quatorze bien nombres.

Here is a coincidence with the number *quatorze* in a previous passage in B. on the occasion of the election of Agamenon.

B. 5,013—4. Altresi riches i ot dus
Comme il (= Agamenon) esteit, quatorze et plus.

Later in B., when the Greeks arrive at Athens, the number is given as much greater: B. 5,687. „LX et nos furent par non." Therefore the mere coincidence of quatorze can have no weight. We mention it simply to show how far one must go to find even a semblance of B's influence upon M. That M. attached no importance to this number fourteen, is shown in Palamides' words, when he speaks of the arrival of the Greeks in Thenedos (8,037) „Et sont bien dix ou douze roys".

2) Menesteus and Agamenon greet each other and proceed together to Athens.[1]) A Trojan merchant, Sentipus, sees the

[1]) M. thus agrees with G. in having no intermediate stopping-place between Menelaus' kingdom and Athens. In Joly's text of B. an intermediate locality is mentioned:

B. 5,029 A Temesse dreit el rivage
Assenbleront tot le parage.

In the Variantes to this line 5.029, Joly says (P. 552) that Mss. B. has „Athenes" for Temesse. This is probably the correct reading, as Joly's text army, and hastens to Priam to acquaint him with the rumors as to its meaning. (5986—99). Menesteus then calls attention to the beauty of his city:

(6,006.)
Et si y a universite
De clers de grant auctorite,
Qui congnoissent tous les sept ars,
Et son par leur habilite
Bien introduitz de toutes pars.
Ie scay de vray, qu'en tout le monde
N'en a point de si bien peuplee
Ne de science si parfoude
Ne de si grans clers honnoree

Menesteus places his city entirely at Agamenon's disposal and the latter thereupon bids all the Greeks rest. — — King Thoas then prepares to go to Athens with his men Cadimas and Basaam. Rumor has told him that the Greek kings are assembling there. He arrives and is gratefully welcomed by Agamenon (6,101).

Chapter VIII.

Council of Priam. — The Oracle of Apollo. — The Arrival of the Greeks at Thenedos.

M. 6,102—8,001. B. 5,695—6,054. G. G 2 v 13 — H 1 v 22.

61. The Trojan merchant, Sentipus, arrives from Athens before Priam, where are assembled all the Trojan kings. He announces the assembling of the Greek host[1]) and its purpose. Sentipus is true to his calling, for his main anxiety is lest the Greeks „destruiront la marchandise" (6,132). Priam asks three times in refrain „Amy ditz tu vray par ta foy?", receiving always the reply: „Ouil sire ie vous affie". Thereupon Priam addresses the Trojan kings, who rise at his voice. He reminds them of their high lineage, of their descent from Teucer (see

contains no subsequent mention of Temesse. Guido therefore probably took his reading from a member of the group of Benoît manuscripts, of which Mss. B. is a representative.

[1]) Milet's idea of the strength of the Greek forces is given here: There are sixty kings (6,115) and 40,000 (!) ships. Elsewhere the total force is given as over 100,000 men: 7,964; 8,443; 22,099.

Proper Names § 243), and of their duty to shield it from dishonor. He also asks for advice. Especially does he appeal to Hector and Paris. With the latter we note the beginning of Milet's emphasis of the idea, that Paris is to blame for the whole matter. We shall find more striking examples of this, later, as the disaster thickens (see Index for references). B-G. have no trace of such a censuring of Paris:

M. 6,199. „Paris, paris, c'est par ton fait
Car ie scay bien qu'ilz veullent dire“ etc.
and 6,205 Pour toy ie souffriray martire
Et pour helene qui tant est belle
Puisque c'est pour toy mon beau filz
Il t'en convient bien traveiller.

Anchises in a long speech (6,223—326) says Helen must not be given up, for the Greeks are in the wrong and will be conquered. Thus will Priam's vengeance be complete. Anchises also suggests the wisdom of consulting the will of the gods, and advises sending Calcas to learn the oracle of Apollo. Priam must also summon the kings who are friendly and allied to him. Anchises names them and their kingdoms (6,291—315).

62. M. continues this council-scene, which is completely original to him, by introducing now the relation of a dream by Hector and its interpretation by Helenus. This desire to introduce dreams on all possible occasions is a marked tendency in the drama and there are many examples (see Index for references). Hector relates that he dreamt Paris was an „esprevier nouveau de branche“ (6,340) and had carried off with violence“ une coulombe belle et blanche“ (6,342). His father had become an eagle and, joining the „esprevier“, defended it:

(6,347)
Si venoit ung griffon moult grant
Qui l'aigle des pies devoroit,
Et l'esprevier bel et plaisant
De ses griffes esgratignoit.
Lors tous les petis espreviers,
Qui estoient de la nyee,
Si vindrent mettre des premiers
Cuidans deffaire la meslee;
Mais il vint de grant randonnee
Ung dragon volant par le vent,
Qui devoroit en sa volee
Les espreviers cruellement;
Ainsi a le griffon reprise
La coulombe et emportee
Et en a fait tout a sa guise
Et la dedens son nic boutee.

Hector asks the meaning of this dream. Anthenor says dreams are not to be trusted, explaining them generally with

6,379.

Il est bien vray quant on espoire
Aulcunes choses advenir,
Qu'on en a en dormant memoire
Pour acroistre le souvenir.

Paris seconds Anthenor's attempt to explain the dream, by saying that Hector had probably lost an „esprevier", killed by an „autour ou escouffle sauvage", and that the dream is a result of his grief. Helenus however speaks up and explains the dream: The dove is Helen, the „griffon" Menelaus, the dragon Agamenon. The eagle is Priam and the „espreviers" are the other Trojan kings who, together with Paris, will perish miserably. Paris ridicules this, „car telles exposicions sont toutes pures fictions" (6,456—8). Troillus supports Paris, saying his valor is not lessened by such words and that he is ready to die piteously to defend his father's honor.

63. There now follows the advent of Cassandra, to which we have already referred (foot note § 45) as transposed from its earlier place in B-G: „adont doit seurvenir cassandra come toute forcenee et criera en telle maniere tout au milieu du conseil ce qui s'ensuit". Her speech is very vigorous: Restore Helen at once, else all will perish and the city be utterly destroyed. Paris is severely blamed for his „amour desordonnee" (6533). Her language becomes more excited; „lors cassandra se gettera aux piez du roi priam et en pleurant dira": She begs him not to support Paris and „sa follye" (6553); she urges him to return Helen and attempt to secure Exionne in exchange. Paris beseeches his father to make Cassandra stop (6,569): „Ie cuide qu'elle est en fureur | Ou qu'elle n'a pas la teste saine" and again (6579) „Ie voy bien qu'elle n'est pas saige | Elle est a demy forcenee. | Si deshonnore son lignage." Cassandra's reply is very spirited: „Paris vous mentez faulcement | Sauve l'onneur de la lignie" and „Pardieu ie ne m'en tairė mie | Tant que i'auray langue ne bouche". She ought to hate him; he has no right to Helen; his act offends the gods,

(6614) „Car tout plainement ie vous dy
Qu'il n'est point plus mauvaise taiche".

After further altercation Cassandra relapses into silence at the request of Priam „sur peine d'inobedience" (6634.) and returns to Heccuba.

In this scene Milet's originality consists in the spirited dialogue. He does not follow B-G. in having Cassandra imprisoned, but reserves this incident for a later appearance of Cassandra § 95[4].

Priam now (6647) addresses his lords: He will summon his allies, and send Calcas to consult the oracle of Apollo. Merion and Enee approve. Calcas is despatched, going away with his assistant Finees. Priam thereupon gives Macabrum a list[1]) of kings to be summoned and Macabrum departs.

64. The scene now shifts to the Greeks (6732 ff.): Agamenon asks if they are ready to advance on Troy, and exhorts them to courage and fidelity. Dyomedes assures him of his zeal. Ajax speaks of their strength and, with Prothesillaus, urges immediate departure. Ulixes now upholds his reputation for wisdom by reminding the Greeks that the gods are the final arbiters of all destiny, and by suggesting that, as they are near to Delon „ou Apollo est honnore" (6861), they select some one to go learn the divine will. In B-G. it is Agamenon who makes this suggestion (B. 5765 ff.; G. G 3 v 10 ff.). Menelaus seconds this proposition and Agamenon thereupon appoints Achilles and Patroclus to go (6,908—920). Achilles declares

---

[1]) In this list we note the name of „merion", 6722, in all prints. There is considerable confusion about this name: Macabrum summons him (7,444) and although nothing is said of his starting (It is always Milet's custom in other cases to mention the act of starting), he, Merion, is represented as meeting the other kings on the way to Troy 7,878, and as arriving with them 7,929. Yet all this time he is at Troy, having just spoken (6,671.) Another confusion exists between Merion and Menon: Anchises gives Priam a list of kings to be summoned (6,291—314; see § 61 end). This list Priam repeats in slightly different order, only omitting Pillon (6,715—26). In this second list Merion is substituted for Menon (in all prints), the order for the neighboring names being the same:

First list: Boetes, Menon, Theseus
Second list: Bouettes, Merion, Theseus.

Both these confusions are undoubtedly due to paleographical misreadings, it being easy to mistake a Gothic ri for an n, and vice-versa. The prints however give us no clue to the correct solution of this small mystery. I know not whether a similar confusion exists in the Mss. Under „Menon" and „Merion" in Proper Names § 241, will be found an attempt to solve this confusion.

himself unworthy of such a mission, but finally yields. Patroclus pleads in like manner and emphasizes his friendship for Achilles:

(6,948.) Achilles vous savez assez
Et vous et moy n'avons que ung cueur
and 6,960 Vous et moy sommes bien amis
Si sommes aussi freres d'armes;
Si doivent estre tous unis
Noz vouloirs, noz corps et noz ames.

They go away together. There now follows the series of scenes in the temple of Apollo, in which Milet shows great originality and departure from his source. Yet a number of things point unmistakeably to G. as M's starting point.

65. M. is indebted to G. for the location of the oracle: B. had said (5,778 and 5,786) it was located at *Defeis* but gives no further description; B. makes no mention of its being an island. G. says (G 3 v 12 and G 3 v 22) „*delphos insulam*", and proceeds with a long description of the place (G 3 v 27): „Erat autem predicta insula delphos mari undique circumfusa que pro certo creditur quod fuerit insula *delos* que scriptorum forte vicio fuit adjuncta que insula in medio insularum *ciclados* sita est in mari scilicet elespontico *constituta,* quare de predictis insulis cicladum principalis est una, (then follows half a page wherein Guido sets forth the connection of this island with mythology. This does not concern us here).

M. does not have *Delfos* but only *Delos:*

M. 6,279 (Anchises to Priam):
Pour ce me semble que en ce cas
Seroit bon et bien convenant
Que vous envoyssiez calcas
En delos qui est bien avant
Et en ciclades constituee."

6,686 „Car il vous fault aller en l'isle
De Delon, loing de ceste ville (= Troy)
6,860 Or sommes nous (Greeks at Athens) pres de delon.
6,903 Que en l'isle Delon envoyons
6,967 La ou est l'isle de Delon
6986 d Qu'ilz soient venus jusques en l'isle de delon.
7,657 Et en l'isle delon venir.

Although B. does not say *Defeis* is an island, Achilles and Patroclus are represented as having come thither in a ship (B. 5,827). This was probably why Guido substituted the idea of an island, and the beginning of the process of thought whereby he changes Delphos to Delos. Although, as we have seen, Milet says an island, he makes no mention of sailing to arrive thither. G. emphasizes the fact of sailing throughout the whole incident.

66. Achilles and Patroclus arrive at Delos and Achilles says it is time to go „au temple de phebus" (6,992). In 7,273 *phebus* occurs again: „la responce de phebus". For this name M. is probably indebted to G., who uses it as a synonym of Apollo (G 4 r 13). It does not occur in B. The original element in M's version consists in the sacrifice of animals[1]): Achilles bids his servant Basaac procure (6,996) „ung aignel debonnaire", later (7,004.)

— — — ung blanc aignel
Allecte bien nouvellement,
Aussi qu'il soit ieune et nouvel
Et qu'il soit moult tendre de pel
Et ayt la layne bien pignee,
Afin qu'il en semble plus bel
Pour hostie sacriffiee.

While waiting for the animal, Achilles says, they must go to the temple to pray:

(7,021) Si nous enclinerons a terre
Et aurons chappeaulx de l'osier
Quant nous vouldrons le dieu prier
Lesquelz nous mettrons en la teste
Quant nous saccriffirons la beste
and later (7,031.) Saindons nous tous deux d'une corde
Et mettons les bandes a point.

7,034 d. „lors se saindront de cordes et envelopperont leurs testes de touailles et mettront chascun ung chappeau d'osier". Achilles forbids his Mirmidons to enter „l'oratoire" (7,039), (Their accompanying Achilles here is an invention of Milet.) and then goes in himself with Patroclus. The two kneel down and say together:

Kirios kirios kirios[2]) | Athanatos athanatos | Ythirios ythirios

---

[1]) It is to be noted that in M. there is no mention of other gifts to the god than animal sacrifices, whereas B. and G. speak of other gifts and omit the animal sacrifices, at least in this scene, not however in a later one (§ 211; 212).

[2]) Greif has made a transcription of this word as lirios. I have not seen the Dresden edition itself, but, judging from his transcription, I imagine that the type it has is the same as that in the Paris edition of 1498 and the Paris edition of 1508. These have a peculiar letter which looks most like a Gothic l and r. Hence Greif's transcription as such. Stengel in the Introduction P. VIII to the „Vervielfältigung" of the Dresden edition points out that the type-setter used lr to take the place of f, which last letter he did not possess. The edition of 1485, (one year after the first edition of 1484) publish-

This invocation is followed by Achilles' prayer, which opens with a long introduction in rhymes of — ité, and — ence (7,046 —88). Patroclus then gives him the lamb. (7,124 d)" lors patroclus tendra la teste et achilles le sacriffira sur l'autel en le parissent par le millieu, en ung vaisel d'argent rȩndra le sang." Achilles then continues his prayer for enlightenment as to the wishes of the gods (7,125—61).

67. The reply of the god Apollo shows several things of interest:

1) B. makes no mention of a statue of the god Apollo, but simply says: B. 5,795 „*Li respons* li (=Achilles) a dit en bas" and later 5,805 „tot ço que *li respons* a dit | Achilles a mis en escrit". (The idea contained in the last line finds no expression in G-M.)

G. however says (G 4 r 20.) „in hoc igitur templo erat maxima ymago tota ex auro composita et in honore predicti dei appollinis". Then follows in G. a long chapter (to G 6 r 29.) on the nature, the wickedness and the history of idolatrous worship, which does not here concern us. Our only interest is to note that M., under the influence of G., says: 7,161 d „lors *l'idolle* du temple respond en *grosse* voix (in B-G. *subdued* voice, 5795, G 6 v 4) comme tonnerre et — — Achilles et Patroclus enclineront leurs faces contre terre". Then 7,162 *L'idolle* Appollo „Entendez" etc." Also later to Calcas 6251 d. „*l'idolle* en voix terrible".

2) B and G. both emphasize in this place the prophecy that Troy will fall in ten years (B, 5,797—800; G 6 v 7) Curiously enough M. omits here this important point, and the only statement of the idea is later, in the words of Calcas to Achilles (7,296.), where it is not explained how Calcas learned it. The idea is moreover differently expressed:

(7,296)

Car dedens dix ans ou avant	Que priam n'aura nul enfant
Vous aurez troye si bas mise	Qui ne soient mors a vostre guise.

Cassandra says later (10,559) La cite perdrez ains dix ans.

---

ed in Lyon in Gothic has unmistakeably a f, likewise the latest edition of 1544, also at Lyon, but printed in Latin type. In place of ythirios the edition of 1544 has yschiros.

3) Another point of M's contact with G. is in the begining of Apollo's reply:

G 6 v 4 „achilles revertere ad grecos tuos a quibus missus es et dic eis pro certo futurum se salubriter ad troyam ituros."	M. 7,164 Premierement ie vous respons Que vous prevandrez saulvement Au port de troye briefment.

B. contains no such thought.

4) M. alone feels the necessity of explaining the cause of the divine wrath against Troy:

(Apollo to Achilles 7,171.) Car les dieux si ont ordonnee La chose estre en ce contre point Et ont leur mauldisson donnee Sur troye la tres fortunee Pour leurs pompes et leur orgueil. (Apollo to Calcas, 7,258) Il fault que les troyens ie voye Destruire car deservy l'ont.	(Calcas to Agamenon. 7,665) Mais ainsi comme i'aparcoy Les dieux ont la cite de troye En hayne pour son desaroy, Car le peuple trop si desvoye; Ilz vivent orguilleusement Et oultre raison sont pompeux, Mangent delicieusement Et si sont par trop curieux.

See also 21,194—5. Later, in Anthenor's dream of the appearance of Hector, the latter says that the gods desire to avenge the rape of Helen (22, 587; § 189).

68. At the close of Apollo's reply to Achilles and Patroclus, the latter say in unison:

„Chere kirios kirios | Chere kirios kirios | Cere athanatos"

and retire from the temple in great joy. As they go out, they meet „Calcas le troyen qui doibt estre habille en guise de prestre selon l'encienne façon" (7204 d). A sharp little dialogue of greeting follows:

7,205	Calcas:	Dieu gard seigneurs.
	Achilles:	Et vous aussi.
		Dont venez vous, ie vous emprie?
	Calcas;	Je viens de troye tout droit cy.
		Dieu gard seigneurs.
	Achilles:	Nous mettrons troie en grant soucy.
		Certes ie le vous certiffie.
	Calcas:	Dieu gard seigneurs.
	Achilles:	Et vous aussi.

Calcas learns whence they have come and begs them wait until he returns. He enters the temple with his clerc Finees, and speaks „el rabon" three times in alternation with „osanna cecilos „spoken by Finees. Calcas then prays for divine favor for the Trojans and sacrifices „ung thoreau blanc — — comme les grecz ont fait“ 7,231. The idol replies „en voix terrible“.

69. This reply shows the following similarities in M. and G.:

1) The address is the same in M. and G. „Calcas, Calcas“ G 6 v 18. M. 7252. B. does not have this vocative.

2) Calcas is forbidden to return to the Trojans: G 6 v 18 Calcas, calcas, caveas ne ad tuos redire presumas.

M. 7252 Calcas, Calcas ie te deffens que tu ne retournes a troye. In both cases this negative command is followed by the affirmative command to go to the Greeks, which latter command is the *only* one in B.

3) M. and G. agree again: G 6 v 21 „numquam discessurus a grecis“. M. 7260 „Si ne te pars iamais des grecz“.

Calcas thanks the god and, leaving the temple, joins Achilles and Patroclus. All go to Athens.

70. There now follows (7,308—622) on the Trojan side a scene of summoning, as Macabrum executes the orders given him by Priam (6,713 ff. § 63 end.). In general it is the same as like scenes already examined (see list in Index), except that it takes place very much more rapidly:

Sixtus Passagoniens leads Macabrum to his master Philimenis, who replies that he will come in two days (7,361).

(7,349.) Car ie suis bien tenu a luy
Car une foiz en pareil cas
Il se monstra mon bon amy.

Macabrum next goes to Glancon and Serpedon of Licia (7370—444); and thence to Merion (7,445—464; see foot note to § 63), who promises to come in eight days (7,458). Macabrum now goes to Ampheneas of Liconnye, to Huppon, to Pillon (Priam had not mentioned Pillon 6,713—28; Anchises alone had done so, 6299; see § 61 end, and § 63 foot-note). Pillon will come in two days (7,501). Bouetes de Bretonnie is then visited, and also Theseus of Thierres (7,526). Macabrum next passes quickly to Epistropus „qui a cent et vint ans ou plus“, who promises to come to avenge Laomedon's death:

Car ie estoie encor petit garson
Quant au premier fuz en sa compaignie.

Priam will see him „ains sepmaine et demie". Macabrum now returns to Priam. In the intervening pause the Trojan allies arm, each having men to carry the standards and the lances (7,595 d). Macabrum then reports that the allies will all come in two days.

71. 1) The scene changes now to the Greek side: Achilles tells Agamenon that he has brought a Trojan priest who will relate the result of their visit to the oracle. Calcas announces the reply of Apollo who bade him leave the Trojans and go over to the Greeks. Patroclus upholds the truth of Calcas' words and advises an immediate departure. Agamenon then also urges departure, and this meets with the approval of Diomedes, Ulixes and Nestor. M. thus differs radically from B-G., where it is Calcas alone who counsels the immediate departure (B. 5,908; G 7 v 3). We shall note other instances of this suppression by M. of the rôle of Calcas, so important in B-G (see Index for references).

2) In the final scene of departure, however, G's influence is again seen: G 7 v 21 Agamenon statim mandavit ut universi exercitus *per tube sonitum* moveantur quod illico naves ascendant [ascendunt] ab athenarum portu feliciter descensuri. Nec mora *a tubete sonitu* [ad tube sonitum] universi naves ascendunt etc.

M. 7732 Agamenon: Faictes les trompetes sonner
Si entrons en la mer salee.

7738 d. — — — et chascun s'en yra en sa nef et devant eulx les *trompettes*. B. has no mention of trumpets in this connection. M. makes continuous use of trumpets throughout the drama, particularly in the battle-scenes.

72. The action now shifts to the Trojan allies who, in a series of scenes, start to go to Priam. They meet after recognizing each the other's banner. Nothing is said of Merion's starting but yet he joins the others (see footnote to § 63). While similar to other scenes of assembling (see §§ 14, 55, 56, 57), this one is much more rapidly accomplished, and we note M's haste in the way he bunches several meetings together (7,842—905) instead of, as before, according to each a separate treatment. Joining company in successive groups, these groups finally unite and come before Priam, to whom Epistropus speaks greeting in the name of all and offers their united services. Epistropus, in so doing, repeats the names of all the kings. This repetition of names probably served only to impress upon the spectators the various actors (see § 13). Priam welcomes and thanks all, bidding them repose until the arrival of the Greeks. Each one goes to rest upon the „petits eschauffaulx“ (7,977 d).

73. The Greeks now move with blast of trumpets „jusques ad ce qu'ilz soient arrivez au port de thenedon qui est a trois lieues de troye“ whereupon Agamenon mounts „sur l'eschauffault“, announces their nearness to Troy and bids each one rest until the morrow when they will meet in council. After a brief dialogue, „lors se partent et par ainsi se finist la premiere iournee et corneront les trompetes et s'en yra on soupper (8,001 d)[1]).

---

[1]) In thus having the Greeks come undisturbed to Tenedos, M. omits several important episodes in B-G: (B. 5,923—6,054 — G 7 v 23 — H 1 v 22): There arises a severe storm. Calcas finds that Diana is angry because they neglected sacrificing to her. He bids them repair at once to Elida (G. island of Aulis), where Agamenon must sacrifice in person to appease the goddess. This is done and the goddess is pacified. In M. the only trace of all this is in the words of Prothenor 7,992 „Nous avons eu moult grant traveil | Sur la mer“. — In B. the Greek pilot Filotetes (B 5,997) plays an important part in the voyage. G. had transferred him from this episode to be the pilot of Jason's expedition (A 7 r 14, A 7 v 1.), and mentions no pilot here. Hence M. does not. — In B-G. there is an attack upon a castle before reaching Tenedos (G. calls this castle Sarronaba G 8 v 7); there is also the resistance offered by the inhabitants of Tenedos. Both these conflicts G. relates in greater detail than B. M. omits them completely, and later we shall note frequently this omission of all fighting except that before the city of Troy itself. M's only references to hostile encounters beyond the neighborhood of the city itself, occur: 1) In Priam's speech to Panthasilee 21,631. Mes champs desheritez | Mes chasteaulx et citez. 2) In Ajax Thelamonius' speech, claiming the Palladium (see 233[1], [3], [4], [5]).

The Second Day of the Drama.

Chapter IX.

The Arrival of Palamides. — The Embassy to Priam. The First Battle.

M. 8,002—8,756; B. 6,054—7,561; G. H 1 v 23 — I 6 r 18.

74. The second day opens with a pleasing scene between Palamides and his father Naulus[1]). Palamides has heard that the Greeks have arrived in Asia (8,008) at Thenedon. He is grateful to the gods for restoring him to health „d'une tres griefve maladie" (8,021), so that he can now fulfil the promise made two months ago (8,035) and go join the Greeks. Naulus bids him good-bye with affectionate advice and fatherly blessing, exhorting him to acquire fame honorably. Palamides departs with his company and with Agalion, his banner-carrier, for Thenedon. The scene shifts thither. Agamenon is holding a council, and reminds the Greeks of their high lineage from Hercules. He urges immediate departure to besiege Troy and many approve.

75. There now follows the scene of the arrival of Palamides, which M. relates with considerable vivacity and originality: In M., Palamides arrives *before* the embassy of Ulixes and Diomedes to Priam and seconds Ulixes in counselling the same (8,293—300). In B-G. he arrives long after the embassy (B 6,933 — I 1 v 18). — In M. Ajax bids the Greeks look

(8,149) Vers la mer car ie voy venir
Une navire bien fournie.

---

[1]) Wunder in giving his abstract of this scene says (Page 16) „So hören wir Naulus (Nauplius) in E u b ö a seinen Sohn Palamides ermahnen" This name Euböa however does not occur in M.

It may contain Trojans coming to assault the Greeks. Menelaus recognizes those approaching as Greeks and sees by the standard (8,164—71) that it is Palamides, son of Naulus, whom they must receive with great honor. Cediron suggests sending kings to honor him: He will go in company with Prothesillaus. They go „andevant de l'eschauffault" (8,209 d). Prothesillaus greets Palamides who mistakes their motive and says (8,214):

Seigneurs vueillez moy pardonner Den ce point pour moy desplacer
Vous me faictes ycy oultraige Mais c'est signe de humble couraige.

The misunderstanding is removed when Cediron asks him to come to Agamenon. Palamides greets all the kings and explains that sickness prevented his coming sooner. Now he is cured, thanks to the gods:

8255 Si n'ay plus qu'un peu le cueur vain
Et la teste ung peu defournye.

Yet he is ready to fight at once, if they wish to begin. In this scene M. omits all idea of Palamides being blamed for not coming sooner. B-G express this idea (B. 6943; I 1 v 22).

76. Ulixes sustains his fame for wisdom by warning against pride and by suggesting, since Priam is a powerful king, a preliminary embassy to him to demand Helen. Palamides and Prothenor second Ulixes, whereupon Agamenon appoints Diomedes and Ulixes as ambassadors. In B-G. it is Agamenon who both discourses against pride, and suggests the embassy (B. 6,063—6,188. H 2 r 16 — H 3 r 22). — M. makes no mention of opposition to the idea of an embassy, as do B-G. (6,192—4; H 3 r 22—25.) — Diomedes and Ulixes depart at once and arrive at the court of Priam. We note in G. and in M. complete absence of descriptions of the richness of attire, which B., here (6204—32) and elsewhere, emphasizes so strongly. — G. and M. also omit mention of the ambassadors being accompanied by servants (B. 6,234; 6265). — In M. the ambassadors come at once before Priam. M. thus omits all allusion to the wonderful tree in front of the palace (B 6,251—263) (H 3 r 27 — H 3 v 7).

77. There now follows the dramatic scene of the ambassadors at the court of Priam. B. and G. already had this largely in the form of dialogue, so that we are enabled again to trace M's close contact with G., and the absence of such contact with B. Comparison yields the following results:

1) Ulixes addresses Priam: The first part of the speech in M. (8,342—71) is wholly independent of B-G., who are here in the closest accord. — There then follows a statement common to B. and M., but absent in the 1477 edition of G. through a corruption of its text; as the statement, however, is found in other editions of G., we need not be embarrassed by its absence in the edition of 1477. We will, nevertheless, speak of this case as an excellent illustration of the need of a critical edition of Guido:

B. has (6,290) Se tu lor (the Greeks) vels fere dreiture,
La dame (Helen) rendes et l'aveir,
Et faces dreit a lor voleir,
Ço te mandent qu'il lo prendront,
Et en lor terre s'en riront.
and M.: 8370 Mais qu'elle soit restituee
Tout nostre ost s'en retournera.

2) In the 1477 edition of G., the statement is much weaker and there is no promise to return: H 3 v 18. „quod si feceris (i. e. restore Helen) salute sani consilii potieris". The above similarity of M. and B. might perhaps be easily caused by the context, but yet it is rather striking. A glance, however, at another edition of G. (that quoted as No. 5507 in Copinger's Supplement to Hain, Part I, Page 172), (f 5 r 10) shows that the edition of 1477 omits the important sentence: „nam ipse rex (= Agamenon) statim cum *universis suis redibat* in greciam et omnis erroris causa deinceps inter te et nos sedata cessabit: quod si forte contempnes respice quanta etc."[1]) Thus, as all three versions contain the promise to return to Greece, this apparent resemblance of M. to B. alone, falls to the ground.

[1]) The edition of 1477 has a curiously corrupted text here: „nam ipse rex statim forte contemnes sed ipsa respice quanta." The s. a. et l. edition (No. 871 in Campbell; No. 4 in Brunet), and the editions of the Strassburg group were evidently made upon the basis of the group to which the edition of 1477 belongs, for they only have a corrected version of the reading of 1477, and, like the latter, say nothing of a promise to return to Greece: „Quod si feceris salute sani consilii pocieris. Si autem hec implere forte contempnes ipse respice quanta etc."

3) It would, however, have been greatly invalidated by the next lines in M., which are taken directly from G.:

M. 8,372—81	H 3 v 19—23
Mais s'elle nous est reffusee, Agamenon vous assauldra, Si verrez vous ceste cite Estre en ruine convertie, Qui est en grant prosperite; Vous mesmes y perdres la vie, Et troye qui est bien garnie Sera mise a pouvrete, Voz enffens et vostre lignie Tous tuez par grant cruaulte.	— forte contemnes sed ipsa respice quanta tibi et tuis sint mala finaliter proventura, nam tu infelici morte succumbes universi tui in crudeli nece peribunt et hec tua nobilis civitas tota cassabitur ex ruina.

B. expresses himself very differently (B. 6,299—6,309):

Car se vos ço ne volez faire, Tel damage ne tel contraire N'avint onques com en iert fait; Jusqu'a M. anz sera retrait. Legierement puez adrecier Ço que te puet tant damagier.	Le mal qu'en peut venir sor tei, Puez or mielz covrir de ton dei, Qu'a brief terme de M. escuz. Se gie de ço ne sui creuz, M. homes n'i valdront que trei.

78. The reply of Priam to Ulixes contains several ideas common only to G-M.

1) M. 8,382—5.	H 3 v 24—5.
Ie m'esmerveille moult forment De la requeste irraisonable, Que vous me faictes follement, Car elle m'est mal agreable.	de narracione verborum vestrorum admiratione multa commoveor.
2) M. 8,389—95.	H 3 v 26—8.
Vous estez par trop mal fondez; Cuidez vous doncques avoir puissance Encontre moi, c'est grant follye, Moy qui ay en obeyssance La plus grant par de toute Asie, Et qui suis en ceste partie Craint, honnore, et redoubte.	Nec puto grecos vestros adversus me tantis viribus prevaluisse quod ad faciendum quod dicis cogi deberem.
3) M. 8,401—5.	H 4 r 1—2.
Et qui plus fort est, vous avez Ma seur, laquelle maintenez Non pas par maniere royalle, Mais on en fait ses voulentez Par euvre ville et desloyalle.	Abduxerunt sororem meam exionam que utinam more regio tractaretur sed vili more meretricio deturpatur.

B. has none of the above ideas, although many others in common with G. alone.

In all versions Priam reminds the ambassadors how badly

the Greeks treated his envoy Anthenor, and commands them to depart, for he cannot bear the sight of them. Thereupon Diomedes replies scornfully:

M. 8,438.	H 4 r 15,
O roy si tu es si esmeu	O rex si solis nobis inspectis sine
Pour ung seul regard de nous deux,	ira non estis toto ergo tempore vite
Et pource que tu nous as veu	vestre non eritis absque ira
Devant toy qui sommes tous seulz,	— — — H 4 r 21. Et si de solis
Bien devras estre douloureux	nobis inermibus tanto dolore contra-
Quant tu verras plus de cent mille	pungeris quanto potius condolebis cum
Des grecs puissans et vigoureux,	plusquam centum milia grecorum con-
Qui vendront assaillir ta ville.	tra te inspicies armatorum etc.

B's expression of the same idea is quite different:

B. 6372
Par de, biaus reis, iames sans ire
Ne sereiz donc, se si vous vet;
Jusqu'a un meis orreiz tel plet;
Voeir en porreiz C. milliers
Trestoz armez sor lor destriers.

79. 1) At these words of Diomedes (8,445 d) „lors plusieurs des assistens comme eneas, polidamas, et merion prendront leurs espees toutes nues et feront semblant de vouloir courir sur eulx". Amphorbius reproaches the Greeks for their insolent words, and the fiery, young Polidamas says (8,449):

Peu s'en fault que tout maintenant
Je n'en metz ung a mort villaine.

The above stage-direction is from G. (H 4 r 27): „Multi ergo de astantibus ad dyomedis verba commoti in ipsum irruere subito voluerunt — et nudatis ensibus". B. expresses himself otherwise (6393): „dui cent en saillirent en piez."

2) Priam stills the tumult: B. had said (6397.)

En ma cort n'a regart messages
Quels que il seit, ou fous ou sages.

G. enlarges considerably the idea of „fous ou sages": (H 4 r 31.)

„cum non sit sapientis stulto secundum suam stulticiam respondere et proprium stulti sit suas demonstrare stulticias et sapientis in sua sapientia tollerare stultorum errores; sicut enim stulto liberum est stulta verba diffundere sic sapientis cedit ad laudem auscultare quod dixerit et auscultata ridere. In verbis igitur stulti cognoscitur stulticia proferentis."

This contrasting of the wise and foolish is reflected in M. 8460 —3:

En apres il convient souffrir
Des folz et les doit on ouyr,
Car le saige doit differer,
Quant il escoute ung fol parler.

3) The speech of Eneas to Diomedes in M. is little more than a translation of G: (M. 8464—8487; H 4 v 12—22).

Likewise Diomedes' challenging reply: (M. 8488—99; H 4 v 23—29). Both speeches in B. are expressed very differently (B. 6,403—6420; 6420—6451.). The above passages are too long for quotation here.

4) At the close of Diomedes' speech in B., Ulixes simply says: (B. 6452) „desore est let" and then addresses Priam. G. and M. show another point of contact: (H 4 v 29). „Ulixes autem dyomedis verba sagaciter interrumpens monet eum ut ne pluribus verbis utatur"; M. 8,500:

Diomedes, ie vous supplie,
Que vous ne vueillez plus parler;
Prenons congie ie vous emprie,
Il est temps de nous en aler.

Ulixes' speech to Priam is essentially the same in the three versions. The ambassadors now return to Thenedon, and there follows immediately in M. a council relative to the first attack upon Troy[1]) G. inserts here a long notice about Eneas (H 5 r 11—29).

80. A council of war is held to consider the best means of attacking Troy. There is considerable hesitation. Thoas (8,522) suggests a night attack, which Ajax Thelamonius disapproves: Patroclus urges an attack by day. In B. this hesitation is abruptly broken by Palamedes (B. 6,977), who blames the Greeks for their dilatoriness, and urges immediate advance on Troy by sea. This speech is closely followed by G. who, however, curiously enough, substitutes for Palamedes, Diomedes (I 2 r 9)[2]). M. does the same (8546). This speech of Diomedes (Palamedes in B.) has the same general tone in B-G-M. B-G. are quite identical.

[1]) M. thus omits a long section in B-G. (6,498—635; H 5 r 30—H 8 v 3), the contents of which are: the expedition of Achilles and Thelefus (son of Hercules) to Messa for provisions; the battle with the king of Messa, Theucer (G. = Theutran, Teutran); the latter's defeat, and the bequeathing by him of his throne to Thelefus, because Thelefus had saved him from the indignity of having Achilles cut off his head, and because of Theucer's friendship for Hercules. Telefus remains in Messa so as to keep the Greek army supplied with provisions, while Achilles returns to the Greeks. M. certainly showed judgment in not disturbing the unity of his drama by such a digression. There then follows the enumeration of the Trojan allies (B. 6,636—932; H 8 v 4 — I 1 v 17), after which comes the arrival of Palamedes (B, 6,933—56; I 1 v 18—31). This latter incident M. has transposed (see § 75).

[2]) Could this be an indication of the group of Benoit manuscripts used by G.?

M. is much shorter and omits the idea that the attack be made by sea. M. thus forgets that he has just called Tenedos an island (7,978), and the first battle is not, as in B-G, an attempt to make a landing (see Thenedon in Proper Names § 241). Yet the speeches of Diomedes in G-M. show a few lines in common:

M. 8558	I. 2 r 15
Il a ia ung an plainement, Que nous sommes en ce rivaige, Tous ravis d'esbayssement, Qui n'est pas signe de couraige. C'est bien petite hardiesse, Quant nous n'osons d'icy partir.	quod iam est unus annus elapsus et plus quod in hanc terram venimus nec ab ea recedere nos aliqua audacia potuit animare ut troyam adire vel videre possemus.

Menelaus, Palamides, and Prothesillaus agree with the advice of Diomedes, and Agamenon immediately acts upon it by arranging the lines for the first battle.

81. 1) Before passing to the account of the first battle, we will say a few words about M's battle-scenes in general: In B-G. the battle-scenes are given at great length, and in far greater number than in M. The necessities and limitations of the stage prevented M. from introducing such a vast array as he found in G. In M., therefore, the battle-scenes take up relatively little space in comparison with the enormous space accorded to them in B-G. For instance, M's first fight takes but 93 lines (8663—8756). In B. the same fight requires 461 lines, and in G. a like length (I 2 v 19 — I 6 v 18). A similar proportion holds good for the other battles, in so far as these are the counterparts of battles in B-G. This shortness and sharpness of the battles in M. adds to their dramatic vigor. The abrupt termination of M's battles is also noteworthy.

2) As we come to the various battles in M., we shall find that nearly every battle is not the reproduction of any particular battle in B-G., but is composed of various combats and episodes, selected quite independently from among the great quantity in his source. This is only natural, for M. must, in his eight short battles, reproduce all the most important incidents of the twenty-odd battles in B-G. He therefore makes one important incident (such as the death of Patroclus; of Hector; of Deyphebus and Palamides; of Troillus; of Paris and Ajax.) the centre of his battle, and groups about it other episodes,

selected, often at random, from a previous, a following, or the same battle in B-G., or sometimes even invented by himself. He does not depart from B-G. in the order of sequence of these chief incidents. We shall see therefore, that Meybrinck (Page 18—25) errs in classing the first eight battles in B-G. as equivalent to the eight battles of M.

3) M. still further shows his independence by giving quite other lists of the leaders of the battle-lines than those in his source. He makes more general than in B-G. the exchange of challenges, and also the taunting of the vanquished by the victor. In B-G. such challenges and taunts are rare; in M. they are scarcely ever omitted. Exhortations to valor are also far more numerous. These greater extensions are of course largely due to the need of having material for dialogue. Original to M. is the frequency with which „amies" are mentioned, either for encouragement of the heroes, or to increase the mortification of the vanquished. We mention this as tending to render doubtful Meybrinck's idea that the women are not represented as spectators of the battles (Meybrinck P. 41—2).

4) Horses are not used in M's battle-scenes, and so the several episodes in B-G of their capture are omitted. Thus, when Diomedes vanquishes Troylus, it is the latter's sword, not his horse as in B-G., which the victor sends to Briseida (§ 115¹). Thus too, when the incident of the dragging of Troylus by the horse of Achilles occurs, a horse has to be specially introduced (§ 151). The only mention of horses in battle occurs in verse 8,676, where Ulixes says:

Vueilles amployer voz destriers.

and this is undoubtedly an inadvertence on M's part.[1])

5) We have made a most careful comparison, first, of G. with B., and second, of M. with both B. and G. and we are forced to the following conclusions:

a) G. follows B. in all the battle-scenes, even in the most trifling details. His deviations from B. are few in number.

b) There is absolutely nothing in M. which B. *alone* could furnish, since G. incessantly reproduces B.

---

[1]) Horses are, however, used in the return of Paris to Troy with Helen (2781 d. § 42).

c) On the other hand, there are several instances in M., where the influence of the few deviations of G. from B. is clearly seen. We shall treat these instances in their proper places in the various battles.

82. Let us now pass to a consideration of the first battle: Agamenon's arrangement of the battle-lines (8,609—31) is entirely original to M. He exhorts them:

8,638 Soyes hardis comme lyons
Et chaultz ainsi que escorpions.

As we have already noted (§ 80), there is no mention of ships, or of fighting for a landing, as in B-G. The only possible reference to landing, and that but a vague one at best, is in the words of Agamenon after the battle (8,766): „Nous avons sur eulx gaigne terre.“ The Greeks advance. Athamas shouts to the Trojans to arm. The trumpets sound. Prothesilaus kills a Trojan. Merion exhorts the Trojans. Ulixes fights valiantly. Hector enters the fight impetuously with two of his brothers. The whole scene is most spirited and dramatic, as indeed is the case in all of M's battles. For the combat of Ulixes and Philimenis M. is indebted to B-G. Philimenis is carried to Troy „a demy mort“. Meybrinck mentions this frequent carrying of the wounded to Troy as characteristic of M. (Meybrinck § 19), but we think it is just as common in B-G. The combat of Hector and Prothesillaus is the chief episode of this first battle, and is repeated from B-G. M. forgets to state that Prothesillaus is killed, and we do not learn of his death until Agamenon speaks of it after the battle (8773). The battle ends with an attack by Palamides and Achilles and a stout Trojan defence by Troylus and Deyphebus. The Trojans drive back the Greeks and return to Troy.

In this battle-scene we can detect G's influence in two minor points only:

1) Hector retires permanently from the battle *before* the arrival of Achilles: B. speaks of „seven or ten“ successive appearances of Hector (B. 7517) but it is not at all clear that he withdrew permanently before Achilles comes. G. also says Hector came and went „eight or ten“ times (I 5 v 15), but he specifies at last *distinctly* Hector's final departure (I 5 v 17): „sol

igitur iam vergebat ad vesperas cum hector quodammodo armorum fatigatione laxatus urbem intravit et relictis ceteris qui proelium accerrimum committebant etc." Then comes Achilles (I 5 v 20). M. follows G: (8748 d) „et apres hector lasse de ses membres s'en yra en bataille". Then comes Achilles (8749).

2) In the last Trojan defence that day M. and G. give an important rôle to Deyphebus (I 6 r 14; 8756). B. does not mention him.

Chapter X.

Council of Greeks. — Council of Trojans. — Election of Hector. Preparations for Battle. — The Second Battle.

M. 8756—10,369. B. 7,562—10,268. G. I 6 r 18 — L 1 v 7.

---

83. For this entire chapter M. is quite independent, building up at will long and wearisome dialogues, of which prolixity and even an art of saying *nothing* in many words are the chief characteristics. — Agamenon holds forth in a long speech (8,757—860): They have arrived before Troy by force, although it has cost them the death of Prothesilaus. He asks for counsel. The Greeks are right in this war, but they must act wisely. He relates a commonplace parable about two men missing each other, (8829—41):-

Pour monstrer clerement
Que celuy a la teste folle,
Qui fait sans fin commencement.

Ulixes gives another parable about three roses (8869—80) to illustrate the need of patience and perseverance. Palamides declares that Ulixes has „parle tres subtilement" (8,910) and exhorts them to continue their attack vigorously. Menelaus approves (8,925). Agamenon asks them not to forget

8,936 Les douleurs et les destourbiers
Qu'avez euz puis deux ans entiers[1]).

---

[1]) See § 245 A. for list of references to the chronological progress of the siege in M.

These griefs should sharpen their courage and their desire for revenge, without which they cannot honorably return. He therefore bids them be ready to sally forth „quant la tronpette sonnera“ (8,958).

84. The scene now shifts (8,964) to Priam's court, where a council is in progress. Priam expresses his grief that the Greeks, his malefactors, are so near him. His words are quite allegorical (8,977—96), a tendency that is very marked throughout the whole drama. He asks their advice and their knightly aid, without which he cannot resist his enemies. He bids them elect

„Ung homme remply de vaillance
Qui sache bien vostre ost conduire.“

Then follows a long scene, in which Hector is elected. Having already amplified a similar scene in the election of Agamenon (§ 59), M. felt constrained to do likewise for the Trojan side. In B-G. the starting point is of the briefest: In B. after the return of Anthenor, Priam in his speech to his sons, had said (B. 3,737):

Hector, biau filz, tu iés li maire
Sire seras de cest affaire;
Tu en seras li chief de toz
Car tu ies molt sages et proz.

Later, after the enumeration of the Trojan allies (B. 6,899) we read:

Et de toz cels qu'a Troie vindrent
Et qui contre Grezeis la tindrent,
Fu Hector sire a son plesir;
Les coveneit toz obeir.

Later again, an election is hinted at (B. 7,630):

Cil qu'il o r e n t f e t conestable
Seignor et prince et sire et mestre,
C'est Hector qui bien le dut estre etc.

G. has similar passages (E 1 r 9; I 6 v 24). In M., on the other hand, there is an actual election of Hector, which is much drawn-out: Enee approves Priam's request for a leader „car les brebis qui n'ont pas chief“ come to grief. He reminds them too that Philimenis is severely wounded, whereat Priam bids that the best of care be given him. Priam then repeats his wish for them to select a leader:

(9,061) Car quant a moy ie suis ia vieulx
Et ne puis plus armes porter.

These lines are noteworthy in view of Priam's energetic share in the second battle (see § 91). Enee suggests Hector whose ability and valor are known. Anthenor supports Enee,

(9,098). Car ung nom crainct espovente autant,
Que les coups en une armee.

Amphorbius however fears for the loss of Hector, which would be irreparable, if he leads the army with his well-known valor, and therefore suggests „Glancon le roy de licie“ (9,120), without thereby doubting Hector's greater ability. Glancon thanks Amphorbius for this honor, which he declines on the ground that it would be a great crime for a stranger to lead the armies of Priam and thereby, perhaps, bring defeat to his arms. Hector must be the leader and as such he will have Glancon's loyal support. Liconius says Glancon decides wisely, but begs him to pardon his brother Amphorbius, who had only desired to show Glancon honor. Merion approves the choice of Hector and all the other kings beg him not to refuse.[1]) Priam then (9,277) says that Hector ought to thank the princes for the great honor and accept it for their sake and to please his father. Although Priam has

9,310 „plus dant qui ne chancelle“

he would rather enter the fight himself than give back Helen. Hector (9,325) declares his desire to obey and to avenge his father, and thanks the princes for their favor, although he would have preferred that they elect another, wiser and better than he. Turning to Paris, he tells him that he undertakes this charge for the sake of Paris and Helen, although he knows

9,370 „Qu'il y a faulte aulcunement“

which carries us back to Hector's objection to the sailing of the expedition to Citharee (1338—1448; § 22).

Hector then exhorts his brothers to duty and valor, and asks Helenus to pray for divine protection. Paris (9,421—556) expresses love for Hector, and obedience to him, and justifies his own conduct in a long discourse upon the power of love over young people: Love makes them

9,431 — „faire plusieurs tours
Et dancer mainte estrange dance.“

Venus and „son filz amour“ are all powerful. He cannot resist

[1]) In the speech of Epistropus, a slight error occurs 9,194. He is addressing Hector when he says: „Que laomedon, vostre pere, ont tue.“ The error is repeated in all editions. (Haepke, bottom of P. 19 shows that „grant“ has been omitted.)

her. A long allegory on the symbols of love now follows, which Hector interrupts:-

(9,559.) Mais le parler ne vault cy rien
De son amy ne de sa myc.

They have talked enough, and must now prepare for action against their mortal enemies. Hector bids them prepare, and asks Priam to put on armor (9,591), „Pour garder les derniers estrois“ and aid them if need be.

85. The preparations for the second battle now continue, and we come once more to passages, in which the contact of M. with G. is evident: Priam promises to obey Hector 9,599,

Car ie te prometz, qu'il n'est rien,
Ou i'ay espoir si fermement,
Apres les dieux premierement,
Que ie faiz en ta saulvegarde,
Si ne puis aler maisement,
Beau filz, mais que ie ne te perde.

which points to G. (I. 8 v 22) „Non enim est michi post deorum auxilium spes alia neque fides nisi in tue virtutis brachio et in tui providi sensus gubernatione discreta diis humiliter supplico ut te michi servent incolumen et ab omnibus tueantur adversis.“

and not to (B 8,019):

Prianz respont: „issi pult estre.
Filz molt me fit en ta main destre,
Que par lie seit m'ire apaiee,
Et nostre desenor vengiee;
Gar que sovent vienges a mei!
Li Deu seient garde de tei.“

Priam is helped to arm, and Hector arranges the Trojan host. M. is here, as before, very independent. In B-G., there are nine divisions, in M. but four. Troylus leads the first in company with Theseus. Hector admonishes his brother to be careful. Similar speeches are in B-G, but M. shows several ideas common to G. and absent in B (7730—44.)

1) (9626) Car ie vous ayme cherement. I 7 r 21. Summa leticia cordis mei.

2) (9637).
Car certes ce noz ennemis
Avoient ioye de vostre follie,
Vous en seriez trop fort repris
Et en pourriez perdre la vie.

I 7 r 26. Ne inimici nostri affectantes quamplurimum casus nostros de tua facilitate [variation = infelicitate.] letentur.

3) (9645)
Alez ou non de tous les dieux,
Et vous et vostre compaignie.
Et retournez victorieux
Par leur tres haulte courtoisie.

I 7 r 28 Vade igitur feliciter in nomine deorum nobis faventium et victor et incolumnis ad civitatem tuam redeas sicut opto.

86. Huppon will lead the second line (9661), with Amphe-neas, Bouetes, and Deiphebus. Glancon, Enee, Paris, Epistropus,

Serpedon, and Merion will lead the third line. In B-G. Paris leads the eighth line. B. contains no admonishing of Paris by Hector (B. 7931); G. however: (I 8 r 22) „et ipsum ammonuit quod quamvis ad alias acies festinet accedere non tamen bello se ingereret nisi se (= Hector) presente".

M. contains a longer warning in which, however, the above occurs:

(9710).
Ie vous prye que vous vous teniez
Pres de moy, car ie vueil ycy,
Que tout ades vous me suyvies,
Et que point vous ne vous boutes
Trop avant sans ma compaignie.

Paris promises strict obedience (9,717). Enee exhorts to valor (9741). Hector prays Jupiter to guard them. He himself will lead the fourth line with Anthenor, Amphorbius, Menones, Liconius, Polidamas, and with his natural brothers Casmabor, Amphibilaus and Margariton. Each brother willingly agrees. In this place B-G. speak of Hector's horse, Galathea, (B. 7,990—99; I 8 v 2), „de cuius magnitudine fortitudine et suis aliis virtutibus mirabilia scripsit dares"[1]). Hector's horse is not mentioned in M. — Hector now (9785) asks Priam to remain near the city and cover their retreat, if necessary, B. specifies no number of soldiers who shall remain; G.-M. agree in assigning a number, but it is not the same, in G. 1500, in M. 1,000. (9,788.) All place themselves in line and the trumpets sound.

87. 1) The scene changes to the Greek side (9,801). Agamenon bids Citheus call to arms, and the Greeks assemble around the banner of Agamenon. Meanwhile, a pleasing scene takes place between Achilles and Patroclus (9829): Achilles says he cannot bear arms that day, for he was wounded in the first battle. (There was, however, no mention of his wound there.) He therefore bids Patroclus take the Mirmidons with him and to be most careful of himself in the fight:

9842. Car se mal vous y advenoit,
I'en seroye aussi douloureux,
Comme se la mort me prenoit.

---

[1]) Dares does not mention Galathea (Joly P. 887). This is one of the many interesting points, cited by Joly (P. 883—887) to show that Guido did not know Dares, and that, when he says a thing is from Dares, he is only quoting Benoit. He unhesitatingly believed Benoit's assertion, that Dares was Benoit's source. Indeed Guido practically thought Benoit but a translator of Dares, and thus, as here, he often declares a thing to be from Dares, when, in reality, it is only from Benoit.

Patroclus asks his friend not to be anxious, for he fears no man. Achilles expresses great grief, and separates from his friend with the refrain:

Adieu patroclus, mon amy.
Mon frere d'armes et de ieunesse.

The skeleton of this agreeable scene is identical in B. (8,135—8,144). and in G. (K 1 r 16—22).

2) Agamenon arranges his men. M. is again utterly independent of B-G. In B., 28 „batailles“ are formed (although immediately after their enumeration, B. says (8279) there were thirty!). In G., 26 are formed (K 1 r 13—K 1 v).[1])

In M. Agamenon, after exhorting the Greeks to valor, divides them into four „eschelles“ (9,916). There is therein no resemblance to B-G., other than that Patroclus is in the first „eschelle“ (9918) and that Agamenon leads the last (9939). Citheus bids the Greeks hurry, for the Trojans are already in the field. He describes the standards of seven of the Trojan leaders (9955 ff.).

88. The second battle now follows (10,022—369). M. is independent in his choice of combats; the first in all versions, however, is Hector versus Patroclus: In M. there is a short dialogue of challenge, „alors frappera hector le dit patroclus tellement qu'il se lerra cheoir en la place tout mort“. Hector then says that he will have the armor of Patroclus:

(10,051) Car ie ne vois barons ne roys,
Qui ayent le harnois si plaisant.

He tries to take the armor. At this point in B-G. (B. 8,330; K 2 r 15) it is Merion who attacks Hector and prevents the despoiling of Patroclus. M. has no Merion on the Greek side and accordingly substitutes Prothenor (10,058).[2])

---

[1]) In B. there are a couple of oversights: B. assigns to battle-line twelve, Diomedes and Merion (8,192), but Merion already leads line two (8,145), and Diomedes is mentioned later as in line twenty-three (8,247). G. does not make these errors. B-G. are essentially the same, except in the assignments to the last few battle-lines. A study of these lists of proper names might aid in the determination of what group of Benoit manuscripts served as G's source.

[2]) A Greek Merion is mentioned (13,893) in the list (13,884—901) of kings killed by Hector, but, as with many of the names there given, the drama contains no further record of him. (see § 121[3]).

1) In the challenge of Prothenor (respectively Merion), we see again G's influence: B says (8,333) „leus enragiez". G. (K 2 r 21). Lupe *rapax* et *insaturabilis*. M. (10,053). Loup *ravissant non saciable*.

2) A slight numerical coincidence between B. and M. exists in the lines:

B. 8341.	M. 10,057
En estrange leu descendoies	Car tantost verras arriver
X. M. chevaliers voieies;	Bien dix milles chevalliers fors,
N'i a celui qui son poeir,	Qui vendront pour toy surmonter.
Ne face de ta teste aveir.	

G. says „quinquaginta milia" (K 2 r 24), but, aside from this difference of number, the phrasing of M. is exactly that of G: „Quod statim *videbis* contra te plusquam quinquaginta milia pugnatorum."

3) In B-G. there now follows an extended fight for possession of the body of Patroclus (B. 8359—432; K 2 v 1—24). M. simply summarizes this in the stage-direction (10,064 d) „lors prothenor impetueusement, avec ses gens et les autres grecz, se mesleront dedens la bataille a grans sons de trompettes et lors les grecz emporteront le corps de patroclus en l'eschauffault d'achilles etc." In the same stage-direction the words „touteffoiz ilz vendront deux corps avecques leurs gens qui feront reculeur hector et cheoir sur ses genoulx" point to G. (K 2 r 29). „in terram flectere genua fuit coactus". B. only says (8348)." „Hector chaï enmi la veie."

4) The rescue of Hector by his servant follows. In B. the servant's name is „Dodaniez del pui de Vir" (B. 8446). G. gives him no name and M., forced to find one, selects Erupius (10,065). In M. Troillus and Deiphebus complete the rescue of Hector (10,072—77 d).

89. 1) M. now skips a long general fight in B-G. (B. 8,487—688; K 3 r 20 — K 4 r 19), and, reaching ahead in his source, selects the combat of Eneas and Ajax (B. 9268—9369; K 6 r 14—25): The usual challenge and reply are exchanged (10,078—93), „lors se combateront tellement qu'il getteront l'un l'autre a terre". B., however, has (9360) „Mes d'els ni ot *nus* qui chaist"; while G. reads (K 6 r 24) „unus impingit in alium sic viriliter et potenter quod *se sternunt* ab equis".

2) For the combat of Menelaus vs. Polidamas, the capture[1]) of Polidamas, and his rescue by Hector (10,094—123), M. turned back again to G. (K 4 r 19 — K 5 r 22 = B. 8689—922), selecting the above episodes from among many others and cleverly uniting them.

3) The episode of the capture[1]) of Troylus and of his rescue by Hector follows immediately (10,124—203). M. adapts it very freely from B-G. (B. 8487—8620; K 3 r 20 — K 4 r 4). There the chief actors are Menesteus and Troylus with their respective followers; in M. however the combat is between Nestor and Troylus. The rescue by Hector is the same as in B-G., except that the reproach of Troylus by Hector is original to M; Hector reproves his brother for his too great zeal, and commands Troylus to keep always near him in the future:

(10,168) Si vueillez penser la destresse,
Que nostre pere auroit pour vous,
Si esties prins par tel hardiesse.

Troillus is very sorry for having transgressed his brother's wish, which he will assiduously follow in future. (10,180—203.)

4) Troillus next defends himself from Cediron and kills him (10,204—35). This episode has no equivalent in B-G.

90. M. now makes a combination of an event in this second battle of B-G. with another episode in the fourth battle of B-G.: Thoas attacks and kills Amphibilaus (10,236), the natural son of Priam. In the corresponding battle in B-G. Thoas kills a natural son, but his name is Cassibalan (B. 9,079; K 5 v 23); later, in the same battle (B. 9,715; K 7 r 18) Thoas is captured, but he is immediately rescued by Menesteus (B. 9721; K 7 r 26)., and he is not captured for good by the natural brothers until the fourth battle (B. 11,426; L 5 r 10), when he is led to Troy by Anthenor and Deyphebus. M. joins adroitly the killing of Amphibilaus by Thoas with the latter's capture. The actual capture is effected by Eneas (10,247). Troylus wishes to kill Thoas, but Hector intervenes and orders Thoas carried to Troy

---

[1]) In both these scenes of capture we note M's insistence upon the binding of the prisoners (10,109 d; 10,158), where B-G. say nothing of it. This might well be cited to explain the similar mention of the binding of prisoners in Cytharea (§ 37).

(10,252) as a prisoner and as a present to Priam. No particular Trojans are named as taking Thoas to the city (10,259 d).

A short connecting scene of M's invention unites this capture of Thoas to the coming of Priam into the fight: Ulixes appeals to Diomedes to aid their men who are hard pressed, even in flight (10,262). Diomedes agrees and the Trojans are driven back (10,275 d).

91. Hector thereupon appeals to Priam. This has its parallel in B-G. but a marked difference exists in M's treatment of the incident: In B-G. no mention is made of an actual entry of Priam into personal combat. Hector simply asks him for reenforcements (B. 9,795; K 7 v 4). and requests him to follow with the rest of his force. In B-G. Priam does not fight personally, until after the death of Hector. M. changes this: Priam actually fights in person (10,303 d), killing a Greek and speaking the vigorous lines (10,304):

Va meschant aux ames dampnees, Que les troyans par leurs espees
Et leur porte ceste nouvelle, Ont bien soustenu leur querelle.

92. In B-G. a long series of combats now follows (B. 9819—10,071; K 7 v 7—K 8 v 30), terminating with the encounter of Hector and his cousin Thelamonius Ajax, son of Thelamon and Exiona. M. omits all these intermediate combats and passes directly to the meeting of Hector and Thelamonius Ajax. This scene calls for a few remarks: In M. Ajax Thelamonius discloses his identity (10,320). In B. the recognition is mutual:

(B. 10,071). A Hector s'est taut combatu,
Qu'il se sont entreconeu.

In G. (L 1 r 8) „agnovit illum hector esse filium" etc. B-G. say that Hector wishes his cousin to go to Troy with him, but that Ajax Thelamonius refuses (B. 10,074; L 1 r 12). M. omits this idea entirely and only gives the request of Ajax Thelamonius that Hector withdraw the Trojans for the love of Exiona. Hector does so. The Trojans return to the sound of trumpets in G-M.:

10,344 Avant trompettes or sonnez, and 10,351 d. (L 1 r 19) tubete sonitu.

Priam congratulates the „barons" on their victory, bidding them disarm and thank the gods (10,352). Hector approves and the Trojans „se desarment et se vestent de leurs robbes" (10,369 d).

93. 1) Following the end of the second battle, B. has a charming passage (10,125—239) which G. omits[1]) entirely (L 1 r 28). This passage contains suggestions for several scenes, which, had M. known B., he might well have written, particularly as they are episodes similar to those, for which M. elsewhere shows an especial fondness. The contents of this passage in B. are briefly:- The Trojans are grieved at being recalled from their successes of that day. Hector is acclaimed by all as their savior. He is most affectionately greeted by his parents:

B. 10,157 Sa mere le prist en ses braz.

His sisters and Andromache remove the armor from his wounded, fatigued, body, and „li mires Goz“ (B. 10,183) attends to his wounds. Priam is not told of the death of Cassibalan:-

B. 10,205. Celerent li, si firent bien,
Car il l'amot sor tote rien.

The „dames“ bestow praise upon the other heroes of the day, Troylus, Polidamas, Paris, and the natural brothers.

2) Common to B-G., but absent in M. is the sending of messengers by the Greeks to ask truce in order to bury their dead, just as the Trojans are preparing to go forth again to the fight (B. 10,240—68; L 1 r 28—L 1 v 7). M's first truce occurs after the third battle, immediately before „disner“ of the second day (11,424. § 105).

Chapter XI.

Burial of Patroclus; of Amphibilaus. — Lament of Cassandra. — The Greeks plan to destroy Hector. — The Trojans discuss the fate of Thoas. — The Third Battle. — Truce.

M. 10,370—11,424 („disner“ of second day). B. 10,240—12,930. G. L 1 r 31 — L 8 v 7.

---

94. Basac informs Achilles that Patroclus has been killed by the slayer of Prothesillaus, whereat Achilles shows great grief. In

[1]) Could this omission and like ones in G. be of service in determining the manuscript-group of B., which served as G's source?

G. the description of this event is very short: (L 1 v 8) „Achilles vero qui de morte patrodi solari non poterat, de morte ipsius mestus et flebilis in multo flumine lacrimarum diutius lamentatur.“ B. and M. enter more into details, and certain resemblances merit attention, although the nature of the incident sufficiently explains them:-

1) M. 10,377 d. Lors achilles ambrasse le corps de patroclus et se pasme *a terre* demy mort etc.

B. 10,271 *Desus le corps* C. feiz se pasme; B. 10,307 Lors se pasma. This resemblance is, however, somewhat restricted, when we compare the italicized words.

2) B. and M. give monologues by Achilles, in which we find two ideas in common: hate of Hector and regret that Achilles was not in the battle. The words of these two monologues (M. 10,378—421; B. 10,272—307) show otherwise no resemblance. M. alone has the thoughts: Achilles bids Death take him, as well as Patroclus. — Achilles upbraids Fortune.

3) The actual burial is related in M. in a very naïve manner:

10,417 Achilles: Apportez moy ycy endroit
Ung tombeau de riches cypres.

In B-G. the material is marble: B. 10,323; L 1 v 7. The „tombeau“ is brought, and (10,427 d) „Lors achilles fera semblant de le envelopper d'un drap et enveloppera une aultre chose et apres le mettra dedens le thombeau et puis dira.“ Then follows (10,428—75) a prayer for the soul of Patroclus.

4) Meybrinck has called attention (page 67) to the absence in M. of all reference to games, in connection with funeral rites or on other occasions. This is a curious omission for an author, one of whose main merits, as Meybrinck shows, is the desire to reproduce the atmosphere of antiquity. At this funeral of Patroclus B. mentions games (10,312—320), but G. has none and M. likewise none.

95. The scene now moves to the Trojan side:- Priam mourns Amphibilaus (10,476—515), finally giving directions for his burial. Another naïve stage-direction is (10,515 d.) „Lors les serviteurs prenent le corps d'amphibilaus et faignent de l'ensevelir“. The burial is in the temple of Venus in B-G-M.

(B. 10,349; G. L 1 v 23; M. 10,515 d.) In M., as the servants of Priam return from the temple of Venus, they meet Cassandra, who begins a lament (10,516—63). There is a similar lament in B-G. (10,355—84: L 1 v 24—L 2 r 2). We note many points of contact between G. and M.:

1) M. 10,532 Pour quoy ne querez aveir paix
Avec les grecz, voz ennemis?
L 1 v 27 Cur pacem grecorum non queritis.
B. says only (10,365) Car fetes pes. —

2) M. 10,540.

Car vous verres les pouvres meres
Pleurer la mort de leurs enffans,
Et mesmes les pouvres peres
Finer a grand doulcur leurs ans,
Lesquelz sont vielz et enciens,
En servitude perdurable.

L 1 v 30. Et antequam parvulis matres eorum [ex] orbate perpetuas ipse et ipsi defleant servitutes. B. has no such thought.

3) M. 10,548 Ie vous ditz que helene n'est myc
Acomparer de si grand pris

L 1 v 31. Non fuit helena tam dolorosa tam exiciosa precio comparanda. In B. this idea is absent.

4) For this lamentation and reproach, Cassandra is imprisoned to prevent discouragement spreading among the Trojans. B. says:-

(10,388) Mes il l'ont en tel leu enclose
Ou assez fu puis longement
N'en isseit pas a son talent[1])

G. and M. agree in having Priam order her imprisonment (L 2 r 3). Quam — — rex priamus capi mandavit et sub firmi claustri custodia tempore multo detrudi[1]). M. puts very brutal language into Priam's mouth: (10,564).

Cloantus et vous adastus,
Alez moy ceste garce prendre,
Et la mettez en lieu obscus.
Qu'on ne la puisse plus entendre.

After a few words of persuasion by these servants, Cassandra obeys: „Lors la meinent en ung eschauffault derriere et la mussent en une courtine etc.“ (10,581 d).

96. 1) The Greek side again claims our attention, and we have another example of M's expanding and rendering into dialogue. The Greeks discuss plans for the death of Hector. In B-G. the corresponding passages occur after their third battle (10,849—968; L 3 v 4—21), which third battle in B-G. (10,496—848; L 2 r 11—L 3 v 4.) has no equivalent in M. In

---

[1]) There now follows in B-G. (10,392—496; L 2 r 4—11) the first criticism by Palamides of Agamenon. This is omitted by M. who only has one such fault-finding (§ 122). Perhaps the slight importance given in G. to this first instance was the reason M. left it out.

B. Agamenon is the principal speaker. G. only says that the Greeks discuss plans *together*. M. therefore allows a general discussion, which is particularly interesting because of the individualization of the participants, especially of Nestor:-

2) Agamenon says that Hector must be destroyed by fair means or by foul. One idea in his speech points to G:-

10,603 Car, tant qu'il ayt convalescence,
Ne pourrions nostre fait parfaire.

Diomedes voices the same thought (10,649):

Car certes, tant qu'il soit vivant,
Nous ne pourrions venir a chief.

L 3 v 11. Dixerunt enim nisi hector ab hac vita deficiat et semper insistat in bellis troyani nunquam potuerunt sic offendi quod greci possint de eis ad victoriam pervenire.

In B. the ultimate victory of the Greeks is not stated as dependent upon the death of Hector, B's only corresponding passage being much weaker:

B. 10,903 Sovent serons par lui malmis.
S'il est alques longuement vis.

3) Agamenon had upheld the use of underhand means to get the better of one's enemy (10,615—24); Diomedes thereupon suggests that Hector be drawn into an ambuscade (10,657 ff.) since he cannot be killed otherwise. Ajax Thelamonius, forgetful of Hector's generosity to him in the last battle, suggests another plan. Let some enemies of Hector in Troy be bribed to assassinate him. The aged Nestor, however, censures all these treacherous plans (10,697 ff.):-

Car ia homme de renommee
N'aura de par moy faulcete.

Greece would be eternally disgraced. Hector must be killed in honorable fight. Nestor therefore proposes Achilles as the most worthy antagonist of Hector. Prothenor and Menesteus approve, the latter using the argument that Hector's death by treachery would be a charge of cowardice against the Greeks. At Agamenon's request (10,793) Achilles agrees and promises to do his utmost (10,801). Two things show G. and M. still in touch:

a) In B. Achilles' main thought in accepting is to avenge Patroclus (B. 10,948). G. and M. omit that idea in this place.

b) In G-M. there is no intimation that the other Greeks will also try to kill Hector. B., however, says (10,961): Altretel a chascuns pramis.

97. M., having inserted in his second battle the capture of Thoas (§ 90), now passes to the council held by Priam concerning his fate. By so doing he skips the entire fourth battle in B-G. (10,969—11,625; L 3 v 23 — L 5 v 5), taking from its vast array of incidents only the capture of Thoas, mentioned above. After this fourth battle in B-G.[1]), follows the discussion of the fate of Thoas, at which point M. again comes in touch with his source: (M. 10,825—952; B. 11,625—721; L 5 v 5 — L 6 r 4). We once more have many points of contact between G. and M.:-

1) The opening words of Priam's speech are identical:

10,827.

Chascun de nous ne ignore mye, Du fort roy thoas lequel i'ay
Ainsi que pour certain ie scay, En mes prisons mon prisonnier.

L 5 v 13. Noscitis qualiter regem thoas carcer noster tenet inclusum. B. only says (11,641): „Li reis Thoas est pris."

2) In B. Priam merely asks for counsel, whether Thoas „sera raainz ou se'l pendrons" (11,650). In G-M. Priam expresses strongly his own preference for the execution of Thoas:-

L 5 v 16. Quare mihi iustum videtur ut per nos iniqua morte periret qui voluit nos perire ut vel sit furca suspensus vel alio modo nequiter detruncatus.

M. 10,831 Sie vueil tantost et sans delay
Qu'il soit pendu comme meurtrier.

M. adds Priam's reason: (10,833) Il a mon filx amphibilaus | Mis a mort dont i'ay grant tristesse. B-G. give no such reason.

3) In Eneas' speech, disapproving this harshness, G-M. have an important point in common, which is absent in Eneas' speech in B., the idea that Thoas be kept safely, so as to be exchanged for some Trojan, whom the Greeks may yet capture:

L 5 v 27 qui pro aliquo nostrorum in bello similiter intercepto posset recuperationis vel permutationis beneficio commutari.

---

[1]) At the close of this fourth battle, G. omits several scenes in B. (11,549—624): Hector visits and comforts the wounded, although suffering from many wounds himself. His armor is then taken off by the ladies of the court, and he is clothed in rich garments. With Troylus and the whole court he reposes in the palace. Helen goes to visit him. He greets her most affectionately (11,608) and tells her of the great combat that day between Paris and Menelaus. Helen says she trembles at these encounters. The passage ends (10,624). „Adonc plorerent si dui oil". It is extremely improbable that M. could have been blind to the beauties and possibilities of these scenes, had he known them.

M. 10,873. Aumoins le pourriez vous changer
S'aucun est, que a dieu ne plaise,
Qui feust bouté en ce danger.

In Hector's speech in B., however, supporting Eneas, this idea finds expression:-

B. 11,696 N'avez baron de si grant pris,
Si'l esteit pris et retenuz,
Qui por celui ne fust renduz.

G. omits this speech of Hector, saying only (L 5 v 29) „hector autem enee consilium utpote laudabile satis probat.“ M. omits completely Hector's participation in the council, substituting Huppon, Pillon and Merion, who approve of Eneas' counsel. The scene closes with Priam's agreeing, and requesting all to go and arm (10,952).

98. Before giving us the next battle-scene, M., by way of contrast, interposes a short but most pleasing passage (10,953—11,022), the general idea of which is taken from B-G. (11,721—824; L 6 r 4—13). Enee takes Anthenor and Troillus to visit Helen. In B. Polidamas goes too (11,724), and B. even hints at a secret love of Polidamas for Helen (11,801—10). G. and therefore M. omit him entirely, M. names, as in company with Hecuba, „Endromaiche, Polixene, Cassandra et Creusa“ (10,966 d), none of whom, however, take part in the dialogue. In B-G. Hecuba exhorts the princes to valor, and they assure her of their fidelity; in M. Hecuba does not speak. In B-G. Helen is not represented as lamenting. In B. she gives presents to the princes (11,798), a detail omitted in G-M. In B. the only mention of her being comforted is in B. 11,799:-

Et il l'ont molt asseuree,
Et en mainz sens reconfortee.

which idea, in G., is somewhat more emphasized (L 6 r 9). „Eneas et troylus helenam nisi sunt multis affectuosis sermonibus comfortare.“ M. takes this idea of Helen's grief as the central, indeed, the only one in his scene. Enee goes with the distinct purpose (10,957):-

Pour ung peu son dueil depporter
Et luy donner soulaigement.

Helen expresses lament in every word she says. Her grief is very great, for she loves both Trojans and Greeks, and is deeply afflicted to see so many die on her account. This idea of Helen's self-accusation is emphasized throughout M. much more than in B-G. Troylus comforts her with the refrain (10,983):-

Dame helene, ie vous supplie,
Vueillez prendre ung peu de confort.

and Anthenor with (10,999):

Belle, ne soyes si troublee,
Mais vueillez reprendre bon cueur.

All take leave of Helen with the refrain:

Or ca, dame, adieu vous dy.
Ie m'en revois ou i'ay affaire.

They then kiss her and go to arm for battle.

99. In this third battle M. is more independent than in the preceding. He invents much more, and selects from various battles in his source what he wishes, so that it is impossible to make this battle correspond with any single one of B-G., as Meybrinck has attempted to do (P. 20). Agamenon bids the trumpets sound (11,023) and Hector exhorts the Trojans (11,030). The two sides meet „et hector abatra les premiers qu'il trouvera". Then the noise is stilled for the combat of Philimenis and Achilles, of which we find no correspondent in B-G. There is the usual exchange of challenges and then of blows, followed by the mocking words of the victor, Achilles, who is at once attacked by Merion. Achilles and Merion „s'entrefrapperont tellement que tous deux charront a terre". They are separated by the arrival of others.

100. After these two original combats, M. reverts to his source, and extracts from the fifth battle of B-G. the advent of the „sagitaire" and Diomedes' combat with the same (B. 12,194 —12,354; L 7 r 6 — L 7 v 12). In this episode it is interesting to note how M. treats the rôle of the sagitaire. His description of the creature is brief and vague: (11,097) Epistropus comes forth from Troy and says:

Et vueil mener mon sagitaire,
Qui est horrible a regarder.
Si leur (= the Greeks) sera treffort contraire,
Et les pourra fort espoventer.

Agamenon's words are equally indefinite: (11,119)

Car ie voy chose non pareille,
Si est moult fort et moult puissant,
Et moult orrible a regarder.

The sagitaire himself says (11,012):-

„Que ie suis bon homme a ce faire" (i. e. shoot arrows).

On the other hand, B-G. give detailed descriptions of him, which are essentially the same (12,207—35; L 7 r 11—20). B-G., however, do not represent him as able to speak, although his upper body and his head are like a man's. B. says only (12,263):-

Grant noise fait et brait et crie,
Que par trestot en vait l'oïe.

and later (B. 12,326):- Cria en halt, braist et henist.

G. has (L 7 r 15):- et equinos ex ore producebat hynnitus. B. adds the detail that flames issue from his mouth and that he ignites thereby his arrows before shooting them (B. 12,277—83). — In M. the sagitaire speaks like a human being. His master addresses him (11,101—8) and he replies (11,109—16) and he talks also to Diomedes (11,125—32; 11,149—56). M. omits the other deeds of the sagitaire, passing at once to his combat with Diomedes, who, however, in the lines (11,141). „Sagitaire, tu as tue | De mes amis bien largement", hints at previous exploits of his adversary. G. omits an incident given by B., that, after the sagitaire's body was cut in two, the portion resembling a horse continued to run about until cut down by the Greeks (B. 12,341—46).

101. After the death of the sagitaire there follows a combat between Menelaus and Paris, the two rivals. In the challenge of Menelaus, he says (11,165):-

Car, ce prisonnier te puis prendre Incontinent te feray pendre,
Et ta tres desloyalle amye, Et elle sera arse et brouye.

This last line does not harmonize with Menelaus' later attitude toward Helen (§ 220). Paris is more magnanimous:-

(11,173) Menelaus, croy de certain
Que pour helene la tres belle
Tu ne mourras pas de ma main.

We have failed to find in B-G. trace of a similar generosity on the part of Paris. This fight is given a slightly greater importance over others. Instead of the usual exchange of *one* blow, „s'entredonnent chascun *troys* coups tellement qu'ilz abatront l'un l'autre". A curious phrase is in Paris' retort (11,177):-

Et croy hardiment que c'est celle (= Helen)
Que i'ayme autant ou plus que moy.

A similar restriction of Paris' love for Helen occurs later (16,726; § 143):-

Car ie vous ayme sans fausser,
Plus que toutes apres ma mere.

In B-G. there are several other combats between Paris and Menelaus, the following being in their fourth battle:- 11,221—232; 11,449—547; L 5 r 12 — v 4.

102. The two other great rivals, Hector and Achilles, now meet. In M. it is the only encounter before the final one. In B-G., however, there are several:-

B. 10,561—660 — (third battle) = L 2 r 23 — L 2 v 23.
B. 11,077—158 — (fourth battle) = L 4 v 5 — 11.
B. 12,355—400 (fifth battle) = L 7 v 14 — 25. etc. etc.

The fight in M. merits no comment. Both heroes fall and are separated.

103. 1) Drawing from the fifth battle in B-G., M. now introduces the capture of Anthenor. In B. the capture is only mentioned, not described (B. 12,401—20). In G. it is described but no special participants are given (L 7 v 25—30). M. builds up an extended scene: There is first a combat between Anthenor and Agamenon (11,213); the latter is struck, but, instead of returning the blow, he bids Diomedes and the „barons" to capture Anthenor. There follows a fight between Diomedes and Anthenor. Both fall. The Greeks then come up, capture Anthenor and lead him to Agamenon (11,252 d), Menesteus acting as spokesman. Agamenon bids Anthenor be led „en mes tentes" (11,258), which command was probably due to (L 7 v 28) „ad eorum tentoria".

2) In B. nothing is said of an attempt to rescue Anthenor further than the *wish* of Polidamas so to do (B. 12,406—11). G. however says (L 7 v 30): „non obstante quod polidamas antenoris filius qui sui patris non interfuit captioni pro recuperatione ipsius multa commisisset in bello." From this sentence M. moulds a short scene of attempted rescue: Erupius calls to his master Hector, in the refrain:-

Cher seigneur, il fault secourir
A Anthenor, les grecz l'ont pris.

Hector, Polidamas and Deyphebus pursue the Greeks, killing

many (11,270 d), but it is of no avail, and Hector says in refrain:-

(11,271.) Seigneurs il couvient retourner,
Car nous ne le pourrions ravoir.

Polidamas is in despair:- „Las, g'y ayme mieulx demourer.“ The trumpets sound on both sides and all retreat. Thus ends M.'s third battle.[1])

104. After the battle Agamenon calls a council and asks regarding the fate of Anthenor. Shall he be put to death to lower the pride of the Trojans? Nestor, always the good advisor, counsels that truce first be asked and that measures be taken to secure the exchange of Anthenor for Thoas. M. evidently introduces this short scene as a counter-part to the similar but longer scene, where the fate of Thoas is discussed (§ 97). G. (at least the prints) has no indication of this scene. G. therefore has omitted Agamenon's speech in B. (12,439 - 94), wherein he encourages the Greeks, speaks of their rescue from the sagitaire, of the valor of Diomedes, and of the capture of Anthenor. G. also omits the suggestion by Achilles (B. 12,488) of an exchange of Anthenor for Thoas. One is tempted at first, therefore, to see B's influence here upon Milet, but the coincidence is slight. When thoroughly examined, it consists only in the idea that Anthenor be exchanged for Thoas. The suggestors of this idea are, however, not the same, in B. Achilles, in M. Nestor. Moreover M. omits all the other ideas, noted above, in Agamenon's speech. Again, B. differs radically from M. in that there is no suggestion of putting Anthenor to death. Rather will he be useful in securing peace and the wishes of the Greeks (B. 12,479):-

Car si com oi dire et retrere,
Toz noz voleirs nos feist fere,
Pez et concorde a noz agrez.

This idea of exchange M. found readily in the context. It has already been suggested in the similar council on the Trojan side, held to discuss the fate of Thoas (§ 97), and the thought

[1]) Following the capture of Anthenor, B. has a short scene, which G. again omits and which, therefore, is not given in M. (B. 12,420—39):- Hector, Troillus and Paris are greeted affectionately, as they return from battle, by Hecuba, Polixene, Helen, and Priam.

of putting the prisoner to death is there expressed in Priam's speech. The introduction of this latter thought here, therefore, completes the analogy between the two scenes. Moreover, the idea of exchange forms an important incident of the later story (§ 109), and, in M., Priam suggests it a few lines farther on (11,389).

105. 1) In the speech by Nestor, advising that Anthenor be exchanged for Thoas, he also advocates that truce be asked:- The Greeks are weary of war „car il y a six ans passez" (11,321). Let two kings of high rank be sent to ask truce of Priam. Menesteus seconds Nestor, and Agamenon appoints Ulixes and Diomedes who proceed at once to Priam. M. thus omits the sixth battle in B-G. (12,543—626; L 8 r 4—10), after which G. passes at once to the embassy of Ulixes and Diomedes.

2) B., however, has more than the sixth battle, before relating this embassy:- B. describes a great discouragement of the Greeks, the reassuring speech of Calcas (12,627—46) and a seventh battle (12,647 ff.), which lasts eighty days (12,650), and in which there are many encounters of Hector and Achilles (12,657—64). The slaughter is terrible and the stench of the dead becomes unendurable. Agamenon, therefore, suggests a truce, and Ulixes and Diomedes go to negociate it (12,721).

3) In M. the ambassadors arrive directly before Priam. M. thus omits their meeting Dolon (G. = Delon) who conducts them safely to Priam (B. 12,724—88; L 8 r 13—15). M. neglects the detail that Priam is at table with his knights (B. 13,789—806; L 8 r 17—18). In M. he is apparently alone. Only B. has the dramatic feature that all the Trojan princes are wounded in some manner (B. 12,795—803). Priam grants, in M., truce for two months (11,378) for the curious reason:-

Afin que ce pendant ie voie
Tous voz princes et tous voz roys.

In B-G. the truce is for three months (12,821; L 8 r 12) and Hector objects strongly to such a long term. M. has no trace of any such objection, for Priam grants truce at once. In M. Priam sends a warning to Agamenon, not to put Anthenor to death, or else Thoas will be made to „languir" (11,388). An exchange can be effected. We mention this as showing how the idea of an exchange is present in M's mind (see last paragraph). The ambassadors return to Agamenon and deliver Priam's message concerning Anthenor. Agamenon promises that „anthenor n'aura mal par nous" (11,411), and all the Greeks retire to their tents with the refrain, „Or alons nous en, il est temps". „Lors se fera pause pour disner" (11,424 d).

Chapter XII.

Events of the Truce:- Love-scene of Paris and Helen. — Interview of Hector and Achilles. — Exchange of Anthenor and Thoas. — Troillus and Briseida.

M. 11,425—12,747. B. 12,890—13,831. G. L 8 v 10 — M 3 v 31.

---

106. Verses 11,425—640 are a love-scene between Paris and Helen, which has no parallel in B-G., where we find only occasional references to their love. Of the latter there are fewer in G. than in B. Indeed G. strikes out of B. nearly all lyrical elements, this being in harmony with G's systematic attacks upon woman.

Paris asks the reason of Helen's grief and lamentation.[1]) Does Helen regret „de m'avoir reçu a amy" (11,434). He speaks of his sufferings to win her, and asks her to still have remembrance (11,459):-

— — — — du doulx baiser
Et de la plaisante acollee,
Que i'euz la premiere iournee,
En laquelle vous espousay.

[1]) A curious contradiction, one all the more remarkable because found in all the prints, exists between:-

11,427 Or a il des ans plus de dix,
Que vous m'aymes de tres bon cueur.
and 11,441 Six ans a et neuf mois passez,
Que ie passe la mer salee.

„Dix" in 11,427 should beyond doubt be „six" because of 11,441, and also because of 11,321:- Car il y a six ans passez. Stengel classes this as a misprint (Page VII of Introduction to his „Autographische Vervielfältigung" of the first edition of M. under page 184, verse 11,427), but it is curious that the same occurs in all the editions.

He bids her also remember their first meeting in Citharee (11,465). Does she desire to return to Menelaus? If so he would grant her wish, although joy would give place to a longing for death in his heart. (11,490). — Helen assures him that she weeps only for love of him; she fears greatly for his safety in combat:-

(11,523). Car tousiours a mort et a vie
Vueil avecques vous demourer.

She speaks tenderly of their first meeting, ever since which she has been completely his. She relates a dream that has given her great anxiety (11,561—600):- An „esglantier“ was united with an „aubespine“ but a tempest destroyed both. She dreamed also of a Greek who cut off Paris' head. These dreams worry her greatly, for she fears that Menelaus will kill Paris. Paris assures her of his superiority to Menelaus in combat, tells her of their fight, and of his sparing Menelaus only out of love for her (§ 101). Paris now says he must go and see Hector, and kisses her good-bye (11,640 d). The verses of this scene are very pleasing, especially 11,457—72 and 11,513—44.

107. M. now wishes to introduce the interview of Hector and Achilles, and does so in the following manner:- Paris goes to see Hector, greeting him with the refrain:- (11,641).

Hector, beau frere, dieu vous gart,
Et Andromaiche la jolye.

Hector welcomes him affectionately (11,645):-

Vostre tres gracieulx regard
Me plaist tant qu'on ne le scet mye.

Hector then expresses his wish to go see the Greeks and especially Achilles. Will Paris go too? Paris agrees, and Hector through Eurupius summons Deiphebus and Troillus. All four proceed to the Greeks, where Hector asks the way to Achilles' tent and is shown thither by Basam (11,699). The interview of Hector and Achilles brings us once more to M's source:- (B. 12,987—13,234; L 8 v 24 — M 1 v 27). It is again unmistakeably Guido:-

1) Hector asks (M. 11,695) „Ou est la *tente* d'achilles“ because G. had said (L 8 v 26):- in eius (= Achilles) tentorio. G.

adds „Achille petente“, a detail not observed by M. In B. the meeting takes place (12,994):-

Sus la riviere de Charente,
— — — .... en une arbreie,
Sus l'erbe fresche qui verdeie.

2) We have just seen above, that it is *Hector* who goes to see Achilles. So also in G. (L 8 v 24) „Treuga igitur ipsa duranter hector ad grecorum castra se contulit“. B. says (12,987) „*Achilles* vait veeir Hector“. M. Joly seems to interpret this as meaning that *Hector* goes to see Achilles, and other scholars, Meybrinck (P. 30) and Barth (P. 27) apparently agree with him. We are inclined, however, to think that an error has been made here:-

M. Joly, says in a note to verse 12,987 (P. 555):- „La leçon de *notre*[1]) manuscrit est la vraie; *le sens le prouve;* seulement il faudrait Hector*s*. Mais outre que notre copiste en use librement avec la règle de l's, la rime autorisait à la supprimer.“ M. Joly, therefore, construes Hector as nominative case and the subject of *„vait“*. His reasoning might be valid, if we considered only the one verse:- „Achilles vait veeir Hector“. As this verse stands, the question of subject and object can for a moment rest doubtful. The doubt is at once removed, however, if we examine the context, and we are forced to admit that Hector must be the object of „veeir“ and, consequently, „Achilles“ the subject of „vait“. The context is as follows:-

(12,987).
Achilles vait veeir Hector
Sor un destrier d'Espaigne sor
O lui seissante conpaignons
Qui molt erent de granz renons
Li plus povres ert reis ou dus.

a) Now these lines can only refer to the subject of „vait“, and that subject must be Achilles, for, a very few lines farther on, we read (12,997):-

Hector et tuit si conpaignon
V. C. erent trestuit par non
Dont li pires valeit un rei.

[1]) The italics are mine. The criticism of M. Joly, which follows, is based upon what is to me the only meaning of „La leçon de notre manuscrit est la vraie“, namely, the reading which M. Joly has adopted in his text:- „Achilles vait veeir Hector.“ If „notre manuscrit“ signifies Mss. J. of Benoît (see § 107² c) the criticism is not valid.

It is the height of improbability, that *both* these passages refer to Hector, since we find no other lines describing the escort of Achilles. We see in these two passages another of the many examples of B's desire to exalt Hector above Achilles, and we are surprised that M. Joly did not note it among the cases he gives in his article (P. 747—759). B. gives Achilles an escort of *60*, but Hector one of *500*. Not only is Hector's escort thus numerically more brilliant, but its individual members have all *kingly* rank, whereas the splendor of Achilles' escort is intentionally restricted by the words *„ou dus"*.

b) Were another argument necessary to prove our point, we find it in the „destrier d'Espaigne sor". This must be Achilles' horse, for, a few lines beyond, we see that Hector is mounted on Galatee:-

(13,029) Achilles a molt enore;
Contre lui vait sor Galatee.

There is no mention that Galatee was a „destrier d'Espaigne" anywhere in B. Benoît wishes to give Hector a more magnificent war-horse than that, and so he says 7,989:-

Hector monta sor Galatee
Que li tramist Morgan la fee etc.

B. thus assigns the origin of Hector's horse to super-human agents. Had he wished to say it was a „destrier d'Espaigne", he would most naturally have said so in this first mention of Galatee. (B. 7,989 ff,)

The fact that in the first battle Hector is (B. 7477) „sor un cheval d'Espaigne bai", need not disturb us. The horse is not there named. Moreover both heroes have several horses, although Hector usually mounts Galathea (B. 315; 7,989; 10,799; 12,366; 12,375; 13,029; 13,873; 15,492). Achilles has horses from Spain 12,988; from Nubie 10,605; from Léutiz 11,904.

c) M. Joly does not give many „Variantes" in his edition. In a note to B. 12,987, however, he says that Mss. *J.* has:- „Achilles voit venir Hector" in place of „Achilles vait veeir Hector". It is extremely likely, therefore, that Guido's manuscript of Benoît belonged to the group of which Mss. *J.*, with its above reading is a member. Of course the same arguments we have used above (a; b), would preclude (in this reading of J.)

„Hector“ being other than the *subject* of „voit“ G. did not note these arguments, hence his version.

108. The actual interview gives us occasion for several remarks:-

1) M. omits the numerous escort of Hector. He goes only with his brothers, Paris, Deyphebus, and Troillus.

2) Achilles is glad to see him, in M. and G.:-

M. 11,702. I'ay tres grant ioye de vous veoir.
L 8 v 28. Gratum est mihi quod video te.

B. has no such idea, but rather:- (B. 13,033.)

Molt par s'entrefont biau senblant,
Com genz qui s'entreheent tant.

3) M. desiring, as usual, to make all those present take part in the dialogue, inserts the following before the challenge of Hector:- Achilles asks Hector if that is not Paris sitting beside him (11,705), who is so handsome and

„Pour qui nous avons tant de peine.“

Paris answers for himself (11,714):-

Achilles c'est il vrayement,
A vostre bon commandement.
Achilles:
A, paris, la vostre mercy,
Ie vous vouldroye tenir ycy
Et que la triefve feust faillie.
Paris:
Encor ne m'y tenez vous mye,
Mais certes aussi ie vouldroye
Vous tenir ung peu dedens troye
Durant la guerre a mon plaisir.
Ie vous donroye assez loisir
De vous confesser (!) et non plus.
Hector:
Or ca, ca, ce ne sont qu'abus
Ne l'un ne l'autre ne l'aura.

4) In the dialogue between Hector and Achilles in B-G., Achilles speaks at length of his desire to avenge Patroclus' death, also of Hector's valor. M. omits both these thoughts (11,727—34).

5) Hector's reply is essentially alike in all versions, yet one idea binds M. to G:- If Hector lives, he will cause (M. 1 r 22). „quod *non solum* tu *verum* omnes maiores grecorum exercitus — — — — manibus meis amara morte *crudeliter* succumberis“:-

M. 11,747
Se deux ans la vie me dure,
Mourir feray *cruellement*
Non mye vous tant *seulement*,
Mais tous voz princes et voz roys.

6) In B-G. Achilles is terribly angry at Hector's challenge to single combat. (13,171—7; M. 1 v 11—13.) In M. he does not show this anger at all:-

(11,773). Hector, Hector, ie le retien
Car c'est bien mon gre de le faire.

This actual expression of Achilles' willingness agrees with G:- (M 1 v 13). „Et quasi madefactus totus in suo rore sudoris bello *se offert*, bellum recipit animosus." G. then adds an interesting detail, not in B. nor in M:- „et iuxta hectorem appropinquans in firmitatis signum gladium sibi offert quod hector plusquam dici potest animo desideranti recepit." B. is quite different:-

(13,178).

Aprismez s'est envers hector;
La bataille voleit plevir,
Mes il n'ot pas tant de lesir
Qu'il li poïst la main estendre;
Ale le sont sesir et prendre
De totes parz bien XXX reis etc.

7) In B. Achilles is accompanied by his escort during the interview. In G., however, there are no others in Achilles' company during the meeting, although, immediately after, Agamenon and the Greek leaders, hearing the tumult in Achilles' tent, hasten thither and force him to retract his promise. This delayed intervention of the Greek leaders is reflected in M., although there somewhat changed:- Hector, accepting as final Achilles' decision to fight, says that he must now go to Agamenon to see (11,777), „s'il veult point roy thoas avoir". Achilles accompanies Hector, and introduces him to Agamenon. Instead of arranging, however, the exchange of Thoas and Anthenor, Hector speaks again of the proposed combat and its conditions (11,789—804). (It is Agamenon who finally suggests this exchange; see § 109[1].) The Greek leaders oppose the combat, their reasons being the same as in B-G. (11,805—60.)

8) In B-G. the Trojan side makes similar objections to the single combat of Hector and Achilles. All fear the result, except Priam who has the utmost confidence that Hector would win (B. 13,205—34; M 1 v 22—28). All this has no echo at all in M.

109. 1) In M., Hector's motive in visiting the Greeks includes the wish to arrange the exchange of Thoas and Anthenor (11,777), and Agamenon voices the same desire, after his decision not to let Achilles fight in single combat (11,861—76). In B-G. the arrangements for this exchange are made *before* the interview of Hector and Achilles (12,937—51; L 8 v 11—13), and the prisoners are actually exchanged before the same. M.

therefore shows some adroitness in joining the scene of negociations for the exchange, to the scene of the above interview between Hector and Achilles.

2) Another bit of cleverness on M's part is his making the exchange of Thoas and Anthenor dependent upon the return of Briseida, daughter of Calcas. In B. we look in vain for a suggestion of such an idea. In B. the prisoners are already exchanged, before Calcas begs for the return of his daughter. (Return of prisoners 12,945—51; appeal of Calcas 12,952—65.) There is consequently no connection between the two events. In G. on the other hand there exists the possibility of such a connection in the words:- (L 8 v 22—23) „Sed priamus ad petitionem grecorum *inter commutationem* antenoris et regis thoas briseydam voluntarie relaxavit.“

3) M. gives this passage a free interpretation, and connects in the closest manner the episode of the exchange of prisoners with that of the return of Briseida:- Not only does he have them take place at the same time, as we shall see (§ 111) whereas in B-G. they are not synchronous (Exchange of Anthenor and Thoas B. 12,945—51; L 8 v 11—13; Return of Briseida. B. 13,301—684; M 2 v 10 — M 3 r 6.) but M. actually makes the exchange dependent upon the surrender of Briseida, in the following manner:-

Calcas asks of Agamenon:- (11,880).
Et que vous diciez a hector,
Que s'il veult avoir anthenor,
Qu'il me face ma fille rendre.
Agamenon assents:- (11,887)
Elle leur sera demandee,
Car autrement n'auront il pas
Anthenor pour le roy thoas.
Ca, hector, vous retournerez
Au roy priam et luy dires
Qu'il rende la fille calcas,
Et aussi le fort roy thoas,
Si luy sera rendu son frere.

110. 1) Hector and his brothers return to Priam, before whom are assembled all the Trojan princes. In bidding them good-bye, Achilles says:- „Recommandez moy a helene“. Priam questions his sons about their visit. Hector says nothing of his interview with Achilles, but only unfolds the conditions of the exchange of Anthenor and Thoas, namely the return of Briseida at the same time.

2) At the suggestion of Hector, Priam asks for advice (11,942). An extended discussion follows (to 12,265), such as M. always

introduces, whenever opportunity occurs. Priam is opposed to yielding Briseida, since it will please the traitor Calcas. This attitude of Priam is in contrast to B-G:- (L 8 v 23). „briseydam voluntarie relaxavit". B. 12,985:-

> Ne velt que riens qui a lui [= Calcas] taigne,
> Seit en se cite ne remaigne.

Some of the reasons given by the other Trojans for the return of Briseida are peculiar, and quite original to M:- Huppon says (12,050):-

> Et puis quant vous l'aurez perdue
> Vous n'y aurez gaires perdu
> Car elle est de bas lieu venue (!)

Merion suggests that the retention of Briseida may start a scandal, compromising the honor of the royal family (13,087). Ampheneas likewise (12,126 ff.).

3) This long discussion of 323 verses is expanded by M. from three lines in G. (L 8 v 20—23), which in turn are a résumé of B. 12,965—86. Despite this brevity, G. contains an idea, not in B, which idea is expressed by M., namely, the condemnation of Calcas as a *traitor*:- L 8 v 20 „troyani asserentes eum esse nequissimum proditorem et ideo morte dignum" M. voices this thought 11,987—93; 12,018—21; 12,119—21; 12,223; 12,257. B. only has (B. 12,967):-

> Calcas blamerent Troien,
> Dient que plus est vils d'un cien.

4) Priam appoints Enee and Pollidamas to effect the exchange of prisoners and the return of Briseida. Pollidamas expresses great anxiety to see his father, Anthenor, again. Priam then bids Macabrum go tell Agamenon that the conditions of exchange are accepted (12,290). The stage-direction (12,313 d). says „lors machabrum se partira". Strange to say, however, there is no mention of his coming before Agamenon, the only omission of the sort in the whole drama. We are therefore at a loss to know how Agamenon is aware that the Trojans have promised to give up Thoas and Briseida, which knowledge he expresses 12,442—5.

5) There now follows the lamentation of Troillus and Briseida at their impending separation (12,314—441). This is of far too general a nature to allow us to find points of contact

with B-G. G. has a most extraordinary narration of Briseida's grief (M 2 r 2--17).

III. 1) The scene of the return of Briseida comes next. M. combines with this the exchange of Thoas and Anthenor for reasons already suggested in § 109. Aside from this innovation, the scene corresponds closely with B-G :- Agamenon appoints Diomedes, Ulixes, and Ajax to go to meet the Trojans who are bringing Thoas and Briseida. In addition to these three, B. names Thelamon, Menesteus, and fifty knights (B. 13,491). G. only mentions Diomedes by name, although he has a numerous escort (M. 2 v 15). Therefore, a coincidence exists between B. and M. in the introduction of Ulixes and Ajax. As, however, Ulixes is, in M., the constant companion of Diomedes on all occasions (see Index), the coincidence is reduced to the name Ajax, which, in our opinion, is a pure accident, especially as M. omits Menesteus. M. would necessarily have omitted Thelamon since he does not, in M., come to Troy (see §§ 54; 57).

2) Those appointed by Agamenon go first to release Anthenor, in order to conduct him to the Trojans. M. here adds an original idea in Anthenor's words (12,474):-

Ha, pour dieu, dictes moy, barons
Se me voulez faire mourir!

Learning the true motive of their coming, Anthenor is reassured.

3) Enee and Polidamas now ask the sons of Priam to accompany them to the Greeks. Hector and Paris excuse themselves, but Deiphebus and Troillus assent, and all go to fetch Thoas (22,525 d) and Briseida. Troillus takes her by the hand and they proceed toward the Greeks. The two parties, approaching from opposite sides, meet, and then separate, after greetings to the liberated prisoners by their respective countrymen. Troillus and Briseida again mourn their separation, but Diomedes interrupts coarsely:- (12,608)

Taisez vous, belle, taisez vous,
Vous trouverez ung aultre amy,
Qui vous plaira autant que luy.

4) As the Greeks return, the advances of Diomedes occupy only a few verses, scarcely more than the thrice-repeated (12,614):-

Ha dame, ie vous serviray,
S'il vous plaist et de tout mon cueur.

In B. this passage is long (13,502—84). In M. Briseida gives Diomedes a semi-favorable reply with astonishing rapidity and directness:-

(12,630.)
Ie vous pry, sire, doulcement,
Que ne me parliez plus d'aymer,
A tout le moins pour le present. (!)
(12,638.)
Mais se ravoir ie ne povoye
Celluy que i'ayme loyaulment, (!)
Tres bien aymer ie vous vouldroie
De tres bon cueur entierement,
Mais non pas si hastivement
La response donner vous veil.

This is in striking contrast to the far more delicate expression given by B. (13,586—648), or even by G. (M 2 v 21—26.) M. omits all mention of Diomedes' stealing Briseida's glove. (B. 13,673—6; M 2 v 31 — M 3 r 2.)

5) They hasten before Agamenon, who arises to welcome Thoas (12,662 d) and Briseida. The latter he gives over at once to Calcas (12,688). M. thus omits the incident of Calcas' coming to meet his daughter (B. 13,677 — M 3 r 2). — A similar scene of welcome to Anthenor takes place on the Trojan side. Anthenor's gratitude to Priam for his delivery, and his words:- „Certes de toute ma puissance, Desormais ie vous serviray" (12,708) are in contrast to his subsequent treachery. — Priam now (12,720) bids the Trojans arm, for the truce is over; Agamenon likewise commands the Greeks to prepare for battle (12,736).

Chapter XIII.

The Fourth Battle. — Death of Hector.

M. 12,748—13,324. B. 15,187—16,265. G. M 6 v 13 — M 8 v 23.

112. M. now reaches ahead in his source, and selects the episode of the attempt of Andromache to keep Hector from battle. Unquestionably M. has destroyed much of the dramatic effect of the incident, as depicted in B-G.:-

1) In B. Andromache makes a frantic entreaty to Hector to remain, assuring him of her dream and that his death is certain, if he goes that day to battle. It is only in the climax

of her grief at his refusal to listen, that she runs to fetch their child, Asternantes, and falls at Hector's feet, imploring him to stay, if not for her sake, at least for that of their child[1]) (B. 15,381—411). G's relation is less dramatic than B., but the central idea of a climax, culminating in an appeal for the sake of the child, remains (M 7 r 14—22). M. spoils utterly this striking effect. Andromache appeals to Hector's love for his children at the very outset:-

12,764 Las, regardez piteusement
Vostre beau filz, laomedon,[2])
Aussi affremach[2]) mesmement.

2) In M., therefore, there is no mention of Andromache's going to fetch the children; they are with her. We see here G's influence:- B. had said: 15,388

Cort por son fill Asternanten,
Dos ielz plore molt tendrement;
Entre ses braz le charge et prent,
A tot vint el pales arrieres.

G. omits this fetching:- (M 7 r 14) „sed dum hoc vidit andromcta eius uxor multo dolore commota cum parvulo filio suo quem gerebat in brachiis" etc.

3) B-G. mention but *one* child in this scene. B. intensifies the dramatic effect by saying it is the younger (15,200), Asternantes (15,388). G. does not name the child, and says only „cum parvulo filio". M., therefore, not knowing which one it is, mentions both.

4) B. says, in a previous passage, that the older child was five years of age (15,194), the younger „pas onquor treis anz" (15,202). — G. implies a difference of age, but does not state it, saying only of the younger, that he „a matris ubere dependebat" (M 6 v 17). — M. implies a similar difference:- (12,766.)

Aussi affremach mesmement,
Qui est si ieune valeton.

He shows, however, his ignorance of B. by adding:-

Ilz n'ont que chascun environ
Deux ans. — —.

113. 1) B-G. do not relate Andromache's dream, but only mention it (15,208; M 6 v 18). M. yields to his fondness for

---

[1]) For a very interesting comparison of Benoît's version with Homer, see Joly P. 741—2.

[2]) These names are the same in all editions of M. For their relation to B-G. see Proper Names § 242 (Laomedon); § 243 (Affremach).

allegory, and describes the dream in detail (12,796—819):- A lion fights a wolf and a leopard, wounds the leopard and is about to carry off the wolf, when the leopard returns and strangles the lion. Andromache had also dreamt that Hector lay bleeding at her side.

2) Hector pays little attention, except to ridicule her. His words are, however, much less severe than in B-G. As in B-G., Andromache then goes to Priam (12,866), to whom she repeats her dream. M. now lets Helenus interpret the dream, thus giving him another opportunity to show his occult learning. (see other instances in Index):- The lion is Hector, the wolf Prothenor, the leopard Achilles. Hector will capture Prothenor, but Achilles will kill Hector „par traison ou aultrement" (12,892—4).

3) Priam at once goes to prevent Hector's departure, and interrupts him, as he is addressing the barons, preparatory to entering the fight (12,931). Priam forbids his going to battle that day (12,933) „sur peine de inobedience" Hector yields at once, although displeased, and bids Paris assume the chief command in his stead (12,954—70).

This submissivenes of Hector contrasts strikingly with B-G. There his father's first prohibition is not sufficient. He arms despite it. He abuses Andromache. He heeds not the entreaties of his mother, Polixene, and Helen. B. is here (15,323—85). far more dramatic than G., who omits many details, and thus destroys half the effect. In B., Andromache hides his armor and weapons. He finds them. She faints, as she sees him armed. He is resolute and determined. She appeals to Hecuba and his sisters. It is as climax to all these futile efforts, that Andromache runs to bring her child (see preceding paragraph). This passage in B. contains so much dramatic material, that it is incredible, that M. would not have preferred it to G's curtailed and colorless version, had M. only known B. We cannot share Meybrink's praise of this scene in M. (P. 28 of Meybrinck).

4) In B-G. Hector mounts and proceeds to the fight. Andromache makes a last frenzied appeal, this time to Priam, who mounting a horse, hastens after Hector and absolutely forbids his departure. Hector yields only with very great reluctance

and returns to the palace. In B., Hector emphasizes greatly the intense disgrace of his remaining absent from battle because of a woman's dream (B. 15,265—72; 15,512—3; 15,520—2). This idea finds no expression in G. nor in M. Indeed G. is very much briefer in the entire episode. He relates in 56 lines (M. 6 v 18 — M 7 v 12.) what B. requires 326 verses to depict (15,203—529). This scene in B. is perhaps the finest dramatically in his whole work. M. omits to state, with B-G., that Hector keeps on his armor, although this is implied in his promise to aid Paris, if need be (12,969).

114. 1) Paris and Agamenon now arrange their men[1]) In the list of the Trojan leaders we note Serpedon (12,981.) taken from Sarpedon in G. (M 7 r 3). B. does not mention him here (15,298—308).

2) The fourth battle, which now follows, shows the usual independence on the part of M. He takes what incidents he pleases from B-G., and quite at random. For instance, the first combat here is between Diomedes and Enee, and it is taken from far back in the fourth battle of B-G. (11,111—32; L 4 r 11—18). The scoffing challenge of Diomedes (13,036):-

Dieu te sault, loyal conseiller, Qui veulx a ton roy conseiller
Dieu te sault, iuste secretaire, De traison et meutre faire!

has its exact equivalent in B-G. It refers to Eneas' conduct at the time of the embassy of Ulixes and Diomedes to demand Helen, before hostilities are begun (see § 79). In M. Enee fells Diomedes to his knees (13,059 d); in B-G. he strikes no blow. B. and M. agree, by chance, in the effect of Diomedes' blow:-

B. 11,118 Ius l'abati en mi lo tai.
M. 13,067 d. qu'il (= Enee) charra tout plat et estonné a terre.

G. says only „quem (= Eneas) graviter vulnerat" (L 4 r 12). — Noteworthy is M's connecting this combat with a previous scene, by Eneas' words (13,052):-

Tenez ce coup et le portez
A Briseiba, vostre amye.

In B-G., at the time of this combat, Briseida was, of course, still with the Trojans.

---

[1]) In the edition of 1484 the stage-direction 13,003 d. has „grecz" for Trojans, a mistake shared only by the Paris edition of 1498.

115. For the combat of Menelaus and Troillus, the rescue of Menelaus by Diomedes, and the latter's discomfiture of Troillus, as well as for the combat of Diomedes and Polidamas, M. returns to the battle[1]) in B-G. (B. 14,189—307. M 5 r 7—27.) immediately following the truce in which truce the interview of Hector and Achilles had tàken place.

The first episodes of those mentioned above correspond too closely with B-G., to furnish any proofs of M's especial contact with either B. or G. When we come to Diomedes' discomfiture of Troillus, however, several points of interest occur:-

1) Both B. and G. say that it is Troillus' horse which Diomedes captures and sends to Briseida (14,241; M 5 r 12). In M. Diomedes knocks Troylus' sword from his hand, picks it up, and sends it by his „senechal" to Briseida. M. Joly says (P. 848) that this substitution is due to a change in customs, „le progrès des moeurs", in Milet's time. We incline rather to the idea that the exigencies of the stage forced M. to the change, since M. has left out horses completely in his battle-scenes (see § 81[4]).

2) B. names the messenger, by whom Diomedes sends this gift to Briseida (14,259), „li filz Carin de Pierelee". G., however, only says (M 5 r 13) „per suum nuncium specialem", and M. likewise has no name, but only „senechal".

---

[1]) This battle is the next one after that called the seventh (B. 12,649); it is, however, not numbered, nor is the following battle, which begins B. 14,468, numbered. Benoit, therefore, ignores these two battles in his otherwise very careful enumeration, when he calls that battle which begins 15,123 the eighth! It is, of course, really the tenth, and Benoit's own subsequent numbering proves it, as follows:-

	Eleventh	battle,	begins	17,000	unnumbered.
	Twelfth	„	„	18,455	unnumbered,
—	Thirteenth	„	„	19,078	numbered.
	Fourteenth	„	„	19,946	unnumbered.
—	Fifteenth	„	„	20,045	numbered.
—	Sixteenth	„	„	20,405	(numbered 20,585).
—	Seventeenth	„	„	20,807	numbered.
	Eighteenth	„	„	20,867	unnumbered.
—	Nineteenth	„	„	21,227	numbered.
	Twentieth	„	„	22,529	unnumbered, etc.

The reading of B. 15,123 should, therefore, be „dizaine" not „oitaine".

3) In B., Diomedes does not name Troylus in his message to Briseida, but says only „un chevalier“ 14,248. The messenger alone names Troylus 14,265. In G. and M., however, Diomedes names Troylus (M 5 r 15; 13,124).

4) In B., Briseida sends a much longer message back to Diomedes (14,277—302). In it she reproaches Diomedes for thus harshly treating her former lover. She lauds the valor of Troylus, declaring that he will yet give a good account of himself. In G. none of these ideas are expressed, and, consequently, M. does not have them either.

5) The attitude of Briseida toward Diomedes merits attention. In B. her demeanor is more modest and delicate, and the expression of her regard for Diomedes is far more veiled. She says (B. 14,301):-

Et si li di que tort aureie,
Puisqu'il m'aime, si le heieie.

Briseida expresses no pleasure at receiving the horse. In G., however, she receives it „hylariter“ M 5 r 21, which is repeated by M. 13,140 „ioyeusement“. Briseida's message in G. contains a greeting to Diomedes, expressed less delicately than in B. (M 5 r 22). „dic securse domino tuo quod illum odio habere non possum qui me tanta puritate sui cordis affectat“. In M. there is a similar expression of regard, but it is very direct and explicit, all veiling being thrown aside (13,145):

Amy, dictes luy hardiment,
Que m'amour ie luy ai donnee,
Et que de cueur et de pensee
Le serviray dilligemment,
Car tres affectueusement
Ie suis de luy tres bien aymee.

6) In B. there is no record of the delivery of Briseida's message or of Diomedes' pleasure at receiving it. The messenger simply leaves her and returns to the fight (B. 14,303—7). G. and M., however, both have such a record (M 5 r 24—26) (13,153—60):-

13,156 — Et que tres debonnairement
Vous ayme de tout son couraige.
Diomedes (13,160). Senechal i'en suis bien content.

7) After this return of the senechal, Paris exhorts the lords to valor, and Polidamas attacks Diomedes, felling him to the earth (13,184 d). This is all that M. has of the combat of Diomedes and Polidamas in B-G. There Diomedes is knocked

from his horse, and the horse falls upon and injures Diomedes severely. Polidamas captures the horse, and gives it to Troylus in compensation for the recent loss of his own (B. 14,355—86; M 5 v 4—12). This horse of Diomedes is called in B. „Passelande" (14,395). The limitations of the stage prevented M. from introducing the horse, here as elsewhere.

116. For the next episode, the death of Margariton at Achilles' hands, M. looks far ahead to the tenth battle in B-G. (15,767—812; M 7 v 30 — M 8 r 9). This episode presents several interesting features:-

1) B. mentions no attack by Margariton upon Achilles. Margariton has seized Thelamon, when Achilles comes up and kills him. G., however, says (M 7 v 31):- „margaryton — — intercipere conatur achillem, achilles dum ille sibi viriliter restitisset interfecit eundem." M. goes even farther, and says that Margariton felled Achilles to the earth, before the latter arose and killed him (13,200 d).

2) Margariton's body is recovered and carried to Troy. B. does not name Paris in this connection. M. and G. do (13,209; M 8 r 4).

3) In all versions Hector is wild with grief at his brother's death. B. alone has the detail that Hector faints three times (15,790). In B-G., Hector recognizes Margariton at once, and his only question is, *who* killed him. In M., besides this last question, Hector also asks who is the dead one being carried by Adrastus and Erupius, repeating the question twice, as if incredulous.

4) We now come to a most striking point of contact between M. and G., namely, that this death of Margariton causes Hector's *immediate* entry into battle. In B. on the other hand, Hector *wishes* to sally forth at once to avenge Margariton,

— — — mes li reis vint (B. 15,811).
Qui a grant peine le detint.

Hector is thus kept back, and the battle continues a long time, until the Greeks, attacking fiercely, drive the Trojans headlong into the city. It is then that Hector, despite the swooning of Andromache and without his father's knowledge, rushes forth to the battle and to his death (15,971—4).

In G. the only fight described after Margariton's death is the struggle to regain the body of Margariton. The Trojans are driven into Troy, bringing the body with them (M 8 r 5—8). This struggle is not in M. In both G. and M., however, Hector immediately rushes forth, as soon as he learns that it is Achilles who has killed Margariton.

5) Before the final encounter with Achilles, Hector, in B-G., (15,976—16,129; M 8 r 10—31) performs many exploits of valor. M. omits all these, saying merely that Hector kills four Greeks (13,240 d) and introducing a combat between Achilles and Bouettes, in which the latter is killed.

117. The final encounter of Hector and Achilles is divided in all three versions into two parts, a first, in which Hector severely wounds Achilles who retires from the field, and a second, in which Achilles returns and kills Hector treacherously. Both parts have features of interest:-

1) In B-G. it is to avenge Hector's killing of Politenes (or Politetes) that Achilles first attacks Hector. In M. there is no such combat, although, as in many other cases, we find this name in the list of kings killed by Hector (M. 13,894). M. substitutes an attack by Hector to avenge Margariton and Bouettes, and is certainly more logical in making Hector the attacking party. Achilles is wounded severely and retires from battle. M. adds the detail (13,280 d) „et de puis se relevera a grant peine et entraynant ses jambes et clochant.“

2) In choosing the events before the return of Achilles, M. is independent:- Hector attacks Prothenor and kills him. (The stage-direction does not state that Prothenor is *killed;* we learn it by finding his name in the list of kings killed by Hector, 13,889). This combat, in B-G., comes much earlier, 10,802—18; L 3 r 22, in their third battle.

3) B-G. say, that Hector captures a certain king, but give no name (16,166; M 8 v 8). M. says that it is Thelamonius Ajax, Hector's cousin, whom Hector wishes to take to Troy „avecques ceulx de ton lignage“. By thus saying Thelamonius Ajax, M. cleverly explains why Hector did not try to kill him at once.

4) The rest of the episode is essentially the same in B-G-M. Hector, engaged in carrying away his prisoner, lays aside his

shield. Achilles seizes this opportunity to rush at him. B. does not state that Achilles' weapon was a lance, although the context implies it. G. and M. state explicitly that it was a lance (M 8 v 13; 13,319 d). M. says „achilles vient *par derriere* hector". B. implies no such attack from behind (16,172—7). M. probably got his idea from G. „non advertente hectore" (M 8 v 13), although M's attack from behind seems hardly reconcilable with G's statement that Hector had placed his shield „post terga" (M 8 v 10).

5) After Hector's death, the Trojans flee. In B. Achilles kills 500 as they flee (16,206), and there is tremendous fighting at the city gates, in which Mennon and Achilles wound each other, Achilles' wound being very nearly mortal. In G. all this fighting is omitted, except that king Edemon wounds Achilles severely. The Trojans „grecis non resistentibus" (M 8 v 21) leave the field, bearing away the body of Hector (see § 167²). This non-resistence of the Greeks corresponds with M. 13,320—3 where Agamenon orders the Greeks to return. M. omits all further wounding of Achilles.

Chapter XIV.

The Mourning for Hectdr. — His Burial. — The Election of Palamides.

M. 13,324—14,279 (end of second day). B. 16,265—16,998. G. M 8 v 23 — N 3 v 29.

118. The lamentations over Hector's death have, in B., an extraordinary development, and are highly dramatic (16,265—458). G. is much shorter (M 8 v 23 — N 1 r 25), and he leaves out the „lamentationes" as „inutiles", saying only, that it is the nature of woman to express grief „in multarum vocum clamore" (N 1 r 23). M., however, has a long series of scenes (13,324—607), and introduces several original features, although nowhere rising to the dramatic height and intensity of B.:-

1) In B., Cassandra takes no part in the scene of lamentation. G. simply mentions that she shares in it (N 1 r 16). In M. it is Cassandra who first sees the body of her brother and utters her lament, fainting twice (13,331 d; 13,339 d).

2) The body is brought before Priam and Hecuba who swoon upon it (13,355 d). During their unconsciousness, Polixene mourns. Her lament contains a peculiar thought 13,372:-

Las, mon frere, or voy ie bien,
Que a mes nopces ne serez mie.
Or ne me chailloit il de rien,
Mais qu'une foiz en vostre vie
M'eussiez d'un bon mary fournie,
Et qui feust d'aussi hault lignaige
Comme vous. — — —

3) In the laments of Priam and Hecuba, M. inserts an idea quite absent in B-G., the blaming of Paris. This thought finds expression in M. at each succeeding grief of the parents:-

(13,396) Priam:-

Ha, paris, paris, ta ieunesse
M'est ycy endroit bien vendue,
Quant tu me faiz en ma vieillesse
Telle douleur estre rendue.

Priam then faints, and Paris and Deyphebus throw water upon his face (13,403 d). Hecuba also swoons again at the end of her lament (13,459 d) „et paris lui gettera de l'eaue roze au visaige". He then tries to console her, but receives only the bitter reply (13,476):-

A, paris, laissez moy en paix!
Le regard de toy mon cueur serre.
Maleureux, c'est par tes beaulx faiz,
Que nous sommes en ceste guerre.
Il te failloit bien aler querre
La mort de ton frere si loing.

Hecuba even blames Priam (13,484):-

Priam, priam, mon doulx seigneur,
Congnoissez cy vostre follye.
Par vous nous vient ceste douleur,
Pource que ne me croiez myc.

4) Priam now bids Deyphebus and Helenus to summon Andromache. This takes place in a naïve manner. Helenus declares they must go (13,514) „sans monstrer ne muer couleur". Deyphebus thinks likewise:-

Nous fault faire semblant et chiere
De ioye sans gemissement.

Andromache, however, has a presentiment of calamity, despite Deiphebus' words (13,532):-

Il n'y a rien, il n'y a rien
Ne vous en veillez soucier,
Se dieu m'aist, il n'ay que bien.

This summoning-scene is wholly original to M. It has its pendant in the summoning of Helen (see § 173).

5) M's relation of Andromache's grief is commonplace. As she sees Hector, she swoons; she remains unconscious a long time (13,543 d); she then grieves in a lengthy monologue, and faints again at its close (13,607). A naïve feature, here and elsewhere, in cases of fainting, is the declaration of the speaker that he or she must now faint! (13,459; 13,495. etc.) This probably served as a reminder to the actor, and was intended to be such. — Far more natural, and, therefore, more truly dramatic is B's account:- Andromache is so overcome, that she cannot speak and is carried helpless to a bed (B. 16,413—425).

119. Priam now speaks of the need of burial, in words taken from G's observation of the same thought (N 1 r 25—31). G. did not place this thought in Priam's mouth, however, and we are rightly astonished at M's lack of delicacy in so doing:-

13,618 Si est char humaine pourrie, Plus tost et plus legierement,
Quant l'ame fait departement, Que la char d'une beste mue. (!)

Priam wishes a rich tomb for his son, and bids Helenus find the most skilful builder in the world. Helenus thereupon sends Adastus to fetch Sentipus. The latter (13,672 d) „prendra ses intrumens et des potz a mettre diverses couleurs convenables a paintures", and comes before Priam who tells him what sort of a tomb to build (13,682 ff.). Thus does M. introduce his description of Hector's tomb. There is in this description considerable divergence from B-G., although the differences between M. and G. are not as great as between G. and the extravagant description in B. (B. 16,605—99; N 1 v 3—22; M. 13,682—745). Despite these various differences, careful comparison shows that M's description is based upon G.

1) The order of details is the same in G-M., and quite unlike B's order.

2) G. and M. speak of steps before the monument. (N 1 v 14—17; M. 13,706—8).

3) Another resemblance is the *statue* of Hector, sword in hand, facing the Greek army with threatening gesture (N 1 v 17—22; 13,710—21). In B. there is no such statue, and the sword and threatening attitude are applied to the embalmed body of Hector itself, seated on a throne (B 16,743—50). G. also describes at length the embalming of the body and the

placing of it on a throne (He even goes beyond B. in placing a vase full of embalming liquid on Hector's head as well as at his feet. N 1 v 25). G. omits, however, the sword and the threatening attitude as applied to the body, having already used these for the statue (N 1 v 22 — N 2 r 13). — M. also mentions the embalming of the body (13,722—29), but, instead of having the same put upon a throne, it is placed within the tomb (13,624; 13,827 d).

120. 1) After giving the above directions for the tomb, Priam likens this loss of Hector to the earlier loss of his son Ganymedes (13,764; see Proper Names § 241), whom the gods took away in his youth. Despite their infliction of sorrow, the deities must be honored. Priam now commands that Hector's body be removed, although Andromache objects strongly (13,796). Let Priam at least allow her to kiss Hector. She does so and faints again (13,819 d.), after which Priam bids his sons with Enee and Pollidamas to remove the body to the temple of Venus (13,826). This differs from B-G:- In B. only, Hector is kept fifteen days in the temple of Juno (B 16,585) and his final tomb is at the Tymbrean gate in the temple of Apollo. G. only mentions the one temple, that of Apollo, and also says that Hector's tomb is within it (N 1 v 2—4).

2) Priam next orders Sentipus to hasten in the preparation of the tomb. „Alors se fera grant pause tant qu'il (= Sentipus) ait tout disposé et tout fait (13,835 d)[1]. Priam now dictates to Sentipus the epitaph (13,844—51), which Sentipus „fait semblant d'escripre". After this Priam requests all to return and prepare for battle. The epitaph has no particular resemblance to those in B-G. G. gives the epitaph, together with that of Achilles, at the end of his work (T 7 v).

121. The scene changes to the Greek side, where a council is being held, addressed by Agamenon. G's influence is markedly apparent again:-

1) In B. Agamenon's speech is 16,531—67. i. e. *before* the burial of Hector. G. introduces it *after* the burial, and likewise M. (N 2 r 25 — N 2 v 18; 13,868—923.)

---

[1]) A similar naïveté is shown in the building of Achilles' tomb (§ 168⁴).

2) At the beginning of his speech Agamenon says that thanks should be given the gods for this victory over Hector (13,871—5; N2r29—31.) This thought is not in B.

3) Agamenon embodies in his speech a list of the kings killed by Hector (13,884—901; N2v3—8). In B. there is no such list in his speech, the corresponding list being inserted in the epitaph of Hector (B. 16,780—800). G. has a second list at the end of his work (T7r22) which is essentially the same as G's list here. It is difficult to deduce any arguments from these lists in B-G-M., until we possess them in complete, critical form, based in each case upon the various manuscripts of B. and the manuscripts and prints of G., and of M. When that work shall have been done, these lists will, no doubt, help greatly to a proper classification of the manuscripts and prints of the three works and thus enable us to determine what manuscript of B. served as G's source, and also what one of G. served, in turn, for M. M's list is very unlike that in the prints of G., and it seems probable that it could furnish some indication of the manuscript used by M.

4) In G-M. Agamenon expresses the opinion that the Greeks will now conquer in a short time. (M. 13,880—2; N2v11.) M. gives a time-limit of fourteen months.

122. Still following the order of events in G., M. now introduces the scene of Palamides' discontent and his election to the leadership. B. had placed between Agamenon's speech (see last paragraph) and the complaint of Palamides, the whole scene of the burial of Hector (B. 16,579—810). In M. this is the only scene of Palamides' objection. We have already noted M's omission of the previous scene in B-G. (10,409—496; L2r4—11.) (see foot note § 95.) The three versions of this episode are, in general, very similar, but in G-M., particularly in Agamenon's reply, the sequence of thought is the same, differing from B. Other points of resemblance to G. also occur:-

1) At the beginning of his speech Agamenon asserts that the leadership has only brought him great responsibility devoid of joy (N2v29—N3r3; M. 13,966—76).

2) Palamides ought not to be surprised that he had no

word in the election of Agamenon, since he, Palamides, was not present at that election. (N 3 r 9; M. 13,995.)

3) In B. it is Palamides himself, who both suggests and urges his own election to the leadership (B. 16,974—9), an idea which is not repeated in G., nor in M. In G-M. it is Thelamonius Ajax who proposes, and the others who support the candidature of Palamides. This was due to G's general statement that the Greek leaders elect him. M. alone introduces an urging of Agamenon by Ulixes to retain the leadership (14,055).

123. The newly-elected Palamides now suggests that truce be asked of Priam (14,115) for one month (14,117) and appoints Ulixes and Diomedes as ambassadors. This is a change from B-G., where the truce is asked before the election of Palamides and is suggested by Agamenon, and where, also, no ambassadors are specified. The truce in B-G. is for two months (16,564; N 2 v 16). M. builds up a little scene out of this requesting of truce :- The ambassadors go before Priam and make their wish known, which is granted. In Priam's reply he naïvely invites the Greeks to come during the truce (14,199),

— — veoir le thumbeau
De mon filz, qui est le plus beau,
Qui oncques fut, ne iamais sera.

The ambassadors return and announce to Palamides the success of their mission, adding that the pride of Priam is in no wise lowered by the loss of Hector. They, however, make no reference to Priam's invitation to visit Troy. Palamides now bids all to rest during the truce, so as to be prepared for battle at its close. With various expressions of farewell all separate, and the second day of the drama comes to an end (14,279).

The Third Day of the Drama.

Chapter XV.

The Anniversary of Hector's Death. — Achilles visits Troy. — Achilles and Polixene.

M. 14,280—15,403. B. 17,457—18,121. G. N 5 r 1 — N 7 v 4.

124. 1) The opening scene of the third day is supposed to take place on the anniversary day of Hector's death. By thus passing to this incident M. omits a long battle in B-G. (17,000—373; N 3 v 30 — N 4 v 31) in which the main feature is the valiant entry of Priam into the combat to avenge his son, Hector. M. reserves this entry of Priam into battle until after the events of the anniversary festivities (see § 133).

2) The scene opens with a long monologue by Achilles (14,280—14,360). He returns thanks to the gods for his victory over Hector and for his recovery from his wound. He refers also to the promise of Apollo at Delos (14,304) that the Trojans would be conquered. As truce now exists, he wishes to go to see Troy and the tomb of Hector. This expression of a wish to go to Troy is taken from G. (N 5 r 8). B. has no such idea. Achilles starts for Troy with Basaac.

125. A scene of considerable ingenuity is now built up by M. on the Trojan side:- Hecuba asks Polixene, Creusa and Andromache to accompany her to the temple, there to mourn for Hector and to pray for his soul. Creusa assents willingly, saying that her grief is as great as if Enee were dead (14,393). Creusa bids Astanius come with her, and a little domestic scene follows:- Astanius says that he mourns „de mon petit entendement" (14,405) and desires greatly to avenge Hector,

(14,409) Mais ie suis encor en enfance,
Et ne suis pas assez puissant.

Hecuba is pleased at his brave wish, and says to him:-

(14,412). Le cueur me dit qu'un temps viendra,
Que le monde te obeira,
Et sera du tout en tes mains.

Cassandra then prophesies that the Roman people shall descend from him:-

Qui le monde gouvernera,
Et sera sur tous les humains.

No such prophecy exists in B. G. says only that Eneas and Astanius shall found Rome (A 8 r 3: see Proper Names). M., therefore, shows a knowledge of Virgil and of legendary Roman history.

Creusa summons all to go to the temple to pray for the safety of the city. They go and kneel. Hecuba utters a prayer to Venus (14,440) to take pity on Hector. All pray in a like strain except Cassandra, who utters a selfish prayer to all the goddesses:- „Exaulcez moy par voz largesses" (14,473). M's reason for giving Cassandra this selfish attitude is not very apparent. B-G. describe a religious ceremony also, mentioning by name only Hecuba and Polixene (17,481—7; N 5 r 17—19). B. alone adds Helen (17,484) whose omission in G. explains her absence in M. M. shows the slight originality of introducing Andromache. In connection with this ceremony both B. and G. speak of the marvellous preservation of Hector's body; M. omits all reference to it, which harmonizes with M's saying that it was within the tomb, and not artificially preserved outside (§ 119[3]).

126. 1) Achilles now enters the temple to offer his prayer to Venus. M's saying here, that it is the temple of Venus, is in harmony with his locating the tomb of Hector there, whereas B-G. place it in the temple of Apollo (§ 120[1]). This direct specifying of Achilles' entering the temple points to G. (N 5 r 11) „et appollinis templum intravit". B. speaks only vaguely of the „riche sepulture" (17,471). and says that Achilles came so near:-

Que bien poeit o els parler (17,503).

2) The meeting of Achilles and Polixene is told with M's characteristic naïveté. It forms a counterpart to the meeting of Paris and Helen in the temple of Venus in Cytharea (§§ 33;

34). Perhaps the taking of this previous scene as his model here, caused M. to change the temple of Apollo in B-G. into that of Venus, which latter seemed to him the proper meeting-place of lovers. — After Achilles has thanked Venus for his victory over Hector, he „se pourmenera parmy le temple“ (14,448 d). Polixene calls Hecuba's attention to him, as the slayer of her brother. Her growing interest in him despite this fact is shown, however, in (14,490):-

> Car il semble estre homme de pris,
> Il est bel homme, et bien faictis,
> Et moult plaisant a regarder.

also in verses 14,507—8; 14,513—8. These expressions of growing admiration for Achilles contrast sharply with Hecuba's wrath against him (14,499) and Andromache's wish for immediate vengeance (14,503—6). The entire conception of Polixene's rôle here is original, B-G. having no suggestion of the same. Andromache and Cassandra bid Polixene speak no more of Achilles, and their dialogue causes Hecuba to say sharply:-

> Or ca, taisez vous, ie le veulx.
> Dictes voz heures toutes deux
> Sans plus ensemble quaquetter (!)

This is another example of Milet's conception of royal dignity. One is almost inclined to believe that he intended a humorous effect in these words.

3) Achilles now passes several times in front of the ladies „en regardant polixene du coing de l'ueil puis apres se tire appart et dit“ (14,529 d; compare 2,163 d. § 33). Achilles then indulges in a long monologue about the beauty of Polixene, and the hopelessness of ever winning her love. This description of Polixene's beauty is too general to allow it to be compared with B. (17,522—37) or with the very extravagant account of Polixene's charms in G. (N 5 r 22 — N 5 v 7.)

4) The ladies soon return to the palace „illion“ (14,580 d), and Achilles, announcing to Basaac that he will remain in Troy until the morrow (14,585), goes to a place near the temple. In M. Achilles remains in Troy until the negociations concerning Polixene are over (15,403 d). B-G. say that, after seeing Polixene, he returns at once to his tent (17,583; N 5 v 30).

127. 1) In all versions, after the meeting of Achilles and Polixene, there follows a long monologue by Achilles expressing the hopelessness of his love (B. 17,606—716; N 6 r 3—21; M. 14,589—668). The line of thought is, in general, the same, but the opening idea in M. points unmistakeably to G.:- Achilles, whom the most powerful of men could not conquer, is now subdued at the sight of a maiden (14,592—600; N 6 r 3—6).

2) At last Achilles determines to open secret negociations with Hecuba for the hand of her daughter, and to that end sends a messenger to Hecuba. This is alike in B-G-M., except that M. adds the detail of the messenger's meeting Polixene and asking of her the way to Hecuba. Basaac is the messenger. Polixene then goes to her mother and says that a Greek wishes to speak to her. Hecuba replies (14,687):-

> Grec, dieu, comment ie les hay tous!
> Qui peult il estre maintenant?

Polixene answers that she believes the messenger was with Achilles in the temple, and Hecuba consents to receive him.

3) Basaac then delivers his message. Curiously enough he does not name Polixene, and we are at a loss to know how Hecuba knows which daughter he means. Hecuba bids him wait until she has consulted Priam. In B-G. she tells the messenger to return in three days (17,824; N 6 v 22).

128. Hecuba goes to Priam and asks him to summon Paris. Macabrum is sent to bring Paris who takes leave of Helen (14,748). The following interview is, therefore, between Hecuba, Priam, and Paris. Here we see G's influence again:- In both B. and G. Hecuba tells the messenger that she must consult Priam and Paris (17,826; N 6 v 21). B., however, omits all further mention of Paris. G. does not. Paris is depicted as actually present during the consultation:- (N 6 v 27). „regina vero heccuba regis paridis habilitate captata in secreto refert illis etc.“ and later (N 7 v 10) „Paris vero verbis regis auditis consilium regis probat etc.“ From these passages M. constructs the scene 14,751—15,046, in which Paris plays a leading part. The dialogue therein is one of the most prolix in M., all the speeches being very wearisome; we note, however, how Hecuba gradually leads up to the main question, and also the protracted weighing of pro and con as in a lawyers' debate. These peculiarities point to Milet's legal training. Besides the presence of Paris, M. shows dependence upon G. in the following:-

1) The opening thought of Priam's reply to Hecuba:- N 7 r 1 „O quam *durum* animo meo videtur illum in amicum recipere qui etc." In echoing this thought M. has a running play on the root „*dur*" which is very characteristic of his time (14,883):-

Ha, qu'il m'est dur a endurer	Et me fault vivre en endurant!
Tel durete a tousiours durant,	Certes mon cueur va murmurant;
Qui peult durablement durer,	Endurcy suis de si dur dueil.

A similar feat of verse-gymnastics occurs 15,475 ff. § 130.

2) At no part of the negotiations for Polixene's hand in B. is it said that the demand for the return of Helen will be abandoned. G. introduces such a thought. Paris gives his consent to the wish of Achilles all the more readily (N 7 r 12) „pro eo quod iuxta promissa ipsius achillis helena consors sua priori non erat restituenda marito sed penes eum debeat perpetuo remanere". This finds ample reflection in M:- In the speech of Paris 14,971—82; in Hecuba's reply 14,982—98; and in Paris' appeal to his sister 15,177.

129. M. now introduces an episode completely on his own responsibility, one which shows in a clearer light his conception of the character of Polixene. In B-G. Polixene is not consulted at all regarding her betrothal to Achilles. M., however, builds up a long scene wherein she is consulted and finally persuaded to accept Achilles:- Paris, after remarking that Polixene should be allowed to express her mind in this important matter, goes to fetch her. Priam then tells her (15,052—131) that she is of age to be married, that he would have preferred another husband for her, but that the desire to save his other sons forces him to „faire une piteuse accordance" (15,093) and accept Achilles. He then urges her to obedience, and depicts the many excellencies of Achilles. Paris uses similar words (15,132—93) appealing also to her love for himself. Polixene (15,194—241) admits her obligation to obey her father, emphasizes, however, the odious nature of such a marriage:- Surely Hector would have opposed it, and, if he is now among the gods, he will avenge such a disgrace. Paris (15,242—81) argues that it is not wrong to seek peace, and emphasizes her obligation to obey Priam, particularly as her refusal will bring disaster and death to many Trojans. Polixene cannot resist this appeal to her generous nature and yields. Priam gives her his blessing (15,307) and bids Hecuba arrange for the marriage, as soon as Achilles has fulfilled his promise and caused the departure of the Greeks. Meanwhile (15,326) he wishes all to prepare for battle, as he himself intends to take part in it to avenge Hector. Let word be sent to Achilles to enter the fight no more. Hecuba (15,358) reports the decision of Priam to Basaac, who in turn tells it to Achilles. The latter thereupon binds Basaac to secrecy, and leaves Troy to return to the Greek camp:-

(15,393) Car Palamides n'a pas ioye
De ce que faiz telle demeure.

Chapter XVI.

Preparations for Battle. — The Fifth Battle. — Death of Deyphebus and Palamides.

M. 15,403—16,262. B. 18,454—19,002. G. N 8 r 27 — O 2 v 3.

---

130. In B-G. Achilles at once attempts to fulfil the promise made to Hecuba, and tries in a council of the Greeks to persuade them to abandon the siege and return home (18,122—454; N 7 v 4 — N 8 r 9). Although M. now depicts a council of the Greeks, he postpones until much later (16,350—526; § 140). Achilles' efforts to bring the war to a close. This postponement hardly seems justified. — The Greek council in M. has no equivalent in B-G., and is one of the barrenest passages in the drama with a wearisome length of 300 verses:- Palamides says that they have been before Troy seven years (15,404); this does not harmonize with B., where Achilles says that five years have elapsed (B. 18,156; 18,403). — Palamides repeats the cause of their coming and their success thus far, especially the death of

Hector. As an illustration of the wearisome nature of the passage, and as another example of artificiality in versification, we quote the following:- (15,475.)

Or revenons a nostre point	Car certes il est tout a point
Si trouverons de point a point	Quant la chose plus fort nous point
Ung convenable appoinctement	D'aler tost a son (= Helen's) vengement.

Palamides urges an immediate attack and is seconded by Thelamonius Ajax (15,499—514) and Menelaus. The latter says that Hector's death has unnerved the Trojans, and counsels a secret assault. Ulixes and Diomedes also urge action, using illustrations taken from the game of chess (15,539—626). Diomedes' speech is frightfully monotonous, yet Palamides says he has spoken „tres soubtillement" (!) (15,628), which is an ill-disguised self-praise by Milet of his own versification. Palamides in an equally tiresome speech exhorts the Greeks to valor in the coming fight. The Greeks disperse and go to arm (15,718 d).

131. The scene changes to the Trojan side. Priam repeats his intention to lead the army that day (see § 129 end). He therefore bids his sons and the other leaders[1]) to arm. Anchises declares his readiness, and mourns the loss of Hector. The other Trojan leaders are eager for the fray, and go to arm (15,809 d), each one in his own „tente". This is the first mention of tents on the Trojan side, but we shall note others farther on (see Index „tente".)

132. 1) Having postponed (see §§ 130; 140) the attempt of Achilles to make the Greeks give up the siege, and his refusal to fight because they do not accede to his wishes, M. now feels the need of explaining the absence of Achilles from the approaching battle. M., therefore, introduces the following scene:- Palamides asks if all are ready. Archilogus replies, all except Achilles, whereupon Palamides bids him go ascertain the cause of Achilles' absence. Palamides hints at this cause himself:-

(15,820) „s'il a point de desplaisance
De ce que j'ay sur vous puissance."

[1]) In this list (15,735—50) we note the name of Boetes. M. has forgotten that Boetes was killed by Achilles (13,264 d; § 116[5]), and he also continues to use the name in 22,200. We note also that Merion (15,738) and Menones (= Menon) (17,745) are distinct personages (see Proper Names. § 241).

This is, in fact, the reason in M. for Achilles' withdrawal from the fight, or at least Achilles' pretended reason. We see it later in this same scene:- Archilogus says that Achilles has just returned from Troy (15,829), and goes to give him Palamides' summons, not, however, mentioning the latter's suspicion. Achilles replies that he will not come; he gives no reason except that such is his pleasure; he remarks, however, that Agamenon was a sufficiently wise leader, although he (Achilles.) has no grudge against Palamides (15,852—61). — In his report to Palamides Archilogus says, only, that Achilles (15,887):-

Se veult maintenant tenir
En sa tente pour reposer.

Yet Palamides (15,895—902) remains suspicious that his holding the chief command is the cause of Achilles' refusal to come, and that Palamides is right, is shown in the words of Ajax Thelamonius (16,283—6) and of Achilles himself (16,338—42) after the death of Palamides. M. herein shows ingenuity:- Wishing to postpone Achilles' attempt to force the Greeks to return and his withdrawal from their ranks because of their refusal to do so, until *after* the death of Palamides, he felt the need of a pretext for Achilles' absence at the present stage of events. He found it in the passages in B-G. (16,985—98; N 3 v 23—29) after the election of Palamides, where Achilles expresses his discontent at the change of leadership. In thus using this discontent of Achilles as a pretext for his abstaining from battle, M. gave it an importance which it does not possess in B-G.

2) In Achilles' reply to Archilogus we note that he praises Agamenon as a ruler (15,852—6); this praise is taken from N 3 v 25. Thus, in both G. and M., it is in close connection with his discontent with Palamides. B. has no such praise of Agamenon in the corresponding place. (B. 16,985—98.)

3) A second peculiar feature of this scene is that Achilles, although refusing to come himself to battle, sends his Mirmidons (15,868—78). In B-G. this granting of the Mirmidons takes place very much later, after several battles have been fought, after the death of Palamides, during a period of great discouragement of the Greeks, and because of the great urging of Aga-

menon. (B. 20,396; O 5 r 25) (see § 149). M. unquestionably loses much dramatic effect by introducing this episode so early and during a period of Greek success.

133. 1) Both Greeks (15,905) and Trojans (15,926) now arrange their forces for battle. Priam exhorts the latter to take revenge for Hector. Paris relates a curious dream he has had which gives him great anxiety, lest misfortune come (15,943—82):- „Ung nouveau serpent | Qui estoit nomme quoquadrille" followed by over a thousand serpents „a la queue" came boldly toward the city. The „dragon" and the „griffon" had been compelled to yield the leadership to this „quoquadrille," „dont le lyon a grant ennuye." An „autour" went to fight the „quoquadrille", but the serpent vanquished him and was about to drink up his blood, when an „espervier" came to the rescue of the „autour". The „espervier" killed the „quoquadrille" with his beak, and put the other serpents to flight. — Contrary to M's usual custom this dream is not interpreted, although its application to subsequent events is very clear. — Deyphebus (15,983—98) speaks of their great loss in Hector, (15,989):-

Car c'estoit la seulle baniere
Et l'estandart pour nous deffendre.

2) Priam again exhorts to valor and the fight begins. Priam enters the fray himself and, at its very outset, kills two Greeks (16,007 d. and 16,015 d.) in revenge for Hector. This is in so far a deviation from B-G. in that Priam's active participation in the fight (the eleventh in B.) takes place *before* the anniversary of Hector's death and not *after*, as here (B. 17,001—304; N 3 v 30 — N 4 v 24; see beginning of § 124). Moreover in B-G. the chief exploit of Priam is a valiant attack upon Palamedes (17,092—121; N 4 r 9—17). This attack occurs in M. also, but M. has ingeniously reserved it until later, after Palamides has wounded Deiphebus mortally. M., therefore, gives this attack double importance, first, as Priam's vengeance for Hector's death, as in B-G., and secondly as revenge for the mortal wounding of Deyphebus by Palamides (see § 136).

134. Next follows in M. the combat of Troylus and Diomedes. For this, M. reached ahead to the fifteenth battle of B-G. (20,057—110; O 4 v 10—22) long after the deaths of

Palamides and Deyphebus. M's version offers several opportunities for comment:-

1) The taunt of Briseida's infidelity by Troylus occurs in his challenge *before* blows are struck. In B-G. it occurs *after* Diomedes has fallen. This taunt in B. is a far greater slander of Briseida's character than in M. especially the lines B. 20,083—94. G. omits all details, saying only (O 4 v 18):- „Troylus autem tunc amorem bryseide dyomedi in opprobriosis verbis improperat", which very general words served as the basis of the taunt in M. 16,024—30.

2) In M. Diomedes reproves Troylus for this insult (16,040—5). B-G. contain no such censure.

3) In B. Diomedes strikes no blow. In G-M, he does:-

O 4 v 14 „Dyomedes autem in troylum lanceam suam fregit non tamen offendit eum aliqua lesione" M. 16,047 d „alors diomedes le frappe tellement qu'il le fait ancliner a terre".

4) G-M. further agree in that Diomedes is felled to the earth. O 4 v 18; M. 16,071 d.

5) In M. Palamides, who, in B-G., is already dead and buried, now bids that Diomedes be carried to his tent (16,073).

135. M. next introduces the combat of Deyphebus and Palamides, taken from the twelfth battle in B-G. (18,650—76; N 8 v 14—25). M's only additions consist in the exchange of challenges:-

1) G. and M. agree in their description of the wound of Deyphebus:-

B. says only vaguely (18,661.) „parmi la forcele". G. (N 8 v 18.) „lanceam suam in deyphebi pectus immisit et lancea ipsa fracta truncus cum ferro in deyphebi pectore remansit affixus". M. 16,103 d. „et doit le fer du baton palamides qui se rompera au bout demourer au coste de deiphebus empres son cueur".

2) Regarding the carrying of Deyphebus to Troy, we note a contradiction in B:- He says first (18,667):-

Paris li biaus l'en a porte
O tot le trois en la cite.

Yet later, *after* the death of Deyphebus we read (18,997):-

Del cors li ont le trois oste,
Puis l'en portent a la cite.

G. shows no such contradiction. Deiphebus is carried at once to Troy after he is wounded (N 8 v 25). In M. this is slightly varied:- We read that Deyphebus is (16,222) „en la prairye" and is carried *after* his death to the city (16,260).

3) It would seem, therefore, that M., in thus postponing the carrying of Deyphebus to Troy until *after* his death, had been inspired by the above lines in B. (18,997), but this view is untenable because two lines earlier, 18,995, B. says that Deyphebus dies *before* the lance is removed from his body, whereas G. and M. agree in saying that he dies *after* and *in consequence of* the extraction of the lance (16,257 d; O 2 r 28; see end of § 138).

136. M. now introduces a scene which does not occur in this connection in B-G:- Priam, mad with grief at the mortal wounding of Deyphebus, goes forth to attack Palamides. He challenges the latter (16,132—9), but Palamides says that he is unwilling to fight because of Priam's great age, and bids him return „a l'ostel". Palamides, however finally accepts the repeated challenge of Priam, who, thereupon, strikes him to earth (16,171 d), after which the general battle continues. In B-G. this combat of Palamides and Priam occurs in the eleventh battle (17,092—121; N 4 r 9—17). We have already commented on M's introduction of this episode here (see § 133²).

137. Returning now to the normal flow of events in B-G., M. introduces Deyphebus' appeal to Paris to avenge him (16,172—87). The same ideas are found in the appeal in all three versions. In M. alone does Paris reply (16,188), after which he bids Herion to give him his bow and arrow and to follow him. Paris immediately challenges Palamides (16,209). In B-G. he has a long search for Palamides and finds him at last just as Palamides has killed Sarpedon (B. 18,800; O 1 r 8). M's thus omitting the death of Sarpedon, explains the continued appearance of Serpedon in the drama (17,093; 17,100; 17,378; 17,492; 24,581). The last words of Paris' challenge in M. are very commonplace:- (16,240) „Jamais ne mengerez char boulue ne rostie." (!) M. omits to state where Paris wounds Palamides; B-G. say: in the neck (18,820; O 1 r 15). G. says that the arrow was poisoned (O 1 r 15) (compare P 3 v 13. § 170³).

In B-G. there is a very long fight after the death of Palamides (18,822—959; O 1 r 16 — O 2 r 20):- The Greeks are driven to their camp. Their ships are set on fire and many are destroyed. The valor of Thelamonius Ajax alone saves the rest. The Greek camp is plundered, and night alone puts an end to the fight.[1]) M. summarizes this fight in the stage-direction (16,240 d.) „lesquelz les troyans chassent en les tuant et les chassent iusques en leurs tentes lequelz sont contraincts d'entrer dedans".

138. Paris then returns to Deyphebus and tells him that he has had vengeance, not saying, however, of what nature. As Deyphebus had asked for vengeance on (16,181) the „prince des gregois", he here assumes that Paris has avenged him in the desired way. Deiphebus now asks Paris to remove the iron point of the lance from his body, and leaves a farewell for Hecuba and the „barons". Paris removes the iron and Deiphebus expires (16,257 d). This agrees completely with G., where Deiphebus asks (O 2 r 28.) „ab eius vulnere truncum avelli, *quo avulso* illico deyphebus expiravit." — B's reading is quite different:- Deyphebus there also asks that the lance be removed (18,985), but he expires *before* it is actually extracted:- (18,995.)

Clos a les ielz, morz est entr'els, Del cors li ont le trois oste,
Adonc comença li granz dels Puis l'en portent a la cite.

In M. Paris now orders that Deiphebus be carried to Troy (16,258) We have already examined the coincidence of this last with B. (see § 135³.)

Chapter XVII.

Achilles urges Abandonment of the Siege. — Re-election of Agamenon. — Preparations for Battle. — The Sixth Battle. — Death of Troylus. Truce.

M. 16,263—17,493 („disner" third day).

As M. selects these scenes quite at random from B-G., the references to the latter are given in connection with each paragraph.

139. Ajax Thelamonius announces the death of Palamides, and suggests that two princes be sent to bring the news to

[1]) In this fight we note the curious displacement by G. of an episode in B. G. introduces here the incident of the death of Heber in the tent of Achilles

Achilles and to summon him to a new election. They must choose someone to Achilles' liking, in order to gain his support. — Nestor proposes his son Archilogus, and Agamenon offers to accompany him to Achilles. The two go thither, and Agamenon tells Achilles of the loss of Palamides, and asks him to come to a council of the Greek princes. Achilles agrees, but gives expression to the displeasure he had at the election of Palamides (16,338—42; see § 132[1]). Achilles is particularly desirous to go to the council,

> „Car i'ay fain de tel chose dire,
> Present toute leur assamblee,
> Qu'il gardera aucun de rire."

This short embassy to Achilles is wholly original to M., unless the sending of Agamenon was suggested to him by his presence in a much later embassy in B-G. (20,347—406; O 5 r 17—26), which embassy has, however, its equivalent in M. later (see § 147). The introduction of Archilogus, here and in the previous case (§ 132[1]), may be due to a desire on M's part to depict an especial friendship between Achilles and Archilogus, and prepare us for their death together (see §§ 160; 161).

140. 1) The next scene is the council (16,351—614). The first part of it (to 16,526) is taken up with an attempt by Achilles to urge the Greek to give up the siege. In B-G. this attempt took place immediately after Achilles' negociations for the hand of Polixene, seemingly its more logical position. M. preferred to reserve it until the Greeks are particularly discouraged by the loss of Palamides (see § 130). The passages in B-G. are 18,122—454; N 7 v 4 — N 8 r 9. In B-G. Achilles is mainly opposed by Thoas and Menesteus. In M. this opposition is voiced by Nestor (16,407), Ajax (16,447) and Menelaus (16,495). In the use of Nestor's name, and in other minor points, we see that M. has also been influenced in this scene by the relation in B-G. of one of the embassies to Achilles to urge his return (B. 19,395—799; O 2 v 30 — O 3 v 22). A comparison of this passage in M. with both the above-mentioned

---

(O 1 v 16 — O 2 r 16). In B. this episode comes much later, in the 13th battle (19,184—260). Could this displacement by G. have been peculiar to the manuscript of B. which he used?

places in B-G. yields little, for the ideas are essentially the same in all.

2) In B. a violent and sarcastic altercation takes place between Achilles and Diomedes (19,703—65):- Diomedes taunts Achilles with cowardice, and the latter replies with insinuating remarks about Thideus, the father of Diomedes. G. omits this completely, and, therefore, it is not found in M. — Particularly noticeable in this scene of M. is the legal nature of the dialogue. The scene resembles nothing so much as an advocates' skirmish. At its close, having failed to persuade the Greeks, Achilles goes away in wrath, and threatens to return home within a month (16,524), M. follows B-G. closely in this.

3) The rest of this council-scene is taken up with the re-election of Agamenon (16,527—614) at the suggestion of Ulixes (16,566) and Thoas (16,568). In this part of the scene M. has again returned to the main stream of his source, where the re-election of Agamenon takes place soon after Palamides' death (B. 19,037—95; O 2 v 8—10). In B-G. it is Nestor who suggests the re-election (19,057; O 2 v 8). — Agamenon accepts after some urging, and then bids all to withdraw. We are told that eight years have now elapsed (16,614).

141. 1) Briseida now visits the wounded Diomedes and gives him her sympathy and offers of service. Diomedes is very grateful and vows that he will have vengeance in the next fight. She gently bids him, however, to think only of getting well, and soon departs. This scene (16,615—54) is quite pleasing, particularly in the contrasting of the characters of Briseida and Diomedes. The episode is inspired from B-G. (20,194—217; O 5 r 6—17.)

2) B. has a subsequent long monologue by Briseida (20,218—330), in which she reproaches herself for her unfaithfulness to Troillus. G. and M. have no trace of such self-condemnation.

3) Still another link connects M. with G. in this scene:-

G. says (O 5 r 11). „de se (= Briseida) iungenda cum troylo nullam sibi superesse fiduciam“, which is echoed by M. (16,620):-

Car ie scay que ie ne pourroye
A touisours mais plus veoir celuy,
Qu'autreffoiz tant aymer souloye.

This thought is not expressed in B.

142. 1) The Trojan side again occupies our attention:- Eurupius brings before Priam the body of Deiphebus. Priam and Hecuba mourn (16,658—81). The materials for this very short scene (16,655—705.) are in B-G. (B. 18,999—19,017 and 19,386—94; O 2 r 28 — O 2 v 3).

2) In B. Priam's grief is so intense (19,004):-

Que pasmez s'est L. feiz.

G. and M. have no mention of such intense grief. In fact, in M. Priam's sorrow does not seem excessive, for he soon says in apparent haste and indifference (16,698):-

Or ca faictes sa sepulture,
Et si le portez enterrer.

This is in curious contrast to the long-drawn-out laments for Hector and Troylus, and is probably due to the brevity of G. who excuses himself from relating at length the mourning for Deyphebus (O 2 r 30) „cum sit enarrare superfluum."

3) M. shows a slight originality in introducing a prophecy by Cassandra (16,682—97); she predicts a like fate for all.

4) Another point of agreement between M. and G. is the mention of the burial in the same passage with this mourning for Deyphebus. In B. a long chapter (19,018—385) lies between, containing the re-election of Agamenon and the events of the thirteenth battle.

143. M. now inserts a pleasing love-scene between Helen and Paris (16,706—863). It is wholly of M's invention:- Paris bids Helen not to grieve as she does, for he loves her dearly and suffers much. Rather curious are the words (16,726):-

Car ie vous ayme sans fausser
Plus que toutes apres ma mere.

(see § 101). Helen reiterates her remorse that the Trojans suffer such hardships because of her. She voices an idea which does not elsewhere find expression in M. and which finds none at all in B-G (16,776):-

Ie voy voz seurs qui se guermentent,
En disant que tout est par moy.

also (16,800):-

Ore i'en ay beaucoup souffert
Et des langaiges moult divers
Dont voz seurs, ainsi qu'il appert,
M'en ont dit maint mot de travers.

In M. Cassandra is the only one who blames Helen, but in no case in her presence (§ 172).

Paris bids her not to mind this criticism of his sisters. The war will soon be over. He then binds her to secrecy, and tells her of the agreement to give Polixene in marriage to Achilles and of the latter's promise to cause the return of the Greeks, by not taking part with them in battle. Paris now kisses Helen good-bye and goes to suggest battle to Priam. Helen's last words are (16,858):-

Mon doulx amy, ie vous mercye ; Au departir de voz deux yeulx,
De ce baiser vauldray ie mieulx; En engoisse mon cueur lermoye.

144. Original to M. is also the following scene:- Troillus asks Priam to command the Trojans to arm. He (Troillus) will lead them, for a dream has shown him that he will kill great numbers of his enemies that day. He then relates the dream (16,888—903):- He had dreamt that he was a fox and searched for his prey in the fields. There he found „bien cent mille coqs et gelines", which he put to flight and of which he killed a vast number (16,900):-

Mais m'esmerveille moult fort, Il me sembla, feust droit ou tort,
Car ainsi comme retournoye, Que la queue laissee avoye.

Will Priam allow him to lead the Trojans to battle? Helenus interrupts his brother and declares that, if Troylus goes forth, he will never return alive. Helenus, therefore, reminding Priam that he had correctly interpreted „le langaige d'andromache" (16,932), urges his father not to allow Troylus to depart. Troylus scorns the warning of Helenus. The latter repeats in refrain (16,944):-

Or bien, on verra la douleur,
Qui ennuyt nous en advendra.

Priam takes no notice of Helenus and bids Macabrum sound to arms. As the Trojans prepare, Troylus urges Paris to especial valor, and Paris warns Troylus not to be too rash, since the Greeks greatly desire his death. At Troylus' suggestion that they try to surprise the Greeks, the Trojans go forth „pas a pas" (17,001 d). Basaam, however, discovers their approach, and alarms the Greeks. Agamenon gives hurried orders for their defence and the Greeks join battle with the Trojans (17,022 d).

145. This sixth battle is characterized by the usual independence of M. in the choice of scenes, but it shows a slight innovation beyond the other battles:- Before the series of single combats begins, the general fight (17,022 d; 17,049 d; 17,067 d; 17,086 d; 17,100 d.) is continually interrupted to permit short side-scenes. — In the first of these (17,023—49), Diomedes orders his „senechal“ to bring his armor and to arm him. He is cured of his wound, and will now wreak his vengeance upon the knight who wounded him. This episode is quite original to M. In B. the first mention of Diomedes' return to the fight after his wound, is in the sixteenth battle (B. 20,538) but nothing is said of his being cured, or of his desire for revenge. In the corresponding place, G. (O 5 v 30) mentions Diomedes, and adds „qui tunc plena sanitate vigebat“, which, no doubt, suggested to M. the above episode. After Diomedes is armed, he enters the fight which „se renouvellera“ (17,049 d).

146. The second interruption of the general battle is made by Achilles who addresses his Mirmidons, urging them to valor in his absence. Basaac replies in their name, exhorting them to take vengeance for the death of Patroclus. They thereupon enter the battle (17,067 d). The basis for this short scene is from B-G. (20,415—40; O 5 r 26—31), immediately after Achilles has granted Agamenon permission to lead his Mirmidons to battle, although refusing to go himself. Several details of the scene in B-G are wanting in M., particularly Achilles' gift to each Mirimidon of „une porpre chiere vermeille“ (B. 20,416); „rubea insignea“ (O 5 r 30), and Achilles' great grief at their departure (B. 20,427; O 5 r 30). In B. Achilles' grief is because he cannot accompany them (29,425); in G. and, consequently, in M. there is no trace of this as the cause.

147. A third interruption of the battle is due (17,068) to Agamenon who declares that the Greeks must have the aid of Achilles against Troylus „qui met tous noz gens a l'espee“ (17,073). With Achilles they can prevail. Agamenon bids Menelaus to remain in the battle, but asks Nestor and Archilogus to go with him to Achilles. They accompany him. — The counterpart of this embassy to Achilles occurs in B-G., not during a battle, but in a truce between the 15th and the 16th battles (B. 20,347—352; O 5 r 17). B. says:-

Par la sentence et par l'esgart
Que chascons fait de soe part,
I ont Agamennon tramis,
(Sevent qu'il estoit ses amis — Mss. J.)
Nestor i meine ensemble o sei.

In G. Agamenon goes of his own free will. No hint is given of his being delegated to go:- „Rex vero Agamenon infra tempus induciarum ipsarum se contulit ad achillem in ducis nestoris comitiva“ (O 5 r 17). This is also the case in M. It is also noteworthy, that in M. Archilogus accompanies Agamenon and Nestor. This is another example (see §§ 132[1], 139, 160, for others) of M's evident desire to associate Archilogus as much as possible with Achilles before their final death-scene together (see § 161).

148. A fourth side-incident is in the verses 17,087—100:- Troylus declares his purpose to attack the Mirmidons who are greatly harassing the Trojans. Epistropus, Philimenis and Serpedon agree. Paris says he will remain to fight where he is. Thereupon Troylus attacks the Mirmidons. The suggestion for this scene came from B-G. (20,508—34; O 5 v 3, in 16th battle; 21,029; O 5 v 11, in 17th battle) where Troylus attacks the Mirmidons with especial fury.

149. The fifth interruption of the general battle is to allow the dialogue of the embassy mentioned above (§ 147) with Achilles (17,101—48), The corresponding places in B-G. are 20,331—404; O 5 r 17—26. Comparison yields but little. In M. Archilogus has his share in the dialogue, and uses sharper language than the others. M. probably intended that he should, because of his youth (17,119):-

Avez en vous peu de prouesse,
Ou vous estez fort deffaillant.

Nestor also uses threatening language (17,137—40), but Achilles still refuses to come, and they go away. In B-G. it is during this embassy that Achilles, out of his special love for Agamenon, finally grants the help of his Mirmidons. We have already noted M's earlier use of this incident (§ 132 end).

150. There now follows the first single combat of this battle, that between Basaam and Troillus (17,149—72). This is the invention of M., except in so far as it is part of the general attack of Troylus against the Mirmidons (see § 148):-

Basaam[1]) strikes Troylus (17,161) a blow which the latter returns (17,172 d). Basaac[1]), mortally wounded (17,179—188), appeals to Achilles for help, and the latter hesitates no longer, but, abandoning his promise to abstain from battle, enters the fight to help his men. This is far less dramatic than B-G.:- There, in the eighteenth battle (21,038; O 7 r 4), the Greeks have been completely routed and driven headlong to their camp. The tumult of the flight penetrates even to Achilles in his tent. Many shout out to him his danger and the great losses of his men. In B. Achilles is so agitated (21,050) „Qu'il n'en a sens ne remembrance." B. makes no mention of the thought of his love for Polixene entering Achilles' mind at this critical moment. Achilles simply forgets everything, obeying blindly the impulse to succor his men. B. is, thus, far more dramatically true. In G., however, it is implied that Polixene entered Achilles' thoughts, in the words (O 7 r 20) „amore polixene postposito". M. is even more explicit. Achilles says:-

17,194 Car pour amy ne pour amye
Ie ne pourroye endurer, etc.
and 17,201 Iamais ie ne vueil requerir
D'oresenavant d'avoir amye.

151. 1) In B-G. Achilles, once in the fight, makes a fearful onslaught on the Trojans (21,073—117; O 7 r 21—6). Troylus rushes at him and, in the combat, Achilles is severely wounded (B. 21,149; O 7 r 29) and thereby disabled for many days. The fight lasts a week (B. 21,171; O 7 v 5) and it is not until the next great battle (the 19th) that Achilles finally has his vengeance by killing Troylus (21,416; O 8 r 22). M., however, passes completely over all this intermediate fighting, and connects Achilles' vengeance directly with his being wounded by Troylus:- Achilles first receives a blow from Paris (an idea original to M.), and is about to return it, when Troylus prevents (17,237—41)

---

[1]) This passage seems to prove conclusively that Basaac and Basaam are one and the same person. He is wounded as Basaam (17,179) and as Basaac appeals to Achilles. The same differences of spelling exist in all the editions and under the same circumstances as above, i. e. Basaam is wounded and Basaac makes the appeal. That they cannot be two distinct personages seems proved by the extreme probability that the appeal for aid is due to the fact of the wounding.

by wounding Achilles. Achilles thereupon immediately orders the Mirmidons to surround Troylus (17,253). Miselet promises in their name. The battle continues. The Mirmidons surround Troylus, and Miselet summons Achilles. The latter comes and cuts off the head of Troylus (17,274 d). This is essentially the same as in B-G., although the exploits of Troylus are there described at greater length (21,306—417; O 7 v 28 – O 8 r 26).

2) We now come to an interesting point:- In all the battles of M. there are no horses (see § 81⁴). The limitations of the stage probably forbade their use in fight. Here, however, M. is constrained to introduce one, in order to faithfully reproduce from B-G. the outrageous treatment of Troylus' body by Achilles:- Before Achilles had killed Troylus, he bids Miselet (17,272):-

Et faites tantost qu'on m'apreste
Ung cheval, si le traineray.

In B-G. Achilles himself binds the body of Troylus to the tail of the horse (B. 21,421; O 8 r 24); in M. he commands that it be done (17,275):- „Lye le a la queue du cheval" (17,279 d) „Lors le lieront a la queue du cheval et achilles montera dessus et le traynera." G. follows up his relation of this outrage with a curious condemnation of Homer for the latter's praise of Achilles who killed Hector and Troylus only through treachery (O 8 r 26 — O 8 v 22). This conception of Achilles' action as treachery finds frequent subsequent expression in M.

152. 1) In all three versions Menon, (in the Copinger-Hain No. 5507 edition of G., Merion), upbraids Achilles for this outrage and wounds him severely:- M. and G. show uniformity in that Menon calls Achilles a traitor:- O 8 v 30 „proditor".

17,280 Traictre, tu as traicteusement
Acomply deux foiz traïson.

B. uses only such words as „fel" and „cuverz" (21,450–2).

2) In B-G. Achilles is so severely wounded that he retires temporarily from battle; he then returns and again attacks Menon (21,509; P 1 r 13). They are, however, separated, and it is not until several days later (eight in B. 21,515; seven in G. P 1 r 17) that Achilles finally kills Menon (21,553:- P 1 r 31). M., again, as in the case of Troylus (see § 151¹) omits these

intermediate events and joins directly Menon's death to his first and only wounding of Achilles.

3) In B. Achilles bids his men (B. 21,525):-

> Qu'il gardent qu'il (= Menon) seit entrepris,
> Et que pas n'en estorte vis.

and the Mirmidons obey him (21,549):-

> Mirmidoneis s'esvertuerent,
> Tant i ferirent et chaplerent,
> Qu'as Perseis tolent lor seignor.

The idea of surrounding Menon is not, therefore, clearly expressed, although it may exist as a secondary meaning of „entreprendre" (see Godefroy). In G. it is distinctly stated:- (P 1 r 22). „circumcludant" and (P 1 r 27) „ipsum ex omni parte circumdant". G. probably wished to make this scene like the preceding one of the death of Troylus. M. follows him in this:-

> (17,297). Faictez tantost ycy endroit,
> Que le roy menon[1]) soit enclos.
> and (17,321 d) „Lors les mirmidonnes environneront Menones"[1])

Before Menon is surrounded and killed, M. inserts his attack upon Archilogus whose rescue is urged by Achilles (17,306—17). In B-G. after the death of Menon, the Trojans flee to the city gates, where a great struggle takes place. In M. the battle ends abruptly with the death of Menon.

153. The removal of the bodies of Troylus and Menon to Troy, and the asking of truce by the Trojans offer occasion for several remarks:-

1) In M. Paris at once orders that the bodies of Troylus and Menon be taken to Troy. In B. Menon's body was so hacked to pieces (21,565) by Achilles, that it was left on the battle-field (21,746), and the pieces have to be gathered together during the truce (21,771—3). In G. these details are lacking. It is only said that Achilles kills Menon „innumerabilibus vulneribus" (P 1 r 31), followed later by the record of Menon's burial. Thus, there was nothing to prevent M's saying that both bodies were taken to Troy at the same time (17,333).

---

[1]) These two quotations would seem to prove, as Meybrinck (P. 15.) presumed, that Menon and Menones are one and the same person.

2) B. says that Troylus' body was recovered only after great difficulty (B. 21,480) „Par grant proesse et par esforz." G. and M. have no hint of this.

3) In B-G. Priam learns at once of the deaths of Troylus and Menon (21,660; P 1 v 15), and he himself sends ambassadors to negociate a truce (21,757; P 1 v 24). In M., on the other hand, Paris counsels that truce be made and that it be kept secret from Priam „iusques apres disner" (17,345), because, if Priam should learn of this new loss, he might not consent to the truce, but prefer to continue the fight in person. This advice is approved, whereupon Paris appoints Philimenis and Enee to negociate the truce. In the reply of Philimenis we have a second mention by M. of the burning of the dead (17,407):-

— nous voulons triefves avoir,
Pour mettre tous noz mors en cendre.

The first mention is 8788:- De lamenter le trespassé | Et ardoir en feu alumé.

We cannot share with Meybrinck (P. 63—64) the view that Milet has emphasized the cremation of the dead more than his predecessors, for, judging by the fact that there are only two mentions of it in M., we think just the reverse.

4) Paris had bidden Enee to ask for a truce of one month, but Enee states no time-limit as he negociates the truce. Enee bids Astanius to accompany him to the Greek camp, and Astanius again grieves that he is too young to fight in vengeance for all the Trojan sorrow (17,417). After the return of Enee, Paris commands all to rest and recover strength. The Trojan princes take leave of him, and there follows a „pause pour disner" (17,493 d).

Chapter XVIII.

Mourning for Troylus. — Plot to kill Achilles. — Death of Achilles.

M. 17,494—18,571. B. 21,653—22,308. G. P 1 v 15 — P 2 v 5.

---

154. 1) Before M. again makes a direct use of his source, he inserts several scenes of very mediocre merit, the material of which is of far too general a nature to be compared with the earlier versions:- Paris mourns Troillus in the presence of Helen. The body of his brother is there (17,503). He dares not tell his father (17,523). Now is Troillus dead, the second Hector, (17,518), and he alone remains of the sons (17,526). — This disregard of Helenus reminds us of similar neglect in other parts of the drama (see Index), and we shall note it again. Was it because Helenus was a priest, and unable, therefore, to succeed his father? — Paris asks counsel of Helen. Every one will now blame him as the cause of all this calamity. Helen (17,542) declares that she, and not Paris, is the real cause, and counsels that Troylus be shown to Priam; otherwise Priam's grief will only be the sharper. Paris, thereupon, bids Erupius, Cloantus, and Adrastus to take the body of Troylus before Priam. As they do so, they meet Cassandra who speaks a long monologue of mourning (17,605—88.), censuring Paris sharply. She, too, calls Troylus „le second Hector" (17,630) and compares the three dead brothers to three roses (17,653 ff.). Her words are wearisomely redundant. At their close she faints (17,688 d).

2) We have already noted how the keeping secret of the death of Troylus is at variance with B-G. (§ 153³.) The appearance of Cassandra loses all originality, because M. has had her appear in like manner at the bringing to Troy of Hector (§ 118¹) and of Deyphebus (§ 142).

155. The body of Troylus is borne before Priam. In his lamentation he, too, blames Paris severely (17,693). He orders his arms and armor to be brought at once, for he wishes to sally forth and take immediate vengeance on Achilles. Paris (17,728) restrains his father by saying that there is a truce, whereupon Priam desists and speaks to Hecuba, pointing out how Troylus has been dragged (17,747). Surely she was ill advised to place confidence in the word of Achilles. It is fortunate that Polixene has not yet been given to him. Hecuba (17,760) is enraged at the treachery of Achilles, and vows that she will find a way to vengeance. She mourns Troylus greatly, declaring that she has almost lost faith in the gods. Finally, Priam, saying that nothing can now be done except to bury

Troylus, gives orders that the body be taken to the temple of Venus (17,821). B-G. do not state where Troylus was buried (21,780—98; P 1 v 25).

156. M. now again comes into more direct contact with his source:- Hecuba in a long speech (17,826—945), outlines a plan for taking vengeance by decoying Achilles to Troy and killing him. She reminds Paris of the successive treacheries of Achilles, which make it entirely justifiable to pay him in his own coin Hecuba's speech requires examination:-

1) Although Hecuba thinks that Achilles' treachery deserves a like payment, she bids Paris to act secretly, lest Priam should know:- (17,938.)

Car le bon roy est si courtois
Et plain de si noble couraige,
Qu'il vouldroit mieulx mourir ainçois,
Que trahyr aultruy par langaige.

Si empescheroit cest ouvraige
Si'l le povoit avant savoir,
Car se luy sembleroit oultraige
D'achilles ainsi decepvoir.

Paris voices the same idea in a later speech (18,167):-

D'autre coste, se priam le savoit,
Ie sais de vray que point ne le vouldroit,
Car il craint trop d'aler contre raison.

This emphasis upon keeping the matter secret is not in B. It was probably suggested to M. by G. (P 2 r 1) „demum accersito ad se paride *secreto* etc."

2) Moreover, M. found in G. no hint that Priam would be displeased or attempt to prevent the assassination of Achilles. This tribute to Priam's character is, therefore, wholly original to M. In B. the idea is rather the reverse. Hecuba appeals to Paris:- B. 21,829 Done a m'ame confortement,
Et a ton chier pere ensement.

3) A striking coincidence between G. and M. is Hecuba's justification[1]) of the proposed treachery, in view of Achilles' many treacheries. B. has no such justification:- (P 2 r 5—8) propter quod dignum esset et *iustum* quod sicut ipse (= achilles) *proditorie* orbat parentes interficiendo filios alienos sic et ipse *proditorie* interfectus penam similem patiatur. M. 17,836:-

Si le serviroy de tel mes,
Qu'il ma servic et saluee,
Car puisqu'il a sa foy faulcee,

Et commis telle traison,
Sa mort doit estre pourchassee
Traicteusement selon raison.

[1]) Compare also Priam's justifying himself in the attempt to assassinate Anthenor and Eneas (§ 194[3]).

G. probably found a hint for his words in Benoît's own observation (B. 21,812):-

Nus hom ne s'en deit merveiller
Ni a grant mal n'a blasme torner.

(see, however, the foot-note to the next paragraph.)

157. The attitude of Paris to his mother's proposition merits careful examination:- In G. there is no intimation of opposition on the part of Paris:- (P 2 r 15) „quod (= Hecuba's request) paris pias matris motus ad lacrimas matri similiter lacrimendo devote concessit“[1]).

In B. and M., on the other hand, Paris hesitates before agreeing to his mother's plans (B. 21,895—910; M. 17,946—77), and one is tempted to see, in this coincidence, B's influence upon M. An examination of the two passages, however, reveals important differences:- In B., Paris hesitates between obedience to his mother and fear for *his own* honor (B. 21,900):-

Bien sai que vos dei obeïr,
Mes ci a molt grant mesprison,
Puisque il torne a traison;
Si a honte cil qui la fait;
Trop m e sera en mal retrait,
Abessier en criem m o n v a l e i r.

There is, thus, no mention of Priam. In M. the alternatives are disobedience to his mother and fear of displeasing his father. This latter alternative is stated first 17,946:-

Madame et ma tres doulce mere,
Certes bien envis ie feroye
Chose, qui despleust a mon pere
Et tres envis le courseroye.

and is, beyond doubt, suggested by the words Hecuba herself has just spoken (17,938—45; quoted in § 156[1]). In M. Paris says nothing of his own honor. He only declares (17,962—6) that he would prefer another method, a thought also contained in

---

[1]) This omission by Guido leads us to suspect that he had before him, as source, a Benoît Manuscript, of the group to which Manuscript G. (Joly P. 157) belongs. Joly says, in the „variantes“ to verse 21,895 where B. speaks of the opposition of Paris. „G. supprime mal à propos la résistance de Paris“. Another indication that the group represented by Manuscript G. is the source of Guido is that M. Joly says, as a note to B. 21,812:- „Nus hom ne s'en deit merveiller | Ni a grant mal n'a blasme torner.“ „G. paraphrase longuement cette pensée mauvaise“ Hence Guido's similar interpretation (see § 156[3]). Yet the variation to Benoît 21,932, would seem to render doubtful the idea that Guido used manuscript G. i t s e l f:- Mss. G. reads that the message summoning Achilles is given in P o l i x e n e ' s name, not, as in other Mss. of B. and in G-M., in H e c u b a ' s name.

Hecuba's words. Paris even agrees with his mother that, in this case, treachery is justifiable, and, indeed, (17,960) „sans nul blasme de faulcete", an idea which, also, is simply an echo of Hecuba's expression of the same thought (17,836—41; quoted in § 156³). This is, however, wholly at variance with B., where Paris remains convinced of the dishonor of the affair, but yet agrees to endure this dishonor for his mother's sake.

The coincidence between M. and B. is, therefore, reduced to the simple fact that Paris hesitates, and we believe that this hesitation is readily explained from the context of M. alone. In M. the only reason of Paris' hesitation is because Hecuba has just told him that Priam would be displeased.

158. 1) The arranging of the plot to entrap Achilles is much alike in all versions, except that M. substitutes the temple of Venus (18,015; 18,188; 18,332) for the temple of Apollo in B-G. Later, however, (25,973) M. forgets this and says that Achilles was killed in Apollo's temple (§ 213³). B. alone reminds us that Hector was buried there (22,049). The references to the temple as Apollo's in B-G. are 21,881; 21,941; 22,046; 22,118; P 2 r 21; P 2 r 29.

2) M. forms a scene out of the arranging of the plot by Paris. The latter explains and justifies the proposed affair to Amphorbius, Enee and Polidamas (18,026—169), closing with the words (after 18,085) „quia illis non est servanda fides qui fidem non servaverunt". This is not, as might be supposed from previous cases, a quotation from Guido. At least we have failed to find it in the G. prints accessible to us.

3) An interesting passage, which has no equivalent in B. or G., is found in the words of Paris (18,094):-

Car la commune renommee
Dit qu'il (Achilles) ne peult estre pugny,
Si'l n'a le pie percie par my
D'une sagette envenimee.

Also a few verses beyond (18,107):-
Et ie (= Paris) trairay de deux costez
Tant que i'auray mes trais bouttez
En ses piez aupres des talons.

Two later mentions of this vulnerability of Achilles occur, the first in the Latin epitaph of his tomb (§ 168³; 19,504) the second in Paris' words (19,783; § 170³). Yet, strange to say, nothing is said of it, when Paris actually strikes down Achilles (18,371 d; § 161).

4) In B-G. there are twenty in the party that is to attack Achilles (22,042; P 2 r 17). M. only speaks of „neuf ou dix“ (18,149). B. alone has the division of these men into four groups which shall attack Achilles from four sides at once (22,051—4). G. and M. know nothing of such an arrangement.

159. The sending of the messenger to Achilles now follows. In G. the message is not related at length. Indeed, G. shows a desire to epitomize most briefly the entire episode of Achilles' death. The words of the messenger in B. and M. (B. 21,932—70; M. 18,170—92.) have only the most general resemblance. Only in B. is it said that Achilles shall come by night. The messenger bids him do so (21,938) „Ainz que la lune seit levee“, and Achilles promise to come (21,992) „— einz que l'aube se respande“ :-

(21,993) — kar ne voil pas Que ceste chose seit seue
A ious n'a certes ne a gas, Ne par nul home aparceu.

Despite all this, Benoît represents him as going *after* moonrise (22,101—6). Neither G. nor M. even say that it shall be after dark. B. is also the only one to mention the detail that the messenger finds Achilles just gone to bed (B. 21,929). In M. the last line of Achilles' reply to the messenger Machabrum :-

Et luy (= Polixene) porteray ung annel.

reminds us of the ring-episode in the marriage-scene of Paris and Helen (see § 46).

160. A little scene is now introduced by M. in which Archilogus takes leave of his father to go to see Achilles. Nestor bids his son to follow Achilles as an example of knightly conduct, and sends a greeting to him. Achilles welcomes Archilogus, saying that he was on the point of sending for him to accompany him to Troy. Both set out, Archilogus expressing great friendship for Achilles. Arriving at Troy, Achilles shows to his companion the strength and beauty of the city, declaring it would be a pity to destroy such, „pour une femme“ (18,321). Archilogus, ignorant of Achilles' compact with Priam, replies stoutly that Priam deserves to lose all for the crime of retaining Helen. They then enter the temple and are immediately attacked by Paris and his companions.

161. The death of Achilles and Archilogus is told very briefly by G. (P 2 r 21—30) but at much greater length in B.

(22,113—305) and in M. (18,336—571). The scene excites our interest for several reasons:-

1) In harmony with the plan in B. (see § 158[4]), Paris and companions attack Achilles from four sides at once (22,123—30); G-M. know nothing of this.

2) B. alone says that Achilles and Archilogus become anxious and fearful as they first enter the temple, but, nevertheless, push bravely on (B. 22,113—22).

3) The dialogue in M. becomes, during this scene, very spirited.

4) B. alone has the dramatic detail that, after Achilles and Archilogus have killed several Trojans, (22,161)

Des cors ont fait chastel et mur.

5) In G. no time-difference is expressed between the deaths of the two Greeks. B. and M. make one, but there the similarity ceases, for the details do not correspond at all:- In B. Archilogus, being the younger, is first overcome (B. 22,191), and Achilles finally dies defending to the last the body of his young companion. The version in B. is hence highly dramatic. M. loses all of this. Both are struck down at the same time (18,371 d). Achilles, however, dies first (18,479 d) and Archilogus makes a long farewell speech before expiring (18,525 d).

6) A resemblance of M. to B. is in the regret of Achilles that he is the cause of the death of Archilogus. (B. 22,195—7; M. 18,444—7). This is, however, merely a natural thought under the circumstances, and only G's brevity (P 2 r 21—30) prevented his giving expression to it.

7) Certain features peculiar to M. merit notice:- Paris allows Achilles a chance to say a last word (18,400—7) and Achilles makes use of the privilege (18,408—79).

8) In this last speech of Achilles he mourns his valor now laid low, he takes leave of Pelleus his father (18,441), but his final words are a message to his beloved Polixene:- After asking Paris to tell her that love of her has caused the death of himself and of Archilogus, he adds a last message of love to Polixene (18,456):-

Et luy dictes que ie luy prye
Qu'elle me vueille pardonner,
Si ie luy ay fait villenye
Ou tort de ses freres tuer,

Pour dieu, vueillez la saluer,
Et luy dictes que ses beaulx yeulx
Me font a grant regret finer,
Dont elle me doit aymer myeulx.
Certes ie prens en gre la mort,
Puisque c'est par ma loyaulte,
Et prens en mon cueur reconfort,
Quant ie pense a sa grant beaulte.
Son cueur aura grant cruaulte,
Si'l n'a pitie aulcunement
De veoir mourir par faulcete
Celuy qui l'ayme loyaulment.

9) Achilles then dies (18,479 d), whereupon Archilogus mourns his death, recounts all the misery caused by Paris (18,493—509), condemns the latter, utters a curse upon him (18,510—7), and says a farewell to Nestor, his father, with his last breath.

162. A striking point of contact of M. with G. now occurs. Paris says (18,526):-

Seigneurs prenez incontinent
Les corps d'eulx deux et les portez
Aux chiens pour estre devores.

Helen, however, suddenly appears (18,529) and begs Paris to moderate his wrath and to have pity for the dead,

— — — en faveur
De la terre ou ie feuz nourrie.

Paris yields to her entreaty; the bodies shall only be publicly exposed to rejoice the Trojan people. To this Helen agrees, and Paris bids the bodies be taken „enmy la place.“ The bodies are carried „devant priam et toute la ville“ (18,571 d). This scene is directly inspired from G. (P 2 r 30).

Paris vero corpus achilles [et antilogi] corvis et canibus exhiberi mandavit sed precibus et monitu helene a templo tamen appollinis eiecti sunt in plateam ut ab omnibus troyanis videre volentibus possent liquido intueri. gaudent itaque troyani de morte achillis.

B. says only (22,248):-

S'ai en l'escrit Daires trové
Que il (=Paris) les a toz detrenchiez,
(which is an idea not repeated in G-M.)
Issi a ses freres vengiez.
Fors del tenple les a gitez
Ainz qu'il parust del ior clartez.

In this scene it is the *appeal of Helen* which is the crucial point of contact between M. and G. The desire of Paris to throw the bodies to the dogs is expressed in Manuscript *J.* of Benoît: („Variantes“ to verses 22,293—4; P. 560 of Joly)

Mangier le volt faire as mastins,
As avoutours, as corbins,

(Manuscript J., therefore, belongs to the group of Benoît manuscripts, which served as Guido's source.)

We see readily whence G. took the idea of Helen's intervention:- B. says that, when Agamenon learns of the death of Achilles and Archilogus, he asks for the bodies (22,287) and that Paris wishes to refuse, (22,302):

Mes Helenus prist a retraire
Qu'il n'esteit pas reisons ne droiz etc.

G. substitutes Helen for Helenus, and M. follows G.

Chapter XIX.

Grief for Achilles and Archilogus. — Discouragement of the Greeks. Menelaus is sent for Pirrus. — Burial of Achilles.

M. 18,572—19,558. B. 22,257—22,528. G. P 2 v 5 — P 3 r 4.

---

163. 1) Githeus brings the news of the death of Achilles and Archilogus to Agamenon (18,572) before whom stand all the Greeks (18,577 d). Githeus says that the bodies (18,588):-

— gisent sur le pavement
Ou mylieu du marchie de troye.

This can only have been based upon G. „in plateam“ (P 2 v 1), for B. merely says (22,251):-

Fors del tenple les a gitez.

2) G. and, consequently, M. do not mention the grief of the „mesniee“ of Achilles and their starting for Troy to recover the body of their ruler, all of which is in B. (22,275—83).

3) Nor have G-M. the thought of B. that the sorrow of the Greeks would have been keener, had not Achilles met his death by treating treacherously with the Trojans (B. 22,271—4).

4) The grief of Nestor is expressed at length in M. (18,590—696). In G. only one line is devoted to it (P 2 v 7), and B. does not say much more (22,309—22). In M. Nestor's grief is mingled with reproaches of Menelaus (18,606—21) and he contrasts at some length the joyousness of his youth with his sorrow in old age. Agamenon tries to comfort him. — B. alone says (22,421—30) that Nestor sends Archilogus back home for burial.

164. There now follows in M. a long passage (18,697—937) wherein the Greeks express their discouragement and are only prevented from returning home by the warning of Calcas. This really is no other scene than that in B-G. (19,780—940; O 3 v 22 — O 4 r 26.) where it occurs after the death of Palamides and during the continued refusal of Achilles to re-enter the fight. M. preferred to reserve it for the period of greatest disaster to the Greeks, i. e. when they have lost Achilles completely and forever. B-G. also depict briefly the discouragement of the Greeks after the death of Achilles (B. 22,431—74; P 2 v 16 — 28), and M. took the chief feature of this later discouragement, namely, Agamenon's speech, and used it as a prelude to his own scene which, in other respects, is copied from the earlier passage in B-G., as we noted above. — M's scene is thus a union of the two passages in B-G. Its general tone, however, is so much like B-G. that comparison is of little use. Yet the following points suggested themselves:-

1) In G-M. Agamenon's speech raises the question to be discussed, namely, shall they return or remain? In B. Agamenon simply asks for counsel, without himself stating the alternatives. M. goes farther than G., making Agamenon a supporter of the policy to go home, although ready to defer to the will of the majority. We note in Agamenon's words (18,718) a contradiction:-

> Et certes ie croy que les troys (= Hector, Troylus and Achilles.)
> Les plus vaillans de tout le monde
> Y sont mors en moins de huit moys.

M. forgets that Hector had been dead a year (14,354) before Troylus was killed.

2) In G. it is Ulixes and Nestor who attack Menelaus (O 4 r 6). In B. Ulixes and Diomedes. In M. it is also Ulixes and Diomedes. We do not, however, think that B. here influenced M. In M. Ulixes and Diomedes are constantly associated, holding the same opinions in council, and going together on embassies in many cases where B-G. do not mention them. Moreover, we cannot exclude the possibility, that M. used a G. manuscript with Diomedes in place of Nestor (although Nestor is the reading of all the Guido prints). Or, assuming this last as improbable, M. may have omitted the Nestor he found in G. because

Nestor has just, (in the previous scene 18,606—21), voiced sharp complaint against Menelaus. M., therefore, desiring a substitute for Nestor, would most naturally select Ulixes' friend, Diomedes.

3) The forensic nature of the council is particularly shown in Ulixes' speech (18,810—57) and in the opening words of Menelaus' reply (18,866):-

Pour souldre voz arguemens
Et voz raisons adnichiller.

4) M's love for proverb and allegory crops out again in Menelaus' speech, where, as an illustration to prove the need of finishing their work by continuing the war, Menelaus speaks as follows:-

(18,874.)
En ung tonnel a plusieurs troux
Par lesquelz peult entrer le vent,
Et quant on les estouppe tous
Et qu'on en laisse ung seulement,
Le vent y entre plainement
Et y peult faire grant dommaige,
Ainsi qu'avant l'estouppement.

5) In all versions Calcas restores confidence by reminding the Greeks of the promises of the gods, and warning them not to disbelieve the same.

165. 1) After the reassuring speech of Calcas, Thoas talks in like strain and then speaks of arranging Achilles' tomb. He urges that they send to Priam:-

(18,942)
Et qu'on trouvast aucune voye,
Feust par argent ou aultrement,
Que nous feissions une monioye
Dedens la cite proprement
Et que achilles feust mis dedens,

in order that his name may be immortalized and that there be written on his tomb,

Comment il a eue victoire
De hector en guerre de droitture.

Menesteus and Ajax Thelamonius approve this counsel, whereupon Agamenon decides that the siege of Troy shall continue, until Helen is won, and meanwhile (18,979):-

Que nous alions priam requerre,
Qu'il nous vueille tant seulement
Donner quinze pies de sa terre.

2) Agamenon thereupon appoints Menesteus and Thoas as ambassadors to negociate with Priam (18,993).

(Ajax then speaks of sending for the son of Achilles. We reserve this for the next paragraph, wishing to speak here only of the location of Achilles' tomb.)

Although Agamenon has appointed Menesteus and Thoas, M. seems to have forgotten this fact, for, later (19,074—89), he lets Agamenon ask the Greeks to select some one, whereupon Ajax Thelamonius and Menesteus offer their services.

In the offer of Menesteus we note (19,109) the lines:-

Yrons nous deux, se c'est vostre plaisir,
Vers les troyans leur donner souvenance
Du fort hector, que achilles fist mourir
De qui le corps fut rendu sans faillir.
Au roy Priam, sans or et sans chevance.

This is the first of three passages in M., indicating M's forgetfulness of the mediaeval version and his leaning toward the antique (see §§ 167[2]; 224[7] for the others). In the mediaeval versions (B. 16,267—8; M 8 v 18—24; M. 13,319 d) the body of Hector is carried to Troy immediately after his death (§§ 117, 118[1]) and Achilles has nothing further to do with it.

M., therefore, in these three passages, contradicts himself, and shows his knowledge of the classic version, as told in the Iliad, Book XXIV, and in the Aeneid, Book II.

3) Menesteus and Thelamonius Ajax now receive instructions from Agamenon. In these the following verses attract our notice (19,122):-

Et aussi vous luy requerres,
Que aupres de la porte timbree
Soit enterre duc achilles.

When the messengers arrive before Priam, Menesteus speaks (19,264):-

Tu nous vueillez donner de terre
Dix pies plus n'en voulons requerre.
(compare with „quinze" quoted above in 18,981.)

Menesteus says further:- (19,275.)

Si te prions tres humblement,
Que tu donnez consentement,
Que au pres de la porte timbree
Soit le corps mis.

(19,283) Si seront les deux ennemys,
Les deux plus fors et plus hardis,
Qui ont dessoubz le firmament eu renommee,
En ung lieu enterrez et mys.

Priam at first refuses (19,312—26) but yields to the persuasion of Anchises. Menesteus again refers to the location of the tomb in (19,403):-

Et pour le lieu le plus propice,
Eslisons la porte timbree.

This curious idea of locating the tomb of Achilles within Troy is taken directly from G. (P 2 v 12):- „ibique achilli constituunt magni precii sepulturam rogantes regem priamum ut sepulturam achillis in civitate troye locari permittit qui in introitu porte tymbree sepulturam ipsam edificari concessit.“

B. has no trace of a location within Troy. Although he does not specify exactly where Achilles' monument is located, the verse (22,409):-

De Troie fu tot cler veue.

indicates that it was at a considerable distance from the city.

166. In the same council where the deliberations noted in the last two paragraphs occur, Ajax arises (18,994) and says:- Since Achilles is dead, he knows of something

(19,001.)
Qui vous doit bien a trestous plaire.
Vous savez que licommedes,
Qui est roy de tres grant puissance,
Gouverne le filz d'achilles,
Et le garde des son enffance.

Without this son of Achilles, they cannot take Troy. Let some one be selected to go fetch him. — Agamenon then appoints Menelaus to go. In the latter's acceptance of this mission, we first learn the name of Achilles' son:- (19,040)

C'est pirrus, qui est de ieune aage.

After a parting speech (19,155—210) in which Helen is blamed for all his troubles, Menelaus sets out:-

Vers licommedes et vers pirrus.

The arrival of Menelaus there forms the opening scene of the fourth day (see § 176).

This sending for Pirrus affords us a number of interesting points:-

1) In B-G. it takes place *after* the burial of Achilles, in M. *before*.

2) In B. the Greeks are so anxious and uncertain what to do after the death of Achilles, that they finally decide (B. 22,473):-

Qu'ore envoient prendre respons.
— — — — — — — —
Esleuz ont cels qui i allent,
Que il quident, qui plus i vaillent.
Gie ne truis pas escriz lor nons,
Mes ço lor distrent li respons,
Que il facent querre et cerchier,
Sans demorer et sans tardier,
Lo germe Achilles et son eir,
Car ço sachent enfin por veir,
Par lui iert fins de la bataille;
A ço ne puet pas aveir faille.
Issi en est la destinee,
Que par lui seit l'ovre achevee.

It is after this reply of the oracle has been told to the Greeks that Ajax interprets it by bidding them send to Licomedes. G. and, consequently, M. omit completely the sending to the oracle and all hint of its reply. In G-M., Ajax speaks of the son of Achilles, without any reference to an oracle (P 2 v 28; M. 18,994).

3) In M. we find no trace of a blood-relationship of Pirrus to Licomedes:- The only references to the mother of Pirrus are 20,675; 20,708; 21,494 (see § 176.) and in none of them is it said that she is the daughter of Licomedes. All these references imply that the mother still lives. The only other verse which might suggest the relationship of Pirrus to Licomedes, is that where Menelaus declares that Licomedes sends Pirrus,

(21,328) Sa norriture qui est belle et iolie.

The meaning of „norriture" (Littré) is „*ward*"; it can be stretched to include „child", but certainly not „grandchild". In B-G., however, Licomedes is the grandfather of Pirrus:-

B. 22,495:- Car il (= Licomedes) fait norrir un vallet,
Filz de sa fille, alques grandet.

G. (P 2 v 30) „avum". G. names the daughter later (S 8 v 10) Dyadamia. This last fact is another indication that Guido used a Benoît manuscript of the group to which Mss. *J.* belongs. Mss. *J.* also gives the name Deidamia (see Joly P. 561, variante to verse 23,705).

4) In B. we learn (22,501) that Pirrus,

Forme et ymaige et contenance
Sanz un sol point de messenblance
A, autel com sis pere aveit.
Qui oncques vit l'un, l'autre veit;
Ja ne dira que riens vivant
Puisse estre a altre si senblant.

See also B. 29,091—5; 29,277—9. This idea is not in G. nor in M. (see § 182² for the only references in M. to the appearance of Pirrus).

167. 1) We have already spoken in § 165 of the embassy to Priam regarding Achilles' tomb. Its only mission is in the interest of Achilles. There is no further mention of the body of Archilogus, and, as Achilles is buried in Troy (§ 168), nothing is said in M. of carrying his body to the Greek camp. In B-G., on the other hand, the embassy asks for and obtains *both* bodies which are carried to the Greek camp (B. 22,305—38; P 2 v 6—9). In G., therefore, the request for locating Achilles' tomb in Troy implies a second embassy (P 2 v 13).

2) In M. Menesteus says to Priam, in support of this request (19,251):-

Si te souveigne de l'accord
Qu'il (= Achilles) te fist pour ton reconfort.
Et comment par belle façon,
Hector ton filz
Te fut rendu par ton deport,
Pour toy donner ioye et confort.
Bonne eure requiert bon guerdon.

We have noticed (§ 165²) the inconsistency of these words with the mediaeval version of the fate of Hector's body. Another repetition of the same is found, later, in the words of Priam, just before his death (26,785; § 224⁷):.

Jadis fut hector, par luy (= Achilles) mort;
Par luy me fut le corps rendu.

G. shows a like contradiction in his epitaph of Hector (T 7 v).

168. 1) After Priam has granted permission to erect Achilles' tomb in Troy, Menesteus and Ajax Thelamonius leave his presence. The latter, in thanking Priam, declares that, if the city is taken:-

(19,413) Bien vous sera la courtoisie,
Que vous nous faictes, acquitee.

The two Greeks then meet Sentipus, and ask if he knows of a suitable workman. Sentipus recommends himself, saying that he made the tomb of Hector, and that he is always called upon to make the sepulchre, (19,427)

quant aucun de la noblesse | De troie fine par nature.

Menesteus thereupon commissions him to make Achilles' tomb and gives him a long description of the same (19,431—506).

2) For this description M. is not indebted to G., as the latter gives none (P 2 v 15):- „Ejus autem sepulture preciose formam et modum describere superfluum visum est.“ B. (22,343—421) gives a detailed account of the tomb, but it bears no resemblance at all to M's description:- In B. the main feature is a statue of which it is said that the makers (B. 22,366):-

— — — molt se penerent
Que Polixenain fust senblant.

This statue represented her as in great mourning and as holding in her arms a vase containing the ashes of Achilles (B. 22,393—22,400), Achilles having been so wounded that it was necessary to burn the body (B. 22,395). In M. no mention is made of cremation or of a statue of Polixene. M's tomb is in the shape of a table with twelve images, five on each side and one at each end. On one side, Jupiter, Juno, Saturn, Mercury, Venus; on the other, Pallas, Atlas „sur luy la terre figuree" (19,458), Diana, Vesta, Neptune. At one end of the tomb (19,472) Mars,

„Et a l'autre le dieu nouveau,
Hercules, le desmesuré."

Each has a sword in the hand „en faisant aide aux gregois." The Gothic nature of the architecture seems indicated in

19,451 Et en façon de couverture
Aura chascun son pavillon.

3) Around this table, the epitaph is to be engraved in two languages, (19,487) „Premierement en ton (= Sentipus) langaige." (no doubt Milet, loyal to the legend of the Trojan descent of the French nation, meant French by this). The French epitaph follows (19,489—95), and then the Latin epitaph (19,504):-

Hectoris cacides domitor clam incautus in armis
Occubui parides traiectus arundine plantas (see § 158³).

Greif (P. 67 § 80) and Meybrinck (P. 66) have said that this epitaph is taken directly from „Achilleïs" of Gualtherus ab insulis (edition Müldener I. 473). It bears no resemblance to that given by G. (T 7 v.)

4) We note the same naïvité here, as in the construction of Hector's tomb (§ 120):- Sentipus finishes his work quickly and then says (19,515):-

Si vous plaise de me payer.
Ajax Thelamonius:- Tu en auras pour ton loyer
Deux cens francs, tien, es tu content?
Sentipus:- Ouy messeigneurs, vraiement.

After this, Ajax Thelamonius and Menesteus return to Agamenon (the stage-direction 19,526 d. has the phrase „en grece", which is probably only meant to designate the Greek side of the stage). They say that Achilles is magnificently buried, whereupon Agamenon commands the Greeks to arm for the next battle.

Chapter XX.

The Seventh Battle. — Death of Paris. — Death of Ajax. Grief of the Trojans.

M. 19,559—20,567. B. 22,529—23,054. G. P 3 r 4 — P 4 v 6.

---

169. Before the next battle, in which Paris is killed, Milet introduces a scene of considerable originality and beauty:- Paris addresses the Trojan barons (19,559—609). He asks them to obey him since all his brothers are dead (19,572). In this statement we again note the neglect of Helenus. Paris has a presentiment that his life will end in the coming battle, and, if it should be so, he entreats them always to serve Priam, their rightful, their noble king. He then bids them wait while he goes to say farewell to Helen. This scene with Helen takes first rank among the lyrical passages in M. and merits lengthy quotation:- Paris finds Helen in trouble (19,607):-

Dame Helene, comment va, doulce amie?
A vous veoir, il ne me semble mye,
Que vous ayes le cueur gaires ioyeulx.
Helene: Mon doulx amy, bien ie vous certiffie,
Pour vostre amour tout le cueur me fremye,
Si ay du mal assez pour voz beaulx yeulx.
Paris: Deportez vous, helene, c'est le myeulx;
Tout yra bien, s'il plaist aux tres haulx dieux.
Mais baisez moy doulcement, ie vous prye.

Paris then tells Helen of the impending battle and of his presentiment of death, after which he says (19,622):-

Si vous vueil du cueur requerir,
Qu'il vous vueille bien souvenir
De moy et de ma loyaulte;
Car certes, s'il me fault mourir,
Ce sera pour vostre beaulte.
(19,643.)
Ie ose dire que puis le temps,
Que furent faiz premierement
De troye les grans fondemens,
Et des rues le pavement,
Home n'ayma si fermement
Femme, que ie vous ay aymee,
Ne ne garda si loyaulment
Sa voulenté et sa pensee.

Et se de vous ie me depars,
Il le convient, ie n'en puis mais,
Ie laise mon cueur en deux pars,
Si aures l'une a tousiours mais;
Et ie vous iure et vous prometz,
Que s'il me convient deffiner,
Mon ame ne pourra iamais
L'amour que i'ay en vous, finer.
Si vous lairray pour souvennance
Cest annel lequel, s'il vous plaist,
Vous porterez en remembrance
De celuy qui du tout vostre est.
Et croyes que ie suis tout prest
De mourir pour vostre gre faire.

Helen then bids him take heart, and says that, if he should die (19,678):- La chose me seroit si dure,
Que me fauldroit contre nature
Mourir par mes mains proprement.

With her parting words, however, she encourages Paris (19,683):-

Si prenez cueur et hardiesse;
Quant de moy il vous souvendra,
Lors doublera vostre prouesse,
Et vostre force ne fauldra.
Ia vaillant cueur ne se rendra,
Se bien luy souvient de s'amye,
Car s'amour bien le gardera
Et de mort et de maladie.

Paris expresses gratitude for this comfort. His own last words are (19,695):-

Pardonnez moy, ie vous supplye,
Se oncques envers vous ie meffiz.
Se vous avez este m'amye,
Ie vous en rens cinq cens mercis.

„Lors se partira de helene en pleurant et rancontrera anthenor.“ Anthenor notes his troubled state (19,699):-

Gentil damoisel, qu'avez vous?
Vous avez la chere marrye.
Il semble advis qu'ayez courroux,
Ou aulcune melancollie;
Soyes ioyeulx ie vous supplye,
Pour donner cueur a vostre armee.

Paris manfully smothers his grief (19,709):-

Non suis, i'ay ung peu mal es yeulx,
Pource me vont estincellant,
Mais quant ie pense maintenant
A hector et a troillus,
Qui souloient aler devant,
I'ay tel dueil que ie n'en puis plus.

Anthenor bids Paris to think only of vengeance and of the battle, whereupon Paris exhorts the Trojans who enter the fight.

170. The seventh battle now follows. It is of very short duration (19,731—810). Although in B-G. there are many other combats besides that between Ajax and Paris, M. selects this one alone. He is evidently somewhat in a hurry:-

1) Eneas (19,731) and Ajax (19,739) exhort in spirited lines their respective sides. The words of Eneas are particularly energetic.

2) M. (19,743—6) follows B-G. (22,539—46; P 3 r 11—13) in saying that Ajax enters the fight without armor. B-G. say that he only had his sword (22,748; P 3 r 13); M. that he has nothing (19,745): Fors seulement mon iaseron,
Et la hache et mon arc turquois.

3) In M., after Paris has killed several Greeks (19,755; 19,763; 19,771), Ajax forces back the Trojans (19,778 d.) „a

grant puissance de gens". Paris thereupon declares that he will go against Ajax (19,783):

Pour luy tirer de bonne entente
Une saiette au droit du cueur,
Ainsi que ie feiz en la plante (see § 158³)
D'achilles par grant deshonneur.

lors getera la sagette contre aiax et le navrera et se commencera la bataille plus fort.

B-G. also state that Paris' weapon was an arrow, G. alone adding the detail that it was poisoned (B. 22,711; P 3 v 13; compare § 137).

4) Ajax now addresses Paris (19,787—802). This speech shows the influence of G. (P 3 v 16—20):-

a. The general sequence of thought is the same.

b. 19,799. Car il est temps de departir
Ton corps de s'amour desloyalle.

P 3 v 19. Necesse est enim ut ab iniusto amore helene — illico sepereris.
B's expression differs (22,738). „Ici dessevre vostre amor | Et l'Eleine —".

5) Ajax kills Paris (19,802 d,) and soon expires himself (19,810 d). B. alone has the detail that Ajax lived until the arrow of Paris had been pulled out (B. 22,765). The last words of Ajax in M. are very human and dramatic (19,807):-

Si requier au dieu immortel.
Qu'il ayt pitie de mes enffans,,
Et du premier, qui est si bel,
Qui n'a pas encores dix ans.

6) In M. the battle ends abruptly, as usual, with the deaths of Paris and Ajax. In B-G. the Greeks drive the Trojans into the city.

171. There now follows (19,811—20,492) a long passage devoted to the mourning for Paris. G. is here very brief (P 4 r 3—26); he speaks at length only of Helen's grief; the rest is rapidly epitomized. B. has a longer passage (22,821—23,016). The following features deserve notice:-

1) In M. Eneas sees that Paris is dead and bids the Trojans take the body before Priam. B. says that the body was carried upon Paris' shield (22,781). G-M. omit this detail.

2) B-G. both declare they cannot express in words Priam's sorrow (22,828; P 4 r 8—11). M., however, has Priam vent his grief at great length (19,827—970). This speech is very prolix and commonplace, and merits but little attention:-

He has borne all else patiently (19,875):-

Mais la grant beaulte de paris
Me faisoit le cueur resiouir,
Car en trestous mes aultres filz
Ne prenoye si grant desir.

B-G. do not show this preference of Priam for Paris. We note the continued disregard of Helenus in the lines 19,891—8, where Priam says that there is now no prince to succeed him and that a powerful king must be found as the consort of Polixene. Priam himself abdicates the royal power (19,905):-

Car c'est bien mon entencion
De devenir beste sauvaige.
Dedens ung bois vueil demourer
Pour le demourant de ma vie;
Et la incessaulment pleurer
Et regretter chevallerie.

Priam then asks for Paris and faints over his body (19,918d). Returning to consciousness he continues his lament:- The gods have destroyed Paris, being jealous of his beauty (19,935). Venus is particularly to blame, to thus deceitfully reward his giving her „le don" (see § 23 b⁴). It would have been better to have given it to Pallas (19,944). Priam then bids Hecuba to hold Paris, for he himself can do so no longer.

3) B-G. declare also their inability to adequately express Hecuba's grief. M., on the contrary, attempts it in another long passage (19,971—20,042). The lament only merits notice in one particular, namely, the complete omission of Helenus in the enumeration of her sons (19,995—20,002). Hecuba says that Hector was first born, Paris second, Deyphebus third, *and Troylus fourth.* Helenus is thus completely ignored, which is all the more remarkable, because he is present during the scene (20,171)! B-G. agree in saying that *Helenus* was the *fourth* son (2,927; D 1 v 18; E 3 v 10) and *Troylus* the *fifth* (2,931; D 1 v 20).

Hecuba at the end of her lament bids Polixene hold Paris (20,038), Car en moy fault toute raison.

172. Polixene continues the lamentation (20,043), recounting the beauties of Paris, and their joyous childhood together. She closes by calling Cassandra's attention to the sad fate of Paris. Cassandra is, however, not moved thereby, but blames Paris most severely:- (20,107.)

Helas, il a bien achettee
Sa folle et mauvaise ieunesse;
Or luy est bien retribuee
Son oultraigeuse hardiesse.

She also blames Helen (see § 143) and urges Priam to make

peace with the Greeks by giving Helen back, else he will suffer a fate like that of Paris. This rouses the ire of Priam, who speaks sharply, even coarsely:-

(20,131.)
Ostez ceste garse, ostez,
Elle me fait le cueur crever,
(20,135.)
Quant ie la voy ainsi parler,
Sans faire le dueil de son frere.

(20,141.)
Il procede de grant orgueil
Quant ie voy qu'elle n en tient compte.
Ha, garce, n'as tu pas de honte,
Quant tu vois que le cueur me fault
Par la douleur qui me seurmonte
En gemissant, et ne t'en chault?

Cassandra replies that she, too, is greatly disturbed, but that the death of Paris is a smaller calamity than was that of Hector. Would only that Paris had died before he became the cause of all this trouble! (20,163):-

Mais ie m'en tais, puisqu'il vous plaist,
Au departir baiser le vueil
Et son beau visage qui est
Tout seignant, de quoi i'ay grant dueil.

The entire conception of this scene with its characterizations of Polixene, Cassandra, and Priam is original to Milet.

173. Priam next bids Helenus (20,171) to summon Helen without telling her that Paris is dead. Helenus asks Anthenor and Enee to accompany him; the latter bids Ascanius to come, and Ascanius again has his little rôle:-

(20,203.)
Chere pere, c'est moult grant dommaige
De la mort du tres beau paris.
Et se ie feusse assez en aage,
Ie alasse sur ses ennemis.

Helenus:-
Gentil enffant, cinq cens mercis
De vostre bonne voulenté.
Ains que ayes des ans trente et six
Aures le monde seurmonté.

They come before Helen and bid her return with them. She feels that some great calamity has occurred, but they assure her all is well. This whole scene is almost the same as that in which Andromache is summoned at Hector's death (see § 118[4]) to which it, therefore, forms the pendant. Its originality is thus mediocre. — All return before Priam who begins by assuring Helen that he will never give her back to the Greeks (20,234). He next speaks of death in general and its divine mission as the end of all human misery. Then bidding Helen to courageously restrain her grief, he announces abruptly (20,260):-

Voy la vostre amy, qui est mort!

174. 1) Helen faints at once. Upon regaining consciousness, she curses fate, the Greeks generally, and even her father (he is not named 20,295), and then vents her grief in a wearisome speech.

2) In Priam's attempt to comfort her, the following thought is expressed:-

(20,369.) Belle, se vous voulez estre remariee,
Ung home vous querray pour estre espousee,
Le plus bel qu'on pourra finer en ma contree.

The indelicacy of expressing this idea at the present juncture is somewhat modified in the next verses (20,372):-

Et se vous aymes mieulx estre vefve gardee,
Iamais ne vous fauldray, tant que i'auray duree.

3) Helen continues her lament by a description (20,376—421) of the beauties of Paris now destroyed, a rather ghastly recital. Needless to add it is absolutely unnatural in a lament of Helen for her to speak thus.

4) The lament of Helen in B. is characterized by a trait which is not reproduced here in G-M.:- In B. it is a self-condemnation of the sharpest sort and an expression of astonishment that the Trojans do not at once kill her, the cause of all their disasters (B. 22,855—916). The entire episode in B. of Helen's grief is far more truly dramatic than in M. (see particularly B. 22,917—57).

5) In all three versions Helen's grief so touches Priam and his family that they love her exceedingly, even as one of his daughters (B. 23,009; P 4 r 22; M. 20,430).

6) In M. Hecuba again expresses the idea already (20,369) suggested by Priam:-

(20,447.) Se vous voulez avoir ung roy
A mary, on le vous bauldra.

They will even make peace with the Greeks and restore her to Menelaus, if she so will (20,449—52). Helen, however, replies to the last proposition:- (20,453.)

Moy lasse, bien faulce seroie
Et de parverse voulente,
Se mon mary ainsi trompoye,
Qui m'a aymee en loyaulte.
Ce seroit grant desloyaulte,
Se a ceux iamais ie m'accordoye,
Qui le m'ont maintenant hoste.
Bien faulcement le trahiroye.

7) After Helen has finished expressing her grief (20,461—84),

Priam bids that Paris be taken „en sepulture" and that all retire for the night. Helen goes away with Hecuba. No place of burial is designated. In G. Paris is interred in the temple of Juno (P 4 r 23); in B. there is a contradiction:- Verse 22,821 reads temple of *Juno*, but 22,961 has *Minerva*. G. and, therefore M., omit the striking detail in B. (22,984—89.) that Priam places his ring, crown, and scepter with the body of Paris.

175. 1) The scene changes for a few moments to the Greek side. Agamenon (20,493) felicitates the Greeks upon the death of Paris, and mourns with them the death of Ajax. The following verses are peculiar, as applied to the rashness of Ajax entering battle without armor (20,506):-

(20,510) Car il convient en brief langaige
Chascun ses meffaiz comparer.
Pource le convient oblier (!)

2) Agamenon then says that Menelaus has been gone six days for Pirrus (20,521), and bids the Greeks to repose while awaiting his return. The Greeks separate in accordance with this command. Menesteus says (20,552):-

Ie n'ay pas le cueur trop chargie,
Car pieça ne tastay viande.

3) The friendship of Diomedes and Ulixes, found throughout the drama, has additional expression in the lines (20,560):-

Ulixes:- Diomedes ie vous emprye,
Que avecques moy venes soupper.
Diomedes:- Ulixes ie vous remercye.
Ulixes:- Diomedes ie vous emprye.
Diomedes:- Ie ne le reffuseray mye,
Puis que m'en voulez inviter.
Ulixes:- Diomedes ie vous emprye,
Que avecques moy venes soupper.

Cy finist la tierce iournee de la destruction de troye la grant (20,567 d).

The Fourth Day of the Drama.

Chapter XXI.

Arrival of Pirrus. — Arrival of Panthasilee. — Preparations for Battle.

M. 20,568—21,999.
Arrival of Panthasilee, B. 23,283—23,432. G. P 4 v 20 — P 5 r 8.
Arrival of Pirrus, B. 23,703—23,744. G. P 5 v 15 — P 5 v 28.

176. The fourth day opens with some scenes wholly original to M. In B-G. nothing is related of the doings of Menelaus while absent to fetch Pirrus. M. builds up a series of scenes:- Menelaus comes to the kingdom of Licomedes, thanks the gods for his safe arrival, and prays for their help in the recovery of Helen. He then goes into the presence of Licomedes and Pirrus, announces to the latter the death of his father, Achilles, and asks him, in the name of the Greek princes, to come and avenge this loss. In the lament of Pirrus (20,664), we have two references to his mother, but it is not stated anywhere in M. that she is the daughter of Licomedes (see § 166[3]). Pirrus says 20,675:- Bien sera madame dolente.
and again in 20,708, he declares that he must also avenge

— — — la griefve douleur
Que en aura madame de mere.

A third reference to the mother is in the later words of Thelamonius Ajax:- May Pirrus avenge his father, (21,494)

Tant que soyes en recouvrance
A vostre tres notable mere.

In all three of these passages, therefore, the mother is thought of as still living. — After expressing his grief, Pirrus declares that he must seek immediate vengeance. He thanks Licomedes (20,698) for all his kindnesses. Licomedes mourns the death of Achilles, and praises the filial affection of Pirrus in desiring vengeance. He then gives Pirrus much advice as to his future conduct:- Let him be courteous, generous and never haughty, for the victor of one day is the vanquished of the next. Let him remember that (20,806)

La racine de tout honneur
Est sens avecques diligence
Et le tronc de tout deshonneur
Est laschette et ignorance.

Let him also bear in mind that old age will yet overtake him. Licomedes gives Pirrus as parting gift a „bauldrier", saying (20,831.) Et vous souviegne bonnement,
Qu'un vieillart le vous a donne,
Qui vous ayme bien tendrement.

Pirrus thanks Licomedes and promises never to fail him in any distress. Pirrus and Menelaus then depart „pour venir a troye". For their arrival see § 180.

177. We note in the stage-direction at the opening of the fourth day (20,567 d):- „Et panthasilee en *son royaulme* acompaignee de ses damoiselles." The references to this kingdom are in M. very meagre. He has omitted the detailed description of it in B-G. (23,225—300; P 4 v 6 — 23), although retaining a few of its features:-

1) The name of the kingdom is „Femenie":- In Panthasilee's exhortation to her maids she says:- 20,908

Faictes vous par tout redoubter
Que l'en puisse par tout parler
Du royaulme de femenie.

Later she calls herself (21,790):- „moy la reine de *femenie.*" This is also the name in B-G. (24,077; K 4 v 8.)

2) B-G. indicate only vaguely that the kingdom is in the Orient (23,230; P 4 v 6). M. says that the queen, to come to Troy, must go (21,041)

— — — vers septentrion
Et venir en la region
D'inde mineur et clef d'asie.

3) The only inhabitants of this place are women, and they are called in G-M. *Amazonnes* (P 4 v 5—7; I 3 r 27; 20,890). B. has the longer form *Amazoneises* (23,603), and he also calls their country *Azoine* (23,231).

4) In B. the distinction is made that only the virgins of

this kingdom practice warlike deeds (B. 23,273—82; 24,003; 24,117; 24,129). In G-M. no such statement is given, and certain passages in M. (see § 179) seem to imply the contrary.

5) The only other verses in M. describing the country are:-

(20,938)
La coustume de ce pays
Est telle, que les ieunes filz
Sont mis hors de la compaignie
Des femmes, car il m'est advis,
Se sur nous avoient le pris,
Qu'ilz auroient tantost envye
De gouverneur la seigneurie.

B. alone says that the male children are kept by their mothers *one* year (23,266).

178. 1) In B. and G. it is clearly stated that Priam expected the aid of Panthasilea and her subjects:- B. 23,050:-

Oiez dont il esteit certains,
D'un secors merveillos et fier,
D'un grant, d'un riche, d'un plenier,
D'un plus biaus, qui onc fut fet.

and later (B. 23,308):- Prianz ne lessot porte ouvrir,
Qu'il les (= Panthasilea and her maids) atendeit a venir[1]).

P 4 v 4. „quod rex priamus indubitabilem spem habebat de quodam succursu ineffabiliter obtinendo ab amazonum regina."

2) In M. we have a curious and inexplicable contradiction upon this point:- Panthasilee says to her Amazons before she leaves her kingdom:- (20,900).

Car priam m'a envoyee querre
Pour luy aider a ses dangers.

which is supplemented by her words later to Priam (21,571),

Or m'a este compte | Que avez adversite | Pour ung cas mal propice.

and yet Priam says to her (21,589):-

Qui vous a advisee
D'amener vostre armee
En ces marches d'asie?
Royne, gente et iolye,
Ie ne cuydoye mye,
Que eussicz eu la nouvelle,
Comment ma seigneurie
A este apouvrie
Par fortune rebelle.

[1]) Greif failed to note these two passages in Benoît, although he quotes a passage in their immediate neighborhood (23,291) to prove that they did not exist! (See Ausgaben und Abhandlungen Vol. LXI, § 59, page 46.): „allein auch bei ihm [= Benoît] wird mit keinem Wort berichtet dass die Amazonen von den Trojanern erwartet wurden, sicher ein klarer Beweis dass ihm [= Benoît] eine ausführlichere Redaktion unseres Dares nicht vorlag. Unser Dichter giebt nur an, v. 23,291:- Por Hector que voleit voeir
Et por pris conquerre et aveir
S'esmut por venir al secors."

This argument of Greif must certainly be abandoned. Fischer (P. 59) had already (1883) noted that the Amazons were expected.

179. 1) M. introduces quite a long dialogue between Panthasilee and the Amazons before they start for Troy. In B-G. there is nothing of all this, scarcely more being said than that she begins her journey:- Panthasilee makes a long speech to her subjects (20,878—21,005), bidding them arm to go and aid the Trojans (20,894):-

Car si les troyans sont vaincus | Ce sera grant perte a ma terre.

She tells them of the origin of the Trojan war, of Paris and of Helen (20,981—6); „lors (20,901 d) les damoiselles de panthasilee despouilleront leurs vestemens et prendront leurs armeures".

2) A dialogue then follows between Panthasilee and three of her maids, Galienne, Esglantine and Mabille. The queen exhorts them to bravery to show the superior valor of women. She then speaks of Hector and confesses her admiration for him because of his bravery (20,969—79). In this M. touches again his source:- B. had said Panthasilee went to Troy (23,291) „Por Hector, que voleit voeir", but G. states clearly *why* she wished to see him, i. e. because of his valor (P 4 v 21—6), which reason we see repeated in M. as above. In G. a love is expressed for Hector (P 4 v 26), and this, too, is found in M., in the words of the queen. (20,974):-

De cestuy desir ay ie fort
Le congnoistre le sens, le fort,
Et avoir de luy congnoissance.
(20,979)
Si est bonne son accointance.

(20,999)
— — Pour savoir
Se hector se vouldra descouvrir
Vers moy pour accointance avoir[1]).

3) In the replies of Galienne, Esglantine and Mabille, each professes a similar interest in one of the other princes of Troy. M. got the idea of these passages from Panthasilee's preference for Hector. Galienne says:- (21,012)

Car de baiser et d'acoller
Et de frapper scay le tournoy.
— — — — — — — — — — —
Madame, i'ay moult grant desir
De veoir ung nommé troillus,
Qui scet assez de coupz ferir;
Si le vouldray a mon plaisir
Regarder pour la grant valeur
Qu'on dit dedens son corps gesir
Dont il acquiert partout honneur.

---

[1]) M. even speaks of a relation between Panthasilee and Agamenon. The latter says he had loved her:- „tres longtemps aymee" 21,976 (see § 184⁴). In B. we find evidence of a love-relation between Hector and Panthasilee in 13,016—18 and 23,331, although this seems contradicted by 23,315—6.

4) Esglantine says of the unmarried Polidamas (21,026):-

Se ie povoye bras a bras
Avoir de luy ma voulente
Oncques ie n'euz si grant soulas
Car i'ay en luy mon cueur boute.

5) Mabille speaks of Paris:- (21,050.)

Et certes puisqu'il c'est voue
A aymer si tres belle dame,
Il sera de moy regarde
Sans y penser aucun diffame.

After these replies Panthasilee orders (21,054) all to follow her, and departs for Troy.

180. The scene is now transferred to the Greeks:- Agamenon bids the herold Citheus call a council, for he is anxious at the long absence of Menelaus. Agamenon then asks Diomedes, if it is advisable to send after Menelaus. Diomedes „n'y entend mye" (21,089 d), but declares that he sees an approaching „mesgnie", „venans de la mer d'esurie" (21,094). There now follows the scene of the arrival of Pirrus, which is original to M. and is very similar to the previous scene of the arrival of Palamides (§ 75):- Diomedes recognizes by the standard (21,098—105) that the approaching party belongs to the house of Achilles, and concludes, since they come „des marches de morienne" (21,113), that it is Menelaus bringing Pirrus. Other Greeks think likewise, whereupon Agamenon bids them go and meet the approaching party, „et luy menez les menestrelz" (21,138). They obey, „et menelaus qui est dedans la *nef* monstre a pirrus troye en luy disant". We thus note that Menelaus arrives by sea. In B-G., however, neither in the arrival of Pirrus nor in the departure of Menelaus to fetch him, is there any hint given of a sea voyage. Even M. himself, at the departure of Menelaus, gives no such hint; rather is the implication that the journey is by land (19,155; 19,210). The introduction of a ship here is probably due to M's wish to have the scene like that of the arrival of Palamides (§ 75).

181. Menelaus calls the attention of Pirrus to the beauties of Troy. In the request of Menelaus „levez l'ueil vers *occident*", we note the usual mediaeval neglect of geographical detail. One would not be told to look to the *west* if approaching the Trojan coast from the sea. — Menelaus then perceives Menesteus and Ajax Thelamonius coming to meet them. Pirrus (21,164) admires the view of Troy and regrets that it must be destroyed to avenge his father. They then land and are greeted by Menesteus who tells what has occurred since Menelaus' absence. In (21,213) „Et troye est tous les iours fermee" we learn that fact for the first time, M. not having stated it after the last battle. It is in B-G. (23,045; P 4 r 30). — Moralizing upon the death of Paris and his separation from Helen, Menesteus, in a long digression, speaks of the instability of love (21,224—55), and at its close says (21,252):-

Or ca, c'est par ung incident Par maniere d'esbatement
Que i'ay ainsi parlé d'amours Afin que le temps ayt son cours (!)

This naïve confession is equally explanatory of the many other long-winded additions and digressions scattered throughout the drama. — Pirrus then asks Ajax Thelamonius to conduct him to Agamenon (21,284), and, with Menelaus, he comes before the latter and kneels (21,296 d). Agamenon bids his brother arise and sit beside him (21,307).

182. Menelaus now makes his report:- As in B-G. (23,705; P 5 v 15) he has been absent two months (21,313).

1) B-G. make no attempt to locate the kingdom of Licomedes. M. says (21,314) it is „es marches d'assurie", which, while in harmony with (21,094) „venans de la mer d'esurie" [de surie?], is hardly so with (21,113) „Vient des marches de morienne."

2) He has brought back Pirrus, the „norriture" (21,328), the ward, of Licomedes. In the description of Pirrus which follows, we note that nothing is said of his *exact* resemblance to Achilles, as in B. (22,501—6, also 29,091—5; 29,277—9). G. had omitted this also. The only lines comparing Pirrus with Achilles are vague (21,332):- „Car d'achilles n'est il gaires *moins* bel." — (21,336) „Car de corsaige luy [= Achilles] *peult* il ressambler." (see § 166[4]).

3) Passing then to the affair of the war, Menelaus declares his willingness to relinquish all else, if they will secure from Priam the return of Helen (21,376). This attitude of Menelaus is an innovation of M., introduced only to precede and explain the energetic opposition of Pirrus to such a course, which opposition is also original to M. Pirrus voices his hostility to an abandonment of the war in a vigorous speech (21,392—429), which comes as a surprise to us, showing that M. does, occa-

sionally, rise to dramatic heights, even in the midst of a plain of commonplaceness:- The question is now much more than the recovery of Helen. It is vengeance for the dead. Pirrus is very severe in his condemnation of Menelaus:- Menelaus forgets the fallen and cares not for them. Verily (21,407) „Ingratitude est mauvais vice". Pirrus will be content with nothing less than the total destruction of Troy, as vengeance for his father:- (21,416.)

Et s'aucun est qui m'en desdye,
Ie presente ce gan pour gaige,
Qu'il est traictre, quoy qu'on en dye
Et qu'il n'a pas loyal couraige.

He has come with all his „bernaige" to avenge his father, and will not suffer this talk of peace, for great will be his grief, if he cannot have vengeance. He closes with an appeal to the „barons" to uphold his views.

4) Another original feature of M. is his introduction of Nestor as the ardent supporter of Pirrus. This is quite natural, for Nestor lost his son at the same time that Pirrus lost his father. M. is clever in thus uniting Nestor and Pirrus in a demand for revenge, and both continue this rôle to the end of the drama (see §§ 199³; 228¹).

Nestor's speech (21,440—62) is also highly dramatic and vigorous:- Never shall Helen be taken back, before (21,456):-

— — verres les murs de troye,
Et le hault chastel d'illion
Bruler, et le sang par la voye
De la troyenne nacion,
Tant que par desolation
Ne demourra piece sur piece.

183. Pirrus now (21,463) asks that he be raised to „l'ordre de chevallerie". This brings M. again to his source (B. 23,719—36; P 5 v 21—9). The relation of the knighting of Pirrus is essentially the same in all three versions. A few points, however, deserve notice:-

1) In M. Pirrus asks Thelamonius Ajax to perform the ceremony of girding the sword (21,470) „Car il est de ma parenté". Later (21,480) Ajax Telamonius calls Pirrus „*cousin*". Nothing is said in B-G. of a relationship.

2) G. alone has the detail that two Greek princes bound golden spurs on to Pirrus (P 5 v 25).

3) A point of contact with G. is that it is *Agamenon* who delivers to Pirrus, the arms and the inheritance of Achilles.

(P 5 v 26; M. 21,500.) G.:- „omnia arma sui patris eius tentoria et res alias". M.:- „l'eritaige"; „les armes"; „toutes les gens et son bernaige". In B. Agamenon does not figure as the giver, and only the „armes" are spoken of (23,721).

4) M. omits all mention of festivities, which, in B-G., take place in connection with this knighting. Pirrus simply thanks Agamenon and retires to his father's tent.

184. 1) Panthasilee now arrives before Troy. In representing her arrival after that of Pirrus, M. departs from his source where just the reverse takes place, and where, even, Panthasilee defeats the Greeks several times in battle before Pirrus arrives (B. 23,343—702; P 5 r 4 — P 5 v 15).

2) Panthasilee tells her followers that they are in the country of Troy and must take care lest the Greeks prevent their entering the city. They enter by the „porte timbree" 21,540. This precaution is only found in M. G. specifies no detail in the arrival (P 4 v 26). In B. we have (23,317):-

Troien sorent sa venue | Contr'als s'en est la genz issue.

These lines are indefinite, since they may refer to a demonstration inside, as well as outside, the city.

3) Panthasilee kneels before Priam and, in easy-flowing verses, explains why she has come. In Priam's reply we have already noted the contradiction implied in his astonishment at seeing her (see § 178[2]). Priam recounts his sorrows and tells of the loss of his sons (21,586—669). As in B-G. Panthasilee is greatly grieved at the death of Hector and declares her wish to have immediate vengeance; M. has her express the thought:- (21,684.)

Car i'eusse prins plaiser et ioye | D'aler avec luy combatant.

She asks Priam to open at once the gate. Priam assents, bidding the Trojans to sound to arms. All assemble „ou millieu du grant eschauffault" (21,781 d.) where, in a prolix speech (21,782——871), Panthasilee exhorts them to duty and valor in defence of their king. Enee adds his exhortation and urges haste, whereupon the Trojans depart for battle.

4) On the Greek side, Agamenon exhorts his followers to

be brave (21,912—99), bidding them remember their wives and friends and (21,938):-

— — — l'argolicque lingnee | Dont vous estes trestous nasquis.

In his saying *ten* years (21,948) there is a contradiction with Priam's *nine* years a few verses above (21,622). He proposes to destroy Troy utterly. He has heard of the arrival of Panthasilee whom he had „tres longtemps aymee" (21,976). Despite this fact he will destroy her if he can. With blare of trumpets the battle begins (21,999 d).

Chapter XXII.

The Eighth Battle. — Death of Panthasilee. — Attempts to urge Priam to make Peace.

M. 22,000—23,126. B. 23,553—24,567. G. P 5 r 14 — Q 2 r 4.

---

185. In M. all the combats up to that between Pirrus and Panthasilee are taken from those battles in B-G. which happen *before* Menelaus arrives with Pirrus (B. 23,343—702; P 5 r 4 — P 5 v 15; see § 184[1]).

1) The first of these is between Diomedes and Panthasilee. This occurs in B-G. (23,553—61; P 5 r 14—20). G. adds the detail that Panthasilee seizes his shield and gives it to her maids (see below, 3). M. adds the rescue of Diomedes by Agamenon and the other Greeks (22,016).

2) In B. it is said (23,521—25 and 23,906—10) that the Amazons have a peculiar and beautiful war-cry or song, when they enter battle. G. and, therefore, M. show no knowledge of this.

3) In B-G. the next combat is between Panthasilee and Thelamon. Since, in M., Thelamon remains at home (4,124; § 54), M. substitutes here his son Thelamonius Ajax. In M. Panthasilee „oste l'escu a aiax" (22,035 d) and gives it to her maids, which incident is borrowed directly from the above-mentioned (see 1.) seizure of Diomedes' shield in G. (P 5 r 19). In M. Panthasilee

takes Ajax Thelamonius prisoner unaided. In B-G. it is with the aid of Philimenis, that Thelamon is captured. In all versions Diomedes rescues the prisoner. The Greeks are driven back in response to the urging of Philimenis. There is then a lull in the battle which corresponds to the end of that day's battle in B-G. and the return to the city (B. 23,633; P 5 v 10).

4) During this lull Agamenon exhorts the Greeks, pointing out the disgrace of letting a woman defeat them (22,064—111). In B-G. a similar reproach is made by Pirrus (23,987—95; P 6 r 25) who, in M., makes none.

5) The fight recommences with a combat between Panthasilee and Menelaus. He strikes her, but she fells him to the earth. This combat is also taken from among those in B-G. previous to the arrival of Pirrus (B. 23,549—52; P 5 r 11—13); M., as usual, omits the capturing of the horse of Menelaus. In place of *Menelaus;* the 1477 edition *alone* of Guido has *Menesteus,* an additional indication that, if its reading goes back to a manuscript previous to 1450, Milet did not use that manuscript.

186. The next episode is the death of Panthasilee at the hands of Pirrus:-

1) In B-G. there are two encounters before the final one, in both of which Pirrus is worsted (B. 24,027—56; P 6 v 2—14 and B. 24,133—149; P 6 v 28 — P 7 r 1). B-G. also speak of many other combats between them for a month preceding the last one (B. 24,185; P 7 r 12). M. divides his combat into two portions. In the first „pirrus la cuilde frapper et elle destorne le coup de sa haiche" (22,142 d); „alors panthasilee gette a terre pirrus" (22,158 d). The two sides then separate and the battle continues a long time, after which comes the final encounter.

2) After the first encounter Pirrus declares (22,160) that he is severely wounded, but will have vengeance. M. then introduces his slaying of Panthasilee. In B-G. there is no surrounding of her, but M., remembering this method used at the killing of Troillus and of Menon, employs it again here. Muselet tells Pirrus that they will surround Panthasilee as they did Troillus and knock off her helmet (22,175—80).

3) After an exhorting of their respective sides by Pirrus and Panthasilee, Pirrus „abat polidamas", and bids the Mirmi-

dons capture him. Philimenis, thereupon, urges Panthasilee to the rescne. Polidamas is rescued, but Panthasilee is surrounded by the Mirmidons. This incident of the capture and rescue of Polidamas is taken from the first appearance in B-G. of Pirrus in fight, *before* any of his encounters with Panthasilee (B. 23,796 —837; P 5 v 28 — P 6 r 4). M. inserts it here immediately before the death of Panthasilee.

4) Panthasilee being surrounded, Pirrus comes and kills her after saying:- (22,223)

Mais ie vouldroye ton corps partir	Qu'on ne pourroit ensevelir
En tant de pieces et de morceaulx,	Ains seras viande aux oiseaulx.

These verses are based upon the recital of the mutilation of Panthasilee in B-G. (24,213—30; P 7 v 1 - 7). M. omits the dramatic detail of B-G. that Pirrus falls unconscious from loss of blood and has to be carried to his tent. In B-G. the battle ends only after the Greeks have pursued the fleeing Trojans. M's battle terminates, as usual, abruptly; the Greeks „sonneront a la retraitte et s'en yront en leurs tentes".

5) Curiously enough there is no further mention in M. of the body of Panthasilee. M. neglects completely the passages in B-G. where it is later spoken of:- In B-G. the Greeks throw the body into, in B., the river Achandre (24,359); in G., a swamp (P 8 r 18). It is, however, ultimately given up (B. 24,842; Q 3 r 18), and taken back to her country by Philimenis (B. 25,667; Q 7 r 22; §§ 200[4]; 201[2]).

187. (22,226 d.) „Quant tout sera apaise priam parlera". What follows is a long lament by Priam (22,227—354) which does not require much attention:-

1) Of interest are Priam's words to Helenus, which, in a measure, correct and explain previous omissions of him as a son of Priam (see Index for references).

22,275	Tu scez peu de chevalerie;
Or sont tous tes freres occis.	Tu congnois assez de clergie,
Il n'y a plus que toy en vie.	Mais cela ne prouffite mye
Helas, heleuus, mon beau filz,	A homme de telle vieillesse.

2) Priam has only one other request to make of the gods:- If Troy is to be destroyed, may he die before he must witness it. Only twice has he wept in his life, first for Laomedon, his father

(22,328) and again for Hector (22,332). Now he must weep a third time (22,333):- — — pour ce pays
Que ie voy exillé a tort.

(This is a curious omission of his grief for the other sons). Never was so mighty a king laid so low. — Just as, in the many instances of fainting, the actor first announces what he is to do, so here Priam says (22,352):-

— Ma barbe trop est empiree.
Il fault pour le dueil ou ie suis,
Que par mes mains soies tiree.

lors priam arrache sa barbe et helenus se met a genoulx et luy dit:-

3) Helenus urges resignation (22,355—418). The world (22,373) — — n'est fors ainsi que une roze
Qui se passe et ne dure rien.

Amphimacus speaks in like strain, but more hopefully (22,419—26).

4) In Priam's reply we note the lines:- (22,435.)

Helas, et ie n'ay plus enffant
Legitime fors helenus,
Des naturelz semblablement
Ne m'en sont que sept retenus.
De trente cinq filz que i'ay euz,
Legitimes et naturelz,
Maintenant ie n'en n'ay plus nulz
Fors huit, dont tu (= Amphimacus)
es le main nez.

This is the only passage in M. where the number of his natural sons is stated. The thirty corresponds with B-G. (2948; D 2 r 1). The „main nez“, as descriptive of Amphimacus, is from G. (P 8 v 22) „Ex suis filiis naturalibus iuniore“. B. says of him (24,479.) „li *mieldres* des filz Priam“ and applies „li meins nez“ to quite another son, namely Tharez (B. 9,933—4) B. uses the word „menor“ for Amphimacus later (24,576), and for Polidorus (26,620). Priam finally becomes silent, in order to:-

22,449 — penser a mon affaire
Et au fait du gouvernement.

188. We now come to the defection among the Trojan leaders which culminates in their betrayal of the city. Its treatment by M. will offer us many points of interest. M. builds up the following scene as a sort of introduction to this new phase of the plot:- Anthenor (22,451) sends Athimas to summon Anchises and Enee:-

Pour une besongue acomplir | Que ie luy diray sans arrest.

M. thus gives Anthenor the rôle of the initiator in the defection, which rôle B-G. do not assign him specifically. — Athymas obeys. Anchises has a presentiment of the meaning of the summons:- (22,471.) Ie pense bien pour quoy ce soit.

While awaiting his friends, Anthenor says (22,478):-

Polidamas, gardez vous bien
Que ne me desdiez de rien,
Mais soyes bien de mon accort
Et me soustenez tousiours fort.
Polidamas:
Aussi feray ie a mon povoir.

Anchises and Enee now arrive before Anthenor, who addresses them.

189. This speech of Anthenor is a long one (22,483—641). It has no counterpart in B-G. where there is not even any dialogue (24,373—83; P 8 r 18—26). Its main feature in M. is Anthenor's relation of a dream in which Hector appeared to him. This dream is undoubtedly inspired from the second book of the Aeneid, where Hector's ghost appears to Eneas; Tivier had noticed this probability (P. 216 of his 1868 thesis; see § 7[5]). For the sake of comparison we give the main features of M's version of this appearance of Hector (22,510—611). Antenor says:-

I appeared to see Hector „dechiré moult piteusement". The sight was so cruel that I cried and groaned incessantly. How different was Hector now, grieved, melancholy, and full of care, from that Hector, who defeated Achilles gloriously and was an example of prowess and virtue.

(22,528.)
Si me souvint de sa prouesse,
De sa vertu et hardiesse,
Et du sens qui en luy estoit,
Du grant renom, de sa noblesse,
Et de haulte gentillesse.

Moved at once to learn his thought, I addressed him as follows:-

„How can one of such high lineage and nobility be so troubled? Pray, what brings you hither, alone and so sad?"

Hector replied:- „Before the gods young and old are equal, and all suffer severely for their crimes, the rich and the prosperous much more than the poor and the downtrodden. Therefore am I (22,572) „En ceste griefve pestilance", because of the wrongs and sins I did, in ignorance, in wishing to

(22,576.)
— — soustenir l'offence,
Le grant meffait et l'inconstance
De mon frere, le beau paris,
Lequel par grant oultrecuidance
Entreprinst ceste folle dance,
Dont fut par luy ce cas commis.

I will now tell you why I come before you; I know for certain,

(22,587)
Que ce lieu sera confondu.
Ie scay bien que tout est perdu,
Et que toute la grant vertu
De troye sera mise au bas.
Si en soyes tout ressolu,
Car les dieux l'ont ainsy conclu
Pour venger ce criminel cas.

And know that, if it had been decreed that this city should be defended and saved, here is that right hand which would have done it. This hand is, however, (22,603) — „au bas boutee“.

Therefore, De deffendre ceste contree
N'aiez iamais nulle esperance.“

After Hector had thus spoken, I thought to approach him,

Et veoir se toucher le pouroye
Mais tantost plus ie ne le vy
Et de ma veue le perdy
Et sans savoir par quelle voye.

Thereupon I began greatly to grieve and to think how the danger to our city could be averted. I, therefore, came to the conclusion that peace must be made with the Greeks and that Helen must be given up. Let us go and urge such action upon King Priam.

By introducing this dream, Milet adds a reason for the defection of Anthenor and the others, which places it upon a very different basis from that in B-G. In the latter they are only moved to snch action by the continued defeat of the Trojans.

190. Milet adds life to the scene by representing the opposition of Anchises to Anthenor's plan, and his finally being persuaded to join it:- Anchises points out the difficulty of gaining Priam's consent. They are all four related to him, and Anchises does not esteem their proposed action as loyal. Anthenor and he are old and need no longer fear death. Therefore, let Priam's will be done, for he is too noble (22,672):-

Qu'on ne doit riens que loyaulte
Aler envers luy pourchassent.

Enee reasons with his father that, in urging the king to make peace, they are only doing him the greatest service. Enee upholds Anthenor. — Polidamas declares that they have not, in the past, shirked sacrifice, but that peace is now the best course. They are powerful enough, as the near relatives of Priam, to enforce their will upon him. Anchises finally agrees to join them in their plan.

In B-G. there is no trace of an opposition of Anchises (24,373—83; P 8 r 18—26). A similarity of M. to G. exists in the emphasis given to the idea that they mnst save their lives. (P 8 r 21) „qualiter possent vitas eorum salvas facere ne perderentur a grecis“. M. 22,630—5, also in line 70 of the *„Instrument“* after verse 23,386. — In G. we note the sudden introdnction of their determination to betray the city, if Priam does not make peace (P 8 r 23). B. had more reasonably reserved this determination until after they learn Priam's intention to assassinate them, and M. is also clever enough to realize the prematureness of G. in this matter; he postpones it, as did B. (see § 195[3]).

191. The short narrative in B-G. is again resolved into a long dialogue:- Anchises opens it with a lengthy recital of their fruitless endeavors to save the fatherland, fruitless because the gods oppose. All resources are now exhausted. He asks Priam to save Troy by yielding all to the Greeks including their demand for Helen. (We are a bit surprised that no one makes any further mention of Anthenor's dream). Priam, after declaring his great grief (22,831) says that he will take counsel with others and give reply (22,859) „dedens quatre jours ou six". This asking for delay harmonizes with B-G. G. gives a slightly more definite time-limit, (P 8 v 29) „per dies aliquos", than B. who says only „enpres" (B. 24,402).

M. now makes Enee (22,863) the spokesman of the request that Priam accept their counsel then and there without delay. Priam then permits them to give their counsel at greater length. In his reply there is a thought common only to G-M.:- He says that they ought not to object if he can find better advice than theirs (22,879—86; Q 1 r 2—4).

192. In the council, which comes next, all versions agree in having Anthenor speak first. In this speech M. comes in closest contact with G., having not only the same succession of thought, but also the following ideas, absent in B:-

1) The gravity of the danger cannot remain longer hid from Priam's wisdom, for the Greeks encircle the city. M. 22,887—901; Q 1 r 5—10.

2) He is so helpless that he dares not open the city-gates. M. 22,909—14; Q 1 r 10—13.

3) All his sons and the greater part of his people are dead. M. 22,927—30; Q 1 r 15—17.

4) Of two evils the lesser should be chosen. M. 22,935—6; Q 1 r 17—18.

All three versions conclude the speech with the exhortation to restore Helen and all the wealth taken with her.

M. and G. again name Cytharea (22,944; Q 1 r 23); B. does not. M. alone designates the wealth as „joyaulx“ 22,944; compare 2,536.

193. There now follows (22,959—90) the spirited reply of Amphimacus. The contact of M. with G. still continues:-

1) Amphimacus emphasizes the idea that they of all others should continue loyal to Priam even unto death. M. 22,963—9; Q 1 r 26—30.

2) Before their request is granted, 20,000 men shall perish. M. 22,980—1; Q 1 v 3—4. B. says that 10,000 shields will be pierced (B. 24,490).

3) In all versions Eneas tries to calm the excited Amphimacus by declaring that peace is the only escape from present and future disaster. The rest of the scene agrees in sequence of thought with B-G:- Priam replies angrily to Eneas. — It is disgraceful and cruel of them to demand peace, for it was Anthenor who counselled sending Paris to Greece and led Priam to disregard the contrary opinion of Hector (23,025).

4) The expression given to the following thought by Priam points to G:- (23,035.)

Moy qui estoie en paix rassis   Se tu ne m'en eusse requis
Ne ne feusse point mis en guerre   Car i'estoye en paix en ma terre.

Q 1 v 21. „Nunquam a mea processisset audacia guerram contra grecos in tanta mea pacis tranquillitate movere“. This emphasis of his being at peace does not occur in the corresponding passage in B. (24,534—8).

5) Priam then turns to Enee and blames him for not preventing the capture of Helene by Paris. The following words are noteworthy:- (23,051.)

Helas, luy [= Paris] conseillas tu pas   Certes, tu l'en amonnestas
Qu'il mist peine a prendre helene?   C'est une chose bien certaine.

We have already (§ 35[3]) noted how these lines do not harmonize with the attitude of Eneas in Cytharea.

6) The next two lines are again from G.:-

(23,055) Toy mesmes feuz le conducteur | Et aidas personnellement.
Q 1 v 26. Et tu etiam fuisti personaliter adjutor ipsius [= Paris].

7) Although they are thus the cause of Priam's being at war, yet they dare to urge him to make peace! In M. Priam ends his speech with great dignity:- (23,093.)

Se vous en ouvres follement, | Vous congnoistrez que ie suis roy.

Enee now speaks very sharp words to Priam (23,095), declaring that they are not afraid of his menaces. Original to M. is it that Priam then orders them to leave his presence (23,111). In B-G. they leave Priam of their own accord. In M. alone does Priam express his distrust of them and his suspicion of treachery. In departing, Anthenor utters a threat.

Chapter XXIII.

Priam's unsuccessful Attempt to kill the Conspirators. — Their Determination to betray Troy. — They force Priam to agree to Peace.

M. 23,127—742 („disner" of fourth day). B. 24,568—24,721. G. Q 2 r 4 — Q 2 v 23.

194. Priam, after first lamenting the present crisis, determines to outwit the conspirators. Only in a most general way is his speech inspired from B-G.:-

1) We note M's emphasis of the idea that Priam has raised the conspirators up to their present power (23,147):-

Se ie suis pugny, c'est bien droit,
Car i'ay ces gens cy avancez,
A qui pas il n'appartenoit
D'estre si tres haulx exaulcez.
Ie leur ay baille le baston,
Dont ilz me batent maintenant.
Ie leur ay monstre la façon,
Car ie les ay mis trop avant.
I'ay fait chascun d'eulx gouvernant
Et roy sur ceste grant cite.

This idea of their being so indebted to Priam is original to M.

2) Priam continues:- They served him during his prosperity, but become traitors, when his fortune changes. It is always so. Friends are plentiful when Fortune smiles. Would that Hector or Troylus were here to lower their pride! He must find means to forestall their evil designs.

3) Although Priam has never yet done a treacherous act nevertheless such is justifiable under the present conditions (23,191—8). This is an echo of Q 2 r 16. B. has no such thought. This justification of treachery in payment of treachery reminds us of Hecuba's similar plea regarding the killing of Achilles. (see § 156³.)

4) The idea of inflicting on the conspirators what they desire to do to him, is not expressed in B. G. and M. give it prominence:- (Q 2 r 16.)

Et ideo non est invicium ut ipsi cadant in foveam quam intendunt aliis preparare.

(23,201.)
Et le fait mesmes maintenir,
Qu'il ont contre moy appreste.
(23,239.)
Il est iuste et convenable,
Que ceulx, qu'envers leur seigneur
Pensent trahison detestable,
Soient frustres de leur labeur,
Et qu'ilz encourent la douleur
Qu'il veullent faire vers aultruy.

5) Priam arrauges that the conspirators shall be summoned to a council, and that Amphimacus with trusty men shall put them to death. B. alone adds another pretext for summoning them (B. 24,607):-

Et por faire un devinement,
Et un grant sacrefiement,
Enpres les ferai conjurer,
Que il remaignent au souper.

In B. alone, also, Priam expresses the idea that, with the death of the traitors, there will be nothing further to fear from the Greeks, since the walls of Troy are too high (24,615—19).

6) Amphimacus promises to execute his father's will, and Priam sends Macabrum to summon the traitors.

195. 1) In B., Rumor brings the news of the counter-conspiracy, not only to Eneas, but also to Anthenor, Polidamas, Anchises, — — „quens Dolon | Et li sages Eucalion" (B. 24,626—34). We note especially the last two names, which do not occur elsewhere in B., and not at all in G-M., as fellow-conspirators with the others.

2) In M. another point of contact with G. is that Eneas is the one who hears of the king's plot:- (Q 2 r 25.)

„Ignoratur qualiter ad Enec pervenit noticiam consilium regis priami."

In M. Enee speaks (23,291) (compare 23,300—5):-

Mes beaulx seigneurs, il nous convient
Bien garder, car il me souvient
Que hier me fut dit et conte,
Que le roy, qui troye maintient,
Et qui ceste grant cite tient,
Nous veult faire desloyaulte.

3) In all three versions the betrayal of the city is now resolved upon. We have already (end of § 190) noted G's earlier introducing of this resolution. M's recital here presents a few original features. — In M. it is Eneas who makes the proposal (23,311). The others agree except that Anchises expresses greater regret, for he witnessed the first destruction of Troy (23,351). Anchises then urges the need of their signing an agreement for

mutual protection and for secrecy. He will write it out and submit it to their criticism. „lors fera semblant d'escripre et puis aura ung papier ouquel est escript ce qui s'ensuit“ (23,386 d). This introduction of a signed agreement bespeaks the legal training of Milet, but an examinaton of the *„Instrument“* which now follows presents a singular picture of that training.

196. The „Instrument de la trahison de troye la grant“ is a curious example of naïveté and contradiction:- It opens with a recital of the cause and result of the war, and then gives, as reasons for the betrayal of the city, their desire to atone for their crime in sustaining Paris (line 66), and also their wish to avoid death (line 70). They have made fruitless efforts to persuade Priam to make peace (lines 90—106), and he replies by seeking their destruction (line 110). They, therefore, have agreed to surrender the city to their „ennemis ançiens“, desiring (line 118) „secourir au bien publique, a la fragilite d'icelui roy, a noz femmes, enffans et possessions“. They promise secrecy and mutual confidence. The „Instrument“ is written in prose and terminates thus:- „et ainsi le promettons, iurons et certiffions, tesmoings noz saings manuelz et noz seaulx cy mis et appliques a ce present contraict l'an de nouvelle fondation de troye la grant XXXVIII le XXIII iour de may“. A few features of this document merit a passing notice:-

1) The first lines contain an inexplicable contradiction. The conspirators give, as the reason for their action, their desire to avoid that which they have already (23,312—4; 23,359—62) declared would result from their action!:- „Pour *eviter* (!) plus grans inconveniens vault mieux et est expedient aulcunes personnes mourir et aulcunes personnes estre saulvees que souffrir et permettre desolation totale d'un pays la mort et perdition de tous les habitans“.

2) With equal ingenuousness they withhold Priam's name (line 18), although naming his son Paris, the extent of his dominions, and the various events of the war „pour aulcunes causes touchant l'onneur de nous et de noz personnes“ (!). And with all this, they sign the paper!

3) The anger of the gods at the sacrilege of the temple of Venus in Citharea is given (lines 44—65) as the cause of

all the disasters of Troy. A list of the offended deities then follows.

4) A Latin quotation is inserted in line 74, which we cannot find in Guido:- „quia agentes et consentientes pari pena puniuntur."

5) They only take this action after ripe deliberation (line 78), „par les autoritez des philosophes d'athenes et par la loy que nous tenons des sainctifies regens du ciel".

It is almost incredible that this ridiculous „Instrument" was faithfully reproduced in all editions of Milet, including the late one of 1544.

197. When Anchises has read the „Instrument", he obtains their approval of it. He signs first, and the others follow. They then decide to go before Priam, and Anthenor suggests their taking 200 armed men (23,427). Despite this large figure they go, accompanied only „de pluiseurs gens d'armes". Macabrum (23,435) tells Priam that Enee is approaching with a large army, whereupon Priam bids him at once order Amphimacus (23,440):- Qu'il ne face pas pour meshuy,
Ce que ie luy ay commande.

The conspirators then come before Priam where are assembled all the princes of Troy. — The above corresponds, in the main, with B-G.

There now follows (23,461—734) the council wherein M. has, as usual, expanded into dialogue the few lines of narrative in B-G:-

1) Priam voices grief at his loss of authority and fall from power. His friends have all deserted him. No trust is to be placed in men. He can no longer talk as ruler, but only as servant (23,521):-

Ne m'appellez plus vostre roy!
Vous ne dires pas verite,
Doresenavant appellez moy
Le vieulx seigneur desherite.

His sorrow is even greater than his father's, yet he will be resigned (23,539). Thanking the allied kings for their services he begs them to return and no longer to labor in his behalf.

2) In Enee's speech (23,681—96) one idea points to G., namely, that peace will be made despite the king:-

(23,686.)	Q 2 v 14
Nous le ferons, vueillez ou non,	ad quod reniteris domine rex velis
Et si vous dy bien sans flater,	nolis de pace tractabitur et si et etiam
Que malgre vous nous le ferons.	te invito.

The resistance of the king is also more emphasized in G-M:- Q 2 v 14; M. 23,665—80. B. only says (24,707,) „O Eneas tença li reis".

3) Priam is finally forced to agree, and asks that some one be selected to negociate with the Greeks. B. gives no hint of any selection being made at this time, although, as in G-M., Anthenor goes to the Greeks later. G. has (Q 2 v 21) „Anthenor igitur eligitur in legatum", and, in M., Enee begs Anthenor to go (23,709).

4) Priam reminds Anthenor of their family ties and bids him act loyally. Anthenor replies evasively: (23,721.)

Sire, ie feray mon debvoir
Si bien que homme d'entendement
Ne m'en devera mal gre savoir.

He then says that it is time to dine, and invites his fellow-conspirators to dine with him. All go away from the „tente priam" 23,734 d. and the morning's performance ends.

Chapter XXIV.

Anthenor negociates the Treason with the Greeks. — Departure of the Trojan Allies. — Long Lament of Priam.

M. 23,743—25,202. B. 24,719—25,132. G. Q 2 v 23 — Q 4 r 1.

198. 1) Anthenor has Achinas bring some olive-branches, and, showing these, Anthenor goes toward the Greeks. Diomedes sees his approach and Agamenon bids the Greeks likewise to show olive-branches. This relation differs from B-G:- In B. Eneas[1])

[1]) It is not absolutely certain that „cil" in B. 24,722 refers to Eneas who has recently spoken (24,709—17), for „Priant" occurs in 24,720. The context seems, however, to imply Eneas, because - 1) it would be improbable that Priam

first mounts the wall and displays olive-branches. In G. (Q 2 v 22) *troyani* — muros — ascendunt. The nature of the return-signals by the Greeks is not specified in B-G.

2) M. introduces Thoas (23,783) who welcomes Anthenor, recalling that, as prisoners, they were exchanged *seven* years ago (23,786). This is a chronological contradiction, for Thoas' remark would mean that they were exchanged in the *third* year of the siege, and yet in 11,321 and 11,441, *before* the first talk of an exchange (11,771; see § 109), we learn that *six* years have gone by since the siege began.

Thoas now leads Anthenor before Agamenon, which act is suggested by G. (Q 2 v 26) „eo agamenoni presentato", inasmuch as B. does not mention Agamenon at the meeting.

3) In G. *Agamenon* immediately (Q 2 v 27) entrusts negociations „cum grecis regi crete dyomedi et ulixi", there being no preliminary speech by Anthenor. In B. it is Anthenor who asks for the appointment of negociators after first (B. 24,739—94) recalling the main events of the war, but it is the *Greeks* who do the appointing, and Agamenon is one of those selected; there is no discussion. (B. 24,798):-

Agamenon i ont eslit,
Lo rei de Grece, et Ulixes,
Et avec els Diomedes.

There are thus *three* appointees in B. and *three* also in G. although in G. Agamenon is *not* one of them, his place being taken by „rex crete" whose name, later (S 1 v 11), is given as Ydumeneus. That G. meant three is seen in the next words (Q 2 v 28) „et quidquid dicti *tres* cum *quarto* eis anthenore adjuncto". M. either purposely or unintentionally neglected this line, being, perhaps, confused by the idea that „regi crete" was in apposition with „dyomedi"; he, therefore, restricts the number to two, Ulixes and Diomedes. As in G. it is Agamenon who finally appoints them (24,101), after a long discussion (23,878

---

himself would mount the wall under the circumstances. 2) an antithesis between „Priant" and „cil" is evidently intended. 3) Anthenor cannot well be meant by „cil" because he has not been mentioned since 24,651, and it is he who, later, in consequence of favorable signals from the Greeks, „s'en ist des murs" (24,728). In Dictys, however, Anthenor also mounts the wall (P. 84,33).

—24,101) has taken place, probably suggested by „cum grecis" (Q 2 v 27).

199. This debate in M. presents a few points of interest:-

1) Anthenor recalls the great destruction caused by the „prise villaine" of Helen, but says, (23,846) that the Trojans can still hold out for 100 years (in 23,857 he reduces this time to „dix ou vintg"). It is, therefore, wise for the Greeks to retreat with Helen; Priam will pay the indemnity.

2) Agamenon, in asking the opinion of the Greeks, declares that he is willing to accept these conditions. In his reply we note another example of artificiality in M's versification:- (23,914).

Par quoy ce debat soit oste, Et aussi la dixiesme annee este,
Vecy ia le dixieme este, Que avons devant cy este.

3) Diomedes (23,934) and Ulixes agree to this settlement but Nestor (23,958) swears that he will never depart before he has had vengeance for his son, and appeals to Pirrus. The latter also demands vengeance for his father, and declares that Agamenon will be his enemy if he accepts any conditions short of complete revenge for Achilles by the destruction of the city. This opposition of Pirrus and Nestor is original with M. and continues that already expressed (see §§ 182[4]; 228[1]).

4) Anthenor helps to quiet these objections. He first promises a great indemnity in the name of Priam:- (24,037.)

Et s'il ne si veult accorder, De vous faire dedans entrer,
Ie m'en faiz fort sur tous noz dieux Malgre ses dens, devant ses yeulx.

Thus will the Greeks be victorious and can wreak their will upon the city. This passage is noteworthy because of the conditional clause in 24,037. Anthenor does not live up to it at all, for, although Priam grants the indemnity (24,406), Anthenor nevertheless betrays the city.

5) Anthenor asks them to appoint some kings to whom he can disclose his plans. Diomedes and Ulixes are suggested by Menesteus and appointed by Agamenon. These two and Anthenor promise loyalty to Agamenon and withdraw to the „eschauffault" of Diomedes (24,161 d).

200. The agreement arrived at between Anthenor and the Greek negociators is essentially the same in all versions:-

1) In M. Anthenor emphasizes the idea that it is Priam's treachery which has determined him to surrender the city.

2) As in B-G., Anthenor insists upon the condition that they spare (24,224.) — — les domiciles
Qui sont a moy et a enee.

3) B. contains a promise of the Greeks which is not repeated in G-M., namely, that Polidamas shall have half the kingdom of Troy (B. 24,827).

4) M. omits Anthenor's request for the body of Panthasilee which is made in B-G. (see § 186⁵).

5) Omitted also is the incident in B-G. (24,848; Q 3 r 14) that the aged king Taltibius goes back to Troy with Anthenor.

6) Anthenor returns alone before Priam and his whole court, and makes a long speech (24,242—381). At its beginning (24,241) and twice during its course (24,291; 24,357), M. introduces a Latin quotation taken from Anthenor's corresponding speech in G. (Q 3 v 11—12):- „melius est marsupiis peccuniariis accommodare dolores cordis quam continuis doloribus anxiari.“ The only difference is that M. has „cordis quam“ instead of „quam cordis“. This might or might not indicate the group of G. manuscripts used by M. All the editions of G. and M. respectively have the difference above noted.

7) Except in this quotation the speech of Anthenor contains nothing that does not occur in both B. and G.:- He says that peace must be bought with a great sum of gold and silver, and asks that Eneas return with him to continue negociations with the Greeks. To these two propositions Priam finally assents (24,406), exhorting Anthenor and Eneas to act loyally.

201. M. now introduces the departure of the Trojan allies, which episode B-G. had deferred, placing it after the building of the horse and before the final ratification of peace (B. 25,640—704; Q 7 r 16—26). Perhaps M. inserted this episode earlier, in order to intensify the misery of Priam which is expressed in the latter's long monologue (§§ 202—205). Certain differences are apparent between the version in M. and that in B-G.:-

1) In M. Priam himself (24,430) dismisses his allies, thanking them for their great services and saying that their presence is now no longer necessary, since peace is to be made. They

regret the peace, but only Serpedon speaks of it as a „vitupere“ (24,586). In B-G. the allies go of their own accord, declaring that they cannot be partners to such a disgraceful treaty (B. 25,644 ff.; Q 7 r 16).

2) Although Philimenis is among those who go away „en divers lieux“ (24,624 d), nothing is said of his carrying back the body of Panthasilee to her land, as in B-G. (25,667; Q 7 r 22; see § 186⁵).

3) In departing, Philimenis says to Priam „Sire, prenez en patience“. These words Priam takes as a theme for a lament at the loss of his power and prestige (24,510—73). After the allies have gone, Priam says to the others (24,629):-

Ie me vueil retraire une piece
A part, moy, si vueillez aler
Tous de voz besongnez penser,
Et me laissez ung peu ycy.

They obey and Priam is left alone to speak his long lament of 570 verses (24,633—25,202). This corresponds with G. (Q 3 v 19):- „priamus colloquo *dissoluto* suam se *secreto* recepit in aulam“, where he gives himself over to lament (to Q 4 r 1). In B., on the other hand, a similar although much shorter lament takes place (B. 25,089—132) but *before* Priam agrees to peace or leaves the council.

202. There now follows the longest monologue of the drama 570 verses (24,633—25,202). If Priam had to speak these without interruption, we are not surprised at the naïve stage-direction at their close:- „priam pourra boire si veult“. In this passage, M. gives his allegorical taste free play. Priam contrasts in symbolical language the happiness of his youth with his wretchedness in old age. Although the allegory is of the most mediocre sort, we feel obliged, for the sake of completeness, to give a résumé of this passage. Greif believes that the sixth book of the Aeneid influenced Milet in this place (see § 7¹²) and Meybrinck (P. 49) shares this view.

1) As an introduction, Priam declares that his great age, over 100 years (24,673), and his many vicissitudes entitle him to speak upon Fortune:- He first arrived at a wonderful tower (24,683) of which he gives an extraordinary description; passing through this he traversed a beautiful field. Under a large oak in its centre was a woman of great beauty called „dame liesse“

(24,773) who gave him some water to drink that drove away all care. She then led him to a wondrous garden full of beautiful birds and sweet-scented trees, and traversed by a river in its bed of precious stones. This garden was called (24,839):-

Le lieu de delectation, | Que les latins nomment tempte.

No one can have sadness there.

2) They then passed to a room where were depicted Chaos, (24,860), Form, Matter etc., ruled over by Soul (24,880). There also were Thought, Nature, God, and the Chariot of Fortune (24,894). — Crossing this room they came to the „haulte sale“ (24,905), where Fortune held in her hand Priam's heart. Greatly did she honor him, and give him for many years happiness and power. In order, however, to show him that she still retained all control over his destiny, Fortune led him and Dame Liesse (24,949) through a black cavern, full of rocks, which they traversed only with great pain, to a desert covered with thorns and brambles, and alive with serpents. This desert was „le lieu de souppir“, „ung lieu de tourment“ (24,966). In its centre was a filthy lake full of snakes and vermin.

203. 1) From this desert they came to (24,993):

— ung lieu tenebreux
Ou resident les malheureux.

Here was a wheel whose uppermost part was made of gold. Its right side was formed of silver, its left of copper, and its lowest part of black iron. Within this wheel were seated „deux chamberiees“ (25,005), engaged „a tourner les cas des humains“. Of these two the upper one was called Prosperity (25,018), the lower one Adversity (25,021):-

La premiere certainement
Recoit celuy benignement,
Que celle d'embas luy envoye,

Mais adversite rudement
Recoit tres rigoureusement
Celuy qui descent en sa voye.

On this wheel were inscribed the names of all who were under Fortune's control. Priam saw his name at the highest point above all others. Then Fortune turned the wheel and he fell to the lowest place (25,041) despite his appeal for clemency. At the same time the names that were lowest took highest place.

2) In the lament of Priam in G. (Q 3 v 18) there is no mention of this allegory of the wheel of Fortune. In B., however we find it:-

(B. 25,112).
Sor le plus halt de la roele
M'asseistes et me posastes,
Mes quant vos vos i atornastes
Trop ledement sanz demorer,
Me ravez fait jus devaler,
Qu'ore sui gie desoz voz piez
Povres, vils et desconseilliez etc.

The presence of this allegory in both B. and M. needs no particular explanation. It is one of the most common figures of speech in all literatures, and it would be strange if M. who is so given to allegorical descriptions, had not introduced it. (see Godefroy under „Roele"; also „Larousse"; see also in the article by Dr. J. E. Matzke, Publications of the Modern Language Association of America. New Series Vol. I. Page 327 ff.)

204. Milet makes use of the allegory of the wheel of Fortune to introduce a passage referring to the fortunes of his sovereign, Charles the Seventh of France:- Among the names which, by the turning of the wheel, rose to the top, Priam saw written (25,064) „Charles septiesme fortuné" and asked of Fortune, „qui devait estre le seigneur?" Fortune replied:- (25,070.)

C'est ung prince de grant valeur,
Le quel viendra a grant honneur,
Mais ainçois aura du malheur,
Et des desplaisirs griefz et grans,
Si sera roy et gouverneur
De france, a tres grant labeur,
(25,076.) Avant qu'il passe cinq mille ans. (Compare Prologue 272.)

(This last line is interesting as revealing Milet's idea of the date of the siege of Troy.) Fortune will treat this prince exactly the reverse of Priam. Charles will have trouble and sorrow in his youth, but honor and glory in his later life:- (25,089.)

Devant cestuy seront plusieurs,
Qui seront ses predecesseurs, (!)
Moult nobles hommes et vaillans,
Mais cestuy aura des honneurs,
Quant passé aura ses douleurs,
Plus que les aultres en son temps,
Ja soit ce que, ses premiers ans,
Ses desplaisirs seront si grans
Qu'on ne les saroit raconter,
Car ses ennemis ençiens,
Qui seront pour l'eure puissans,
Le cuideront desheriter,
Mais ainsi que tourné ie t'ay
A bas, ainsi le tourneray
En hault, et tout en ung moment
Sa noblesse releveray,
Sa puissance redoubleray,
Tant que dessus le firmament
N'aura prince, qui nullement
Ose faire son mal talent,
Et celuy roy, que ie te dis,
En ses armes certainement
Si portera tant seulement
Trois moult plaisantes fleurs de liz.

It is worthy of note that Milet does not repeat in this passage anything regarding the descent of the royal house of France from the kings of Troy, which he had emphasized in the Prologue to the drama.

205. After Fortune had thus told Priam of the future king of France, Priam cries out against her cruelty (25,113) in forcing him to bear adversity after prosperity. Surely it is easier to first suffer adversity, if all ends in prosperity. Fortune, however, left Priam, leading away Dame Liesse with her, after first showing him the road „d'aler en tristesse". He goes thither and finds — — la chamberiere

Qui ce faisoit nommer tristesse.

She and „Liesse" are sisters but hate each other, quarrelling incessantly. Tristesse gave Priam to drink

(25,162) „D'une eaue venimeuse et noire"

which intensified the memories of his former happiness and made him so wretched that he left the tower, only to learn that all his friends were dead, and that he must endure his misery alone. Priam concludes by declaring again that he has experienced the whole range of fortune shown to mortals. Happy in his youth, he is wretched of all men in his last years and is abandoned by all his friends. He bids all future kings to profit by his sad experience.

Chapter XXV.

Preliminaries of Peace. — The Palladium. — Sacrifices. — The Wooden Horse. — Ratification of Peace. — Feigned Departure of the Greeks.

M. 25,203—26,693. B. 25,183—25,903. G. Q 4 r 1 — Q 8 r 26.

---

206. At the close of Priam's long allegorical monologue Helen arises. She is anxious for her safety in the event of agreement with the Greeks, and goes to Anthenor to beseech him to intervene in her behalf:-

1) Her opening words are taken almost literally from G.:-

(25,203) I'ay entendu qu'on veult traiter | La paix aux grecz — —

(Q 4 r 1) „Helena vero sciens quod pax erat tractanda cum grecis."

B. expresses himself otherwise:-

(B. 25,183.) Cist parlement furent retrait | A dame heleine.

2) In B. she asks Anthenor to address his appeal to the *Greek princes;* Menelaus is not specified (B. 25,195—7); moreover the appeal is actually addressed to the Greek princes (B. 25,209). In G-M., on the other hand, she begs Anthenor to appeal directly to *Menelaus* (Q 4 r 4; 25,215; 25,244; 25,264; 25,337) and Anthenor does address Menelaus in her behalf (Q 4 r 17; 25,379).

3) A feature of some interest, illustrating a difference of custom between M's century and that of B., deserves notice. In B., Helen fears that her husband „la face desmenbrer" (B. 25,193). In M., „que ie soie arse et brulee" (M. 25,221). In G. no punishment is specified.

4) In M., in some unexplained way, Helen knows that Anthenor and Enee are to betray the city.

25,239. Puisqu'ainsi va, que voullez rendre | Aux grecz ceste noble cite.

207. 1) In accordance with the decision of the council (see § 200⁷) Anthenor and Enee go to the Greeks and meet Diomedes and Ulixes. With these they reaffirm by oath the conditions of the treason: on their side the betrayal of the city, on the Greek side the sparing of the (25,312) „parens et heritaiges" of Anthenor and Enee. All four then go before Agamenon and the other Greeks where Diomedes recounts the agreement (25,354) „iuré sur saintes et sur sains". At the suggestion of Agamenon, Diomedes and Ulixes are commissioned to go to Troy, Pour veoir priam et ses subgetz (25,378).

2) Anthenor now adds his plea for Helen, and M. constructs quite an animated and original dialogue between Menelaus, Agamenon and Nestor.

(25,387):-
(Menelaus en soubzriant)
Ha, la faulse, ie l'entens bien,
Quant el ne peult plus resister,
Elle veult trouver le moyen
Par prieres de moy matter.

Yet he loves her, despite all the grief she has caused him. He asks Nestor if she is worthy of pardon. Nestor replies sharply:- (25,403.) Faictes en ce que vous vouldres
Pleust aux dieux qu'elle fust brulee!

She caused the death of his son, and, although she is his cousin,

(25,408)
Ie regnie le cousinaige,
Quant a par sa folle pensee
Deshonoré tout son lignaige.

Menelaus has a „cueur d'enfant" (25,411), but, as he is nearer in relationship to Helen, let him do with her as he wishes,

(25,425.) Car i'ay assez et largement
D'aultres besongnes en la teste.

Agamenon thereupon calms the brusque Nestor, saying that Menelaus is naturally glad to hear of Helen's repentence:- (25,433.)

Car ung cueur d'amoureux desir, Certes, il ne se peult tenir
Quant on luy parle de s'amye, Que tout le corps ne luy fremye.

Agamenon begs his brother not to allow Nestor to influence his decision. Menelaus then replies to Anthenor:- Helen is pardoned

„doulcement | S'elle se repent, i'en ay ioye."

Yet, if ever she does the like again, the Greeks will wish her burned (25,474). Although she has caused him and the Greeks untold woe,

Touteffois le cueur me resserre
Que ne luy puis nul mal vouloir.

Anthenor thanks Menelaus, and, with Enee, Ulixes and Diomedes, returns before Priam and all the kings of Troy (25,498 d).

208. In the council-scene which follows, we note again a series of points of contact with G:-

1) In all versions Ulixes is the first to speak, but his opening words are the same in G-M:-

M. 25,514.
Deux choses nous font cy venir,
Pour nostre parlement tenir.
M. 25,520.
Nous demandons premierement
Admende et restaurement
De nostre grant et grief dommaige.
Nous demandons semblablement
L'exil et le banissement
D'amphimacus au fier couraige.

Q 4 r 24.
Ulixes — — — dixit illis grecos videlicet duo petere restaurationem damnorum in auri et argenti maxima quantitate et quod amphimacus perpetuo relegetur ab urbe sine spe aliqua redeundi.

In B. (25,231—8) only the exile of Amphimacus is emphasized at this time. B-G. say that this was demanded at the secret insistence of Anthenor (25,231; Q 4 v 28). M. omits all hint of Anthenor as the instigator.

2) There now arises a tumult among the Trojan people. B. gives no other cause thereof than (B. 25,249):-

Que ço fussent li fill priam,
Si chevalier et si servant,
Qui les deus reis venissent prendre.

G. and M., however, say, in addition, that the demand for the exile of Amphimacus is the cause:- (Q 4 v 16) „propter relegacionem amphimaci". M. 25,532:

C'est pour l'amour d'amphimacus,
Que ces gens cy sont esmus,
Pour cause du banissement.

The council is now dismissed by Priam (25,536), and Anthenor leads Ulixes and Diomedes to a secret place.

209. In the secret interview which now follows, Anthenor tells Ulixes and Diomedes about the Palladium. The contact of M. with G. is very marked in this passage:-

1) In B. there is no expression of impatience on the part of Diomedes or Ulixes at the delay in surrendering the city. In G-M. Ulixes expresses impatience (25,540—7; Q 4 v 23—4). G-M. further agree in having Anthenor declare that there exists a difficulty (25,554; Q 4 v 27), also in having Diomedes continue the dialogue by replying to Anthenor (25,555; Q 4 v 29). All three of these things are absent in B. where Anthenor begins his speech at once (B. 25,263) without any introductory dialogue. In this speech which explains the origin and nature of the Palladium, several things are common only to G-M.:-

2) In stating that Ilius (M. 25,561; Q 4 r 31; in B. Ylus 25,273) was the founder of Troy, M. omits to mention, with B-G., that the castle of Ilion was named after him.

3) B. says that he built a temple in honor of Minerva (B. 25,278). G-M., as usual, substitute for this the Greek name Pallas (25,566; Q 5 r 1). While this temple was still incomplete, there came from heaven a wonderful thing which fastened itself to the inside of the temple.

4) The nature of this wonder is differently expressed:- B. calls it (25,281) Uns signes, fiers et precios,
Et sor toz altres merveillos.

and says further:- (25,290)

De fust est, mais ne sai a dire
Ne la façon ne la matire,
Com faitement fut manovrez,
Et entailliez et conpassez.

G. repeats this, essentially unchanged:-

(Q 5 r 3) „quoddam mirabile signum et quadam res nimium virtuosa."

and adds (Q 5 r 9—12) that it was for the most part of wood, but of what wood or how it was made into its present form no one knew. M. follows these ideas closely, but adds another, which shows, even more than with B-G., his ignorance of the fact that the Palladium was a statue of Pallas:-

(25,557.)	Et ne peult on certainement
— — ung merveilleux ymage.	Savoir comment elle est fondee.
(25,580.)	(25,600.)
Si a figure d'un serpent	Iceluy serpent — —
Et semble de bois composee	(Compare Meybrinck P. 60.)

5) B. only says (25,297) „appelez est Palladion", without stating why. G. and M. state why:- (Q 5 r 19.)

pro eo quod a dea pallade creditur esse datum.

M. 25,596.	25,600.
En l'onneur de celle pallas	Iceluy serpent appellerent
— — — — — — —	Palladin par son droit nom.

6) All versions agree that, as long as the Palladium is within Troy, the city cannot be taken; as to the possibility of removing the Palladium, they differ:- (B. 25,295.)

Onques puis ne fu remuez	Qui l'adesereit de sa main,
Ne atochiez ne adesez.	Que li celeste soverain
(B. 25,310)	Le destruiroient demancis.
Ço savon bien et ço creon,	

Thus, B. feels obliged to say when the actual theft occurs:-

(25,556.) Mes Minerve le consenteit.

He, however, makes no exception in favor of the guardian of the Palladium. G-M. make such an exception:-

(Q 5 r 6.)	(M. 25,776.)
Et a nemine se baiulare permittit	Si est chose trop perilleuse
a loco scilicet ubi est nisi a custodibus	De la vouloir du lieu retraire,
suis tamen et nunc a solo suo custode	Et a home tres dangereuse,
videlicet a sacerdote.	Mais le prestre le puet bien faire.

7) G. and M. further agree in letting Anthenor close his speech by saying that the Greeks ought to comprehend the delay under all these circumstances (25,610—1; Q 5 r 23—6.)

8) In B. it is Ulixes who replies to Anthenor (B. 25,320—37.) In G-M. it is Diomedes, and his reply is in quite similar words (25,612—9; Q 5 r 21—3).

9) The answer of Anthenor is alike in G-M. (25,620—35; Q 5 r 26 — Q 5 v 1):- He assures them that by bribing the priest he can obtain the Palladium, and that, when this is once outside the city, there can be no further hindrance to the Greeks.

210. M. now passes directly to the episode of the corruption of the guardian-priest of the Palladium. He thus omits the council where Anthenor sets forth the money-conditions of the peace (B. 25,350 - 91; Q 5 v 12—22.), deeming his previous mention of these conditions (§ 200[1]) sufficient. The scene of the bribing of the priest continues to show M's direct dependence upon G. (B. 25,504—68; Q 5 v 22 — Q 6 r 16; M. 25,639—810.)

1) As in previous scenes (death of Achilles; appeal of Helen to Anthenor) M. omits the idea emphasized in B-G. that the incident took place after dark.

2) Although B. speaks of bribery (B. 25,519—21; 25,533—4; 25,542—4), the promises all refer to the future. In G-M. the bribery takes place on the spot by an actual transfer of money. (Q 5 v 25—29; M. 25,647—54 d; 25,711—18; 25,731—34 d). M. even states the bribe as „deux cens besans" (25,732).

3) Interesting also is the idea found only in G-M:- With the aforesaid money the priest can ever live in luxury, not only he himself but:- (Q 5 v 28) „tu et heredes tui"; (M. 25,717) „Vous et voz enffans".

4) In all three versions the priest makes considerable resistance, which gives M. a chance to expand the dialogue. In his objections in M. one or two things are noteworthy:- He, Thoas, is guardian of the Palladium in place of Calcas (25,676). — M. quite cleverly grades the overcoming of his objections:- At first he absolutely refuses 25,677—86; his second refusal is much weaker 25,703—10; in his third he is only actuated by fear of detection (25,719—26) and he finally tries to quiet his conscience by offering a prayer for forgiveness to Pallas (25,745—50) saying that he does this act „pour faire fin a la bataille".

5) G's influence is also seen in Anthenor's assertion that he is as anxious for his own reputation as the priest for his (M. 25,687—92; Q 6 r 1—4). B. does not have that idea.

6) The actual removal of the Palladium also presents several points of interest:- In B. it is Anthenor who takes it from its place (B. 15,552):- Quant Anthenor l'ala sesir.

G. implies the same (Q 6 r 11):- „Thohauz — — palladii subtractionem anthenori sponte concessit.“ M., however, remains true to the idea previously expressed by himself and G. that only the priest could take it (Q 5 r 6; 25,776; § 209[6]); he has the priest take the Palladium and give it to Anthenor.

7) G. and M. have no reference to a punishment for this corruption. B., however, has (25,552):-

Ses ielz repont que il nel veie.
Quant Anthenor l'ala sesir,
Bien l'en déust mesavenir;
Si féist il par tel endreit,
Mes Minerve le consenteit,
Que senpres perdist les deus ielz.

The above punctuation is according to Joly who interprets this passage (note to 25,557):- „il ferma les yeux pour ne pas voir; il eut dû en perdre les deux yeux; mais Minerve y consentait.“ The confusion of pronouns in the passage renders it difficult to determine whether Benoît thought that the priest merited the punishment, or Anthenor.

8) In B. Anthenor himself brings the Palladium to the Greek kings who, in turn, transmit it to Ulixes (B. 25,558—65). In G-M. Anthenor sends it by messenger directly to Ulixes (Q 6 r 13—5; M. 25,767—801). Original to M. is Anthenor's command to his servant to ask that Ulixes

(25,772) — die tout publicquement, | Qu'il a sustrait par sa cautelle.

This last is due to (Q 6 r 16):-

„postea vero fama dictante publice dictum est quod ulixes sua sagacitate illud interceperat a troyanis.“

9) At the close of the episode of the theft of the Palladium, B. has an additional council of Anthenor with the Greeks (25,569—611). G. has an interesting passage (Q 6 r 16—26) in which he attacks most severely the priesthood for their cupidity and corruptibility. M. passes directly to the sacrifical scene and its ill-omens for the Trojans.

211. M. follows G. in placing this sacrificial scene after the theft of the Palladium. In B. the order is the reverse (B. 25,392—503; Q 6 r 26 — Q 6 v 26; M. 25,814—994.) In B. the first attempt to light sacrificial fires is made in the temple of Minerva (B. 25,395) and, when this fails, the people run „dreit a l'autel appollinis“ (B. 25,422) where the eagle carries away the unburnt animal-sacrifices. In G. and M. both episodes occur in the temple of Apollo (Q 6 r 29; 25,854). M's relation of the first attempt merits lengthy notice. We shall see how both episodes in M. remind us of the former sacrificial scenes at Delos (§ 66):-

Anthenor goes to Priam and asks that sacrifices be made, first to Apollo, then to Diana (25,820). Macabrum is sent to summon the Trojan princes and Priam's family who come and „se serront en consistoire“ (25,866 d). Priam bids Thoas, the guardian of the Palladium, and his „clerc“ Cidrac, as officiating priests, to begin.

(25,879 d.) „adont thoas vest les habillemens convenablez pour sacrifier aux dieux et tous les troyens se mettent a genoux et fauldra avoir de la genefve afin que la fumee ne face mal aux yeulx et thoas dira a son clerc nomme cidrac qui sera aussi revestu comme thoas mais il n'aura point de chappeau en la teste“.

At the bidding of Thoas, Cidrac brings fire, whereupon Thoas prays to Apollo (25,883—90) „alors fait semblant de mettre le feu ou genefvre et ne se doit point alumer ains fait grant fumee“.

Astonished at this, Thoas says (25,899):-

Zebay ferme cidrac | Zebay ferme cidrac | Gesi sabaoth cayaulx.
and Cidrac:- Belchi mepsi exanictos | Belchi zoe athanatos | Holy hely belsanitos.

Thoas once more (25,905—12) prays that the fire be allowed to kindle, „lors veullent mettre le feu au bois et ne peult sinon fumer“

Thoas thereupon declares that they must propitiate the god with animal-sacrifice. — Comparing this first part of the sacrificial scene with B-G. we note several features:-

1) M. speaks only of the failure to light the fire, and reserves the actual animal-sacrifice as a means of propitiating the gods until the second scene. B. (25,409) and G. (Q 6 r 31), however, speak of sacrifices being offered before the attempt to light the fire.

2) B-G. mention no priests as officiating.

3) B. omits all hint of smoke. G-M. emphasize this detail. (Q 6 v 5) „ignis statim extinctus resolvebatur in fumum“; in M. the above three stage-directions (25,879 d; 25,890 d; 25,913 d).

4) B. declares that Diomedes and Ulixes were present (25,392—402). M-G. agree in not mentioning their presence.

212. The second part of the sacrificial scene follows immediately (25,921 d. — 94):- Thoas

„prent ung mouton blanc qui a cornes et le prent par les piez de devant et son clerc par ceulx de derriere et puis quant il y est il le fent en disant.“

Thoas then beseeches the gods to accept the sacrifice;

„alors respent du sanc sur l'autel",

after which he continues his prayer (25,935—42)

„adont tire des entrailles et les met sur l'autel" :-

Tres haulx dieux, prenez ceste oaille,
Que nous vous offrons de bon cueur,
Et vous plaise qu'elle nous vaille
A effacer vostre fureur.

O dieux, nous vous faisons honneur
Par immolation sacree;
Recevez du sanc la liqueur
Et des entraillez la fumee.

En disant ces quatre lignes dernieres doit descendre par artifice une aigle qui les emportera et les prendra."

Compared with B-G. this shows but slight variation:-

1) B-G. say nothing of shedding the blood as one means of propitiation.

2) Instead of one animal, B-G. speak of a large number, although not specifying of what sort (25,424; Q 6 r 31).

3) M. omits the detail in B-G. that the eagle carries the entrails to the Greek ships (25,443; Q 6 v 11); M., therefore, omits the interpretation of this incident given by Calcas (25,464—7; Q 6 v 24).

213. 1) In M. the priest now asserts that it is useless to offer further sacrifices, as the gods are displeased (25,943—6). The result of the sacrifices, therefore, remains most ominous for the Trojans. In B-G. further and propitious sacrifices are made.

2) B. alone speaks first of another unsuccessful sacrifice made by Hecuba to Apollo and Minerva (B. 25,470—81).

3) In all versions Cassandra declares that Apollo is angry because of the violation of his temple at the death of Achilles: M's words here (25,973),

Pour achiles qui par esclandre | Fut en son temple destroussé.

show that he has forgotten that he describes Achilles' death as occurring in the temple of *Venus* (see § 158[1]).

4) M., however, does not follow B-G. in Cassandra's command that the Trojans go where lies buried, in B. Hector (25,492), in G. Achilles (Q 6 v 20), and kindle there a sacrificial fire. She prophesies that it will be successful and her prophecy is correct (B. 25,497; Q 6 v 22). G's substitution of Achilles' tomb for Hector's seems appropriate, for, as Apollo is angry at the assassination of Achilles, expiation should be made in the

latter's name. This substitution was the more possible in G., because he had said that Achilles' tomb was in Troy near Hector's (see § 165[3]).

5) B. alone declares that, in consequence of this successful sacrifice, the Trojans (25,502)

Grant ioie ont quant li dampledé | Se sont vers els apaié.

G's omission of this idea of reconciliation may in part explain M's total neglect of this successful sacrifice.

6) In B. Cassandra does not interpret the carrying away of the entrails by the eagle. In G-M. she does, which affords us still another point of contact:-

(Q 6 v 22.)	(M. 25,978.)
Cassandra troyanis asseruit proditionem civitatis apud grecos sine dubio esse tractatam.	Que troye doit estre rendue Aux grecz et de voz mains perdue Par fraude et par trahison.

7) When, in M., Thoas, the priest, says that it is useless to sacrifice further (see this paragraph [1]), he discloses, at the same time, the loss of the Palladium (25,951):-

Car le paladin est pris,
Et l'a ulixes emporte,
Et si tres cautement surpris
Par sa grande subtilite,
Que oncques ne m'en suis advise,
Tant que i'ay entendu les ditz
De gens, qui ont en l'ost este
Qu'on la veu dedans son logis.

Nowhere in B. is it said that the Trojans learn of the loss of the Palladium (see § 214[7].) In G. they do learn of its loss (see also § 214[7]), but nothing is said of it here in this sacrificial scene.

In M. the sacrificial scene closes with a speech by Priam (25,983—94) who declares his resignation to the divine will.

214. 1) The next scene takes place on the Greek side and contains the counsel of Calcas to build the horse. M. thus has the same order here as G. In B., however, the theft of the Palladium is introduced between the sacrificial scenes treated above and the following building of the horse.

2) In an introductory speech (25,995—26,042) Agamenon declares that the fall of Troy now seems near at hand and that they must find means to hasten it. As the best one to devise such means Agamenon introduces Calcas:- (26,031).

Vecy Calcas qui longuement
Nous a par son bon sentement
Gardé de ce pays laiser,
Car prins avons consentement
Plusieurs fois de departement,
Et de la guerre delaisser.

This passage atones, in a measure, for the less attention paid to the rôle of Calcas in M. than in B-G.

3) The advice of Calcas to build the horse now follows (26,043—66). M. thus does not mention the first suggestion of Calcas that sacrifices be made, which, in B-G., precedes his counsel to build the horse. M. also omits the name of Crises as the associate of Calcas in these sacrifices and in connection with the building of the horse (B. 25,618; Q 6 v 26). In B. both Calcas and Crises *advise* the building of the horse (B. 25,620—6), but Crises alone tells how it is to be constructed (B. 25,634). G., thinking, therefore, that Crises was the principal actor in the matter, has him both advise and describe the construction of the horse. M., not introducing Crises at all as a „personage", has Calcas alone.

4) In B. Calcas declares to the Greeks that the horse be built:- (B. 25,621.) Por le tenple qu'ert violez,
Dont li pallades ert enblez,
Que Minerve n'en fust iric.

and that this is said in all sincerity, without any connection with the treacherous purpose of the horse, seems further substantiated by B. 25,629—30, and B. 25,760—77. In G. and M., on the other hand, Calcas states openly that this propitiation is nothing but a ruse to induce the Trojans to allow the horse to come into the city (Q 7 r 7—12; M. 26,102—4; 26,139—44.)

5) In B. the interior construction of the horse is not specified. B. simply says (25,638):-

Quant la chose vos iert retrete,
A grant merveille vos torra.

and gives nowhere a description of its interior. Stranger still is it that B. contains *no* hint of the horse being intended to hold armed men, *no* word of armed men being put into it, or of their issuing forth from it.[1]) It is only said of Sinon later,

---

[1]) Dunger (P. 38) says that Benoît mentions armed men in the horse. Dunger's work is based on Fromman's selections from Benoît in Pfeiffer's Germania II. (Joly's work had not then appeared.) These selections, however, do not contain the passages referring to the horse, but only such in which Herbort v. Fritzlar „von Benoît abweicht" (Dunger P. 32). Dunger, therefore, bases his opinion regarding the armed men in the horse upon Herbort, since he says

who lights the signal fire for the Greeks to come and capture the city, that he (B. 25,916) „dedens lo cheval esteit". *No others* are mentioned as placed within the horse. In fact, in B., the *only* trace of the classical idea of the horse is that the Trojans break down a part of the city-walls to allow it to pass (25,814—9), through which breach the Greeks ultimately enter the city (B. 25,939; see § 218[4]).

In G-M., however, the classical idea of the horse's use, to hold armed men, finds abundant expression:- In G.:- (Q 6 v 31) „ut in eo saltem possint *mille* milites constipari", also Q 7 r 6—7 with the same number, 1,000. These soldiers in the horse issue forth and join their countrymen in the sack of Troy:- (Q 8 v 2) „egredientibus militibus qui in equo extiterant constipati etc." Even so in M.:-

(26,055.)	(26,096.)
Qui feust cavé si sagement	Tant qu'il y puisse a une fois
Que gens d'armes y peussent estre.	Dedans quarente hommes armés.

See likewise 26,133—6. M. also builds up a scene (26,161—87) where Pirrus and his men enter the horse:- (26,187 d) „lors entre dedans le cheval pirrus luy [= Synon] tresiesme" (the editions of 1485 and 1544 have „pirrus et toutes ses gens"; the number is therefore uncertain); and M. further has another short passage where „pirrus et ses compaignons saudront dehors" (26,705 d).

6) B. does not state the material of the horse. G. says „ereum" (Q 6 v 31; Q 7 v 15); M. „bois", probably after Virgil (26,054; 26,095; 26,107). M. describes the arrangements which enable the men within the horse to breathe, and also emphasizes their being able to look out (26,057—8; 26,098—101). G. is only anxious for the openings through which they may see and also make their exit (Q 7 r 3; Q 8 r 30).

7) In B. the *Trojans* are not told that the horse is a substitute for the stolen Palladium. Calcas gives this reason *only*

(P. 32) „Wir können daher überall wo Frommann nichts erwähnt aus Herbort auf Benoît zurückschliessen und diesen aus jenem ergänzen." Herbort, in truth, mentions armed men in the horse (Frommann's edition — Quedlinburg and Leipzig 1837), verse 15,957 (?) and 16,158 ff., where the number is given as thirty (compare M's forty and G's thousand).

to the Greeks (B. 25,621 see this paragraph [4]). Indeed, it is nowhere said that the Trojans learn of the loss of the Palladium (see § 213[7]), and the only reason given to urge Priam's acceptance of the horse is that (B. 25,775):-

Minerve quiert et velt cest don,

and that, by his accepting it, she will honor Troy and save the Greeks from the perils of the sea (B. 25,765—74).

In G-M., on the other hand, the horse is given with a distinct understanding that it is in reparation for the theft of the Palladium, of the loss of which, therefore, the Trojans learn:- Q 7 r 8—12 (in the counsel of Crises); Q 7 v 18 (in the urging of Priam) „pro furto palladii". In M. 26,139, Calcas says:-

Vous ferez semblant de donner
Au temple tres devotement
Le cheval pour l'amendement
Du paladin qu'on a pris.

and Agamenon says to Priam:- 26,424

Vous scavez bien par quelle guise
Ulixes a prins en l'eglise
Paladin desoulz palas.
26,429.
Afin qu'elle soit appaisee
Nous avons voulu composer
Ce cheval pour luy presenter
En la remuneracion
De la griefve execution.

In M. the Trojans learn of the loss of the Palladium from their priest Thoas, even before the horse is offered to them as a substitute (25,291; see § 213[7]).

215. In the preceding paragraph the analysis of the nature and purpose of the horse has forced us to select disconnected passages and abandon temporarily the continuity of events as related in M. His treatment of the preparation of the horse, however, merits notice:-

Calcas, after advising the building of the horse, bids the workman Apius be summoned (26,060). At Agamenon's command, Citheus fetches Apius to whom Calcas then describes the construction of the horse:- It must be made to hold forty armed men (26,098):-

Et, si tresbien le composez,
Qu'il puissent avoir leur alaine,
Et voir la clarté toute plaine
Par les pertuis de la machine.

Apius replies (26,106):-

Ie l'auray tantost acomplye,
Car i'ay du bois a grant foison,
Qui ne fait riens en ma maison.
(26,113.)
Tant que ie l'auray amene,
Ie ne quiers boire ne menger.

A very naïve stage-direction follows:-

„lors s'en va et prent le cheval qui sera tout fait apres qu'il aura ung peu muse en estant hors de la veue des gens et y aura pause de menestrelz apres laquelle le dit apius amenera le cheval.“

Apius delivers the horse to Agamenon, who asks (26,121) Calcas what is its use. Calcas explains (26,129—60) its strategical purpose:- It shall be filled with armed men, given as a pretended reparation for the stolen Palladium, and carried into Troy. The Greeks shall then go away, only to return at a signal from those within the horse. Agamenon approves this plan and asks for volunteers to enter the horse (26,161). Pirrus offers himself and his man Sinon:-

The line „Si aura [Sinon] lez *clefz* du cheval“ points to G. (Q 8 r 10) „Symonem cui greci *claves* assignaverant“, inasmuch as B. says nothing of keys. — Moreover Q 8 r 10—15 served as source for 26,177—82. — Pirrus and his men enter the horse (26,187 d.), and there ensues the scene of the ratification of peace.

216. Preparations for the ratification of peace now follow. The scene does not show many points of contact with G. but is chiefly interesting because of the way M. handles it:-

1) Agamenon (26,188) says that Priam must now be summoned to ratify peace, and sends Citheus to deliver the message. B-G. say indefinitely that the scene takes place outside the walls (B. 25,641 and 25,708; Q 7 r 28). M. specifies

26,192 „Es prez de la porte tybree.“

2) A slight point showing G's influence is the following:- In B. the context seems to show that „saintuaires“ are carried out *from Troy* (B. 25,706—8):-

Ont fait porter les saintuaires
De fors les murs en unes aires.

G. and M., however, say that the *Greeks* set them up:- (Q 7 r 28) „extra muros sanctuariis ordinatis *a grecis*.“ In M. (26,199), Agamenon says to Citheus:-

Et luy (= Priam) dy aussi que ie foys
Porter les dieux enmy la pree.

3) G. does not specify any deities by name. B. and M. do, but the names are not alike:- B. says (25,727—9) „Jupiter, — Apollo, — Soleil et lune et terre et mer“.

M. (26,207)
Mercure, le dieu des marchands,
Venus aussi, d'amours deesse
Et palas, dame de sagesse.

4) Agamenon bids Diomedes swear to the peace:-

(26,216).
Comme anthenor la demandee
Ainsi ne sera point faulsee
Nostre promesse et nostre foy.

and Diomedes swears this way, later (26,387—8: see § 217[2]). This scheme to avoid perjury is equally emphasized in B-G. (25,737—9; Q 7 v 2). B. alone states that Anthenor and Eneas had arranged it so. It calls forth from G. the moralizing remark (Q 7 v 5) „qui artificiose iurat artificiose periurat".

5) M. alone has the additional detail of Nestor's being delegated to „porter les dieux", because he is the oldest (26,223—27 d.) Interesting also is (26,227 d):-

„lors nestor aporte trois ymages faiz en façon que les sarrazins pandoient [in editions of 1485 and 1544 „faisoient"] leurs dieux et les mettra sur une table bien paree ou millieu de l'eschauffault."

6) Citheus meanwhile summons Priam who, in turn, bids Anthenor, Enee, Anchises and Polidamas to accompany him to the place of ratification.

217. The actual ceremony of ratification is the next scene. M. treats it with considerable originality:-

1) A preliminary interview between Priam and Agamenon is not without pleasing features:- Agamenon salutes Priam and addresses him (26,273):- He regrets that Priam has had so much trouble Pour ung de voz filz seulement,
and refers to Priam's age, beauty and magnificence.

(26,307) Et a regarder voz deux yeulx
Samblez bien avoir grant couraige.

In Priam's reply (26,309) he says

Agamenon, moult estez saige,
Moult estez plaisant en langaige,
Mais ie ne vous dois pas aymer.

Priam then speaks of his great sorrow at his terrible losses and ends with a generous plea for Helen (26,324—44).

2) Both sides now proceed to the giving of oaths:- In all versions Diomedes is the first to swear (B. 25,714; Q 7 r 31; M. 26,375). He swears to the peace (26,387)

Comme il a este apointe
Par anthenor et enee.

(see § 216[1]). In B. *all* the Greeks swear (B. 25,726) after the leaders, Idomeneus, Thoas, Emilius, Nestor, Menelaus, Thelamonius Aiax and Neptolemus have sworn. G., however, speaks only of „majores grecorum ceteri“ (Q 7 v 6). M. still further restricts it. Only Ulixes, Diomedes' colleague in the negociations, repeats the oath (26,389). G. and M. omit all hint of the two sacrificial fires between which in B. (25,730—6) the Greeks pass, as an extra assurance of good faith. M. has a similar restriction of the oath-taking on the Trojan side:- In B. the Greeks (25,743) „ont fet a cels dedanz inrer“, but Priam is not specially mentioned. In G. (Q 7 v 7) „Priamus itaque cum omnibus troyanis suis deceptus et ignarus pacem ipsam non ficticie sed absolute iuravit.“ M. understood this as meaning that Priam *alone* took the oath, and he so represents it (26,398—419).

218. 1) Agamenon expresses satisfaction at Priam's oath. He then urges him to accept the gift of the horse. This last episode we have already analyzed in § 214[7]

2) In B-G. Priam makes no reply (B. 25,778 — Q 7 v 20). In M. he expresses his want of faith in the Greeks:-

(26,457.)
Las, m'oseray ie bien fier
En vous et en vostre promesse?
Certes se seroit grant simplesse.

3) In all versions Priam yields to the persuasion of Anthenor and Eneas. Anthenor's chief reason is original to M.:- One cannot with impunity prevent another from making a sacrifice to the gods (26,468—71).

4) Priam finally gives orders for the horse to be brought to Troy (26,489). Enee (26,495) „Pour donner aux aultres exemple“ „prent une corde et la lie au col du cheval“, whereupon Anthenor and Amphorbius „mettront la main au cheval“. The horse is, however, not drawn into Troy until after the feigned departure of the Greeks (26,680 d). In B-G., on the other hand, the Greeks do not go away until the horse is within the city. They even aid in the labor of hauling it thither (B. 25,790—821; Q 7 v 26 — Q 8 r 5). In M. nothing is said of the need of breaking away the walls to admit the horse. In B-G. such a tearing down is necessary. We have already noted (§ 214[5]) that in B. this breaking of the walls is the only relic of the classical purpose of the horse. In B. *alone* the Greeks take advantage

of the horse being within the breach in the walls to enforce the payment of the indemnity (B. 25,821—32).

219. The restitution of Helen varies in the version of B-G. from that in M.:- In B. Priam beseeches for clemency toward Helen (B. 25,750—9), but the Greeks secretly decide not to receive her until the city is taken (B. 25,846—58), and they tell Priam that they will send for her as soon as they are at some distance from Troy on their way home. Their leaders give as excuse that, if they take her at once, the common people will put her to death (B. 25,863—72). Helen is finally taken captive by Menelaus during the sack of Troy (B. 26,091—4). G. follows this in the main (Q 7 v 10—13; Q 8 r 18—21; R 1 r 24—25) but in the first of these passages (Q 7 v 10—13) it is not only said that Priam beseeches for clemency toward Helen, but also that he „helenam grecorum regibus restituit". M., therefore, ignoring the subsequent passages regarding Helen, takes this line as the basis for his version. Helen is given back before the sack of Troy, and nothing further is said of her in M. until the discussion of her fate is precipitated by the demand of Thelamonius Ajax for her death (see § 228).

220. Milet's treatment of this restitution of Helen is as follows:- After consenting to receive the horse, Priam exhorts the Greeks to keep their faith and to depart immediately. He will give them Helen (26,502—18). Agamenon asks for the immediate surrender of Helen, and Enee and Anthenor are sent to fetch her. A pleasing scene of farewell between Helen and „Hecuba et ses filles" follows (26,533—82):- Helen takes affectionate leave successively of Hecuba, Creusa, Andromache, Polixene and Cassandra, who all express great grief at her departure. To Helen's prayer for pardon (26,573):-

> Se par moy ont perdu la vie
> Voz freres — —

Cassandra replies generously:-

> Aussi faiz en bonne foy,
> Belle seur, ie le vous pardonne,
> Car vrayement il n'est personne
> Qui vous en deust mal gre savoir.

Helen then comes before Priam who declares (26,591) that he loves her dearly, tells her of the agreement of Menelaus to receive her, and bids her accept the inevitable. Priam then beseeches the forgiveness and clemency of Menelaus. Although Helen has been the cause of his (Priam's) utter ruin,

(26,607) — neantmoins de tres bon cueur
Luy pardonne mon desplaisir.

Priam then bids Helen to kneel before Menelaus and to add her own plea for forgiveness. Helen does so (26,631), beseeching Menelaus to remember that she was powerless to resist at the time of her capture. Menelaus reprooves Helen, but pardons her all (26,639—50).

221. 1) Menelaus now (26,651) bids Priam farewell:- The Greeks return home „Ou ne feusmes des ans a dix". Priam in turn bids them good-bye, wishing them god-speed, although they have laid low his fortune. „adont (26,662 d.) tous les grecz entrent dedans les nefz ou ilz estoient quant il vindrent premierement". M. has omitted to speak here, before the departure of the Greeks, of the actual payment of the indemnity, which in B-G. (25,821—35; Q 7 v 24—6) forms an important part of the conclusion of peace.

2) Agamenon next (26,663) bids the Greeks to steer the ships „tout droit — — Dedans *l'isle de tenedon*", whence they will return for the final vengeance upon Troy. „alors s'en vont en *l'isle de thenedon* c'est assavoir la ou arriverent quant ilz vindrent a troye." Other references to *Tenedos* in this connection are M. 26,147; 26,182; 26,697. This is another striking proof of M's dependence upon G. In G. the Greeks tell Priam that they are going to *Thenedos* (Q 8 r 17) there to receive Helen; and they actually go thither (Q 8 r 25). In B., on the other hand, they go to *Sigeon* (B. 25,860; 25,900).

3) After the departure of the Greeks, Priam (26,673) commands the horse to be drawn into Troy „iusques au temple". It shall be placed within the temple on the morrow (26,683). Priam then bids all retire to rest; „alors tous les troyans feront semblant de dormir et y doit avoir une couche ou priam se reposera" (26,693 d).

Chapter XXVI.

The Sack of Troy. — Death of Priam; of Polixene; of Hecuba. — The Dispute over the Palladium. — The Greeks disperse.

M. 26,694—27,984. (End of the Drama.) B. 25,904—27,156.
G. Q 8 r 27 — R 4 v 28.

---

222. The return of the Greeks presents several interesting features:-

1) In B-G. the return takes place *before* the fire-signal is given by Sinon (return, B. 27,906; Q 8 r 28; signal, B. 25,913; Q 8 r 31). The Greeks approach the city and await the signal in order to enter it. In M. the return from Thenedos is *after* the signal and in consequence of it (signal 26,708 d; return 26,732 d).

2) Although all versions speak of ships at the departure of the Greeks, only B. mentions them at their return (B. 25,907). „Des *nes* issirent as chans fors." G. and M. do not mention ships but say only:- „se contulerunt" (Q 8 r 28); „s'en doivent venir" (26,732 d). Indeed, despite M's recent insistence upon Thenedos as an island (see § 221²), he lets Agamenon say (26,724):-

Mais il m'est advis que mieux vault
Aler par t e r r e de present
Que par mer, car ie voy le vent
Qui n'est pas bon pour le besoing. (!)

3) M. alone has the detail in the words of Sinon (26,694),

Ie voy ia la lune levee.

4) We have already (see § 214⁵) noted B's total omission of armed men within the horse, and M's accord with G. concerning their rôle on this occasion.

5) As M. has no hint of a breach in the walls to admit the horse (see § 218⁴), he of course omits (26,732 d) saying that the Greeks enter the city by that breach, thus differing from B-G. (25,939—43; Q 8 v 1).

6) In G. and M. the silence of the return is emphasized (Q 8 r 29; 26,713—15). In other respects M's version of this return is not noteworthy except for Agamenon's exhortation (26,709—32) and for the nature of the signal-fire (26,708 d), „adont ilz alumeront trois *gluis de paille*".

223. The general sack of Troy is introduced by M. with:- (26,732 d.)

„adont les grecz s'en doivent venir tout doulcement a l'entree de troye et doivent trouver deux troyans ausquelz ilz copperont la gorge.“

Diomedes bids that no quarter be given. Agamenon commands (26,736) that the houses of Anthenor and Enee be spared (26,741).

Mais vueillez en tout aultre lieu
Mettre tout a sang et a feu,
Hommes, femmes, petis enffans,
Soient ieunes ou anciens.

Pirrus adds (26,746):-

Or ca, par ma foy, il nous fault
Bouter le feu parmy la ville
Et envoier de noz gens mille
Pour prendre priam au palays.

(26,750 d) adont les grecz alumeront grant feu de fagotz de genevre et feront semblant de bruller toutes les tentes de troye et n'y doit rien demourer entier que ylion et le[1]) temple et l'eschaffault d'anthenor et enee.

Of the special attack upon Ilion in B-G., led by Anthenor and Enee (B. 26,028—38; Q 8 v 25—9.), M. only mentions, in the words of Hecuba, that the Greeks are in the palace (26,769). A later stage-direction (26,890 d.) continues the general destruction and implies that Ilion has been razed:-

„alors les grecz font de grans cris et de grans clameurs et renouvellent le feu de genefvre iusques a ce que troye sera brullee du tout excepte le temple de palas.“

This general sack simply summarizes the description in B-G. (25,943—96; Q 8 v 1—14). The account in B. is particularly terrible and tragic.

224. 1) The death of Priam is the most dramatic event of this sack of Troy:- In all versions the noise awakens him. B. says:- (25,998.) „Sot et conut qu'il ert traïz“ which may refer either to the treachery of the Greeks or to that of Anthenor and Enee. G. and M. agree in specifying the latter (Q 8 v 14: 26,760).

2) B-G. do not distinctly say that Hecuba and her daughters were present at the moment of Priam's being killed by Pirrus. M. adds to the tragic effect by representing them as present (26,771 d; 26,817).

3) It appears also that Enee was present, since Hecuba addresses him at once after Priam's death (26,819), and says

---

[1]) This „le“ proves to our thinking that but one temple served on the stage for the oft-used temple of Apollo or of Venus, or, in 26,878d., of Pallas.

(26,830—4) that Enee led the assassins to Priam. This would then seem to be due to G's statement that both Anthenor and Eneas were present (R 1 r 1). B. does not specify their presence in 26,039—52, but later in Hecuba's speech to Eneas the lines:-

(26,065) Que len ci endreit, vos veiant,
A detrenchie lo rei priant.

would prove at least the presence of Enee.

4) M. still further enhances the tragedy of the scene by adding an episode unknown to B-G, namely the killing by Pirrus of Amphimacus in the arms of his father Priam (26,776 d). This, as Tivier has pointed out, is taken from Virgil, Aeneid II, the murder of Politenes.

5) In the flight of Amphimacus and Priam to the temple, M. emphasizes that they are clothed only in their „pourpoint" (26,771 d; 26,776 d). This was no doubt suggested by (Q 8 v 4) „et indutis vestibus quibus [priamus] potuit". B. neglects such a detail.

6) A slight difference in M. is that Priam is killed in the temple of Pallas (26,771 d). In B-G (26,005; Q 8 v 18 and 30), it is in that of Apollo.

7) Following the killing of Amphimacus is a speech by Priam (26,777—800) in which the latter upbraids Pirrus for his cruelty, and declares that Pirrus cannot be a son of Achilles who never showed such inhumanity. Two lines are of especial interest (26,785):-

Jadis fut hector par luy [= Achilles] mort;
Par luy me fut le corps rendu.

We have noted (§§ 165²; 167²) other passages containing this idea and its contradiction with the mediaeval version. This speech of Priam (and the scene generally) is undoubtedly inspired by Virgil's Aeneid II.

8) Pirrus replies brutally to Priam:-

(26,801.)
Viellart, vous mentez faulsement.
D'achilles suis ie propre filz,
Mais vous yres presentement
Avecques luy pour voz mesdis.

(26,808 d. adont lui coppe la teste.)
Or, allez devers achilles
Et luy demandez hardiment,
Qu'il vous di tout par expres,
Se ie suis son filz proprement.

At sight of their father's death, the daughters implore divine mercy.

9) In the stage-direction 26,808 d. Pirrus cuts off Priam's head. This agrees, strangely enough, with B. 26,043:-

La li fist si lo chief voler.

whereas G. only says (R 1 r 2) „regem priamum coram altari nequiter interfecit". This accidental agreement with B. is too isolated and too easily suggested by the context, to possess any weight. M. has Pirrus later decapitate Polixene, quite independently of such a manner of death in B-G. (see § 230[5]).

225. In all versions Hecuba attacks Eneas for his treachery. Her speech in G-M. contains several ideas not found in B.:-

1) Priam had exalted Eneas. Eneas, therefore, owed him complete loyalty. 26,825—9; R 1 r 8—11.

2) Yet he leads Priam's murderers against him (26,830—4; R 1 r 10).

3) Eneas betrays his *natal* city. 26,847—8; R 1 r 11—13. B. only has „Par vos est oi Troie esseilliee" (26,069).

4) Is Eneas not horrified at this conflagration of Troy? 26,849—53; R 1 r 13—4.

5) In B., Hecuba swoons twice, once, before beseeching Eneas to save Polixene, and again afterward (B. 26,074—5; 16,085) G-M. omit all mention of either swooning.

6) In G-M. in Hecuba's plea for Polixene, she exhorts Eneas to do at least one good act amid all his crimes. 26,854[1]—9; R 1 r 14—7.

7) In G-M. Hecuba's chief anxiety for Polixene is expressed as follows:-

R 1 r 19 „qui eam interficiant et turpiter dehonestent."

26,860. S'elle est tenue par les grecz, | Il luy feront aulcune esclandre.

B. does not have this idea.

8) On the other hand G-M. both omit the thought which in B. Hecuba expresses:- (26,083—4)

S il ocire ne me voloient, | S'ai gie deus mains que m'ociroient.

---

1) Greif neglects to number a verse between 26,852 and 26,854 in M.; He has made the contrary mistake by numbering the name Cediron as verse 8,180. Both these errors are not noted by Stengel.

9) Eneas promises Hecuba to rescue Polixene. In his reply the words (26,875)

Ca polixene, doulce amie,
Vueillez moy suivre, ie vous prie.

point to G. „eam incontinenti secum *ducit*.“ In B. Polixene is unconscious and Eneas has to carry her away in his arms (B. 26,086—90).

226. The last episode of the sack is the rescue of Andromache and Cassandra by Thelamonius Ajax (26,079—90). This short scene also shows relation to G. (R 1 r 21—3), and absence of such to B. (26,107—11).

1) G-M. omit to say that Ajax Thelamonius had to defend them against the Greeks. B. says that the Greeks took them from the temple, but

Li corteis, li prouz Aiax | Les deffendi come vassaz.

2) Although B. probably meant Ajax Thelamonius, since Ajax is already dead (B. 22,768) he has Ajax (26,111). G-M. obviate all ambiguity by saying Thelamonius Ajax.

3) B. says only „Andromacha la proz la bele“. G. has „quondam hectoris uxorem“, which M. repeats in Andromache's reply to Thelamonius Ajax (26,883):-

Que de hector fus femme iadis.

4) The sack of the city concludes with a general stage-direction partially quoted in § 223 (26,890 d). This continues:- „et apres ce que tout sera brullé et le feu estainct et les clameurs cessees tous les grecz s'assembleront au *temple* palas devant agamenon.“ This was because G. said that the assembly took place (R 1 v 1) „in magno *templo* mynerve“. B. had said (26,141) „en la *tor* minerve“.

227. A long speech by Agamenon follows next (26,891—27,034):-

1) The first part of this speech (to 26,999) is M's invention:- Agamenon first speaks of the respect and pity due to Priam for his excellent qualities and terrible misfortunes (26,915—71), and moralizes upon the vanity of glory and wealth and the fickleness of fortune. After this, Agamenon (26,974 d) „oste son bonnet et sa couronne et tous les rois ostent les leurs aussi.“ Agamenon then thanks them for their loyal obedience in his

own and in his brother's name, and declares that he and Menelaus will not forget those who have lost their lives in the war (26,975—98). The rest of the speech is M's version of B-G.

2) In B., before Agamenon speaks (26,143),

Agamenon la s'umilie,
Tos les deus aore et mercie.

This idea is not repeated in G-M.

3) In M. the lines (26,999):-

— — — vous vueil questionner
Sur deux poins et araisonner.

point to (R 1 v 3) „Agamenon de *duobus* eos sollicite requisivit."

4) Verses 27,002—4:- Premierement ie vueil demander
Se nous devons la foy garder
A ceulx — — etc.

come from (R 1 v 4). „Uno scilicet si *conservanda* sit *fides* illis". B's expression is different (26,157):-

Or si gardez quel la ferons,
Saveir se nos lor retendrons
Ço dont il ont noz seurrances
Nos seremenz et nos fiances.

Only in M. does Agamenon express distrust of the betrayers of Troy (27,006—10; 27,117—22).

5) In B. the question of the distribution of the booty is not treated in Agamenon's speech, but is spoken of in narrative form (26,171—4). In G. and M. Agamenon broaches the question himself.

6) In all versions the Greeks agree to hold faith with the betrayers, and to divide equitably all booty. In M. Diomedes is the chief spokesman of this agreement and the others approve (27,035—80). Diomedes uses a curious argument to show that the betrayers of the city have not been traitors (27,051—62)!

228. In all versions Ajax Thelamonius now urges that Helen, the cause of the war and all its attendant misery, be put to death.

1) B-G. say that he was supported by many others, but do not specify any names (B. 26,177; R 1 v 14). M. cleverly makes Nestor and Pirrus again (see previous cases §§ 199[3]; 182[4]) the advocates of vengeance. Pirrus adds to the general reason his continued desire to avenge his father (27,115), and Nestor the wish to complete the vengeance for his son (27,123).

2) In all versions it is Ulixes who rescues Helen. B. says (26,184) that Menelaus appealed to Ulixes, but G-M. know noth-

ing of this appeal. B-G. do not indicate Ulixes' arguments and M. is, therefore, thrown upon his own ingenuity:- In M. Ulixes opposes to the sorrow of Nestor and Pirrus their joy at the ultimate victory and glory. He further urges that vengeance on a woman of such high birth would be infamous. Moreover, they came to please Agamenon and Menelaus and their demand for Helen's death would alienate all thanks on the part of those brothers. Ulixes' main argument, however, is that they must bring Helen back to Greece as proof positive of their success. — Menelaus bids them take everything at Troy except Helen (27,185). Ajax Thelamonius and Nestor finally agree to spare Helen out of their respect for Menelaus and their desire to avoid further strife.

3) Agamenon, in thanking them, asks that Cassandra be given to him. In B. the reason given is (B. 26,198):-

Merveilles l'aveit aamee.
Sor tot riens la desirot,
Sacheiz que pas ne s'en celot,
Molt par iert de s'amor espris.

This reason is not in G-M. who still further agree that Agamenon asked for her as a reward for his labor:- (R 1 v 22.) „in sui *laboris* premium"; (M. 27,245) „J'en demande pour mon *labour*."

229. 1) The next episode in Milet is the death of Polixene upon the tomb of Achilles. M. thus omits B-G. (26,205—84; R 1 v 23 — R 2 r 11) in which passages the following events occur:- Anthenor and Eneas beg for the lives of Andromecha and Helenus. Helenus, in turn, beseeches for the safety of Hector's two sons, which is also granted. (In B. 26,248 Helenus further entreats them to pardon Hecuba, and this is also done). The Greeks then decide to set sail for Greece, but a violent storm prevents; in explanation of this storm Calcas declares that Polixene must be sacrificed to appease the divine wrath because of the assassination of Achilles.

2) M., however, passes abruptly to the demand of Calcas for Polixene's death. There is no mention of a storm having occurred, unless it be vaguely in

(27,263) Ou aultrement sans en mentir
Vous n'aures le vent propice.
and (27,334.) Et pour avoir la mer saisie.

In B-G. (26,294—306; R 2 r 15—18) Pirrus now enquires the whereabouts of Polixene. M. omits this enquiry, touching B-G. again in Agamenon's summoning Anthenor to give up Polixene (27,281).

3) We then have another link in the evidence binding together G. and M.:- In B. Anthenor demands of Eneas the surrender of Polixene, but Eneas refuses (B. 26,309—17) and Anthenor then searches for her himself. G-M. agree in omitting this appeal to Eneas, and only have Anthenor's fetching of Polixene. All versions describe a violent seizure of Polixene by Anthenor (B. 26,322; R 2 r 27; M. 27,293 d; M. 27,299 d).

4) M. builds up a short scene out of this incident:- Anthenor promises to fetch Polixene (27,289—93).

lors anthenor vient au lieu ou est cachee polixene et quant elle le voit elle se met a genoux et dit.

Ha, sire, ie vous crye mercy.

anthenor la prent entre ses bras et dit,

Certes, polixene, m'amye,
Ie ne vous puis saulver la vie.
Venez devers agamenon.

Polixene:
Ha sire, et pour quoy non?
Ie n'ay point la mort desservie.

adont la tire de tous poins dehors du lieu ou elle est cachee et la mainne a agamenon et quant hecuba la voit elle dit

Ha traictre, plain de felonnie!
Meurtrier, meurtrier, traictre, larron
Laisse ma fille, ie t'en prie!
Acomplir veulx ta trahison, (27,301.)

Verse 27,301 points to a phrase in G. (R 2 r 22):-

„anthenor — — volens omnes prodiciones suas finaliter percomplere."

Anthenor surrenders Polixene with only a slight plea for her life (27,306):-

Ie vous iure qu'elle est pucelle, | Et s'elle meurt, vous aurez tort.

5) In B. it is now Ulixes who says that Polixene must be killed at once. In G-M. Ulixes does not appear; it is Pirrus (27,315; R 2 r 29). In B-G. the fate of Polixene excites great pity (26,337—64; R 2 r 30 — R 2 v 6). In B. it is the people who sympathize; in G. both kings and people. In M. Ajax Thelamonius gives the only expression of this pity (27,323—38). B. alone mentions the possibility of a ransom being paid for Polixene (B. 26,436).

230. In M. the last words of Polixene are introduced by her being allowed by Pirrus to speak them. They merit some attention, although the general line of thought follows B-G. closely (B. 26,369—432; R 2 v 6—28; M. 27,342—425):-

1) M. emphasizes that Polixene *loved* Achilles (27,350):-

Las, achilles, vaillant seigneur,
Ie vous aymoye si loyaulment.
27,363
Ia dieu ne m'en face pardon,
S'oncques la pucelle medee
Ayma plus loyaulment iason.
Ie fus pour vostre mort marrye,
Car i'avoye ia mys mon cueur
Pour vostre grant chevalerie
A vous amer sans deshonneur.

B-G. do not go beyond her expressing great regret at his death.

2) G-M. agree in:-

R 2 v 15

Quare dixit melius sibi succedere in patria sua mori quam per exilium in paupertatis angustiis vitam ducens anxiose adire provincias alienas.

27,390

Si m'est advis qu'il me vault mieux
Mourir en ma propre cite,
Que de regarder de mes yeulx
Ce pays en adversite,
Et servir par grant vilite
Ceulx qui ont mys a mort villaine
Mon lignage et mon parente.

3) B. has two thoughts omitted by G-M.:-

a) Surely they ought to be satiated with their other slaughter without demanding her blood (B. 26,382—95).

b) It is Envy who has pursued her thus relentlessly:-

(26,426—32) Qui de ma bialte se plaingneit
Et qui tant me par haïsseit.

4) The keynote of all versions is her joy at dying a virgin. M. employs here effectively five-syllable verses (27,398):-

Viegne donc la mort
Moy donner confort!
Ie me rens a elle.
Se ie meurs a tort,
C'est mon reconfort
Que ie meurs pucelle.

G-M. agree in the following idea:-

R 2 r 19.

et virginitatem suam diis omnibus et ipsi morti grata voluntate libare.

27,410

O dieux, recevez
Et en gre prenez
Ma virginite.

5) At the close of Polixene's speech, Pirrus, declaring that he does so in vengeance for his father (27,428):-

„— — — qui pour l'amour
De vous est mort a grant douleur"

„luy coppe la teste". This last is interesting, for B-G. do not have this detail. B. says „detrenchiee" (26,442); G. „occidit" and „eius corpore truncato" (R 2 v 22). M's preference for decapitation explains why he agrees with B. in the manner of Priam's death (see § 224[9]). M. follows B-G. in emphasizing the shedding of Polixene's blood upon Achilles' tomb (B. 26,446; R 2 v 23; M. 27,429 d).

231. 1) At the sight of her daughter's death, Hecuba loses her mind:- (27,432)

Hahay, ie forsenne, i'enraige,	De dieu iupiter et venus,
Que mauldit soit tout le lignage	Juno, palas et saturnus.

She throws stones, runs after the Greeks, biting some and striking others „en telle maniere (27,435 d) que ame ne se doit trouver devant elle."

2) Thereupon Agamenon commands her to be taken

— — en une isle	Laquelle est aulide appellee
Qui est aupres de ceste ville	Et que elle soit lapidee.

This is taken directly from G. both in the name and location of the place:- „*aulidam insulam* troye *vicinam*" (R 2 v 31), and in the fact that Hecuba is stoned to death *after* her removal thither (R 3 r 1). In B. the place, (not an island), is „*loin* du port" and called Albidee („variante" = Abydos). Hecuba is stoned to death *before* her removal.

It is there that her sepulchre is erected (B. 26,462—6). In obedience to Agamenon's command, „adont la prenent et la mainent puis la lapident insques a la mort" (27,445 d).

3) Agamenon then continues:-

(27,446.)	Et desormais par chascun iour
Si aura ce lieu present nom,	Sera dicte l'isle de plour
Le lieu de consommacion,	Iusques en perpetuaulte
Car cy endroit est consommee	Pour la pitie et cruaulte
De priam la noble lignee,	Qui est en ce lieu advenue.

M. thus follows B-G. in giving a special name to the place of Hecuba's death, but varies from them in his more sympathetic thought:- B. had said (26,467):-

Por lie, qui si faitierement	Et sanz amour et sanz raison.
Se fist ocire molement,	Ço distrent puis et ço lison,
Apelerent lo leu engres,	Qu'ele se fist fole a escient
Por ço que lo cueur ot pervers	Por receivre mort et torment.

G. translated this „engres", „locus infestus" (R 3 r 6). The episode of Hecuba's death closes in all versions with the mention of a sepulchre (B. 26,465; R 3 r 4).

27,454 d. „lors doit avoir des gens qui feront une elevation de terre en façon de sepulcre.“

232. At the close of the last incident Agamenon bids all return, to hold a council relative to their departure. Ajax Thelamonius assents, declaring his desire to make a request there. After all are seated, he arises and argues his claim to the Palladium. The scene which follows (27,464—665) has its equivalent in B-G. (26,485—981; R 3 r 8 — R 4 r 21). It is a difficult scene to compare with B-G., for almost the same thoughts occur. We present, however, the following points as proof that G., not B., still serves as M's source:-

1) The general plan of the scene is alike in G-M.:- *first* an attack of Thelamonius Ajax on Ulixes, *then* the latter's reply, and *finally* the decision of Menelaus and Agamenon. The *only* variation is that M. divides the speech of Ajax Thelamonius into two parts, one before, and one after Ulixes' speech. In B. the arrangement is quite different:- *Diomedes* (who in G-M. is not mentioned in this connection) first makes a claim (26,513—28; also 26,921—6). Ulixes then supports his own right and is, in consequence, violently attacked by Ajax Thelamonius, after which comes the decision.

2) In the individual speeches the order of thought is wholly the same in G-M., and only partially the same in B. Even where B. has the same order of thought as G-M, there are important differences in other respects, which render impossible B's influence in those places. Moreover, B. has a number of important things, which G. and M. alike neglect. — The three following paragraphs contain the details:-

233. Of Ajax' two speeches, the second contains such a general appeal that it admits of no comparison with B-G. We, therefore, need only consider the first speech (27,464—527). For the last part of this speech, the sequence of thought is alike in all three versions (see this paragraph:- 3, 4, 5, 6).

1) Ajax Thelamonius says that he often supplied the Greek host with food, thus rescuing them from famine (M. 27,480—3 R 3 r 22—4). In B. he mentions and describes at more or less length *specific* instances (B. 26,629—33; 26,640—7; 26,653—7; 26,675—91), besides those times when, in company with Achilles,

he procured supplies (B. 26,734—8). G. and, consequently M. unite all these in the above general statement.

2) He often rescued the Greeks from defeat in battle (27,484—7; R 3 r 24—6). A similar idea is expressed in B. 26,636—8, although the sequence seems to refer to Ajax Thelamonius' exploits elsewhere than before Troy.

3) He killed Polidorus, son of Priam, and relieved the Greeks with the captured treasure (27,488—95; R 3 r 26—30). M. omits the detail that Priam had entrusted Polidorus to the guardianship of King Polinestor (in G. Polimestres) and had given the latter the above treasure (B. 26,615—28; R 3 r 26—8). B. relates the death of Polidorus differently:- He was stoned to death by the Greeks under the walls of Troy and before the eyes of Priam (B. 26,624—8).

4) He killed the king of Frise and took his treasure (27,496—99; R 3 r 30—1). B's passage is 26,639—52. G-M. omit all mention of the king's daughter Temissa (B. 26,648—52).

5) He conquered many kingdoms adjacent to Troy:-

M. 27,500—11.	R 3 v 1—4.	B. 26,661—70.
Gargaires	Gargaros	Botrillancie
Ceridie	Cepresum	Gargare
Larizie	Arisdiam	Cepsim
Gripperie (Griparie)	Larissam	Larissam
		Arisban

These names, as they stand, do not allow us to draw any conclusions, but their study in all manuscripts and prints might lead to results useful in grouping the said manuscripts and prints. The names „Crouceresse" and „Trace" in B. 26,615 are not repeated in G-M.

6) Following immediately in G-M. is the idea that Ulixes performed no deeds of real valor, but excels only in treacherous speech (27,512—9; R 3 v 8—10). In B. valor is not denied to Ulixes; Ajax Thelamonius only declares him *less* brave than himself; indeed the whole idea of comparison between the two is more pronounced in B. than in G-M.

B. 26,699 Qu'il n'est si vaillanz ne si proz.

7) Omitted in Ajax Thelamonius' speech in G-M. is the idea that, had Achilles lived, his greater claim would have rendered all discussion about the Palladium impossible (B. 26,500—2; 26,706). In B. this thought leads to a long account

of the exploits of Achilles, in which Ajax Thelamonius says he helped (B. 26,706—815). G. declares that he omits these as superfluous (R 3 v 6—7), and they are, consequently, not in M.

8) Omitted likewise in G-M. is the passage in B. (26,815 —918) where Ajax Thelamonius relates the quarrel between Achilles and Agamenon regarding the daughter of Crises, Astronomen, and the daughter of Brises, Ypodomia. Ajax Thelamonius contrasts with especial emphasis his peaceful settlement of this quarrel with Ulixes' love of discord and deceit.

234. The reply of Ulixes follows immediately in G-M. We have already spoken of the difference in arrangement in B. (§ 232[1]).

1) In B. Ulixes speech (B. 26,534—84) is mostly an account of *how* he got possession of the Palladium. We note that he therein tells the truth, whereas in G. (R 3 v 29—31) Ulixes declares that he went himself to Troy and got the Palladium. The main emphasis in G-M. is, however, upon the *importance* of his securing it, namely, that Troy would never otherwise have fallen (27,528—35; R 3 v 18—23).

2) An important similarity of G-M. is Ulixes' statement that the Trojans did not themselves know the virtue of the Palladium. (27,536—8; R 3 v 24—5).

3) Ulixes alone discovered this virtue and secured the Palladium. (27,539—43; R 3 v 25—9).

235. In the reply of Ajax Thelamonius and in the relation of the decision regarding the Palladium, M. relies largely upon his own ingenuity:-

1) In this speech M. has ingeniously reserved, as a climax to the plea of Ajax Thelamonius, his argument that it will be a lasting disgrace for the Greeks if they give Ulixes the Palladium, (27,564) Puisqu'il fault que par decepvance
Vous confessez avoir vainçu
Et non pas par puissance.

Ajax closes by urging them to repudiate such an idea and to show that their victory was through valor, by adjudging the Palladium rightly.

2) Diomedes, fearing strife, advises that the „iugement" be left to Agamenon. Thoas suggests the two brothers, Mene-

laus and Agamenon, and the two disputants agree to this arbitration. After a short dialogue, Agamenon and Menelaus decide that Ulixes shall retain the Palladium (27,651). Ulixes thanks them, but Ajax Thelamonius abuses and threatens them. (27,658—65). In this arbitration-episode M. follows essentially B-G, except that he does not intimate, as do B-G. (26,937—9; R 4 r 10—12), that Agamenon and Menelaus so decide because Ulixes had saved Helen from death against the wish of Ajax Thelamonius (see § 228²).

3) B. says (26,934—60) that the Greeks generally are very incensed at this decision, since they upheld Ajax Thelamonius. G. has only the thought that they upheld Ajax Thelamonius (R 4 r 14—6) but no expression of anger on their part. M. omits both ideas; M. further omits the thought that the Greek kings took pains to surround themselves with guards because of the threats of Thelamonius Ajax (B. 26,975—81; R 4 r 19).

236. The death of Thelamonius Ajax and the flight of Ulixes are the next episodes. M. follows B-G. in the main, being only original in the naïvité of his presentation:-

1) B-G. say that Ajax Thelamonius was found dead next morning, his body much mutilated. B., however, does not say that he was found in bed (B. 26,983—7). G. and M. do:- „in lecto" R 4 r 24; „couche" M. 27,666; 27,673 d; „lit" M. 27,750. M. joins this episode very naïvely to the scene of the adjudging of the Palladium:- After the kings have gone away amid the threats of Ajax Thelamonius, the latter says (27,666):-

Pirrus, ie vois presentement
Moy reposer sur une couche
Car ce desplaisir qui me touche
Me contraint aler dormir (!)
Pirrus:-
Or alez a vostre plaisir.

Lors Ajax[1]) s'en va coucher sur une couche et fait len pause de menestrelz et puis dit pirrus.

Ie m'esbahys moult grandement
D'ajax, qui dort si longuement.
Ie le vueil aler esveiller.

---

[1]) M. thus abbreviates the full name here and later 27,672, 27,740. B. had made the opposite abbreviation, Thelamon, in B. 26,531—2; 26,985; 26,997. G. keeps the full name longer but finally also abbreviates to Thelamonius (R 4 r 4; 7; 11; 16; 25; 27; 29; 30; R 4 v 4; 7).

Adont il vient a la couche et le treuve mort si doit crier en soi esmerveillant.

What follows is a lament by Pirrus. M. thus follows B-G. in making Pirrus the chief mourner (B. 27,009; R 4 r 29).

2) In B-G. the guilt of this death is ascribed to Agamenon, Menelaus and Ulixes (26,989—90; R 4 r 28). (By „deus vassaus" (B. 26,990) B. undoubtedly means Diomedes and Agamenon, this addition of Diomedes harmonizing with B's representing him also as a claimant for the Palladium. B. 26,513—28; 26,921—6.) G. adds „sed potius in ulixem", which probably decided M. to allow suspicion to rest only upon Ulixes (M. 27,683; 27,762). M. is still more consistent to this idea by representing Agamenon as grieving greatly (27,753). That M. himself did not think that Ulixes was guilty is seen in the words he lets Ulixes himself say:- (27,737.)

Ie m'en vueil maintenant aler
En mon pays secretement,
Car tres bien ay ouy parler,
Que ajax est mort traiteusement,
Si pourra on aulcunement
Dire que ie en ay este cause.

3) In B. we find no declaration of Pirrus that he will avenge the death of Ajax Thelamonius. There is only a general expression of rage by all (B. 26,993—6; 27,046—7). G. and M., however, have such a declaration by Pirrus (27,698—705; R 4 r 29—31).

4) This episode of the grief and suspicion of the Greeks in M. is related as follows:- Pirrus, after discovering the dead body, goes to tell Nestor who grieves and vows vengeance. Both then go to Agamenon, and meanwhile Ulixes repeating the lines quoted above (27,737 ff.) „s'en va en son pays". Agamenon mourns for Ajax Thelamonius, and the more because he declares that this loss will derange Thelamon's mind, the father of the dead hero. We thus see that M. represents Thelamon as still alive (27,755). Agamenon, before voicing his suspicion of Ulixes, expresses a curious idea:-

27,757 Las il [= Ajax Thelamonius] aloit trop menassent
Et peult estre que ses menasses
L'ont fait mourir, car trop souvent
Meurt le lievre dedens sa place.

Agamenon then bids Citheus to fetch Ulixes, but Citheus declares that he saw Ulixes depart „en son pays". This indefiniteness corresponds with G. who likewise mentions no destination (R 4 v 2). B., however, names „Ismaron“ (B. 27,051). At this news of Citheus, Nestor concludes that Ulixes is guilty (27,778), but the whole affair is quite abruptly terminated by Agamenon's words (27,785):-

Or ca, il n'en fault plus parler
Tant que nous soions retournez.

5) In this episode M. omits two features in B-G., first that Ulixes left the Palladium with Diomedes (B. 27,052; R 4 v 3), and secondly, the obsequies of Ajax Thelamonius instituted by Pirrus (B. 27,012—37; R 4 v 4—7).

237. 1) M. now represents a last council of the Greeks where the question of the exile of Anthenor and Enee is discussed. In B-G. the reason of the exile of Enee is that he concealed Polixene, which plays only a secondary rôle in M. 27,844—53. Moreover, in B-G., the Greeks do not exile Anthenor; he goes away voluntarily (B. 27,153; R 4 v 25). In M. the main reason for the exile of both is lest they and their descendents should rebuild Troy and found again a mighty power:- Agamenon reminds the Greeks of the first destruction of Troy by Jason and emphasizes the latter's mistake of leaving the inhabitants in Troy who rebuilt the city stronger than ever and were able to wage the disastrous second war (27,793 — 806). Agamenon, therefore, counsels (27,810),

Qu'anthenor et aussi enee
Feussent bannis de ce pais
Avecques toute la lignee
Des troyans —

Diomedes upholds this view, saying that both Anthenor and Enee have sons who could restore the city and avenge its destruction. Thoas and Menesteus agree, the latter urging Enee's concealment of Polixene as an additional reason. With the agreement of the other kings, Agamenon sends Citheus to summon Enee and Anthenor.

2) When they come, Agamenon orders (27,885):-

Que sur peine de souffrir mort
Vous vous en aliez de ce port,
Et que meniez tous voz enffans
Et le demourant des troyans
En quelque pays estrangier.

Anthenor at first remonstrates (27,893):-

Dea sire, et par quel raison?
Nous cuidions en nostre maison
Vivre seurement a mercy.

He yields, however, at last, saying (27,898):-

Alons nous en donc, sire ence, | Il nous fault partir hors de troye.

Enee:-

Ic m'en vueil aler mettre en voye,
Pour partir hors de ce pays
Et enmeneray tous mes amys
Et m'en yray en ytalie.

Anthenor:-

Et ie menray ma compaignie
Es ylles devers les angloys
Si feray la dedans troys moys
Une cite forte et garnie.

Enee:-

Adieu troye, cite iolie,
Ie ne te revairray iamais!
C'est raison que pour mes meffaiz
I'endure le pugnissement.
Las, ie faiz aux dieux bon serment
Que iamais en nulle façon
Ie ne commettray trahison.
Plus ycy ne demourray mye;
Adieu, toute la compaignie!

3) M's version of this departure of Enee and Anthenor differs from B-G:- There Enee is allowed to remain at Troy long enough to fit out his ships. Meanwhile Anthenor departs. Enee, however, learns that Anthenor, by his disclosure of Enee's concealment of Polixene, caused his (Enee's) exile, and has the Trojans recall Anthenor in order to wreak vengeance on him. The Trojans then exile Anthenor as well. The latter proceeds to the Adriatic sea and founds a city which he names Corchirre Menelan (B. 27,407; R 5 v 21). There is no further mention of the destination of Enee in B. M's having Eneas go to Italy is, therefore, either due to his knowledge of Virgil or to G's final statement (S 3 r 13), and the departure of Anthenor „devers les angloys" is merely an anachronistic phantasy, perhaps due to M's sense of the fitness of associating the betrayer of Troy with the greatest contemporary enemies of France.

238. The last scene of the drama is the departure of the Greek princes:- Agamenon declares that they have accomplished everything for which they came, and that, therefore, he and his brother intend now to return to their kingdom of Citharee. He further bids all likewise to return to their homes. Menelaus (27,929) thanks them for their aid, hoping to have sometime an opportunity of repaying it. He then, with Agamenon, leads his men away.

M. thus ignores in B-G. the conflict between Agamenon and Menelaus on one side and the rest of the kings on the other, resulting in the hostile departure of the brothers (B. 27,169—92; R 6 r 16—22). The other kings also depart:-

Nestor goes to Pille (27,943) with a last regret for his dead son (27,947—52). Menesteus, Thoas and Diomedes each take their departure, bidding Pirrus farewell who, in turn, goes to „Magnise la grigneur“ (27,958).

As a final refrain Thoas recapitulates twice the leading events of the drama (27,969 and 27,981):-

Or a este premierement
Par les troyans ravye helene,
Et puis les grecz mis en grant peine
Et troye arse finablement.

Pirrus draws therefrom the moral (27,973):-

En fortune n'a nullement
Fiance, c'est chose certaine.

and Diomedes bids farewell to the audience as follows (27,977):-

Si vous pryons tres humblement
Que recevez d'entente saine
Noz diz, car sans chose villaine
Avons ioue l'esbatement.

By bringing the drama to a close at this point, M. omits the subsequent history and adventures of the Greek kings as related in the last part of B-G. M. thus confines himself strictly to the „Destruction de Troye“.

Appendix.

References to Events antecedent to the Drama.

239. Throughout the drama we find freqnent references to those events which Benoît and Guido describe in the first portions of their works. These are — the expedition of Jason for the golden fleece; its capture; Jason's relations with Medea; the refusal of Laomedon king of Troy and father of Priam to harbor the Greeks in this expedition, and the first destruction of Troy by them in consequence. These references are, however, of far too general and vague a nature to furnish us with sure points of contact with B. or with G. alone. They are equally possible from both. For the sake of completeness we will give these references, for even here, in a few cases, M. has allowed his imagination to add some features:-

1) The references to Jason's acquisition of the fleece are meagre:- 3,653—6; 4,862—4. In 5,342—3 „quant il conquesta la toison et les *serpents*", we have M's sole mention of the difficulties connected with the capture of the fleece. Hercules is Jason's companion.

2) All the above passages are connected with the refusal of the „port" or the „passage" to the Greeks by the Trojans, also 3,673. In this connection Laomedon's name is also given 3,290—2. His death is often referred to:- 388, 7,950 etc.

3) Rare again are the mentions of the love of Jason and Medee:- 5,043. Medee's name is most often mentioned because of her faithfulness and suffering in love:- 20,425—8; 27,364—5. In regard to the time of this episode M. (5,042) places it as *thirty* years before the second expedition against Troy. That he, however, attached no importance to this number is shown in

a) „puis certain temps" 695; 5,339.

b) Anchises' words, 15,769, that the first destruction took place *fifty* years before the second.

c) Priam's statement, 377, that he had grieved for the loss of Exiona *ten* years.

4) More frequent are the references to the first destruction of Troy, although even here few details are given. Of the persons who also in B-G. figure as present, we note in M. Jason, Hercules, Thelamon, Nestor and Laomedon. To these M. adds:- Anchises (15,768; 23,357); Antenor (698); Atrides (as singular „d'atrides"!) „et dautres de vostre [= Palamides] lingnee" (3,677—8); Ajax (4,860—7).

Less distinct are the mentions of Belides, father of Naulus, who was with Jason when he was refused the „port" (3,669—73), and of Epistropus, who says that he was much beloved by Laomedon (7,946). Probably M. thought that both were present at the first destruction, together with the father of Patroclus (unnamed) killed by the Trojans (3,531) and the grandfather of Pollidamas (likewise unnamed) killed by the Greeks (1,213; see § 241 Antenor).

It is noteworthy that M. omits Castor and Pollux as present at this first destruction of Troy. In M. as in B-G. Exiona is given to Thelamon (45; 730), which fact ultimately leads to the rape of Helen and the second war. M. gives the limit of the first conquest of the Greeks as „Apertheloppes". From the refounding of Troy to its second destruction Milet supposes thirty-eight years to have elapsed (see § 196; compare also § 239[3]).

The Proper Names in Milet.

(In general the spelling as found in the drama has been used in the thesis.)

---

240. General Survey.

1) In preparing the lists of proper names we were considerably handicapped by the absence of critical editions, which would have furnished a greater number of variations and enabled us, undoubtedly, to show many interesting features regarding the grouping and inter-relation of the manuscripts

and prints. That M. could not use the entire vast array of names which he found in G. is self-evident, but one is truly surprised to find that nearly half his names are not taken from his main source at all, but are either the product of his own invention or else borrowed from other sources than the fund of names common to B-G. For the most part these new names in M. are given to the less important *dramatis personae,* servants, banner-men, and the like, but, even here, it is remarkable that M. preferred other names, instead of adapting to new rôles the many names still left in his main source. We have not felt it necessary to give a list of these names which M. did not use, as their study has little to do with the main purpose of this work. Regarding the names found in M. the best plan seemed to be to divide them into three groups:-

I. Those common to the three works B., G. and M. (§ 241).

II. Those common only to G. M. (§ 242).

III. Those found in M. alone. (§ 243).

In doubtful cases the division is made on the basis of the spelling.

2) For a purpose akin to his use of scenes of family and filial affection, namely, to bind more firmly together the various personages and thus increase our interest in their action, M. emphasizes greatly the friendships and relationships found in G. and adds to their number. For these additions see:- (§ 241) Antenor, Polidamas; (§ 243) Amphorbius, Cediron; also (§ 241) Ajax Thelamonius, Menelaus, Nestor and son Archilogus. Under these last four names and also under Exionne (§ 242) certain inconsistencies are note-worthy.

3) G's influence upon M. is not only found in all names in § 242, but also in the following:- § 241: Armonie, Diomedes, Eneas, Huppon, Menon, Micenes, Naulus, Paphagonnye, Politetes, Salemine, and § 243: Humanus, Philotas.

241. Names common to B-G-M.

Achilles.

Adrastus; Adastus. Trojan servant, 10,564; 13,209. In B-G. he is a king allied to the Trojans (6,646; H 8 v).

Affrique, as territory ruled by the Greeks, 1,401; 5,281 (see § 22 f.).

Agamen(n)on. there is no other spelling.

Ajax. same age as Nestor in M. 4,899. Note also M's reference to his children (§§ 170[5]; 239[4]).

Ajax Thelamonius. M. represents him as a cousin of Pirrus 21,283; 21,480; also as cousin to Menelaus 27,212. In 10,332—6, we note that he is called a nephew of Helen. This last is an inconsistency, for, being the son of Exiona. he is Priam's nephew and Hector's cousin.

Amphimacus, natural son of Priam (§ 187[4]).

Anchises, father of Eneas (§ 239[4]).

Andromecha (many variations), wife of Hector.

Antenor. in M. alone, married to Priam's sister 11,288; 23,774. Therefore, brother to Priam 11,894 and uncle to Priam's children 11,270; 11,290; 22,553. Thus, when Polidamas 1,213 speaks of his grandfather as killed by the Greeks, he probably means Laomedon (see further § 194[1]; § 239[4]).

Archilogus, son of Nestor; in M. only son, 3,995; M. also has him as a nephew of Menelaus 4,040. This is, however, an inconsistency (see under Menelaus).

Archilogus, Greek king. In M. he figures only in the list of those killed by Hector 13,887.

Armonie, daughter of Helen and Menelaus, 2,644. In B. Hermiona (4,231). In G. Hermonia (E 6 v 5).

Asia. M. constantly emphasizes this as the domain of the Trojans, viz. 1,410; 6,149; 6,184; 8,393; 18,060; 19,394; 19,421; 19,903; 19,913; 20,296; 20,863 21,148; 21,591; 27,503—511; (see § 22 f.; h.).

Athens. In M. „fleur de science" 22,127 (see also § 60[2]).

Boet(t)es, Bouet(t)es. Trojan ally (see § 131 foot-note). B-G. have a second Boetes, a Greek, 16,785; L 3 r 8.

Briseida 11,885, daughter of Calcas.

Calcas. 6,281. M. says that he was once guardian priest of the Palladium 25,676.

Carta(i)ge. 2,932. In M. „Juno deesse de Cartage 4,094; 5,232.

Cassandra. 3,005.

Castor. 812 (§ 239[4]).

Citherea, island 4,796. In lines 33—36 of M's „Instrument" (after verse 23,386), it is given as „isle prochaine du royaulme de serpedon" (see Serpedon § 243).

Deiphebus, son of Priam.

Diomedes. In B. he is called „filz Tideus" fourteen times (B. 383; 11,133; 12,311; 12,347; 12,461; 13,499; 14,221; 14,928: 19,750; 22,786; 22,797;

23,624; 25,393; 27,819). Only once in G. is he called the son of Tideus, and that (L 4 r 20) in a passage omitted by M. (see § 97 beginning). Hence the total absence in M. of this second appellation.

Eneas, Enee. Only G-M. give Venus as his mother (H 5 r 13; D 1 r 25 18,134). G. has a passage about Eneas' later exploits (H 5 r 11—29.) (see also Creusa).

Femenie, the kingdom of the Amazons 20,910; (see § 177[1]).

Frise, the king of —. M's only mention of him is that he was killed by Ajax Thelamonius 27,496.

Glaucon of **Licia,** 6,295—6, Trojan ally. G-M. say that he is related to Priam (H 8 v 14; 7,383). Brother of Serpedon.

Hector. 1,026.

Hecuba.

Helene. 2,121. In M. she speaks of her father, but gives no name 20,295.

Helenus. 325.

Hercules. 3,675. Also „gent de grece, gent herculee", 8,100 (see § 168[2] end).

Huppon. Trojan. Hupoz in B. Huppon in G. In B-G. from Larissa (B. 6,681; I 7 v 7). In M. from Lariesse (7,609); Laroisse (7,924); Lariche (6,301). In 7,927, Huppon is given as from Trace, which is evidently a copyist's error, since Pillon is always spoken of as from Trace, and Huppon has just been given in the same list 7,924 as from Laroisse. Huppon would not be twice mentioned in the same list. For Huppon, therefore, in 7,927, Pillon should be read (compare Haepke P. 96).

Il(i)us; Yl(i)us, early king of Troy. 25,561.

Il(l)ion; Ylion, the castle of Troy 959.

Inde mineur, where occurs the judgment of Paris (see § 23b[1]). M. also uses it as a synonym of Trojan territory (21,895.) (see also 7,381).

Jason. (§ 239[1]; [3]).

Laomedon, father of Priam 388 (see § 84 foot-note; see § 239[1]).

Licie, country of Glancon and Serpedon 6,295.

Licomedes, guardian of Pirrus (see § 166[3]); M. says for ten years 20,795.

Margariton, natural son of Priam 9,770.

Medee 5,063. (§ 239[3]).

Menelaus. In M. cousin to Nestor 2,074; 4,849; 4,972; 5,546. He cannot then well be uncle to Nestor's son, Archilogus, 4,040 (see Archilogus)

Menesteus, duke of Athens 5,906.

Menon, Merion. Owing undoubtedly to paleographical causes there exists considerable confusion between these two names in all three versions' in B., however, less than in G-M. The solution of the difficulty in B-G. appears to be as follows:-

There are three Greek Merions. Two of these are killed by Hector, the first one 10,005; K 8 r 20; the second, who is a cousin to Achilles, 14,099; M 4 v 14. In B's list of kings killed by Hector, one of these figures as Merion 16,784, the other as Meriones 16,791. In G's list (edition of 1477) the first figures as Menon, the second as Merion. In the other editions of G. only one name is given in this list, — Merion, which probably accounts for the presence in M's list of but one, also Merion. The third Merion in B-G. is given as the son of Idomeneus of Crete (T 3 r 23; 28,925—7).

On the Trojan side there seems to be but one personage; the spelling varies in B. between Mennon and Mennor (the latter only in the rhyme of 11,008; 12,120, in both cases to Anthenor). B. calls him now the son (11,008) now the nephew (6,833; 17,333) of the Persian king. In G. the spelling varies between Menon and Merion. He is killed by Achilles (B. 21,553; P 1 r 31) — In B. 8,865 it is difficult to know whether the Merion there given is Greek or Trojan. The context seems to require a Greek, the more so as Mss. B. has Dorius, a Greek, in place of Merion. (see B. 5,609—11; 8,180—3).

In Milet the confusion is increased by the addition of Menones (164; 209; 368) on the Trojan side, but that he is identical with Menon has already been indicated (§ 152[3] foot-note). With this fact as a starting point the remaining confusion also becomes clear:- On the Trojan side in M. there then remain two distinct personages, this Menon (respect. Menones) and a Merion. That they are distinct is shown in three places, one of which we have noted § 131 foot-note. The other places are 12,983—4, and in Ulixes' speech, balancing the losses on each side:-

18,846. Pour palamides mesmement
Ilz ont perdu le roy menon
Et merion semblablement
Ou lieu du fort roy cediron (= a Greek).

Now, of these two personages, one, Menon(es), is represented as already in Troy, 164; 209; 368, and the other, Merion, is summoned. During this summoning the spelling Merion is consistently used with one exception. He is summoned as „Merion" in 7,444; 7,445; 7,455; 7,463, and comes to Troy also as „Merion" 7,878; 7,929. The only exception is where he is called „Menon" by Anchises in the latter's list of those to be summoned 6,308. (see foot-note, Page 55.) We suggest, therefore, changing this Menon to Merion. Still another inconsistency is in 6,671. It must there be Menon who addresses Priam and not Merion as in the text, since the latter has not yet come.

In like manner Merion in 10,003 should be Menon:- It is a question of the leader of the fourth battle-line, and in 9,759 Menones is given as such. That Merion is not meant is further seen in the fact that

1. Merion is given as a leader of the third battle-line 9,696.

2. It is Menon's standard described 10,003—10, Merion's having already been described as he came to Troy 7,850; 7,878. Merion would not be likely to have two different standards, and thereby deprive Menon of one, especially as no case of two standards for the same leader elsewhere exists (see § 244).

Although these changes seem so necessary, they bring us to a metrical difficulty. Merion is everywhere counted as three syllables (6,722; 7,444; 7,445; 7,878; 7,929; 12,983; 13,893; 15,738; 18,848). If, therefore, we substitute Merion for Menon in 6,308, we will have a syllable too much and vice versa in 10,003, one too few. We must accordingly either rearrange these particular verses or else ascribe the above mistakes, not to a copyist but to Milet himself.

Menon is, as in B-G. killed by Achilles (§ 152³). Regarding the death of the Trojan Merion there is a slight oversight by M. Merion speaks in 17,491 (i. e. after the death of Menon 17,329 d) and in 18,848 Ulixes mentions Merion as dead; yet between the two passages there is no record of his death. Many similar oversights occur in the list of kings killed by Hector (13,884—901) since most of the names there given find no other mention elsewhere in the drama.

On the Greek side in M. there is no acting personage, Merion. Yet we find a Greek Merion in the list of those killed by Hector. 13,893. (see § 88 foot-note.)

Micenes, city of Agamenon 7,388; also Methenez 3,233; Methenes 15,916. These last two forms evidently taken from G. Mathene, Metenas (G 1 v 29).

Mirmidones, Achilles' warriors 4,491; 7,039.

Naulus, father of Palamides, 3,619. Mentioned oftener in G. than in B; hence importance of his rôle in M. First mentioned in B. 27,551 (see § 239⁴).

Nestor. In M. cousin to Menelaus (see the latter) and therefore to Helen:- 2,636; 3,883; 25,407; (see also § 207²); see also Ajax.

Palamides. M. gives him as only son of Naulus, 8,047. Regarding his death in B. see Joly P. 710—1; G. therein follows B.

Paladium, see §§ 209—210.

Panthasilee, 20,878.

Panteon 7,739. Banner-man to Philimenis. Perhaps suggested by G. Pentheus (B. Pantus), the son of Euforbius (see § 26 foot-note).

Pap(h)agonnye, the land of Philimenis 7,801; 7,824; 21,753. Its inhabitants = Paphagones 22,060; Passagonien(s) 7,313; 7,323. B. has consistently Paflagonie (— goine); G. Paffagonie.

Paris.

Patroclus. In M. he says that his father was killed by the Trojans. No name is given 3,531. (§ 239⁴).

Peleus, father of Achilles. 552. M. agrees with B-G. in representing him as still living, in 15,825; 16,503.

Philimenis, of giant stature in all versions 7,931.

Pille, Nestor's home. 844; 27,943. Usually Pirre in B; Pira in G. Pile occurs once in B. 5,613, and Pylon twice in G. (C 4 r 19; G 2 r 10).

Pillon, (Trojan) from Trace, 6,299. Evidently the same as B. Pelex (6,711). G. Pyleus (H 8 v 26).

Pirrus, son of Achilles. Of interest is the total omission in M. of his second name, **Neptolemus.** In B. this latter occurs five times (24,050; 24,350; 25,725; 26,294: 26,442), but Pirrus is used some 30 times, A like proportion exists in G. where Neptolemus occurs three times: P 3 r 3; P 5 v 17; T 7 r 7.

Polidorus, son of Priam. 27,489 (§ 233³). Only in the Hain 5507 edition of Guido is it said (C 2 v 6) that Polidorus was a further son of Priam by Hecuba „ut scripsit Virgilius", and was killed by the king to whom Priam had entrusted him together with a vast sum of money.

Politetes. In M. only in the list of kings killed by Hector 13,894. In B. Politetes 16,790, also isolated in list. In G. prints Polibetes; also Polibethes in Mss. 𝔄ℭ𝔈 of Milet. (Haepke. P. 49 foot-note.)

Polixenar. Only found in list of kings killed by Hector 13,890; also in B's list 16,788 Polixenart. In the 1477 Guido the name does not occur. In the Hain 5507 edition, however, is Polixenart (K 5 v) an additional indication of M's relationship to this print.

Polixenes. Found only in list of kings killed by Hector 13,892. Probably the same as Policenes in G's list (N 2 v 6) and Politenes in B. This last name does not appear in B's list, but he is killed by Hector B. 16,122—4 (in G. killed as Policenes M 8 r 31). — M. has still another Polixene in the list of those killed by Hector 13,889.

Polixene, daughter of Priam 3,042.

Pollidamas son of Antenor; „qui doit estre de XVIII ans ou environ" 949 d. Cousin to Hector 9,205 (see, for other relationships, under Antenor).

Pollus, Castor and Pollus. 827. (§ 239⁴.)

Priam. Interesting is M's greater emphasis of his age 24,673. He is over 100 years old. **Priamus** in 7,756; 8,350 (See also § 187⁴).

Prothenor. 3,475.

Prothesillaus. 3,604.

Sagitaire, the. (see § 100.) See Epistropus.

Salemine, kingdom of Thelemon; 674; 27,709. (not an island as Wunder, through an oversight, says § 13); always Salemine in G. and Salamine in B. Salomnie figures as the fief of Pirrus M. 20,868, and Salennie occurs 494 as a destination in Anthenor's journey. The latter is evidently also Thelamon's kingdom, but this cannot be said of S a l o m n i e with the same certainty.

Sentipus, only mention is in list of those killed by Hector 13,890. Undoubtedly the same as Xantipun in B's list, 16,786, and Zantipus in G's, N 2 v 6.

Serpedon of Lice (Trojan), brother of Glancon, 6,298. (see § 137.)

Sinon, in the horse § 214⁵. Meybrinck (§ 14) seems to overlook the fact that the name is in B. 25,915.

Thelamon, father of Ajax Thelamonius by Exiona, 691.

Thelamonius Ajax, see **Ajax** Thelamonius.

Thenedon a „port"; 2,619 d; 7,977 d; 3 „lieues de troye" 7,737; 7,977 d. B. does not call it an island; G. does, F 5 r 7, and also M. 7,978; 21,144; (see also §§ 39; 80; 221²; 222²). Wunder overlooked verse 7,978 in saying (P. 40), that M. only calls Tenedos an island in the f o u r t h Day.

Theseus, Trojan ally 6,311 (see Thierres § 242).

Thideus, a Greek whom Paris meets in Cytharea; only mention 2,111. Cannot well be the Thideus in B-G. father of Diomedes; in any event he does not figure as such. (see Diomedes.)

Thoas, Greek king, 6,040 (see under Phabermye § 243). Wunder errs in saying (P. 43) Thoas „kommt aus Aetolien". The name Aetolia does not occur in M.

Trace. In M. Pillon comes thence 6,299; as in B-G. it is, therefore, territory allied to Troy (see under Pillon) 6,300; 7,927. M. does not have Trace as Greek territory, belonging to Ulixes, as in B-G.

Troye.

Troylus, youngest son of Priam. 9,416.

Tymbree, (Tybree, 26,192) a gate of Troy. This is the only one of the six gates in B-G. (3,132; D 2 v) which M. mentions.

Ulixes.

Venus (see also under Eneas),

Ysedius, figures only in list of those killed by Hector 13,893; the same as Yssidus in B's list and Ysidius in G's.

---

242. Names common to G-M.

Apius, the builder of the horse 26,081. In B. Epius B. 25,631.

Bretenie, 6,806; Bretonnie 7,506; Broutonnye 7,607; Brotune 7,928. Land of Boetes, the Trojan. In G. Brotino, I 1 r 8. In B. Botine 6,771; 8,109.

Ciclades (see § 65).

Creusa, daughter of Priam and Hecuba; wife of Eneas, 14,389; 14,395; 25,843; 26,557. Meybrinck says P. 16 „Jedenfalls Virgil entnommen, denn Colonna kennt sie nicht." But she is given in G., as the first daughter of Priam and wife of Eneas. D 1 r 23. Cleusa in edition of 1477; Creusa in Hain 5,502.

Delon, where is located the oracle of Apollo; island (see § 65).

Epistropus, (Trojan) owner of the Sagitaire 11,097. Epistrop(h)us in G. (I 1 r 20.) Pistroplex in B. 12,199. M. gives him the extraordinary age of 120 years, 7,545 (see further § 239[4]).

Exionne, Priam's sister, 36; C 8 r 24. In B. Ysiona, (although the Vienna manuscript used by Frommann has Exionne). In M. Priam calls her his only sister, which conflicts with M's saying that Antenor had married a sister of Priam. (see Antenor; also § 239[4].)

Ganimedes 13,765—9; (§ 120) son of Priam „ravy pour estre avec les dieux". This assigning of Ganimedes as son of Priam is found in the edition of G. marked 5507 by Hain (C 2 v 13) but not in the other editions. This is, therefore, additional proof of M's common source with this print.

Italie, see Ytalie.

Laomedon, child of Hector and Andromecha 12,765; M 6 v 16 (see § 112). B. calls him Landomata B. 15,195; 29,465; 29,478, 29,585.

Manise, city of Peleus, 552; 568; 5,323; „Magnisse la grigneur" 27,958. In G. Municium (D 5 v 7) Menusium, Manussum. B. has Maresse 3,271.

Othimenes, figures only in the list of kings slain by Hector 13,896. G. mentions a „rex ottomenus“ (L 6 r 31) as killed by Hector, but the name is not repeated in G's list. Haepke P. 49 foot-note gives Obthimethone(s) as in Milet Mss. AC.

Pallas, in G-M, where B. has Minerva (§§ 23¹; 209³ etc).

Phebus, as additional name of Apollo (see § 66; also verses 1,074; 5,220).

Sinabor, whom Paris bids take the banner; only mention 12,999. The Hain 5507 of G. has, as one of the natural sons of Priam, the form Cicinabor (G 6 v 5.) which seems to indicate where M. got the name. He is not further described in M. or called a natural son.

Thierres. (7,526): **Thiere** (7,614); kingdom of Theseus, Trojan ally. Certainly resembles more the corresponding Thereo in G. (I 1 r 23) than Theresche in B. 6,853.

Thoas. Trojan priest and guardian of the Palladium 25,663. In B. his name is Theanz, Theans, Theano. In the 1477 edition of G: Thonans-Thonantem. In the Hain 5,507 edition, however, **Thoas** occurs several times beside Thoans-Thoantem. The Strassbourg group of G. prints has Thohans and Thohas.

Ytalie. G-M. agree in having Eneas ultimately go thither 27,903; S 3 r 13. B. (28,127—30) has him go to „Lombardie“.

---

243. Names found only in M.

Abimalet, a Mirmidon 4,494.

Achinas, servant to Anthenor 23,745; 23,751; 25,767, same as Athimas, Athamas.

Adamas, servant to Prothesilaus 4,498.

Affremach (in all editions) younger child of Hector (§ 112⁴). In B. he is called Astarnantes. Asternantem 15,200; 15,388. In G. Astronontam (M 6 v 17) Astronatam, Astionactam, Astionatam, according to the edition. Could M's curious corruption of the name indicate the G. manuscript he used?

Agalion, banner-man to Palamides 8,074.

Alivrelech, a Mirmidon, 15,873.

Amour, as son of Venus 9,436.

Ampheneas, Trojan allied king 7,473.

Amphenor, only in list of those killed by Hector, 13,888; undoubtedy same as Alphinor in G. (N 2 v 5) and Helpinor in B. 16,786.

Amphibilaus, natural son of Priam 10,476; the one killed by Thoas 10,834.

Amphymor. Greek, only in list of those slain by Hector 13,891.

Amphorbius, Trojan, given as cousin to Menon 18,114 and brother to Liconius 153; 974; 1,064.

Annarie. „De riches pierres d'—“ 10,001.

Aperthecloppes as limit of first conquest by the Greeks (§ 239⁴).

Argolique lingnee „dont vous (= Greeks) estes trestous nasquis“ 21,938. G. has E 4 v 31 „ex arginis (argivis) more“. Both B. and G. speak of Argus as builder of Jason's ship.

Ascanius, Astanius, 179; 184 son of Eneas „jedenfalls aus Virgil entnommen" (Meybrinck P. 15).
Assurie, marches d'— 21,314. § 182[1].
Athamas, 8,650 same as Athimas. Meybrinck's reason (P. 15.) for doubting their indontity seems insufficient (§§ 16; 39; 42).
Athimas, servant of Anthenor 489.
Atrides, as singular number with no reference to Agamenon and Menelaus 3,677 (§ 239[4]). B. uses „de la lignee Atrei" correctly 27,172.
Auldimeche, a Mirmidon 10,424.
Aventus, only in list of those slain by Hector 13,899.
Babel, „la tour —" 2,924.
Basaac, **Basam**, **Basaam**, one and the same Mirmidon 7,003; 10,370; 11,696; 15,872. (see § 150 foot-note).
Basaam, servant to Thoas, Greek king, 6,048. Differing from Meybrinck P. 14, we think this another personage than the above.
Belides, grandfather of Palamides 3,669 (§ 239[4]).
Cadimas, servant to Thoas, Greek. 6,048.
Calixtus, banner-man of Boetes 7,765.
Casmabor — natural son of Priam 9767—73.
Cebat, Mirmidon 4,492, same as Sebat 15,873.
Cediron — Greek king 3,476 killed by Troylus 10,219 d. Cousin to Prothenor 4,260; 5,068; related to Helen 4,247
Cedron, only in list of those killed by Hector 13,896.
Cidrac, „clerc" of priest Thoas 25,882.
Cisteron, banner-man of Ampheneas 7,749.
Citheus. Greek messenger 3,457. His rôle like that of Macabrum on the Trojan side.
Cloacus, banner-man of Ulixes 4,615.
Cloantus, servant of Priam 10,564.
Coreas, banner-man of Theseus, Trojan 7,771,
Corinthus, servant of Ajax, 4,803.
Cytheus = Citheus.
Derrons, banner-man to Hector 8,679. Arnons in Mss. 𝔄ℭ (Haepke P. 49. foot-note).
Dolus, only given in list of those killed by Hector 13,888.
Durion, likewise 13,897.
Egenus, Greek, meets Paris in Citherea 2,078 d.
Erupius, Hector's servant (§ 88[4]) 10,065.
Esglantine, an Amazon 20,905.
Faryc, whence come pearls 7,870.
Finees, „clerc" to priest Calcas 7,224 d. (§ 68.)
Florimonde, maid to Helen 2,146 (§§ 32[3]; 36).
Galienne, an Amazon 20,902.
Glaucus, banner-man to Huppon 7,755.
Herion, servant of Paris 16,199.
Humanus, only mention in list of kings killed by Hector 13,899. Perhaps the same as Humers in B.; Humerus in G. Milet Mss. ℭ. has Hnmerus (Haepke P. 49 foot-note).
Licaonie 6,304; Licaone 7,926; Liconnye 7,466, country of Ampheneas.
Liconius, Trojan ally 160.
Mabille, an Amazon 20,914.
Macabrum, messenger of Priam, 94. Greif says (§ 80 end):- „Die Hilfsfigur des Macabrum — erinnert an den Macabrins des Alexanderromans (ed. Michelant, p. 415, 32, Macabruns p. 425,12.)"
Mesebech, a Mirmidon 15,872.
Methenez, Nestor's banner-man 4,741.
Micheus, only in list of kings killed by Hector, 13,897.
Micheus, servant to Prothenor 4,302; 5,083 d.

Miselet 17,261; **Missellet** 4,492; **Musselet** 22,174, leader of the Mirmidons after death of Basaac (§ 151[1]).

Morienne, „marches de —" whence comes Pirrus 21,113; (§ 182[1]).

Nichanor, servant to Menesteus 5,907.

Nuron, only found in list of those slain by Hector 13,898.

Orgiam, a Mirmidon 4,492.

Paralamenon, only found in list of those slain by Hector 13,895.

Pausipus, likewise 13,898.

Permenis, servant of Ulixes 4,615.

Phabernye, kingdom of Greek Thoas 9,927. B-G. give his kingdom as Tholia (5,616; J 4 v 9).

Phanon, only in list of those killed by Hector 13,898.

Philipon. Trojan king; only mention 17,490. B. has a Greek Philipon in list of those slain by Hector 16,791, but not elsewhere. This Philipon in B. would seem from its position in the list to correspond with Phillis in G's list. G's Phillis is actually slain, M 4 r 17, and in the corresponding circumstances B. has „Felis" 13,965.

Philotas, banner-man of Trojan, Epistropus 7,781, perhaps taken from Greek king G. Philoteas K 6 r 26 B. Philitoas 9,375.

Plotinus, servant of Epistropus, 7,786.

Polixene, only in list of killed by Hector 18,889. See Polixenes in § 241.

Protheus. 2,078 d. — Greek who meets Paris in Cytherea.

Salomnie fief of Pirrus 20,868. (see Salemine — § 241).

Samaritaine 20,598 „par tout le monde | De cy jusques samaritaine".

Sebat = Cebat.

Senechal — **Seneschal**, servant of Diomedes. No further name given; 3,565 4,507 etc.

Sentipus, a merchant of Troy 5,984, probably the same as Sentipus the builder of the tombs of Hector (13,657; 19,423) and of Achilles (19,430; 19,512).

Sergestus, banner-man of Cediron 4,308; 5,083 d.

Serpedon, given as kingdom of Menelaus in lines 33; 36 of the „Instrument" (after 23,386); perhaps due to a corruption of Sparta (see § 49[4]).

Simoys, banner-man of Pillon 7,760. (Compare Meybrinck P. 16).

Sisteron 7,752 = Cisteron.

Sitheus 4,481—4 = Citheus.

Sixtus Passagoniens, servant of Philimenis 7,324.

Sorbin, Trojan ship-master 499.

Surie „venans de la mer de —" 21,094. probably = Assurie (§§ 180; 182[1]).

Tencer (Tencer, only in edition of 1544), forefather of the Trojan nobility, 6,156—9.

Thaye, land of Castor and Pollus. 753; 3,466. In B-G. Achaia. M. probably forgot the Latin construction of place without the preposition, and understood a as preposition. The change, ch = th (t) is frequent.

Thedius, only found in list of kings killed by Hector. 13,892. Probably same as Cedius, Scedius in the lists of B-G. Haepke says (P. 49 footnote) that Mss. 𝔄ℭ have Sedamis.

Thimotheus. servant of Menesteus 5,913.

244. The Standards.

In view of the importance given by M. to the royal arms of France in his Prologue (verse 73 fol) and in Priam's long monologue (25,109), and, particularly, (in the Prologue), to the descent of the French kings from the royal house of Troy, it seems most likely that the various standards of the Trojan princes were introduced by M. in honor of the great noble families of France. Wunder's suggestion (P. 39) that the standards on the Greek side are equally emphasized does not appear to us to destroy the above possibility. Unfortunately lack of time prevented our investigation of this question. The references to these standards are as follows:-

Trojan side.

Ampheneas 7,868; 7,882.
Anthenor 9,997.
Boetes 7,865; 7,881.
Enee 9,973—78.
Epistropus 7,856; 7,879.
Glaucon 7,807—20.
Hector 9,989—96.
Huppon 7,829.
Menon 10,003 (see § 241).
Merion 7,850; 7,878.
Panthasilee 21,984.
Paris 9,979—86.
Philimenis 7,792—800.
Pillon 7,846; 7,877.
Priam 10,292.
Serpedon 7,807—20.
Theseus 7,861—7,880.
Troylus 9,955—61.

Greek side.

Achilles 4,515—21.
Ajax 4,839.
Cediron 5,116—45.
Diomedes 4,548—63.
Menesteus 5,946—56.
Nestor 4,878—89.
Palamides 8,160—74.
Patroclus 4,523—26.
Pirrus 21,098—110.
Prothenor 5,116—45.
Prothesillaus 4,644—49.
Thelamon 5,102—7.
Thelamonius Ajax 5,084—95.
Ulixes 4,657—65.

Noteworthy in this list is the absence of the chief leaders of the Greeks, Agamenon and Menelaus. A similar neglect is not found on the Trojan side.

In 9,963—70 a Trojan standard is described as belonging to the second battle-line, but no owner is given. It can belong to either of the two leaders of this line, Huppon (9,661—2) or Deyphebus (9,669). It is undoubtedly the latter's, for Huppon would not have two standards, and Deyphebus, alone of the king's sons (except Helenus, the priest), still lacks one.

245. Some Observations upon the Time-Limits in Milet's drama.

A) We learn from verse 25,076 Milet's idea of the date of the Trojan war. He places it as occurring 5,000 years before the accession of Charles VII of France. As in Benoît and Guido, the duration is ten years. Calcas (7,296) and Cassandra (10,559) prophesy it as such, although in both cases ten is given as the extreme limit (see in this connection § 67[2]).

Throughout the drama the passage of this time is frequently referred to, much more often than in B-G. There are, however, a number of contradictions in these references, showing Milet's carelessness in their use. These references are as follows:-

1) One year between the rape of Helen and the embassy of Ulixes and Diomedes to Priam, 8,353.

2) One year since the arrival of the Greeks before Troy, 8,558.

3) Two years, before the second battle is fought, 8,937.

4) Six years, after the third battle, 11,321.

5) The contradiction between ten years in 11,427 and six years nine months in 11,441, has been noted in the foot-note to paragraph 106; „Dix" in 11,427 should be „six".

6) Six years again, 13,935, after the burial of Hector, and long after the exchange of Anthenor and Thoas (see § 245 A 13).

7) The anniversary of Hector's death (14,354; 15,062) marks the seventh year, as given in 15,404.

8) Eight years in 16,614 after the death of Deyphebus and again eight years in 18,710 after the deaths of Troylus and of Achilles.

9) In 18,718 it is said that Hector, Troylus and Achilles „y sont mors en moins de huit moys", which is a contradiction, since Hector had been dead a year (15,062) before Troylus or Achilles was killed and Achilles had even attended the anniversary festivities of Hector's death (14,354). We noted this contradiction § 164[1].

10) Nine years are passed:- 21,035, after the death of Paris; 21,364, when Menelaus goes to fetch Pirrus; 21,622, at the arrival of Panthasilee.

11) Nine years and eight months 21,948—50 (in the text ten years less four months) at the time of the last battle.

12) Ten years 23,067 after the death of Panthasilee; over ten years 23,806, when Anthenor begins negociations for peace.

13) The contradiction implied in Thoas' words to Anthenor that they were exchanged as prisoners seven years ago, has been noted in § 198[2].

14) Still another inconsistency exists between eleven years in 25,996 and ten years in 26,654; also between ten years in 23,067 and eleven years in line 10 of the „Instrument" (after 23,386).

B) In the use of shorter time-limits, Milet is equally free and equally indifferent to inconsistencies. He seems wholly insensible to the naïvité of long journeys being made on the stage in a few minutes. We have noted the following time-limits:-

1) „ennuyt" 6,059.
2) Two days 3,560; 4,090; 5,081; 5,883; 5,887; 7,355; 7,361; 7,501; 7,598; 7,618; 12,298.
3) Four or six days 22,859.
4) Six days 4,206; 7,478.
5) Week 7,565.
6) Eight days 7,458.
7) Week and a half 7,581.
8) Ten Days 15,835.
9) One month 5,983; 11,864; 16,403; 17,393.
10) Month and a half 3,514; 12,703.
11) Two months 11,378; 11,622; 12,722; 12,737; 15,482; 21,719.
12) „Longuement" in 27,674. where the naivité is particularly noticeable.

C) That anachronisms should exist, is to be expected. The following were noted:

19,496. Latin inscription on Achilles' tomb.

Latin, 24,241, and French, 24,261, mentioned by Anthenor.

The mention of „Sarrazins" 26,227 d.; Carthage 4,094; the English 27,905.

For the discussion of „artillerie" in 3,904, see foot-note to page 46.

246. Refrains.

To show the frequency of the use of refrains by Milet, the references to them are appended. The majority of these refrains are of the variety found in triolets, i. e. a triple repetition at intervals of three verses. In the following list only the first verse of these triolet refrains is given, and in heavier type:-

516; 24; 32; 38 (see § 54 foot-note).
539; 42; 47.
950.
1,234.
1,253; 65; 76; 88.
1,896.
1,988.
2,055.
2,221; 29; 37; 45; 53.
2,443; 47; 49; 53.
2,482.
2,561; 69; 77; 85.
2,716.
2,724.
3,098; 101; 105.
4,352; 60; 68; 76; 84; 92; 4,400; 4,408; 16; 24 (see § 54 foot-note).
6,134.
6,972.
7,205.
7,225; 6; 7.
7,300.
7,888.
9,492; 9,500; 9,509.
9,877.
10,983; 89; 95.
11,015.
11,261.
11,271.
11,417.
11,641.
11,906.
12,321; 29; 37; 45; 53.
12,385; 93; 401; 409.
12,614; 20; 26.
12,679; 82; 86.
12,971.
13,129; 35; 41.
13,221; 27.
14,415; 21; 27.
15,711.
16,311.
16,944.
17,454.
17,486.
18,252.
18,665; 73; 82.
20,548.
20,560.
21,774.
25,921; 29; 33.
25,927; 41.
27,654.
27,953.
27,969; 75; 81.

Of interest in this connection is the effect of repetition produced by 1,847 (see § 28):-

Rappaisez vous dont a ceste heure;
Rappaisez vous, ma doulce amye;
Rappaisez vous, rappaisez vous;
Rappaisez vous ie vous emprye!

The repetition of the refrain especially as a triolet often gives a pleasing effect, see for example § 68; and in similar greetings, see verses 950; 11,015; 11,641 etc.

A. Benoît:-

I) The edition of Joly was the only one available to us as the promised critical edition by M. Leopold Constans has not yet appeared. Besides in M. Joly's edition much study has been given to a proper classification of Benoît manuscripts; the following is at best but a partial list of articles, being such as came to our notice:-

a) Joly. P. 69 ff. of his edition.

b) Stengel. Zeitschrift für Romanische Philologie VI. 463 foot-note.

c) E. Josef. Zeitschrift für Roman. Phil. VII—7.

d) Paul Meyer. Romania 18 (1889); pages 70—102.

e) Carl Jacobs. „Ein Fragment des Roman de Troie auf der Stadtbibliothek zu Bordeaux" Progr. — Beil. der Höheren Bürgerschule zu Hamburg. Hamburg 1889. This fragment corresponds to verses 9,013 through 12,821.

f) Léopold Constans „Notes pour servir au classement des manuscrits du Roman de Troie" in „Etudes Romanes dediées à Gaston Paris". Pages 195 - 238. Paris 1891.

g) In Sommer's Reprint of the „Recuyell" (London, 1894.) is a list of Mss. Vol. I. Page XXII foot-note.

II) A few facts have come to light in the present study, which seem to point out what group of Benoît manuscripts served as the basis of Guido's work. References to these are in the Index under *„Manuscripts:- Benoît"*.

Undoubtedly many more indications would have been found if a truly critical edition of Benoît with all variations existed. The edition of Joly gives but few variations. Another indication of Guido's source is in the variation to Benoît 3,861. Joly's text reads: „vi devant moi Mercurion", but he gives as „variante" of manuscripts C, D. *and G*:- „*vint* devant moi Mercurion" which reading was probably adopted by Guido in „qui ad me statim *accedens*" E 2 v 24.

B. Guido :-

I) In view of the great importance of Guido as the source of so many later versions of the Trojan story, it would seem most advisable that a critical edition of his work be undertaken. The number of manuscripts is very great, although the larger part of them, being of later origin, would be of less importance for critical purposes. We ask leave to insert a list of the manuscripts possessed by the National Library in Paris:-

Index Latinus (Ançiens Fonds):-

Number:-	5,694	Date 1334. Guido alone. 35 books.
	5,695	Date 1350. — complete —.
	5,696	Three last books.
	5,697	Complete — 15th century.
	5,698	„ — „ „
	5,699	Guido alone — 1st leaf wanting — 15th century.
	5,700	„ „ — Complete — „ „
	5,701	„ „ „ — 1419.
	5,702	Complete — — — — — — 1444.
	5,703	„ 15th century.
	5,704	Guido alone — Complete „ „
	5,705	„ „ „ „ „
	5,706	„ „ „ „ „
	5,707	„ „ „ „ „
	6,073	„ „ „ 1458.
	6,357	Guido in 34 books — 15th century.
	7,717	Guido — 1st ten books — „ „

New Acquisitions:- Catalogue-Vol. E.-L. Page 100 (compare Léopold Delisle: „Inventaire des Manuscrits latins conservés à la Bibliothèque Nationale sous les numéros 8823—18,613, et faisant suite à la série dont le catalogue a été publié en 1744. — Paris 1863—1871).

12,505 — — 15th century.
12,506 — — 1474.
14,628 — — 14th century (1370?)
15,016 — — 15th „
16,022 — — End of 14th century.

Most recent acquisition (Page 18 of 1896 catalogue):- Guidonis de Columna historia trojana, XIV s; n. a. lat. 1745. (described by M. Omont in Vol. LVII (1896) of Bibl. de l'Ecole des Chartes, page 178).

A partial list of Guido Mss. is given by Sommer „Recuyell" Vol. I. page XXIV.

II) Of the prints of Guido (see Brunet Vol. 2. P. 170 and Hain) a large number are to be found in Paris. The Mazarine Library possesses:-

1) The first edition of 1477, Cologne.
2) The Strassbourg edition of 1494.
3) The edition s. l. n. d. described in Copinger's Supplement to Hain (Part. I, Page 172 under No. 5507).

In addition to these three, the National Library owns:-

4) The Strassbourg edition of 1486.
5) A Strassbourg undated edition (Hain No. 5503).
6) Two copies of the edition s. l. et s. a. described as No. 4 in Brunet's list (= No. 871 of Campbell); different miniatures.
7) The edition described as No. 5 in Brunet (Hain 5502).

The National Library does not possess the editions marked in Brunet No. 1⁰ (Hain 5505) and No. 3.

A few peculiarities of these prints came to light in the preparation of the list of proper names in Guido:-

1) The Strassbourg editions (marked above Nos. 2, 4 and 5) show little or no variation in proper names and evidently have a common origin. No. 7 also shows the closest relationship to this group and likewise No. 6. In a few instances Nos. 6 and 7 together differ from the others in this group, possessing common deviations.

2) No. 2 is less dependent upon the Strassbourg group, but still possesses many names in common. It contains traces of influences other than those common to the Strassbourg group.

3) No. 1, the first edition, shows the greatest independence of all the prints. It not only differs more widely from the others in its greater corruption of the names, but it alone possesses certain features:- for example, it alone has a sort of genealogical, historical introduction (A 2 verso); it has verses at the bottom of A 7 recto; it omits a list of the names of

Priam's natural sons; and it adds several names to the list of kings killed by Hector (N 2 v 3). Its text is the least correct and good of all the prints, there being numerous mistakes. See also § 77² foot-note, which shows a connection of the 1477 edition with the Strassbourg group.

A few interesting points were discovered, tending to show that, of these prints, that one which we number 3 (Hain 5507) is closely related to the group of Guido manuscripts, one member of which group was used by Milet in the preparation of his drama. For the references to these interesting and more specific indications of Milet's source see Index under „*Hain 5507*".

C. Milet:-

The manuscripts of Milet are described and their classification undertaken by Haepke in his dissertation (Greifswald 1897) paragraphs 13—23.

The prints are described by Brunet II, pages 656—9. Various interesting details regarding their history in book-sales are given on Page 139 of Gustave Brunet's „La France littéraire au XV siècle ou catalogne raisonné des ouvrages en tout genre imprimés en langue française jusqu'à l'an 1500." Paris 1865.

The National Library possesses the following copies:-

1) The edition of 1485. Mathieu Husz. Lyon.
2) Two copies of the edition of 1498. Jeh. Driart. Paris:- one on vellum with fine miniatures, the other on paper.
3) The edition of 1508. Mich. le Noir. Paris.
4) The edition of 1544. Denis de Harsy. Lyon.

That the edition of 1544 is related to that of 1485 seems shown by their agreement in several instances in mutual deviation from the other prints (see §§ 66 foot-note; 214⁵ end; 216⁵).

248. Bibliography.

„Benoît de Sainte-More et Le Roman de Troie" by A. Joly. — Vol. 27 (seventh volume of the third series) of the „Mémoires de la Société des Antiquaires de Normandie". Paris 1869—1871.

Guido de Columna. — „Historia Trojana." Cologne 1477 (the first edition).

Milet, Maistre Jacques — „L'Istoire de la destruction de Troye la grant translatee de latin en francoys, mise par parsonnages et composee par maistre Jacques Milet estudiant es loix en la ville d'Orleans l'an mil quatre cens cinquante le deuxiesme iour du moys de septembre, et imprimee a Parîs par Jehan Bonhomme, Libraire de l'universite de Paris, le XII de may, mil quatre cens quatre vingts et quatre".
Autographische Vervielfältigung des der königlichen Bibliothek zu Dresden gehörigen Exemplars, veranstaltet von E. Stengel. Marburg and Leipzig 1883. (W. Greif did the transcription).

Barth, Robert. — „Guido de Columna." Leipzig Dissertation 1877.

Becker, Karl — „Die Mysterien „Le Siège d'Orléans" und „La Destruction de Troye la grant", eine sprachliche Untersuchung." Marburg Dissertation 1886 (disproves Tivier's idea of Milet's common authorship).

Dunger, Hermann. — „Die Sage vom Troyanischen Kriege in den Bearbeitungen des Mittelalters und ihre antiken Quellen." Leipzig 1869.

Fischer, Clemens. — „Der altfranzösische Roman von Benoît de Sainte More als Vorbild für die mittelhochdeutschen Troja-Dichtungen des Herbort von Fritzlar und des Conrad von Würzburg." — Münster Dissertation. — Paderborn 1883.

Greif, Wilhelm. — „Die mittelalterlichen Bearbeitungen der Trojanersage, ein neuer Beitrag zur Dares- und Dictysfrage. Erweiterte Fassung einer durch die philosophische Facultät zu Marburg gekrönten Preisschrift." In Stengel's „Ausgaben und Abhandlungen aus dem Gebiete der romanischen Philologie." Vol. LXI. Marburg 1886.

Haepke, Gustav. — „Kritische Beiträge zu Jacques Milets Drama „La Destruction de Troye la Grant." Greifswald Dissertation 1897.

(has since appeared (1899) in extended form as Vol. XCVI of Stengel's „Ausgaben und Abhandlungen." It, however, still treats of only the first two days of the drama. That part of our own thesis was already printed).

Histoire Littéraire de la France" — Tome XIII, page 428. 1814,

Jaeckel, R. — „Dares Phrygius und Benoît de Sainte-More. Ein Beitrag zur Dares Frage." Breslau Dissertation 1875.

Koerting, Gustav. — „Dictys und Dares. Ein Beitrag zur Geschichte der Trojasage in ihrem Uebergange aus der antiken in die romantische Form." Halle 1874.

Meybrinck, Ernst. — „Die Auffassung der Antike bei Jacques Milet, Guido de Columna und Benoît de Saint-More, mit besonderer Berücksichtigung der Kampfscenen und religiösen Gebräuche." in Stengel's „Ausgaben und Abhandlungen" Vol. LIV. Marburg 1886.

Parfaict, the Brothers. — „Histoire du théâtre français." Amsterdam 1735.

Paris, Gaston. — Romania III P. 129; Revue Critique 1874. No. 19. P. 289.

Petit de Julleville. L. — „Les Mystères" Vol. I. 315—317; Vol. II. 569—584. Paris 1880.

Sommer, H. Oskar. — „The Recuyell of the Historyes of Troye." 2 volumes. London 1894.

Tivier, H. — „Etude sur le Mystère du siège d'Orléans et sur Jacques Milet auteur présumé de ce mystère." Thèse de doctorat. Paris 1868.

Tivier, H. — „Histoire de la littérature dramatique en France depuis ses origines jusqu'au Cid" (Milet, pages 383—431). Paris 1873.

Wunder, Curt. — „Jacques Milets Destruction de Troye la Grant." — Leipzig Dissertation 1868.

Addenda.

To § **8**[3] end:-

Professor Stengel has just published as an appendix to Haepke's work (Ausgaben und Abhandlungen. Vol. XCVI. Page 130) the „Epistre adjacent et epillogative“ which is attached to Manuscript 𝔊 of Milet. In this curious „Epistre“, in which the moral purpose of the „Destruction“ is much emphasized, the following phrases may be cited as additional acknowledgment by Milet of his source:-

a) Page 130; fourth last line: „je dessus nommé — — ay voulu translater de latin en françois“.

b) Page 135; third last line: „par moy dessuz nommé compositeur et translateur de l'istoire precedent“.

c) The drama is frequently called a „translacion“:- Page 130, line 14; P. 130, eighth last line; P. 131, line 17; P. 133, line 6; P. 135, line 5. In P. 132, line 14, it is called apologetically „une translacion prolixe et artificieuse.“

The following words are also worthy of note:- (Page 130, line 18):-

„— — l'istoire de Dares jadis citoyen de la ville de Troye lequel descript et recita en bon et brief langage etc.“

Is this simply an echoing of Guido's statement or are we to suppose that Milet really knew the book of Dares?

Interesting also, because no doubt explaining the several cases of inconsistency and forgetfulness in Milet's work (see Index: „*Inconsistencies*“ and „*Naïveté*“), are the words, Page 135 middle:-

„— — la presente transgredie laquelle a este composee dedanz l'espace de deux anz inclusivement, et pour dire vray le plus du temps a esté delaissee intercipee et remise sanz y toucher ouvrer ou besongner en aucunne maniere, etc.“

To § **13** foot-note 2:- Compare Haepke (Ausgaben und Abhandlungen XCVI) P. 65; verse 105.

Index.

The numbers refer to the paragraphs and their subdivisions.
See also under Proper Names §§ 241—243.

D.

Misprints.

Page 4; § 5[2] fifth last line: Insert comma after „texts."
Page 12, line 10: „know" should be „known."
Page 13; § 11, line 2: „§ 247 B[24]" should be „§ 247 B[11]."
Page 15; § 13, line 2: Omit comma after „central."
Page 17, line 2: „s'ire" should be „sire,"
Page 31; § 33[1], line 4: „ensuit" should be „sensuit."
Page 61; § 71[2] second last line: „continuous" should be „continual."
Page 75; fourth line: „sa mye" should be „s'amye."
Page 78; § 88[3] third last line: „reculeur" should be „reculer."
Page 83; § 95[9], line 2: „Acomparer" should be „A comparer."
Page 90; § 104, line 4: „advisor" should be „adviser."
Page 112; § 120, line 2: „§ 241" should be „§ 242."
Page 163; § 180, line 2: „herold" should be „herald."

Vita.

I was born in Salem, Massachusetts, U. S. A., December 16, 1871. My father, Samuel Cook Oliver, Brevet-Colonel of United States Volunteers in the War of the Rebellion 1861—1865, died in 1888. My mother, Mary Elizabeth Oliver (née Andrews) survives him. I am a Unitarian. My early education was in the Public Schools of Salem. In the fall of 1889, after a summer spent in France, I entered Harvard University and received in 1893 the A. B. degree. Aside from the prescribed courses of study at Harvard, my work there was mostly in French and German. I then began the study of medicine, but relinquished it and, in November 1894, came to Germany to begin the study of Romance Philology.

After a semester spent in Leipzig, I went to Heidelberg in April 1895, and remained until August 1897. I then passed ten months in Paris where I continued the work of preparing the accompanying thesis. In the summer of 1898 I returned to Heidelberg, and on March first 1899 passed the examination for the doctorate of philosophy. During this period of study in Europe, I have enjoyed the instruction of the following professors:-

In Leipzig:- Professors Sievers, Weigandt, Biedermann and Marcks.

In Heidelberg:- His Excellency Geheimrath Kuno Fischer, Professors Fritz Neumann, Wilhelm Braune, Freiherr von Waldberg, Erdmannsdoerffer, Fr. Meyer, Schneegans, Waag, Sutterlin and Ehrismann.

In Paris:- Mm. Gaston Paris, Paul Meyer, A. Thomas and Morel Fatio.

To all these gentlemen I desire to express my sincere gratitude, and especially to Professor Dr. Fritz Neumann of Heidelberg.

www.ingramcontent.com/pod-product-compliance
Lightning Source LLC
Chambersburg PA
CBHW020348030726
47496CB00007B/2058
* 9 7 8 3 3 3 7 3 9 4 5 8 5 *